Return to Duty

by Dustin Williams

Cover design by Jake Clark © J Caleb Design
Editorial services by Sage Taylor Kingsley

Paperback ISBN 979-8-9891104-0-7

First Edition

Published by
Hypothesis Book House

Printed and published in the United States of America

www.DustinWilliamsAuthor.com

dustinwilliamsauthor@gmail.com

Dedicated to those who selflessly serve and protect
and to those who give their limbs and lives in battle.

Preface

During Operation Iraqi Freedom and Operation Enduring Freedom in Iraq and Afghanistan, more than 1,500 U.S. soldiers suffered from limb loss due to bombs, blasts, or other traumatic injury. Each year, more than 1,000,000 people across the world lose a limb primarily due to vascular disease or trauma. Prosthetics constitute one of the most common tools for returning quality of life to these amputees.

Osseointegrated implant technology addresses many of the limitations that accompany traditional prosthetic socket systems. Specifically, an osseointegrated implant consists of a titanium rod that is surgically inserted into the medullary canal of an amputated bone, such as a femur. The opposite end of the rod is percutaneous (meaning it protrudes through the skin), so that a prosthetic or bionic limb can be docked onto the metal. This aligns the mechanical forces of the system directly onto the skeleton, whereas traditional socket prosthetics load the soft tissues, which can lead to bruising, skin problems, and limited use.

But despite its promise, osseointegrated implant technology has a weakness.

In 2005, I was hired as the microbiologist among a team of scientists and clinicians endeavoring to develop osseointegrated implant technology for transfemoral amputees in the U.S. Why did the team need a microbiologist? Because bacteria can thrive at the skin-implant interface of percutaneous osseointegrated implants and cause infection. Microbiologists specialize in developing antimicrobial strategies to manage bacteria in these and myriad other situations.

Throughout the project, we had the opportunity to visit with Department of Defense officials and amputees. The latter, who had already put their lives on the line, were willing to advance another frontline by becoming the first-ever patients of osseointegrated implant technology in the U.S. I was honored to witness their courage and learned to an even greater degree just how deeply I and all of us are in Service Members' debt.

While working on the development of osseointegrated implant technology, a science-fiction story generated in my mind. Its fruition is in the following pages.

Recognizing that "osseointegrated implants" can be a mouthful to read and say, and to distinguish real-life osseointegrated implants from fictional ones, I created a new term for their fictionalized version—Ozzies—with the help of my friend, Kraig. In the book, Ryker can walk with Ozzies immediately following surgery. This is a fictional portrayal to "move" the story. In clinical reality, patients with osseointegrated implants and accompanying prosthetic legs require extensive healing and physical therapy that take months before full function is achieved. Ozzies' walk, sport, and battle modes presented in the book are also fictional, but who knows what scientists will develop in the future!

This book is a tribute to Service Members, Veterans, and all those willing to square their shoulders and face new frontiers head-on: Service Member, citizen, adult, and child. May Ryker and the team herein figuratively exemplify your hearts and efforts as you display courage beyond compare, whatever your circumstance.

Chapter 1

Paktia Province, Afghanistan

Capt. Ryker Vaughn typically navigated his forward ordnance patrol *around* fields of improvised explosive devices—IEDs as the military acronymized them—but this morning, he intended to lead his team directly *through* them. He squinted to shield the morning sun from his hazel eyes as he scanned the bomb-filled landscape. The undulating hills and endless Afghan sand seemed harmless, but inches below the surface, the soil was riddled with Humvee-crippling explosives.

"You done daydreaming, Cap?" asked Dylan, Ryker's second-in-command and most sarcastic team member.

"No, Captain Impatient! Just remembering how bad I beat you balling last night." Ryker flexed, showing off his athletic six-foot-two build, forged through years of basketball and military training. His thick arms and brawny legs were readily visible even through heavy combat fatigues.

"Ooh, harsh! I see how it is," Dylan retorted, playing calm to hide his nervousness as he loaded a container with water bottles and rations into the back of a Humvee. "Looks like we have a rematch coming up. But hey," he nodded toward the tablet in Ryker's hands, "do you need me to take a look at that thing?"

Ryker held up the tablet. "Dude, we'd end up at a bar if I put you in charge of this! I got it."

Dylan paused and smirked, wiped his bony brow, then shrugged. "Yeah, you're not wrong."

Ryker laughed with the team, then refocused to double check the tablet as the others loaded the last of the equipment. He opened the tablet case and eyed the inside cover onto which was taped a crinkled photograph of his mom, himself, and his lanky teenage brother, Jack, perched on his back. He could still smell the ocean spray that splashed their faces as they took that picture on their latest family vacation. Noticeably absent in the photo was his dad, Paul, who had been killed in battle. Ryker knew that his mom consistently feared the same would happen to him.

I'll be fine, Mom, he thought.

He hoped he was right.

He folded the tablet cover back, putting the photo out of sight, and entered his personal code into the system app, giving him access to the IED-detection software.

"Welcome, Ryker Vaughn," a computerized woman's voice said.

Ryker clicked the "System Check" icon.

"Confirming you want to perform a system check?" the voice asked.

Ryker clicked a "Yes" icon. A slew of numbers, readouts, and information appeared. Based on the data and the green flashing lights on the C-arm-like contraptions hanging off the front fenders of the lead Humvee, the U.S. Army's newest state-of-the-art IED-detection system was functioning normally.

"Readouts are clean," Ryker said. "Ready to go in?"

"I guess," Dylan supposed. "But I'm not thrilled about being a test dummy for this new detection system. IEDs suck, sir!"

"Command says this system's three times more accurate at finding them," Ryker said. He had to display some semblance of confidence in the system to his team.

He'd spent a half hour the night before trying to convince his commanding officer, Col. Samuel Brighton, that he didn't feel the system was test ready. But Col. Brighton and Dr. Sharp, the IED-detection system inventor, had insisted they had enough data to support a field test. The orders stood.

"Command?" Dylan scoffed. "Yeah! What could go wrong?"

"Plenty!" said Deshauna, the sole female sergeant in the group. She opened her big brown eyes wide and spoke in her thickest Georgian accent. "But it's what we do. So, where we headin'?"

Ryker held the tablet up and panned it across the horizon, displaying an electromagnetic map. "Once we roll over that second hill with the three bushes, we'll head west. That area should have the most IEDs."

"Normally, I wouldn't say this," Deshauna said, "but I *hope* you're right."

Ryker took a deep breath and put the tablet aside. He patted his armored pockets to ensure he had his equipment, donned a helmet over his sand-colored hair, then checked his weapons. Satisfied he was ready for patrol and battle, he ordered, "All right, everyone, load up!"

One by one, the ten team members buckled into three heavily armored, camouflage-patterned Humvees.

Ryker watched each patrol member with respect. Just twelve hours prior, they were hanging out in a makeshift bar in Camp Firefox. Now they were carrying weapons of war, willing to pay the ultimate sacrifice for each other and their nation.

Ryker had been chosen to lead and handpick the team field-testing the device. The mission was nerve-wracking; they had to get as close to IEDs as possible to assess proximity statistics and readout potentials. If anything happened to any team member, he would feel responsible.

Deshauna slid into the driver's seat of the lead Humvee, made the sign of the cross over her chest and head, and closed her eyes briefly before asking, "Ready?"

Ryker sat next to Dylan in the back and buckled in. "Ready!"

"It's go time!" Deshauna spoke into the comm to alert the trailing Humvees. "Follow close." She floored it and angled the Humvee toward a pre-determined path that led to the bomb field. For ten minutes, the Humvees lurched over washboard roads and weed-infested landscape.

"Pull up on that ridge," Ryker said, pointing as they approached a precipice. "If everything's reading right, that's where we need to start the measurements." He tapped the tablet screen. *Still working*, he thought. Electromagnetic sensors, ore detectors, resonance frequency modulators, and detonation warning readings were all within normal ranges. "Systems look clean," he announced. "Move forward."

The vehicles eased frontward, carrying the team closer to enemy explosives. In direct opposition to the jovial and joke-filled atmosphere of last night, everyone was reserved.

"There!" Ryker hollered.

Deshauna could see it: a slight mound of dirt concealed the first detectable IED. She pulled the Humvee to the right to avoid it, then continued down a poorly marked road. The trailing Humvees followed her lead.

Nearly eighty feet later, Ryker cautioned, "There!" again.

Deshauna dodged the second one. The two trailing Humvees followed suit.

Ryker continued to monitor the tablet sharp-eyed, looking for signs of the next bomb. Twenty feet down the path, he saw an unusual signal.

"That's odd," he said. He shook the tablet, thinking that might affect the feedback. It didn't.

"What is it?" Dylan asked.

"I'm not ... sure."

"Does it show there's something ahead?" Deshauna prodded.

"Yeah, but—"

"There's no mound." She finished Ryker's sentence.

"Right. It's buried deep," Ryker said. "Much deeper than an IED."

"So, let's leave it be," Dylan pleaded. "We have enough to worry about already."

"But it's not a bomb," said Ryker. "The next bomb is at least a hundred feet ahead." He stuck his head out the window and ensured the green lights on the C-arm-like contraptions were blinking. They were. He sat back down. "The detectors are working. Whatever this thing is, it's producing a completely different signal. Stop here for a sec."

"Is it a weapon?" Deshauna asked and pressed the brake.

"Doubtful," Ryker said. "There's no sign of explosive material."

"It's treasure!" Dylan cheered.

"Now we're talkin'!" Deshauna hollered.

"Ha, I wish," Ryker said as he opened the door. "Wait here."

Dylan pushed his helmet back and watched Ryker exit the Humvee. "Dude, you're not gonna—"

"Yeah, we need to find out what it is. Could be a new reconnaissance system. If it is, we could be ambushed any second."

Ryker went to the back of the Humvee, grabbed a shovel, and threw it on the ground. He used the tablet to maneuver the C-arm-like contraptions and identified the exact location of the underground signal.

"Got it." He picked up the shovel.

"Shouldn't we help?" Deshauna queried.

"No," Ryker replied. "If I'm wrong, I'm responsible."

Ryker walked ten feet ahead and sank the shovel repeatedly into the sand, digging a three-foot-wide pit. Within minutes, he uncovered a piece of black metal.

"Found something!" he announced. He got to his knees and pushed sand out of the way, revealing a six-inch diameter, foot-tall, obsidian-colored cylinder. He pulled it from the ground, surprised at how heavy it was, and held it up.

"Permission to exit the Humvee?" Dylan requested. "I want to see what the heck that is."

"Granted," Ryker approved.

Dylan got out and stood next to Ryker. Ryker angled the cylinder so they could both analyze it.

"Those are some weird markings," Ryker said, tracing his fingers along crevices that ran the length of its surface.

"Is that an animal?" Dylan wondered, pointing at a hieroglyph-like symbol.

"I don't know," Ryker shrugged.

Deshauna was anxious. "So, uh, we gonna have another Jurassic Park incident here, folks?"

"Huh?" Ryker asked.

"Don't worry about it," Dylan cut in. "She's always making Jurassic Park references when she sees something weird. It's her favorite movie."

Deshauna rolled her eyes. "Whatever that is, I say we put it down and get back to work!"

Ryker ignored Deshauna's plea and wiped the cylinder with his sleeve. He didn't realize there were now three more team members from the other Humvees standing behind him, wanting to glimpse the newfound treasure.

Ryker noticed sand still embedded in the cylinder's crevices. He spat on it to wipe it down—then nearly dropped it as several of the crevices lit up, displaying intense blue veins of what appeared to be a viscous liquid.

The light paths traveled to the opposite side of the cylinder then outlined a curved rectangular panel.

The team stepped back, preparing for something bad to happen.

Dylan warned, "Careful! You're making it mad!"

Before Ryker could do anything, the panel illuminated and cycled through a series of indecipherable symbols.

"What do all those mean?" Dylan questioned.

"No idea," Ryker responded.

Deshauna remained in the driver's seat shaking her head. "Jurassic Park, y'all! Don't say I didn't warn ya! And ya better believe I'm outrunnin' all y'all when that first dinosaur comes. Uh-huh, you know that's right. I ain't gettin' eaten first!"

Ryker looked toward Deshauna and promised, "A *T. rex* is *not* going to pop out of this thing!"

"But apparently, it *does* know your name!" Dylan blurted.

"What?!" Ryker begged.

Dylan pointed at the panel.

Ryker looked and saw his name—R.Y.K.E.R. V.A.U.G.H.N.—spelled out in crystal-clear blue letters on the cylinder's panel.

"How the—?" He wiped the cylinder again to remove the remaining sand. The intense blue veins darkened, and his name faded.

"Trippy!" Dylan said.

"Okay!" Deshauna hollered. "This is officially a freak fest. Is this some kind of joke? Dylan, you always pullin' crap on us. You do this?"

"Yeah, Deshauna, I came through here last night, dodged all these IEDs," he panned his arms across the landscape, "and *planted* this big, fat, black cylinder right here in the ground." He threw his arms in the air. "Ya got me!"

Deshauna pursed her lips, raised her eyebrows, and tilted her head. "I knew it."

Dylan rolled his eyes. Deshauna was always being impossible.

"You guys, enough!" Ryker said. "I'm going to call it in." He went to the Humvee and pulled a radio out of a pack. "Col. Brighton, do you copy?"

The deep, middle-aged voice of the team's commanding officer, Col. Samuel Brighton, came through. "Copy, Capt. What's the fuss? We see you on satellite. You'd better have a good reason for digging into dirt where IEDs reside."

"I did, sir. The system found something. Not a bomb. Some kind of cylindrical device. It even knows my name. It turned on, then fizzled out. I think it may be reconnaissance."

"Finish the mission, then bring it in. The Humvee armor should shield any transmission it's giving. We'll have the communications team analyze it."

"Copy, sir."

"We'll await your arrival. Out."

Ryker slipped the radio back into the pack and picked up the cylinder. "Guess we're taking it back. Load up. We still have work to do."

The team obeyed their orders and returned to the Humvees. Ryker hefted the cylinder onto the seat between him and Dylan. He buckled in, grabbed his canteen, and took a swig of water. He half screwed the lid, set the canteen aside, and wiped his mouth as he looked once again at the tablet screen. "Everything's still clean. Let's roll."

"Mother Mary help us," Deshauna prayed as she eased the Humvee forward. "A hundred feet you said?"

"Yes, system shows the next one's at least that far," Ryker confirmed.

As they moved forward, the terrain worsened.

"Bumpy ride ahead," Deshauna said. "Hold onto your butts!"

Ryker reached over and latched a seatbelt around the cylinder.

Dylan smiled. "Precious cargo?"

"Guess we'll find out," Ryker said. He grabbed a handhold above his head to brace himself as the Humvee jostled over the rocky terrain. He and Dylan failed to notice water sloshed out of his canteen, dousing the cylinder. The veins emanated intense blue light, and the panel displayed Ryker's name again, but he didn't notice.

Ryker checked the tablet screen. An unfamiliar set of numbers and letters in the bottom left corner morphed in and out of sequence. The hairs on the back of his neck tingled. Something was wrong.

He looked at the cylinder. The vein-like crevices were pulsating various hues of blue.

No!

He checked the tablet. The screen was wigging out.

It's malfunctioning!

Ryker thrust his head out the window and yelled, "Abort!" But his voice was lost in a sudden explosion.

A shockwave of hot air burned his face, and lava-hot shrapnel scattered in every direction as the trailing Humvee erupted.

The second Humvee lurched to its side. As its passenger door hit the ground, the impact triggered an IED. The Humvee launched into the air and exploded.

The force of the second shockwave ejected Ryker from the lead Humvee. He flailed through the air. Just before landing, the left fender of the second Humvee zipped toward him and sliced through his legs, taking them both off inches above the kneecaps without him realizing it; adrenaline coursing through his veins masked any sense of trauma or pain.

He thudded to the ground and watched as the lead Humvee detonated. He felt an instant sense of loss for the mission. He coughed, cleared sand out of his mouth, and tried to gasp before realizing his was the only breathing he could hear. He assessed the wreckage.

No movement.

Anywhere.

"Everyone okay?" he yelled.

No answer.

He knew then he was the only survivor. He teetered to his side and wailed. A sinkhole developed in his stomach. He had just killed his team. His friends. The sense of loss immediately racked his soul.

I never should have dug up that cylinder!

He wanted to scream, but he struggled to get air into his lungs. He gasped again.

Aching. Legs.

Ryker's brain started to detect that something more was wrong. The ringing in his ears prevented his mind from processing his senses. He tossed his head back and forth, trying to shake awareness into his brain. His balance was wildly off as he tried to sit up.

The throbbing in his thighs was painless at first, then intensified as he gained his senses.

My legs!

He clawed through the sand where his lower legs should have been. Blood-soaked sand, threads of camouflage cloth, and bone fragments slid through his fingers. Panic flooded through him as reality set in; he would be a double amputee for the rest of his life.

No! He shook his head, imagining the nightmare he would live: he would never play basketball again, never walk again, never go on a run, never kneel to pick up one of his future children. A sense of sorrow he had never experienced engulfed his heart.

He threw his helmet at a smoldering Humvee behind him. *I was supposed to do this for my family, not fail in battle.*

He wiped away involuntary tears that he didn't realize were forming. The increasing pain in his legs reminded him that there wasn't time to mourn. Not yet. In a matter of moments, he would be dead, too, if he didn't get his bleeding under control.

Five years of military training and the experience of three tours of duty kicked in. He burst his survival pack open. He dry-heaved and yelled toward the sky; that relieved the pain only slightly. He wiped his brow and tore open two emergency tourniquets. They would save his life. He hesitated briefly ... not sure he wanted to be saved. That was his subconscious talking.

Mom, Jack, he reminded himself.

Focusing his thoughts, determined to fight for his life, Ryker bit a stick between his flattened teeth—worn from the constant stress of combat. He controlled his shaking hands and readied the tourniquets. It was impossible to soothe the pressure as he cinched them onto his mid thighs to compress both femoral arteries. He grimaced and exhaled repeatedly, causing the veins to bulge from his thick neck. The bleeding stopped in seconds.

He slammed his head on the cool ground, rocked it back and forth, and growled in pain. Exhaustion was already setting in. But he knew he didn't have time to rest. Al Qaeda enemies would likely be en route after hearing the explosions.

He reached for his canteen, drank the bulk of its contents, poured the rest on his face to refresh his agonized body, then reached for his M4 carbine. Grunting, he rolled over and looked at the closest overturned Humvee. *The engine block*, he thought. *The only refuge where bullets won't penetrate.*

His six-pack abdomen shifted in pain as he army-crawled toward the crumpled remains of the Humvee; his mind didn't yet know how to deal with lost limbs. He twisted onto his butt and shimmied his traumatized body backward until he could rest against the Humvee's front axle. Taking refuge by the vehicle was a risk—the gas tank or engine components could still explode—but it was a risk he had to take. This would be his best protection from al Qaeda militants.

The triage strategy of Operation Enduring Freedom meant that most wounded soldiers could be accessed within five minutes if they were close to the city. But at nearly ten miles out, Ryker knew he wouldn't be reached for fifteen or twenty minutes and wasn't certain who would show up first: al Qaeda or medical help.

Ryker was never one to back down from a challenge or battle. His grit was unparalleled. He prepared for the worst.

He scanned his proximal surroundings to see if extra ammo or another firearm were within reach. None were, and he didn't have the energy to crawl fifteen yards to reach the next closest weapon. All he had were two extra magazines for the M4, two grenades for the underside M203 grenade launcher, and a 9mm on his hip with thirteen rounds. That wouldn't be enough for most soldiers, but Ryker would have a chance against four or five hostiles; his accuracy with rapid fire was unmatched.

Several minutes passed with no sound but his heavy breathing and the crackle of burning tires, the fumes of which were generating a gag-inducing stench. The throbbing in his legs became unbearable. Morphine, stored in the Humvee, could have taken the edge off, but it had disintegrated in the blast. He yelled again, beginning to not care if the enemy heard him.

Another two minutes passed. If a triage medical unit didn't arrive soon, he would be exchanging fire. Confirming that both weapons were chambered, and the grenade launcher loaded, he placed the 9mm on the sand to his right and readied the M4. If this were the last chance he had to serve his country, he would die fighting, just as his dad had in Iraq years earlier.

Both eyes open, Ryker lifted the M4, aimed toward the horizon, and steadied his breathing as best he could. Two hundred yards out, someone was coming.

Chapter 2

Ten Miles from Ryker's Location,
Communications Tent, Camp Firefox, Afghanistan

Seven personnel in the communications tent—crammed with dust-covered computers, monitors, dials, and readouts—burst into action the moment the Humvee fireballs erupted. Col. Samuel Brighton demanded answers. Was there any movement near the dismantled Humvees? Were there any survivors? What had gone wrong?

"Sir, we have satellite footage," Sergeant First Class Jason Phillips—one of Ryker's closest friends and an accomplished sniper—announced.

"Full screen," Brighton ordered. His deep voice shook everyone's chest.

Brighton was director of the DETECT initiative for the military, otherwise known as the Deployed Experimental Telemetry for Exploration, Combat, and Telecommunications initiative. His presence was commanding. He was a Desert Storm veteran: thick-chested, mid 50s, graying hair that contrasted starkly with his ebony skin, and biceps larger than most men's thighs. His mind was strategically inclined with a Bachelor's in Mechanical Engineering from West Point and a Master of Science in Imaging Systems from MIT.

Brighton was overseeing the first IED field test with Dr. Steven Sharp, the inventor and design engineer of the IED-detection system.

Dr. Sharp sat wide-eyed in the back of the tent. Neither he nor Brighton could comprehend how the system had failed to detect a cluster of high-powered IEDs.

"Full screen on," Phillips said.

All eyes focused on the image of destruction displayed at the front of the tent. Scattered metal and contorted Humvee frames were painful reminders of al Qaeda's relentless desire to make IEDs ever more powerful in response to increased body armor on U.S. military vehicles.

"Give me details," Brighton ordered.

"Sir," Phillips answered, "Ryker crawled from his initial position to an overturned Humvee. I can't determine the extent of his injuries, but he left a trail of blood behind him. I don't see movement from anyone inside the vehicles."

"He's our only survivor, lucky to be alive," Brighton said. In his twenty-five years of combat oversight and experience, fifteen in Afghanistan, Brighton was well-acquainted with the damage and heartache that explosives could cause. "Scan the surroundings. We need to know if enemies are close."

"Yes, sir!" a soldier said.

Brighton turned and locked eyes with Phillips. "Phillips, gather your triage unit and save Ryker! Depending on the extent of his injuries, he may not have long."

Brighton watched Phillips throw his headphones down and rush to the medical triage truck. In less than a minute, the truck was racing out of camp.

"Col. Brighton," Dr. Sharp spoke up from the back of the communications tent, "I know what went wrong with the system. There was a malfunction in the feedback signal due to interference."

"Worry about that later," Brighton stated. "Right now, we focus on our soldier."

"Of course," Dr. Sharp said sheepishly, nestling his toothpick-shaped body back into a chair.

Brighton watched hawk-eyed as a satellite imaging technician scanned Ryker's surroundings. To the southeast, they detected movement—six men heading toward Ryker.

"They ours?" Brighton asked sternly.

The technician focused the image. "No, sir. Al Qaeda."

The atmosphere in the room intensified.

"Get me Phillips on radio!" Brighton boomed as he grabbed a headset. Phillips was on the line in seconds. "Sergeant Phillips," Brighton stressed, "what's your ETA?"

"Maybe ten minutes."

"Ryker doesn't HAVE ten minutes. You're going in hot! Push the truck as fast as you can. Ryker is in immediate danger. I repeat, Ryker is in immediate danger. Al Qaeda are approaching. Engage at will."

~

Phillips shouted over the revving engine so the other three members of the triage team could hear him. "Weapons ready. Hostiles are approaching Ryker!"

Phillips floored it, making the truck jump and spew sand high into the air. Within minutes, they approached a ridge and could see Ryker in the distance, as well as six nearby al Qaeda enemies. Phillips knew they would never make it in time.

He slammed the brakes and brought the truck to a sliding halt. He and the others jumped out of the truck and yelled at the top of their lungs, trying to get the attention of the enemies. But none of them could hear their cries. They were too far away.

Phillips threw open the back door of the truck where his M24 sniper was stored. The other three soldiers continued to yell, hoping they could provide some distraction, to no avail. All the triage team could do was swear violently to themselves and hope Phillips' sniping skills could protect Ryker.

A corporal screamed, "Phillips! You ready? They're moving in."

"I see them! Gimme a sec!" Phillips yelled. He steadied his rifle on a rock atop the ridge. He aimed it at an al Qaeda operative and pulled the trigger. It didn't budge.

"It's jammed!" Phillips yelled.

He yanked the bolt action. It wouldn't budge.

Ryker was on his own.

Chapter 3

Paktia Province, Afghanistan

Ryker ignored the beads of sweat collecting on his upper lip. He fought mentally against dehydration from blood loss, incoherency from pain, and a deep desire to pass out and die. His legs were seizing, and his body began to shake involuntarily. Acid from his stomach tempted him to vomit, but he couldn't afford to take his eyes off the target. *Dad, Mom, Jack,* he reminded himself. *That's who I'm fighting for. Liberty, justice, freedom. That's what I'm fighting to preserve.* The inner strength these instilled bolstered his courage to fight.

He blinked rapidly, wiped his eyes, then looked for movement through his scope. He could clearly make out six al Qaeda soldiers as they came into view. Rays from the midmorning sun highlighted their turbans and gave them away as their heads rose above a sweeping hill on the horizon. One had an RPG, the others machine guns or assault rifles. They moved hesitantly toward the wreckage, not certain if they would be receiving gunfire from potential survivors.

Ryker knew it would take a miracle to survive. A mildly religious man, he asked whatever powers might be to protect him, then assessed the situation. He was immobile, weak, and fading, but determined to make a strong last stand. An offensive approach would be his only option. He would have little chance of survival once the enemies detected him. His heart raced. Calculating his plan of attack, he concluded that he had to throw them off: take them out of their element. They needed to think that there were many against them.

Ryker shifted his right index finger to the forward trigger of the M203 grenade launcher on the underside of his M4.

No turning back!

He pulled the trigger. The M203 recoil nearly knocked him over; his balance was challenged without his lower limbs intact, but the grenade soared well over two hundred yards and exploded close enough to where he wanted it— thirty yards behind the hostiles. All six men jumped forward. Ryker instantly shifted to the M4 trigger and sprayed several three round bursts toward the first enemy on the right.

One down, five to go.

The remaining al Qaeda soldiers scrambled for cover behind a ridge of sand. He sprayed two more bursts to their left as they fumbled, disorienting them enough to where they couldn't determine the direction from which the bullets were coming. Were there two, three enemies? They didn't know.

Ryker watched a hand grenade land roughly fifty yards in the distance and detonate. The enemies were too far away to reach him with a hand throw but were attempting to send a warning signal.

He focused again on the horizon. A turban began to surface. He pulled the trigger and watched an explosion of cloth flitter through the air.

Two down, four to go.

He hurriedly reloaded the grenade launcher during the window of opportunity.

Two hostiles leapt over the ridge and zigzagged toward him, screaming, and shooting wildly in every direction. Another peered over the hill to provide cover. Ryker launched his final grenade. Before it connected with the ground, he unloaded his first magazine toward the militant providing cover, causing him to hide once again and preventing him from getting an accurate shot off.

One of the zigzaggers crumpled to the ground after the grenade exploded. The other dove into the sand like an ostrich burying its head, attempting to find whatever cover was available. Ryker loaded his second magazine and opened fire. He knew the sand was too shallow to provide cover so he aimed for where the ostrich's torso would be. Within seconds, the sand turned a dark red.

Four down, two to go.

Ryker recognized the ping of bullets penetrating the metal and sand around him as he loaded his third and final magazine. A bullet grazed his right arm. Another tore through the fabric where his left shin would have been. Both remaining hostiles had homed in on his position and were determined to end the fight.

Ryker returned fire. His aim became shaky. The adrenaline coursing through his veins, in combination with the trauma he had experienced, were taking effect. Soon, he would black out. He breathed deeply, determined to take at least one more of them out before he succumbed to death.

Ryker aimed toward the adversary carrying the RPG, now squarely atop his shoulder, as the bullets from the second al Qaeda soldier continued to zip by. Ryker fired multiple rounds and missed horribly. The RPG wielder shifted his position, dodging fire.

Ryker wiped hot tears, then steadied his aim and fired his last six bullets. They connected with the RPG holder— five down, one to go—but not before he was able to fire. As the militant slumped to the ground, the RPG soared through the air. Its notorious lack of long-range stability forced it to burrow in the sand thirty feet away.

But the blast created a shower of sand that pebbled Ryker's eyes, blinding him. He threw his M4 aside and scratched at his eyes. Hazy, blurred images were all he could make out. Frantic, he focused on the foreground. Through his fading vision and early signs of fainting, he distinguished the outline of the sixth and final al Qaeda hostile coming toward him. The villain's frame crescendoed in size until it was standing over him.

Ryker sluggishly reached for the 9mm he had placed to his right. It was gone; the RPG blast had launched it out of reach.

The enemy laughed as he held the 9mm high in the air with a glare. *Looking for this*? his expression seemed to ask. The evil inside him lay much deeper than his skin; it exuded through his face, distorting his character.

The hostile spat at Ryker and threw his 9mm past the Humvee, then began to shout vehemently, satiating his desire to rebuke the sinful and wicked American. Ryker imagined his enemy had always dreamed of this experience—the unlikely moment he would tower over a species weaker than his own. The hostile punched Ryker, threw his emptied assault rifle aside, and scowled. He savored the moment until he finally removed his sidearm from its holster and raised it to Ryker's forehead.

Ryker accepted that it was his time. He literally had nothing left to give. The pale of his face was unnoticeable due to a layer of tear-streaked dust. His shoulders sagged, and he struggled to sit up. His right arm was numb where the bullet had grazed, and his left arm was too weak to lift, preventing him from fighting back. The five men who lay motionless in the foreground would be his lasting symbol of determination and incomparable willpower. His death would be an emblem of sacrifice and love for his country, family, and friends.

Ryker rested his forehead on the barrel of the hostile's handgun and nodded, authorizing the militant to pull the trigger. He saw movement out of the corner of his eye and turned his head to a faint scene of soldiers jumping up and down on a distant ridge. He saw a flicker of light, then heard a reverberating blast. He assumed the reverberation came from the handgun of his adversary. The thud of the body in front of him suggested otherwise. Through the grit in his eyes, he could make out a sniper's bullet hole in the head of his cocky rival.

Waves of emotion surged through Ryker's soul. He had never tasted the appetizer of death. His brain was still telling him his final moments had arrived, but his heart refused to stop thumping. He began to sob uncontrollably.

Unable to fight his body any longer, he threw up. He gasped for air as he waved for help from his saviors on the ridge, then collapsed to the ground.

Everything went black.

Chapter 4

Surgical Unit, Camp Firefox, Afghanistan

Ryker's esophagus hurt. It felt like something had irritated it all the way down to his lungs. Something had: a surgeon had removed an endotracheal tube moments earlier. Ryker licked his dry lips and blinked rapidly as he looked around. The beige canvas walls, esoteric medical equipment, and pungent odor of betadine and alcohol gave away his location—the surgery recovery section of an operating theater—a place no one ever wanted to visit. He was nauseous. He groaned as he turned to his right where Phillips was sitting nearby.

"Dude, how you feeling?" Phillips asked.

Ryker tried to clear his throat. "Water," he barely whispered.

"Can I get him a drink?" Phillips inquired the surgeon who was cleaning equipment behind them.

The surgeon nodded and held a thumb and index finger close together, indicating Ryker could have a small drink. Phillips grabbed a nearby thermos, filled a cup less than halfway, and handed it to Ryker.

Ryker sipped a bit then laid his head back on the bed. His mind began to retrace what had led to him laying on a surgical table. It hadn't yet reached the part where he lost his legs. "How long have I been out?"

"Like five hours," Phillips said. "Triage team and I watched what you did. Dude, that was the craziest thing

I've ever seen, taking out five guys like that. That was incredible, man!"

Ryker half smiled. "Was that your sniper rifle reticle I saw flicker in the sun?"

"Yeah. My bolt stuck for a minute, blocked by sand, but I was able to jimmy it just in time to get that last guy. I mean, I *was* going to let you finish but, you know, looked like you needed a hand."

Ryker shook his head. Painful memories were starting to formulate, but not clearly yet. He thought about giving a smart aleck response but said, "Thanks, man," instead. His memory retrieved the explosion. He grimaced. His heart began to ache. "My team?" He already knew the answer but wanted confirmation.

Phillips pursed his lips and shook his head with sorrow.

Ryker closed his eyes and struggled mentally.

"I'm, uh, I'm sorry," Phillips said and put his head down. He shifted his gold-colored eyes back and forth and pushed his fingers through his bushy black hair, then rubbed his ever-present five o'clock shadow. He was trying to think of words of comfort to offer. "But we got you, bro. You'll be all right. It'll take time." Another long pause. "Oh, hey, there's some people here who want to chat with you. I'll get them and catch you later. I think they have some classified things to talk about."

Ryker nodded, and Phillips went to the next room.

Ryker rubbed his eyes, trying to wipe away the memory of the explosion and his team's deaths. Everything felt like a dream. He wished it were.

He watched Brighton and Dr. Sharp enter the recovery room. Brighton was well-groomed yet notably tired. Dr. Sharp was bright-eyed, but his graying, middle-aged hair was a mess, either because he didn't care at all what he looked like, or he had just stepped out of a helicopter—or both. But what Dr. Sharp lacked in looks, he made up for with a scientist's energy.

"Good to see you, Captain," Brighton said and let the flap door fall behind him.

"Uh, yeah—yeah," Ryker said groggily. He made eye contact with Brighton and attempted to salute.

Brighton grabbed Ryker's hand and returned it to his side.

"Take it easy, soldier. Your country is proud of you. Not many would have been willing to fight under those circumstances. I'm going to personally make sure you're rewarded for your efforts."

"Thank you, sir," Ryker replied, knowing that such a compliment from a high-ranking official was an honor.

Brighton continued, "Ryker, you *are* going to make it through this." Brighton knew the difficulty that Ryker would have from dealing with limb loss. It was well known that many soldiers who lost limbs fought battles just as difficult as combat: depression and severe addictions. But with family, continued support, willpower, and determination, full recovery was possible.

"Yes, sir. I ... uh ... Phillips saved me, but I ... I'm sorry." Ryker struggled to speak. "I failed the mission."

"*You* didn't fail anything," Brighton assured him. "The system failed. In fact, IED expert Dr. Sharp here tells me there was interference. We don't know where it came from."

"Sir, I—" Ryker cleared his throat and took a breath. "I do. I know where it came from."

"You do?!" Dr. Sharp probed with raised eyebrows.

"Yeah. The black cylinder thing we picked up that was like a foot tall flickered some characters and even showed my name on a screen. Then it messed up the tablet. I tried to abort the mission, but...." Ryker swallowed hard and took another sip of water to dam incoming tears.

"I knew it! I *knew* there was something strange," Dr. Sharp emphasized. He shifted his lanky frame closer to the recovery table. "That cylinder and your laptop must have blown up in the blast."

Ryker's face paled. The memories began to solidify. The visual of the blast, his team members losing their lives.

My legs! No!

His mind began to panic. His first thought was that he would never walk again. He closed his eyes and tried not to hyperventilate.

"Take it easy, soldier," Brighton said. "Everything will be all right."

Ryker did all he could to obey the order. He compiled every negative thought about not having legs and crammed them all into a corner of his brain that he didn't know existed.

Dr. Sharp must have realized he had struck a nerve and rerouted the topic. "I caught a glimpse of a signal, but the system cut out before I could track it. Any chance you remember the characters you saw?"

"Oh, uh, yeah." Ryker put a hand to his forehead and closed his eyes to think. He distinctly remembered what he observed on the tablet prior to the blast. "I saw typical output, um, normal background signal strength, similar to what we'd seen in practice runs, and the IED composition outputs worked for the first two IEDs that we dodged." Ryker cleared his throat and groaned as he adjusted his weight. The throbbing in his legs was there, but not nearly as bad as he thought it would be; morphine must have been working. "But these six odd characters started showing up in the feedback signal section. Then—" His thoughts trailed for a moment, and he choked back his emotions. He cleared his throat again. "Anyway, the characters wavered a bit, but they were odd, so they stuck in my mind; they were zero-one-alpha-ksi-one-gamma."

"That's it! Just what I was looking for!" Dr. Sharp exclaimed as he jotted the characters on a notepad. Without saying goodbye, he bolted out of the tent.

Ryker wasn't sure why Dr. Sharp had gotten so excited. "Guess he had things to do."

"He's an odd duck, that one," Brighton said. "Like most scientists I know. But listen, when you're up to it, call your family and let them know you're all right. Having family support will help you through this. But you should be up and running sooner than you think."

"Running, sir?" Ryker didn't know how to process Brighton's latter comment; he had just lost his lower limbs. Panic once again started to encompass him. He fought it. *Breathe.*

"Yes. Look at your legs."

Ryker wasn't sure he had the will to look down. The negative thoughts he had forced aside started creeping out of their hiding place. He shook his head and forced that door of his mind closed.

He looked down. He was shocked to see two metal posts sticking out of his leg stumps. Each was cylindrical and about three inches long. They seemed to be attached to his skin and had circumferential inset regions toward the ends, like they could be connected to something.

"What the—What are those?!" he begged.

"*Those* are called 'osseointegrated implants,'" Brighton said.

"Osseo what?" Ryker asked, uncertain how to comprehend metal posts attached to his body.

"Osseointegrated implants," the surgeon who had been hovering in the back of the tent cut in. He wiped a surgical instrument, set it on a counter, and turned to Ryker. "Osseo means 'bone' in Latin. Those are metal rods surgically inserted into what's remaining of your femoral bones. They're the latest in prosthetic technology, developed a few years ago by a team from the University of Utah and the Veterans Affairs."

"That's science fiction!" Ryker proclaimed.

"It used to be." The surgeon smiled.

"Crazy. So, did I ... *ask* for these while I was out? Or am I some kind of test subject?"

"No, neither, but we choose which soldiers get them. Trust me, you'll thank me later."

"I guess." Ryker shifted his gaze side-to-side to get a better look at the posts. "So, what do they *do* exactly?"

"Good question. One side of the metal is inserted directly into the medullary canal of your residual bone, and the other side protrudes through your skin so you can attach a bionic leg to it. That way, when you walk on the bionic, it puts the mechanical force directly onto your bone. They'll give you drastically improved functionality compared to traditional prosthetic socket systems, which would compress your leg and can cause bruising and other issues. These implants also produce minimal pain because they make a connection with your bones and neurons. Your body thinks they're part of you. That blocks the pain signal. You probably notice that your legs hurt less than you thought they would."

Ryker nodded. "Yeah. My legs don't even really hurt. How the—?" He shook his head in amazement. "I'm not sure I followed most of what you explained, but I guess what you're saying is I'll be able to walk with these?"

"Yes, and *much* more if you'd like. Here, I'll show you how they work."

The surgeon stepped into a separate room and reemerged holding two simplistic, yet rudimentary-looking bionic legs.

The look on Ryker's face forced the surgeon to explain.

"Oh, don't worry, these aren't the final products, just temporary ones. You'll get better ones once you get to the states, but these will allow me to demonstrate."

The surgeon clicked the bionics onto the metal posts coming out of Ryker's legs. Each bionic made a whirring sound once it was attached, then lit up with flashing LEDs indicating they were ready to function.

"All right, stand up," the surgeon ordered.

"Stand up? I just lost my legs," Ryker replied, incredulous.

"Trust me," the surgeon stressed.

Ryker exhaled and eased himself to the edge of the bed. He situated the bionics' feet on the floor and started to stand.

His conscience battled with his actions. He felt like he shouldn't be walking already. He had watched several friends suffer through limb loss. They agonized and struggled, appropriately. Was he supposed to just leapfrog all that? He fully expected he shouldn't. It hurt to think about what his life would be like without legs. While his conscience suggested he should go through more agony, his proprioception countered that visceral thinking and pushed him to use his now-composite body.

He obeyed the latter conviction and continued to stand and could hardly believe how easy it was; amputees often took months to stand, let alone walk, following traumatic injuries. Yet here he was, accomplishing the improbable within a day of injury.

I'm standing!

"Go ahead. Take a few steps," the surgeon prodded.

Ryker hesitated, then put a foot out and was amazed at how intuitive it was to step forward. He took a second step with relative ease, then a third. It almost felt like he could run already. But he stopped himself short of doing so and got back on the bed. He didn't feel right about being able to just get up and walk while his team lay dead.

"They feel interesting," Ryker mused, "but I don't think I'm going to remember what you called them."

"Just call them Ozzies," the surgeon said.

"Are they from Australia or something?"

"No," the surgeon chuckled. "It's just a nickname I derived from osseointegrated implants. I apply it to the whole system, including the metal posts and bionic legs."

Ryker took a moment to process what he had just experienced. His thoughts started to spin, and he hurt inside. He had nearly died, and when he woke up, metal rods were protruding through his amputated stumps.

And now he was wearing clunky metallic legs. It was overwhelming.

"Ryker," Brighton noted, "with Ozzies, you could be back on the battlefield tomorrow. We've tested these under carefully controlled experiments. They're the future of soldier care. They'll change your life and allow you to function at full capacity."

Ryker raised his eyebrows. "That's incredible, sir, but I, I'm not ready for that." He bowed his head. "I'm still trying to wrap my head around all this. I just lost my legs *and* my team. I nearly died." Ryker paused to inhale and exhale. "I don't feel well. I … I just need some time."

"We understand, soldier. Give your family a call. And get some rest and take the time you need."

Ryker nodded with appreciation but sank into despair. He could no longer blockade the panic attack. His breathing increased. His head spun. His muscles tightened. He closed his eyes and hit a nearby table with clenched fists.

"Doctor," Brighton queried, "can we get him some meds?"

"Of course."

The surgeon handed Ryker two pills which he swallowed aggressively. Within minutes, Ryker drifted into a deep zone of despair followed by welcome sleep.

Chapter 5

Communications Tent, Camp Firefox, Afghanistan

Dr. Sharp threw open the door to Camp Firefox's communications tent. A dozen soldiers were inside working on various telecom systems.

"Everyone out. Now!" Dr. Sharp yelled.

The soldiers paused, unsure of how to handle an order from someone who wasn't wearing military apparel and who clearly wasn't an authorized commander.

"I'm serious, this is a matter of national security. I need everyone out of this tent, immediately!"

The soldiers looked at one another and shrugged. They'd seen Dr. Sharp in the tent before and knew he had clearance; if he needed the room that badly, he could have it.

Once the room was his, Dr. Sharp opened his laptop.

"Now let's see where that interference code came from," he mumbled as he connected his laptop to the imaging system he'd developed as part of the DETECT initiative. "I'm the dang inventor of this equipment. No one can breach *me*!"

Dr. Sharp typed vigorously on the keyboard and accessed the detection software. He used the code that Ryker gave him to triangulate the location of the signal that interfered with Ryker's tablet. Dr. Sharp watched the computer screen as the software crunched the data. When the result appeared, he cranked his head back and furrowed his brow.

"That can't be right. A signal near ... Saturn?" He was expecting the interference pattern to come from enemy territory. Saturn was a far cry from their location, let alone Earth.

He typed the code in again to repeat the triangulation. The same outcome appeared; the interference signal was coming from somewhere near Saturn.

"Not *on* Saturn, but near it," Dr. Sharp said to himself. "That can't be." The hairs on his neck rose. This could be the scientific breakthrough of his life! "It must be something with an intense electromagnetic signal." He thought for a moment. "I need a picture!"

Dr. Sharp linked the system to satellites that were being used to monitor electromagnetic signals as part of the DETECT initiative. He pulled up the camera function on the satellite that was closest to Saturn and typed in a command to capture a series of images. He tapped his fingers and adjusted his papers nervously as he awaited the results; it took several minutes for images to arrive from that far out in the solar system. When they did arrive and popped up on the giant screen in the communications tent, Dr. Sharp gasped.

"What are you gasping about?" Brighton asked from the entrance, startling Dr. Sharp. Brighton looked at the images on the screen and raised an eyebrow. "Did you seriously come in here to watch an alien invasion movie?"

Dr. Sharp shook his head slowly. "Those images *aren't* from a movie. I just took them ... using a satellite near *Saturn!*"

Brighton squinted. "Dr. Sharp, if you're fooling around, I'm going to throw you off this base with my bare hands, and I won't give a second thought about where you end up!"

"I'm not joking," Dr. Sharp said and pointed at the screen. "*Those* are what caused the signal interference."

Brighton and Dr. Sharp watched the screen in silence; words weren't enough to capture the intrigue mixed with terror that filled their souls.

The satellite images showed three silver ships flanking one enormous black ship near Saturn.

"Are they moving?" Brighton asked.

"I don't know."

"We need to get to D.C. Now! If those *are* real, we need to warn the world."

Chapter 6

The Vaughn Home, San Antonio, TX

Grace stood up sprightly from her recliner. She had fallen asleep last night as she usually did, watching reruns of Perry Mason.

It was early morning. The feeling in her core was all too familiar; the same she'd had when Paul, her husband, was killed in action. She couldn't explain it, but somehow, she knew Ryker, her older son, was in great pain.

She placed a hand over her heart, feeling her protruding sternum that accentuated her bony yet tone frame. She offered a silent, heartfelt prayer—begging that Ryker be protected and able to make it home. She strode down the hall to check on Jack, her fifteen-year-old, lanky younger son. He was breathing. That gave her some comfort.

She sat next to his bed and pulled the sheets over his uncovered feet. He had grown nearly three inches and increased three shoe sizes over the summer, causing his arms, legs, and feet to become disproportionate from the rest of his body. He welcomed the growth spurt; it would make him a better basketball player. One of his prime goals in life was to beat his older brother.

With Ryker gone, Grace made it her responsibility to monitor Jack's free-throw shooting. Ever since her husband had died, she considered it her duty to make sure her boys were addicted to basketball, just like their dad—a Spurs fan through and through—always wanted. Before Paul's death, she had been glad to know nothing about basketball. After he died, she became a season ticket holder to the San Antonio Spurs and a passionate basketball connoisseur—perhaps out of guilt, but mostly to keep their father alive in their minds.

She grabbed Jack's hand, pushed his brown hair above his hairline and kissed his spring-tanned forehead.

"Mom?" Jack squinted. "You okay? Because I'm not sure my hand is."

"Oh! Jack, sorry." She had squeezed his bony hand harder than she meant to and woke him in the process. Her hand strength was a result of endless nights waitressing as a teenager, then, as a mother, doing the yard work that her husband never had time for, and cooking endless amounts of food for boys who constantly emptied their refrigerator, as well as for guests of her bed-and-breakfast, which was attached to their home.

Grace knew that Jack could sense her concern. When she worried, her face tightened, causing the wrinkles around her taupe-colored eyes to intensify.

"Something wrong?" Jack asked, groggily.

"It's Ryker. He's in trouble," she replied, pushing back a strand of her brunette bangs.

"How do you know?"

"I just do. Something—Something doesn't feel right." Her voice trailed off.

"Is he ...?" Jack couldn't bring himself to ask the inevitable.

"I hope not. Let's pray not."

"You know if anybody can survive over there, it's Ryker," Jack assured her.

Grace knew Jack's comment was based on more than the fact that Ryker won every round of first-person shooter games on Xbox. Ryker was driven and firm in the face of trouble—a trait he'd acquired from their dad. Jack was something of a hands-off individual, a let-the-pieces-fall-where-they-may type of teenager. That was a result of being protected by his big brother.

"Do you remember how Ryker always protected me?" Jack wondered.

Grace smiled. "How could I forget?"

"I think a lot about when he stood up for me against those three bullies. I was alone outside. They came up the sidewalk that was all broken up by the oak tree roots out front. I think I was like nine and Ryker was seventeen. They asked me, 'You ever had your bike stolen?' I said, 'No,' and then they tried to take it. Ryker came out with eyes on fire and took all three of them on alone. 'Hey, noobs,' he yelled. 'How about you give my brother his bike back?' Ryker knocked each one of them to the ground. They sure wished they'd never walked by our house."

"I remember. I didn't approve of that fighting, but I still appreciate that he protected you," Grace disclosed.

"Ryker *hated* bullies, Mom. There's a part of me that thinks he still does, and that's why he's over there protecting us from the ultimate bullying."

"I don't think I've ever thought of it that way," Grace mused, "but you may be onto something."

Grace looked around Jack's room. A dozen or more pictures were on the walls: of Jack and Ryker at basketball camps, and of them and their dad fishing, camping, and playing. Grace inhaled and felt a sense of pride. It pleased her that the three of them had a strong bond and had had minimal family arguments. Ryker, in particular, had always had a level head, never one for the dramatic.

Grace stood, exhaled deeply, and walked across the room for a closer look at Ryker's most recent picture of him in full uniform. His military decorations exuded honor and dignity. The crisp collar and medallions enhanced his already-pronounced jaw and muscular features. *Resolute, composed, confident,* and *strong* were words that Grace thought of to define Ryker. Jack kept the picture of Ryker at the forefront of his desk. Though he didn't admit it, Grace knew Jack missed his brother desperately.

Grace's cellphone rang, interrupting their musings.

"Hello, this is Grace Vaughn."

"Mrs. Vaughn," a deep voice spoke. "This is Corporal Nate Olsen with the United States Army. Your son's been injured in battle, but I'm pleased to say that he's here with me and doing well."

Grace slumped to the ground. "Oh, thank you, God! He's alive!"

Jack rushed to her side and hugged her. Grace put it on speakerphone.

"He is, ma'am, and he would like to speak with you."

Grace and Jack waited while there was a shuffling noise in the background.

"Mom, you there?"

"Ryker!" Grace wept, "are you okay!?"

"I'm okay, Mom."

Hearing Ryker's voice elicited a swath of emotions. Grace almost couldn't speak.

Ryker struggled, "But I guess there's not really an easy way to say this ... I lost both my legs just above my knees."

Grace gasped. Jack squeezed her shoulder.

"It's not all bad, though. They put some metal implants in my bones and gave me new prosthetics, er, bionics, called Ozzies. But I can't—I mean, I know I'm lucky to be alive, but honestly the whole situation is messing with my head."

Grace was horrified, but knew she had to be strong, for her and her boys. She breathed deeply. Having lost her husband, she knew just how fragile the life of a soldier was, yet she was acutely aware that it was better to have a wounded warrior than none at all.

"Baby, you'll get through it. We'll be here and will help you in every way. You're alive. That's what matters!"

"Thanks, Mom. Having your support, it, uh, it helps already. But I kind of want to get my mind off this for a minute. So, how's Jack? Is he another inch taller?"

Always one to try and take a jab at his older brother, Jack retorted, "As a matter of fact, I'm *three* inches taller. But before we jump off the subject of your legs too fast, you know, I hear it's good to look on the bright side of things."

"What's the bright side?" Ryker probed with curiosity.

"Now you won't beat me in basketball!"

"Jack!" Grace slapped his shoulder. "What the—"

Ryker huffed in the background. "Dude, you're a complete moron, you know that? Seriously! But truth be told, the total inappropriateness of that comment actually relieves some stress. If anyone but you had said that ... but coming from the imbecility of my teenage brother. Yeah, whatever. But let's be real, you know I'll still kick your butt no matter what. So don't get too high and mighty on yourself just yet. These Ozzies will apparently make it so I can still do *whatever* I used to. Including dominate you in ball."

"The ball and hoop will be ready, bro," Jack said, only half-joking.

Grace raised an eyebrow. "Apparently, not much has changed in the six months you've been gone."

"Obviously," Ryker quipped. "So, in the spirit of *actually* changing the subject, how's the bed-and-breakfast doing?"

Grace and Paul had built the bed-and-breakfast onto their home when Ryker was young. Grace remembered how Ryker would watch the construction workers dig the enormous hole next to their house. She remembered him telling her how he thought the hole was a lot bigger than a typical house foundation. He was right. But it wasn't until Ryker entered the military years later that Grace was allowed to tell him the bed-and-breakfast was funded by the military, primarily built to house Service Members as they worked on classified projects. The basement was a command center for intelligence collection and systems monitoring. There were a select number of secure rooms that only authorized personnel could enter as they provided access to the command center.

Grace and Paul recognized this opportunity would provide a steady source of income and agreed to manage the bed-and-breakfast component while the military maintained the exterior, landscape, and took care of the secure location.

"It's doing well," Grace said. "It isn't a busy season, so I've been able to keep up on it and even redid some of the interiors last week."

Ryker said, "That's good to hear. In fact, I may need some of your biscuits and gravy when I get back." He chuckled, then grew somber. "I just—I need something to get me through this." Ryker paused. "You know, through the pain and anxiety."

Grace's heart hurt for Ryker. He was typically much more upbeat and positive.

"Baby, you get back to us, and I'll bake you any meal you'd like," Grace promised.

"I will. They say they want me to show off my Ozzies at Brooke Army Medical, so I'll be back in San Antonio soon. Kinda crazy. I'll be helping at The Center for the Intrepid, but as an amputee, not a volunteer."

Grace and Jack both understood the irony of Ryker's comments. Natives of San Antonio and nearly all Veteran amputees were well aware of the Center for the Intrepid, also known as the CFI—a 65,000-square-foot military outpatient facility located just off the main Brooke Army Medical Center campus. It had the most sophisticated instrumentation for amputee rehabilitation in the world. The Vaughns had volunteered at CFI several times to help amputee soldiers, provide service to their community, and show their appreciation for those who served.

Grace, Ryker, and Jack talked about Ryker's experiences for another fifteen minutes. The remorse he was going through was obvious. Several times throughout their conversation, he groaned, not at the pain he was feeling in his legs, but the despair he was experiencing.

Ryker concluded the conversation. "Well, guys, they're telling me I need to go. But I should be at Brooke Army within about twenty-four hours."

"We can't wait to see you," Grace said. "Just come home safe."

"I will, Mom. Love you guys."

"Love you, too."

Grace hung up and sighed in relief. She gave Jack a kiss on the forehead. "He's alive, Jack. And he's coming home!"

Chapter 7

Camp Firefox, Afghanistan

"Well, it sounds like your family's doing well," Phillips said, after Ryker's call ended.

"They are," Ryker agreed. "It was good to talk."

"Ready to head back?" Phillips asked.

"Yeah. I appreciate the support."

Phillips grabbed the handles of Ryker's wheelchair and pushed him toward the communications tent exit.

"Sure you don't want to try and walk with the new Ozzies?"

Ryker groaned, "Man, I'm having a hard time getting there. I don't think it's right that I can just get up and walk already, or that I even *ever* should with my team dead."

Phillips didn't argue with him and worked the wheelchair over the exit door threshold. The air outside was mild and muggy, typical of an Afghan spring in the Paktia Province. The sun was lowering and blinded them momentarily.

Ryker looked to his side as Phillips pushed him across packed earth that made up the makeshift roads in Camp Firefox. He could see the airbase tarmac through several openings of a green fence that surrounded the camp.

"Phillips, can you stop here for a sec?"

Phillips halted the wheelchair, allowing Ryker to peer through a fence opening. He could see nine caskets on the tarmac, each draped with an American flag.

Ryker shook his head. "I'm responsible for their deaths. It's not fair I'm the only one who survived."

"Bro, we all know what can happen to us. It's not your fault. They gave what we're all willing to. It wasn't your fault."

Ryker watched in silence as the caskets were loaded into the back of a Boeing cargo plane. He held back tears. "I need to stand for them."

"Of course." Phillips locked the wheelchair in place.

Ryker stood with ease. His shorts fell slightly but didn't cover his Ozzies. Multiple soldiers walking by stopped to stare at the unique legs sticking out of Ryker's amputated limbs. Ryker ignored the onlookers and saluted the caskets. He stood until his body began to wobble. As the last casket was loaded, Ryker's muscles gave out and he fell back into the wheelchair; his body was still weak from trauma—mental and physical.

Ryker admitted, "Man, I need to sleep or something before I fly back home. I gotta find a way to shake this anxiety or whatever it is. My mind—" Ryker hit his forehead, trying to jostle the ill feelings swirling in his brain.

"I got you," Phillips said.

Phillips pushed Ryker back to the recovery unit and told a medic that Ryker was struggling. The medic gave a look of understanding and handed Ryker two pills in a paper cup, then helped him take off his Ozzies. Ryker eased onto his recovery bed and nearly inhaled the pills as he swallowed.

"I gotta get home," he sighed.

After Phillips and the medic left the room, Ryker crushed the little pill cup and tossed it toward a garbage can. He put his hands on his head. Mental anguish encompassed his mind. He slammed his fists on his bed.

"Come on!" he begged for the pills to take effect. "Get me out of this nightmare!" The pills soon allowed him to relax enough to fall asleep.

Chapter 8

En Route to Brooke Army Medical Center

Ryker analyzed the interior of the retrofitted plane for the umpteenth time during the hours-long flight in which he got minimal sleep. The cargo hold resembled a mobile hospital. IV bags dangled from the ceiling, and rows of beds along the walls, one above the other, ran the length of the plane's steel frame cargo hold. The beds were filled with wounded soldiers—those with limb loss, brain injuries, broken bones, burns, as well as the critically ill and distressed. More than a dozen medics traveled with them, constantly monitoring vitals and well-being.

Injured soldiers were strapped to the beds to prevent them from falling when they hit patches of turbulence, and with good reason. During the final approach into San Antonio, the plane's instrumentation experienced several malfunctions as did many other flights across the globe. The plane shook for nearly a minute and sank more than 500 feet. Crew members and passengers alike wondered if it was their time. The pilots had to circle San Antonio for forty-five minutes before the computer systems allowed them to lower the landing gear.

The final approach and landing challenged even Ryker's stalwart stomach.

When the rear hatch finally groaned open, Ryker sighed in deep relief. He was home!

Dusk—Ryker's favorite time of day—was settling in. A brief rainstorm mixed with lightning left the distinct smell of ozone lingering in the humid San Antonio air. It reminded him of summer nights when he, his dad, and Jack would shoot hoops and play H-O-R-S-E in the driveway. Inevitably, they would have to bring out a spotlight to finish their games; it got dark long before they ever wanted to finish.

"We'll empty the rear of the plane first," a medic said to the travelers. "Be patient, and we'll transport you individually to your rooms at BAMC." BAMC was the acronym and commonly used nickname for Brooke Army Medical Center, which everyone pronounced "BAM" followed by "C."

Ryker's heart leapt. He knew his mom and Jack would be waiting in his room. Without thinking, Ryker stood and began to walk toward the rear of the plane. His Ozzies whirred noisily with each step.

"Nice legs," said a tone-bodied, coffee-eyed twenty-something brunette in scrubs as Ryker approached the hatch.

Ryker was taken aback by her beauty. He smiled. There was an instant connection between them. He sensed she was partially flirting with him, but also being serious. And curious. He looked down at his legs: a pair of clunky Ozzies. "Oh." He paused for a moment. "Do you have a wheelchair?"

"Can I ask why? It doesn't look like you need one," the woman said.

"I, uh, yeah, I'd just like one."

"Sure, soldier," the woman said. She went to a nearby transport truck, grabbed a wheelchair from the back, and wheeled it to him. "Have a seat."

Her voice was pleasant, and Ryker wished she *had* been flirting with him. He eased himself into the wheelchair, acting more gimpy than he actually was, and said, "Thanks."

"Where to?" asked the woman facetiously.

"BAMC." Ryker smirked. Where else would he be going?

"Well, you're in luck, that's right where we're headed."

She pushed Ryker to the transport truck, helped him in the passenger seat, loaded his wheelchair in the back, started the truck, and headed for the freeway.

Ryker broke the silence. "I didn't think we were going to make our landing."

"From turbulence?"

"Yeah, I've never experienced it like that. The plane dropped at one point. We all thought we were goners!"

"I'm glad you're okay. I saw a news feed about there being problems with planes while I was waiting. There was something about flights all over malfunctioning. Thousands of airplanes were grounded. It wasn't just you."

"Crazy," Ryker said.

For the next twenty minutes, Ryker's subconscious completely forgot about the pain, anxiety, and depression he had been battling as he and his captivating driver hit it off. Ryker had never made a connection with anyone so quickly. He experienced an overwhelming chemistry between them, and he knew she felt it, too. When they pulled up to their destination, he felt disappointed that their conversation would end.

Ryker looked at the General Hospital of BAMC. It had a light-brown block-based façade lined with dozens of windows that made the building look majestic and welcoming. Well-groomed grass and gardens lined the entrance and were particularly inviting in the evening as carefully placed lights highlighted their beauty.

"I appreciate how well they take care of this place," the woman said. "Gives a sense of respect for those who serve."

"It does," Ryker said. He caught himself looking at his chauffeur for a moment too long and didn't realize she had fully stopped the truck. "Oh, yeah ... I guess this is my stop."

She smiled.

Ryker opened his door, stood on the asphalt, and said, "So, we made that whole trip, and I, uh, I'm sorry, I didn't catch your name."

"That's because I didn't give it to you." The woman winked and leaned against the steering wheel. "But it was a pleasure to meet you, soldier, and take care of those legs, will ya?"

Ryker's heart sank; he thought she would be willing to give him her name, maybe even number, after hitting it off so well. Perhaps he was wrong about what they were feeling. He smiled and nodded. "Good to meet you too, and, uh, yeah, I will." He tried to extend the conversation, hoping to catch her name. "You know, it's not every day—"

"Captain Vaughn?" An RN standing on the sidewalk cut him off.

Ryker turned. "Yeah, that's me."

"I can show you to your room if you're ready. Your family is waiting."

Ryker had momentarily forgotten that his family was there. He closed the car door, turned to his chauffeur, and said, "Well, looks like I gotta go. Thanks for the ride. I, uh ... it'd be cool to see you around."

"It would be," the woman agreed with a flirtatious grin, then put the truck in gear and pulled away.

Ryker felt slightly deflated; he would have liked to solidify a time to talk with her again, but the opportunity was gone, and it was time to see his family.

Ryker eased into the wheelchair and admired the hospital as the RN pushed him into the lobby.

"So, there any chance you know her name?" Ryker asked.

"Sorry, I don't, but I could probably find out for you."

Ryker shrugged. "Yeah, if you get the chance. I'd like to talk to her again."

The RN smiled. "I'm sure you would."

They reached the elevator and took it to the fourth floor. As they exited, Ryker saw Jack peek his head out of a room down the hall.

"Mom, he's here!" Jack shouted.

Grace emerged from the room and ran down the hallway, exuding enough excitement to fill the north wing.

"Ryker!" she sobbed, unable to say anything else.

They embraced for a long moment as Grace cried shamelessly.

"Good to see you, Mom."

Grace pulled away and grabbed his face and said, "I love you. Thank heaven you're alive!"

Ryker grinned ear to ear, speaking volumes without words. Warmth coursed throughout his body. Two days prior, he had wiped his feet on death's doormat, but now he was home!

"Follow me, Mrs. Vaughn," the RN said as he maneuvered Ryker toward his room. Ryker held Grace's hand as she walked alongside.

From ten feet away, Ryker could smell sanitizing solution emanating from his hospital room. As they crossed the threshold, he saw Jack hiding behind drawn curtains that surrounded his hospital bed. "Seriously, dude, I can see you."

Jack jumped out from behind the curtains. "What's up?" he teased. "Glad you could make it."

Ryker chuckled. His brother was always the wisecracker, yet Ryker's heart leapt internally at the opportunity to interact with his brother. "Yeah, yeah, just thought I'd stop by for a visit, you know." Ryker gave Jack a half hug. "Good to see you, man."

"You too, bro. I'm glad you're okay."

Ryker had the RN wheel him to the far side of the room, closer to the bed. Before hefting his bag onto the bed, he decided to toy with Jack.

"Jack, catch!" Ryker called and fake tossed his bag to Jack.

Jack flinched, prepped for the toss. But Ryker held onto the bag, faking Jack out.

"Ah, I see what you did there," Jack quipped. "The good old *pass fake*!"

"Works every time," Ryker said and winked.

He and Jack both laughed. They had used the pass fake countless times on the basketball court.

Ryker grinned and threw his bag onto the bed, fully exposing his bionic legs.

"Dude, what are *those*?" Jack asked in shock, mesmerized by the metal prosthetics connected to Ryker's amputated limbs.

"They're my new legs," Ryker said. "But I—" Ryker shook his head. He was drowsy. "I can't remember what they call them."

"They're called Ozzies," a pleasant voice from the doorway interrupted.

Ryker turned and saw the woman who had been his chauffeur enter the room. She was wearing scrubs and had her hair in a ponytail. He gave an inquisitive look. Not five minutes ago, she was driving his transport truck. He didn't expect to see her again—certainly not this soon—but he wasn't sad about it and suddenly felt a surge of awakeness.

The woman made eye contact with Ryker and smiled. "They're the latest in bionic technology and soldier care. They'll allow Ryker to function at an even higher level than his real legs, and much higher than traditional types of prosthetic sockets."

"That's sick!" Jack exclaimed.

"Yeah. He'll be able to go on runs, play some basketball if he wants, take a girl out on a date," she winked at

Ryker—blatantly revealing her attraction to his striking hazel eyes, sandy hair, muscular torso, and humble attitude—"even ... *return to duty* if he'd like. Ozzies were designed to return soldiers to civilian life *or* the battlefield within days."

Ryker lifted one of his legs and let his family examine the Ozzie technology. He disconnected the Ozzie to show how the bionic leg component of the system connected to the metal post that protruded through his skin. "See this connector?" Ryker pointed to a quick connect component of the metal post. "That's where the connection between the metal in my actual leg and the bionic leg is made."

"You say he'll be able to *run* on these?" Jack asked rhetorically as he eyed the rusty metal on the Ozzies. "No offense, but they don't even look like they would hold up his weight, let alone play some ball."

Grace slapped Jack's arm and gave him a threatening look. *Seriously, Jack, have some decency*, her glare implied.

"Whaaaat?" Jack shrugged. "Honest questions is all."

Ryker looked down at the tattered Ozzies. He couldn't disagree. The temporary bionics he received in Afghanistan were clunky and aged with obvious signs of rust at the hinge points and feet.

"Actually, just so happens that's one reason I'm here," the woman said. "My name is Jessie Bell." She smiled at Ryker. "I'm the physical rehab supervisor here at BAMC and the Center for the Intrepid. I've been tasked to support Ryker with his new legs. Hang on, I have something." Jessie stepped out of the room for a moment.

Ryker looked at Jack while Jessie was out.

"Dude, she's *hot*," Jack whispered.

Ryker nodded. He unintentionally grunted. A little.

"Seriously, you two." Grace rolled her eyes. "She's also smart and accomplished; don't ogle just over someone's looks."

"Hey, you can't discount the basic tenet of biology," Jack said. "Without attraction, life doesn't progress. That's what my science teacher taught."

Ryker fist-bumped Jack.

Grace shook her head and smirked.

Jessie returned holding a pair of carbon-fiber-based, futuristic-looking Ozzies. Ryker noticed the upscaled micromotors and hinges in the knee and ankles. The Ozzies' contours reminded him of sleek lines on a high-end sports car, with blue lighting along the flanks and smooth metallic components that made them unabashedly eye-catching. It was obvious the designers had no intention of making the Ozzies look discreet.

"Think these will do the trick?" Jessie asked Jack.

"Now we're talking!" Jack said with wide eyes as he analyzed the machine-like legs.

"What do you say, soldier, want to try them?" Jessie asked Ryker.

Ryker smiled, then frowned ... and hesitated. His mood slumped. For the last few moments, he'd reveled in the exhilaration and excitement of seeing his family—and meeting Jessie. But these positive feelings were an undersized bandage over the gaping wound of despair deep in his soul as thoughts of his ordnance patrol team resurfaced.

"I mean, I wish I could, Jessie, but ... I'm not ready for that yet. It's like I told my buddy in Afghanistan, I just don't feel right about standing up and walking or running all of a sudden while my team lies dead. I feel like I'd be dishonoring them."

"I respect that," Jessie said, nodding. As a physical therapist who worked with recovering amputees and wounded warriors, she knew that mental trauma affected every soldier differently. But she also knew how important it was for wounded warriors to make physical and symbolic steps forward. "Tell you what, how about I show you some of the features the Ozzies have first? Then we can figure out the next step."

"Uh, sure," Ryker tepidly agreed.

Ryker lifted one of his legs and didn't mind Jessie placing her soft hands under his hamstrings so she could attach the new Ozzies, in under ten seconds. The quick connect feature highlighted one of the superior aspects of Ozzies compared to old prosthetic socket technologies, which typically took patients ten to thirty minutes to don.

"All right," Jessie instructed, "there's a dial right here on the outside of each Ozzie."

Ryker and Grace both leaned over so they could see the dial Jessie was pointing to.

"The dial has four settings: rest mode, walk mode, sport mode, and battle mode. You can kind of guess what each of those means."

"Yeah, that's pretty intuitive," Ryker said.

"Okay, do you mind if I set it to walk mode and you just take a brief stroll around the room? Just so you can get a sense for how they feel."

Ryker inhaled and exhaled slowly. "Mom," he said as he looked Grace in the eye, "could you help me up?"

Grace agreed without hesitation and grabbed one of Ryker's hands, then wrapped an arm around his torso to help hoist him up out of his wheelchair.

Ryker stood with ease. He remained still for nearly a minute, not so much to get his bearings—the new Ozzies were even easier to balance on than the other Ozzies—but to contemplate. *What would my team think of me standing, no, living, with them lying dead?* Ryker stood for so long, he made everyone in the room wonder what he was going to do next. He took another deep breath, then a step forward. The oddest sensation occurred.

"Whoa, wait a minute," he noted. "How is it I can actually feel the texture of the floor under my feet?"

"That's one thing I wanted you to experience with these," Jessie said. "The way these new Ozzies are designed, not only do they provide direct mechanical loading to your bones, they also have a microchip that sends signals directly to your neurons so you can actually *feel* the surface you're walking on. Just like real legs and feet."

"That's trippy," Ryker said. He let go of Grace's hand and took another step forward, then another. A sense of exhilaration filled him. Just days earlier, he'd dreaded the thought of being a double amputee; he was terrified when he clawed through the sand and couldn't find his legs. He didn't think he would ever walk again. Several of his comrades in battle had lost limbs, and it took them months, if not years, of rehabilitation to walk again. If ever. And here he was, upright and walking, within days of losing his legs.

He continued to take steps forward, even nudging Jack aside as he passed him. "And you thought you'd beat me in basketball."

He and Jack both smirked.

The Ozzies flowed with ease as Ryker took step after step. He saw his mom wipe her eyes as she watched him walk; not only did it echo his first steps as a child, but to see a wounded warrior who could function so soon after nearly paying the ultimate sacrifice sparked deep emotion.

Ryker nearly lost all sense of his pain and anguish as he walked. The experience was thrilling. He stepped into the hallway and found a rug. He rubbed the feet of his Ozzies on it and could sense the rough texture under his toes. He shook his head in awe as he looked at his family and Jessie. "This technology is fascinating!" He took a brief walk down the hallway then reentered his room. Everyone was grinning ear to ear to see him overcoming major mental and physical challenges.

Yet, as he passed by the window of his room, Ryker's steps slowed, and he came to a stop. He peered through the blinds. His heart sank.

He watched a cargo plane land at the military base in the distance. He knew it was the very plane transporting the caskets of his team. In an instant, all the remorse, all the pain, all the loss he had experienced the past two days rushed back into his mind.

"No!" he yelled, startling Grace, Jack, and Jessie. He scrunched his face. Tears started streaming down his cheeks. He slammed his body on his hospital bed in uncharacteristic fashion. "Get these things off me!" he demanded and began to fumble to get the Ozzies off. "This isn't right! I should have died with them."

Grace rushed to Ryker's side. "Baby, relax, just relax. We're here for you."

"Mom, it isn't right. I told you it wasn't right!"

Jessie rushed to the hallway and called a nurse. "We need help, now!"

Ryker yelled in pain, not physical—mental. "Why did they have to die? *Why?* It was my fault. I told them it was all clear. It wasn't! The bombs killed every one of them!"

Jessie quickly detached the Ozzies and set them against a far wall. "I'm sorry, Ryker. I shouldn't have pushed you yet."

Ryker ignored her and continued loudly lamenting.

A nurse rushed in the room and injected a solution of meds into a catheter in Ryker's wrist. "This should help calm you down. Hang in there."

Ryker's cries filled the corridor. He hugged his mom tight. "Just stay!" he begged.

"I'm not going anywhere," Grace soothed. "I'm here. I'm here."

For longer than anyone measured, Ryker held onto his mom and cycled in and out of sorrow as she rocked him gently and caressed his hair, tears streaming down both of their faces.

Jack sat on the windowsill bench and cried quietly as he watched his brother mourn. Jack had never experienced firsthand the grief that a soldier goes through after losing comrades or suffering injuries. The reality was clear now, and he didn't envy it. He felt powerless to do anything about it.

Jessie wiped her eyes as she stood in the hallway just outside Ryker's room, giving them the time they needed.

Ryker rocked back and forth as his mom embraced him on his hospital bed. Images of caskets draped with American flags flashed through his mind. Gratefully, the meds began to take effect and he was able to drift off.

Grace felt Ryker's body begin to relax, but she maintained her embrace.

"I'm here, baby. I'm here. We're going to make it through."

Chapter 9

Situation Room, The White House, Washington, D.C.

It was 1330. Brighton waited anxiously for the DETECT initiative board of reviewers to arrive in the main Situation Room of the White House in Washington, D.C. The Situation Room was a complex of offices, as opposed to a single room, on the ground floor of the White House consisting of more than 5,000 square feet. Dozens of people worked in its confines, monitoring world affairs and potential threats 24/7. Brighton had participated in high-profile meetings in offices throughout the world, many furnished with the most lavish accessories, but none had the sophistication of the main Situation Room. Seven flat-panel screens lined the walls, the largest being opposite the entrance. Secure feeds could connect the president or his staff to virtually any area of the world. With its modular design, the room served well as an axis for communications, intelligence operations, military strategy, or lower-profile meetings.

Brighton nervously straightened the brown leather chairs around the conference room table and assessed the flat panel screens. He could only imagine what images had been displayed on those screens over the years: geopolitical unrest, conspiracy information, Top-Secret intel. But what he and Dr. Sharp were about to show, well, he wasn't sure that had ever actually been viewed before. Anywhere. Brighton closed his eyes and took a deep breath; the upcoming presentation would have worldwide implications.

"Col. Brighton," a woman in the corner of the room said, interrupting his thoughts, "they're here."

Brighton straightened his uniform and cleared his throat. "I'm ready."

Dr. Sharp entered first followed by personnel from the Air Force, NSA, Naval Communications, Marines, the Vice Chair of the DETECT initiative—Gen. Shauntel Pearson—and two scientists from NASA: Drs. Pradib Gupta and Hillary Forest.

Gen. Pearson, a commandeering mid-sixties woman with cropped black hair, piercing brown eyes and a coarse demeanor when necessary, had worked with Brighton on a variety of projects and budget committees. "You've been quite the world traveler lately," she said to him as she took a seat. "You were in Afghanistan not two days ago, is that correct?"

Brighton, still standing at the front of the room, nodded. "It's been a busy time to say the least. After we performed the initial field test for IED detection, I finalized several reports, then Dr. Sharp and I took an emergency flight to Houston to work with Drs. Gupta and Forest at NASA headquarters." Brighton acknowledged Drs. Gupta and Forest just as they were taking their seats at the table. He noticed the bags under their eyes that matched his own, indicating they too had barely slept in the past twenty-four hours. "We needed them to help us prepare for this meeting."

Brighton's lead-in piqued everyone's interest.

"Well, we're intrigued to see what you have to share," Gen. Pearson said with a hint of curiosity.

Their conversation was interrupted as the president of the United States entered the room along with his secretary of defense, former Gen. Van Childress. Gen. Childress had been a private citizen for more than ten years, but everyone still called him "General." Old habits were hard to break.

The group stood out of respect for the president. Spry and youthful, his black skin highlighted the brightness of his white shirt and red tie. He was best known for his optimism, but his military experience was limited, which was why he had Gen. Childress in tow.

Gen. Childress was worn well beyond his years. At age fifty-eight, he looked seventy-five. His hair had grayed early. His skin was leathery and anoxic due to an unbreakable smoking habit. Alcohol had become his life's only companion. Work, serving soldiers, and alcohol were all he lived for.

"Good morning, all," the president said. "Please, take your seats. I'm told there's a serious matter at hand. Let's skip any pleasantries and get right to it. What's going on?"

Brighton took charge and stood at the front of the Situation Room with his hands behind his back. His thick chest enhanced the medallions and military ribbons decorating his uniform. "Thank you, Mr. President, and all of you for being here." He spoke in a professional, commanding voice. "For the past nine months, Dr. Sharp and I have led a team performing developmental tests on our new digital communications instruments for IED detection and other advanced weaponry exploration initiatives including high-altitude electromagnetic pulses, also known as EMPs. This week, we obtained critical information that will affect national and global security. I'll let Dr. Sharp explain."

Brighton knew that the attendees sensed his tone, which carried a weight typically reserved for battlefield scenarios.

"Thank you, Col. Brighton." Dr. Sharp nodded as he strode to the head of the table with his laptop in hand. His long, slender legs, which matched his frame and face, carried him swiftly to the front. He removed a key from his pant pocket and undid a lock that secured his laptop cover. "As review for those of you who have not met me yet, my name is Dr. Steven Sharp. I'm an MIT professor of Aeronautics and Astronautics in the Department of Engineering. I'm a consultant to the military on several digital imaging and acquisitions systems that are being used for the DETECT initiative." Dr. Sharp fumbled slightly as he connected his laptop to the projector that hung in the middle of the conference room. His least favorite part of being a professor was public speaking. He was inherently shy and self-conscious. His underlying nervousness was apparent and made more noticeable by the sheen of sweat forming on his wrinkled brow. "As Col. Brighton mentioned, we've been employing several imaging systems to collect intelligence information on IED bombs that al Qaeda manufacture.

"Our initial field test of the system was performed this week. Unfortunately, the system failed due to an external signal interaction."

The Air Force representative asked, "Sorry, Dr. Sharp, what exactly does that mean?"

"It, uh, just means our system was compromised by a form of electromagnetic interference, and that's why it didn't detect the IEDs when it was supposed to."

"Did al Qaeda already figure out how to jam your $50 million system before it was even in use?" the president prodded.

"No, no, sir, we're very familiar with al Qaeda signals that have the potential to disrupt our systems. They use typical binary code outputs. That's why I incorporated a feedback signal into the digital detection system. It would have the ability to detect when al Qaeda was attempting to intercept our signals."

"Then where did the interference come from?"

"Well, as part of the DETECT initiative, I specifically use our detection equipment and software to scan for electromagnetic and radiation signals both on land, and ... in *outer* atmospheric regions.

"This week, Capt. Ryker Vaughn observed an unusual set of codes during the IED-detection field test. The code was not solely binary, which indicated it came from an advanced source. We're lucky he remembered the interference characters because I was able to use those codes and several satellites to triangulate the location of the interference. It came from," he swallowed nervously, "*outside* our atmosphere."

The NSA representative sat up in his chair angrily. "You mean to tell me it was *you* that hacked those satellites this week? We thought that came from enemies! We spent tens of thousands of dollars in manpower and resources trying to figure out who that was and why our satellites were being commandeered. And now here I am, sitting as a DETECT initiative member, and I find out this happened in our own backyard? Dr. Sharp and Col. Brighton, you could be court martialed for this!"

"Oh, I would wait a moment before passing judgment against this ...." Dr. Sharp hesitated.

"Well, you should have let us know before you had us gather for this. I can't believe what I'm hearing."

"Um—" Dr. Sharp tried to go on.

Before he could continue, Gen. Pearson grumbled, "I don't recall the military approving funding for anything outside of our original objectives. Col. Brighton, I'm somewhat shocked that you allowed this to happen."

With the exception of the two NASA board members, the attendees began to whisper incredulously to one another.

"Ladies and gentlemen," Brighton cut in, "I need you all to stop immediately. We don't have time for this bickering. Let Dr. Sharp continue his presentation. Your concerns will be addressed. What he has to share is a matter of *unprecedented* national security."

Brighton obviously wasn't joking. He stared down everyone at the table.

"I agree, let Dr. Sharp continue," the president said.

The chaos settled, and Dr. Sharp went on. "Yes, thank you. As I was saying, when I triangulated the location of the signal, I found that the interference derived from a location near Saturn."

"Whoa, boy." The NSA representative rolled his eyes. His face was flushed and red.

"Enough," the president commanded and shot a stern look at the NSA representative.

Dr. Sharp explained, "I connected our detection systems to the satellite network and was able to capture images of what caused the interference." He wasted no time, pushed a few buttons on his laptop, then turned his head toward a flat-panel screen and clicked the power button. "All right everyone, brace yourselves."

Most of the attendees, in particular the NSA representative, gasped as the satellite images came up on the screen. Those who had naysaid just moments prior felt chagrined for challenging Dr. Sharp. The DETECT initiative reviewers had seen plenty of news reports and conspiracy theories about *Un*identified Aerial Phenomena, but displayed before them were images of *Identified* Aerial Phenomena.

Everyone stared at the semi-clear images of four interstellar ships near Saturn. Three of them equidistantly flanked a larger one. The flankers each had vertical metallic rings wrapped around the circumference of clear domes fused to the vertical ring. They looked like replicas of Saturn rotated ninety degrees, with transparent canopies.

The fourth and largest ship was black and shaped somewhat like a city-sized toy jack. Unlike a jack with a cone-shaped center piece, its core was hexagonal and stretched twice as far in height than depth.

"Each of the horizontal arms you see on the larger ship extends for approximately four miles. All four ships are about the size of a city," Dr. Sharp explained. "And as you can see, each arm houses three, equally spaced turbines, with the third comprising each arm tip." Dr. Sharp paused, then muttered, "And it's appearance is ... threatening."

"Okay, wait a minute," the Air Force representative cut in, "can we slow down for a moment and assess what we're looking at here? First off, I'm not actually buying any of this. I apologize, but we've been monitoring UAPs for decades and nothing has ever been legitimate. And how do we know these images are real? Has anyone verified this information?"

Somewhat skeptical, the president said, "I agree. I've sat in this very room and reviewed hours of footage that showed images and videos of potential UAPs and related events. Can you convince us this is real?"

"We can," Dr. Gupta assured. "Col. Brighton and Dr. Sharp came to Houston and asked, er, ordered Dr. Forest and me to review Dr. Sharp's information. They are real, Mr. President."

Gen. Childress exhaled heavily, grabbing the attendees' attention. "So, let's assume they're real. Do we know if they pose a threat?"

The president responded. "Our protocols state that we are required to *assume* that any independent system outside of our atmosphere poses a threat."

"I agree, Mr. President, but I can't trust in a protocol on a piece of paper to tell me whether they *actually* pose a threat." One of Gen. Childress' pet peeves was the portrayal that government officials gave of knowing the intricacies of battle because they had read something in a document. "If we need to put up a fight, we need to know exactly what we're fighting against. And what their intentions are."

"Understood, Gen. Childress. Col. Brighton, do we have any indication that these ships pose a *real* threat?"

Brighton replied, "At this point, we don't have information beyond what we're showing you. There are no apparent signs of hostility, but we don't have enough data to say whether they're a threat."

Gen. Childress sat back in his chair. "Are they mobilizing, and if so, do we have an ETA?"

"From the information we've collected, it looks as though the ships are maintaining a position near Saturn. For whatever reason, they don't appear to be approaching."

"Why haven't we detected these before? How long have they been there?" the president asked heatedly. "Why would they suddenly appear out of nowhere?"

"That's—well—Unfortunately, we don't have a good answer for that," Dr. Sharp replied.

The president jumped out of his chair and opened the main entrance doors of the Situation Room. "Get me our communications specialist," he yelled down the hall. "I want the CIA and Area 51 directors on screen, now!"

Within minutes, both women directors were on videoconference.

"Directors," the president started as he sat back down, "what we are about to discuss is highly classified information. You will share it with *no one* unless otherwise authorized. Am I clear?"

Both women agreed.

"The team on this videoconference has credible information and gives us reason to believe that there is something in our solar system interfering with our computer systems. I need to know if you are aware of this and if you have had *any* indication of what it is. You will spare us no details! Our security is on the line."

"Of course, Mr. President," the Area 51 director offered. "We have information that, uh, may be helpful. For several weeks, there have been indications that our systems were hacked, but we'd been unable to determine who hacked us."

"You, you have the most secure computer systems in the entire government. How did a hacker get through?"

"Well, we, um, there was an incident ...." She hesitated.

"I said spare no details!" the president shouted. "What incident?"

The CIA director spoke up. "Mr. President, let me explain everything."

"Please do." The president sat slowly.

"Three years ago, we recovered a black metal, I guess you could say *cylindrical* object, maybe a foot tall, from the Gulf of Mexico."

"My gosh!" Dr. Sharp interrupted. "That's also what Ryker found!"

"Please, Dr. Sharp, let her continue," the president requested.

Dr. Sharp shrank back and nodded. "Of course, sorry."

The CIA director continued. "We call it GM-1. A fisherman watched GM-1 fall from the sky and land in the vicinity of Port Aransas, Texas. He found it under water due to some blue flashing lights on its surface. After retrieving it, he called the police. It was ultimately turned over to the CIA.

"For several weeks, we attempted to determine where it came from. As we characterized it, we found that the object was composed of a stable form of astatine. Astatine is typically a highly radioactive material that vaporizes in the presence of its own heat with a half-life of only eight minutes. We believe it came from a celestial source."

"Why do you believe that?" the president asked.

"Sir, less than a gram of astatine exists on Earth in its natural form. GM-1 is made of more than twenty *pounds* of it!" The CIA director paused, letting the information sink in. "The astatine in this object appeared to have been chemically stabilized by methods that our scientists were unable to figure out. To our knowledge, none of our allies or enemies have ever worked with astatine, so we didn't suspect terrorism or warfare.

"We concluded that it was made by a higher life form, perhaps a sign of extraterrestrial life, and we transported it to our specialists at Area 51."

The Area 51 director took over for the CIA director and continued. "GM-1 sat dormant for years in our facility. About two days ago, there was an incident wherein a disgruntled scientist entered the facility in a drunken rage. As security attempted to detain him, he overturned a water jug, and the liquid fell onto GM-1. Several lights on the object began to flicker sporadically, and our computer systems crashed for a brief period. We believe this was the window of opportunity that a hacker used to get into our system."

After a short pause the president asked, "Is that everything?"

"That's all we have at this time," the Area 51 director said.

Dr. Sharp interjected, "Doesn't it seem obvious that GM-1 has some form of water detection technology?"

"Dr. Sharp," the Area 51 director scoffed, "I hope you can appreciate that we considered everything from it being an ancient tool to a toilet accessory. Yes, we've considered it could be a signaling device, but up until this point, we have no indication that that was the case."

"Yes, we do! We do now!" Dr. Sharp exclaimed.

"Excuse me?" the CIA director barked incredulously.

"Mr. President, may I?" Dr. Sharp asked, hoping to inform the CIA director and Area 51 director about the ships they detected.

"Yes, if anybody needs to know, it's these two."

"Thank you," Dr. Sharp said. "Directors, over the past several years, I developed a software program and accompanying instrumentation that has a unique ability to sense electromagnetic waves and corresponding radiation.

We initially developed this technology to detect high-altitude warheads that may elicit EMP attacks. This system works with greater sensitivity than any previous piece of equipment.

"This week, Capt. Ryker Vaughn uncovered a cylinder just like the one you mentioned. It apparently produced some interference and generated a code in our detection system. Gratefully, he remembered the code and gave it to me. I used it to determine the source of interference."

Dr. Sharp turned once again to the president, confirming permission to show the directors the images of the ships they discovered.

The president nodded his approval.

"Using satellites near Saturn, I was able to collect these images." Dr. Sharp shared his screen using an encrypted system.

Both directors gazed in amazement. Dr. Sharp was silently interested to see the look of surprise on the face of the Area 51 director. Dr. Sharp thought, *Hmm. Had Area 51 actually contained aliens or any form of alien ships according to popular belief, she likely would not be so shocked.*

"Director," Dr. Sharp addressed the CIA director, "when that fisherman first retrieved GM-1, he told you the lights were flickering, is that correct?"

"They did for a short period, yes."

"And then it sat dormant for years, until it got splashed with water, correct?"

"Well—I—Yes, that's correct," the director answered with interest.

"There's a simple way for us to determine if GM-1 is a water-sensitive transponder." Dr. Sharp shifted his eye contact to the members of the DETECT initiative, the president, and Gen. Childress. "Pour some water on it."

"What exactly is that going to tell us?" the Area 51 director asked.

"Both times that GM-1 has been wet, the lights flickered. My presumption is that it responds to water. If we pour a cup of water on it, and those ships out there give us some indication that they recognize it, we'll know if it sends a signal. It's a basic science experiment."

Brighton interrupted. "But this is much more than an experiment. What if GM-1 *is* a transponder? What if it's a beacon? If it belongs to those ships and you activate it, do we really want them to find it, or us for that matter? Maybe *that's* what they're waiting for—another signal."

Gen. Childress warned the team, "We need to leave that thing alone. We don't know what we're dealing with here." He gave the president a stern look.

"So, we reduce the risk of sending a signal. We pour water on it briefly and incrementally," Dr. Sharp said. "Pour a small amount of water on it, such as ten milliliters at first, and immediately wipe it off. If it doesn't light up, we increase the amount to twenty milliliters, dry it off, and so forth. See if and when it lights up. That way, we can determine *if* it's sensitive to water and just *how* sensitive it is. The important thing is, we dry it off each time to reduce the risk of letting it send a signal."

The room fell silent. The meeting attendees looked at one another, weighing the possibilities.

"But what if we don't dry it off quickly enough?" the CIA director wondered. "For all we know, the signal may take less than a second to transmit. We shouldn't mess with it."

"And if we don't pour water on it, what happens?" the president contemplated. "We let those ships sit there. Do they come? Do they go? Do we leave our children and grandchildren to deal with them? Are they nefariously gathering data for a worldwide conquest? Do we never say a word to the world that there are in fact signs of life 'out there?' I guarantee that astronomers, amateur or not, from other countries are going to see them soon. Once it gets to the public, the world will be on red alert for an impending attack. Think about the chaos that will ensue. Thousands, perhaps millions, of lives will be lost." The president paused to let his words sink in. "Systems will collapse, and we'll put ourselves in financial and political ruin. The people may suffer worse than if they did come visit us. I propose that we follow Dr. Sharp's advice. We have to remove some variables."

Everyone sat in silence. The president seemed unusually cavalier about the potential of signaling the ships.

"Fine, we'll take a vote," the president demanded. He grabbed a leaf of paper, tore it into small rectangles, and handed each attendee a piece. "Each of you write your vote: checkmark for 'yes,' we pour water slowly on the cylinder, x for 'no,' we don't do that. No need to write your name or any explanation. Just mark your vote and fold your paper. Directors on screen, text me your response."

"This is nonsense," Gen. Childress argued. "This requires federal oversight. Legislation."

"That's not a luxury we have at the moment. Extenuating circumstances require immediate action. If we let administrators take over, we won't have an answer for another decade. As president of this nation and commander-in-chief of our armed forces, I ask that all of you vote. Now. Then pass me your papers."

Hesitantly, the attendees wrote down their decision and slid their papers to the president. He read the responses aloud. "Seven for. Four against. We go forward. Director," the president turned to the screen of the Area 51 director, "do you have video feed in the area where GM-1 is located?"

"Yes."

"Patch us into that room and tell your technician to pour ten milliliters of water on GM-1."

"I'm warning everyone in this room," Gen. Childress shouted, "if we let this continue, we are committing global suicide!"

"I agree with Gen. Childress," the CIA director complained from the screen. "We have no idea what the implications are. I strongly advise against this."

The president deliberated. "Listen, I assure all of you that if those ships do respond to GM-1 and begin to approach us, our atmosphere will be safe. What I'm about to share is beyond Top-Secret, but imperative for this team, and this team only, to know.

"Over the past two decades, NASA and our military have collaborated with multiple countries. We've put several protective measures in place for this precise circumstance. At this very moment, there are high-powered artillery units orbiting the moon and several more orbiting Earth. They are armed with nuclear weapons that have the ability to reach a celestial object more than 500,000 miles away in a matter of hours. I assure you we will be protected. There's a reason why Pluto is no longer a planet."

Brighton and the rest of the DETECT initiative team marveled at the president's words. No one had ever considered the military having armaments surrounding Earth that were powerful enough to destroy a dwarf planet. Brighton noted Gen. Childress' demeanor soften but not fully relax.

"If I seem collected about the situation," the president said, "this is why. Once again, I assure you that what we are about to do is rational. Director," the president ordered, "have your technician pour the water. Slowly. And observe."

"Yes, sir."

The director left her screen and patched into the secure area where GM-1 was being held. The room consisted of 1,000 square feet of lab space located thirty-five feet below the surface of the Nevada sand. The room was temperature controlled and equipped with computers, intricate instruments, and blacktop benches—upon one of which sat GM-1. Consistent with the description that was given, GM-1 was nothing more than a black metal cylinder roughly one foot high and six inches in diameter. The surface was shiny, and it had a rectangular section that delineated a screen of sorts.

"Mr. President, I'm in the containment facility," the Area 51 director said. "I'll have one of our techs pour water on GM-1. Okay," she called to a lab technician, "pour ten mils of water on GM-1."

The lab tech filled a beaker and looked inquisitively at the director, silently wondering if she was kidding.

"I'm serious," the director said. "The president of the United States would like to watch you slowly pour water on that object."

The tech withheld a chuckle and followed her orders. She opened an acrylic case and slowly started to pour ten milliliters of water on the cylinder. She had barely poured half a milliliter of the water when it began flashing blue. The tech wiped it dry immediately.

"Just as I presumed," Dr. Sharp cheered. "What you have there is an object that is sensitive to water!"

"And how do we determine if it's a transponder?" Gen. Childress asked chillingly.

Brighton leaned forward. "Dr. Gupta, can you monitor the status of the ships?"

"Of course." Dr. Gupta turned to his laptop and plugged it into the equipment in the Situation Room. He linked a subset of NASA's secure space exploration technology to his software in order to follow the ships. "Sir ... my readouts indicate that the ships, uh, just began to mobilize."

"And their trajectory?" the president asked.

"Just a moment." Dr. Gupta said. After several minutes of monitoring, Dr. Gupta replied, "It, it appears they're now heading toward us."

Gen. Childress shook his head in disbelief. "What have we just done?"

"There's more," Dr. Sharp spoke up. "My systems are detecting a code, or, wait a second, a message it looks like."

"Put it on screen," Brighton ordered.

Brighton watched with the group as the message appeared on the large flat panel screen. He could hardly believe his eyes when he saw the message:

Justice to Ryker Vaughn.

"What the ...?" Brighton stuttered.

"Ryker Vaughn?" the president inquired. "Isn't he the soldier you mentioned?"

"He is," Brighton said.

"What business would those ships have singling him out? Better yet, how would they even know who he is?"

"I don't know, sir."

"Do we know where Ryker is?"

"Yes," Brighton said. "He's at BAMC in San Antonio, getting support following his injuries."

"Get him on the line, immediately!" the president stressed. "And put him on speaker."

Within moments, a call was routed to BAMC, and a groggy-voiced soldier answered.

"Hello?"

"Is this Capt. Ryker Vaughn?" the president asked.

"It is. May I ask who's calling?"

"Capt. Vaughn, this is the president of the United States. Do you have a few minutes?"

"Ha, ha, very funny, Jack," Ryker gibed. "Buddy, I'm not up to this right now."

"Ryker, this is no joke. I assure you I am the president, and I'm sitting here in the Situation Room of the White

House with Col. Brighton and Dr. Sharp, with whom you are familiar."

"Hello, Ryker," Dr. Sharp spoke. "It's true, we're here with the president."

"Oh, Mr. President, sorry." Ryker cleared his throat. "I thought it was my little brother playing a joke. Sir, what a tremendous honor."

"Ryker, we need you to come to Washington, D.C., like, today. There's a matter of national security that we cannot discuss by phone, but it urgently requires your presence."

"Mr. President, I ..." Ryker hesitated. "It's an honor to receive this call, and I sincerely wish it were under different circumstances, but I'm not, uh, I'm not currently in a state of mind or health to support military operations any further. Col. Brighton knows that I nearly died this week, and I'm not functioning yet. I apologize, but I need to be with my family right now and would like to respectfully decline the invitation."

"Soldier, I'm not sure you understand the gravity of this situation."

"Sir, no, I don't, but I'm not currently capable of travel and I, I just need to be with my family."

The president pushed the mute button so Ryker couldn't hear him. "What do we do with a soldier who won't follow a request from the *president*? He must be in bad shape. I could order him, but .... What is it he's not saying? What do we know about this soldier?"

Brighton responded, "He's top notch, but not himself, sir. I received a text saying he had a breakdown last night. He was the only survivor of his team, lost both his legs, lost his dad to war years ago, and I think it's all taking a toll on him at once."

"Well, I sympathize but this is of global importance. His name is sitting up there on a screen of the most powerful military force on Earth and was apparently sent by some aliens sitting in our solar system. He's involved whether he likes it or not. If he won't come to us, we're going to him. And, as it just so happens, at his house you'll be able to collect the data you need to characterize these ships more fully." The president pressed the unmute button. "Ryker, your mother runs a bed-and-breakfast for the military in San Antonio with Top-Secret intelligence and reconnaissance collection capability, correct?"

"Um, yes, Mr. President, she does."

Brighton imagined that Ryker was surprised the president knew about that, but then again, the president would know more about Top-Secret locations than anyone.

"Tell you what, I could order you here, but don't worry about coming to the White House. I'm going to have a team come to *your* house. Your country needs you, soldier. I'm sorry for all that you're going through, but I need you to muster what strength you can and rise to action."

"I'll, I'll do what I can, sir."

"We'll see you soon, soldier." The president hung up and directed, "Brighton, Gen. Childress, Drs. Pradib, Gupta, and Sharp, pack your bags. You're all going to San Antonio."

The attendees didn't hesitate and started gathering their belongings.

"Mr. President," Gen. Childress commented as he stood from his chair, "I don't like a single thing about any of this." He shook his head and pursed his lips. "All I have to say is ... those had better be some *big* guns you have floating around the moon!"

Chapter 10

Bed-and-Breakfast, San Antonio, TX

"Pull in here," Brighton said to the driver of the black SUV that was transporting him and a selection of DETECT initiative officials from Randolph Air Force Base to Grace Vaughn's bed-and-breakfast. "Where those scrub oak trees line the driveway on either side, that's the bed-and-breakfast."

Brighton glanced briefly at the exterior of the bed-and-breakfast. It was perhaps the nicest Top-Secret building the military owned. He understood why it was effectively incognito; few would have considered that a building with a white picket fence in front, a wraparound porch with dangling plants spaced evenly, southern-style woodwork, red shingles, and sparkling white siding would host some of the world's most covert reconnaissance activities.

Brighton rushed out of the SUV after it came to a stop, put his sunglasses on to block the early morning sun, and opened the back hatch. He saw Grace walking down the front steps of the welcoming abode.

"Mrs. Vaughn, it's a pleasure." He spoke with urgency. "Thank you for having us. I'm Col. Samuel Brighton, one of Ryker's commanders."

"The pleasure is mine. I appreciate you watching over my son. Please, everyone, grab your things and come in. I have food and drinks for you on the table. Your rooms are ready upstairs."

"That's very generous. We'll eat quickly as we have pressing matters to address."

"I prepared finger breakfast food for just that reason."

Brighton got his bag—the only one he'd had time to prepare before their flight from D.C. to Texas—as did Gen. Childress, Dr. Forest, Dr. Gupta, and Dr. Sharp. Brighton led the way into the house with a swift pace and put his bag down in the main room. He noticed the slanted walls just inside the main entrance. They contained hidden doors, behind which were surveillance systems and stations with mirrors so guards could see out, but no one could see in. A similar clandestine station, designed to look like a shed, was behind the house. The interior of the bed-and-breakfast was modest, not extravagant, consistent with a military-funded venture. The walls were gray-toned, the floors were white oak-like laminate, and the décor matched accordingly.

"Please, help yourselves to some mini breakfast burritos with salsa, fruit, cinnamon rolls, coffee, and fresh-squeezed orange juice," Grace invited as she pointed to the spread on the dining room table. She then showed them the stairs at the end of the main hallway. "Your rooms are right up those stairs. I think you each brought your own access codes, so I'll let you find your way around up there."

"Much appreciated, Mrs. Vaughn," Gen. Childress said as he aggressively ate a burrito.

Brighton watched Dr. Sharp stuff his face. Salsa hung from the corner of his mouth, and he made no attempt to clean it off. Brighton shook his head; he was intrigued by the odd scientist who seemed to always be in his own world and didn't care a whit what anyone thought of him. Drs. Gupta and Forest, on the other hand, seemed more attentive to their hygiene and presentation. They both ate with notable refinement—napkins in hand and no food drippings on their faces.

"All right, hurry and eat so we can begin Project Galago," Brighton said.

The president had formalized their endeavor of learning more about the celestial ships as Project Galago, symbolic of the nocturnal animal with exceptional night vision, hearing, and nimbleness so it can track tiny prey in the dark.

Brighton asked Grace, "How is Ryker?" while wiping his mouth with a napkin.

"He's a little better today, thank you. I'm heading over to pick him up soon."

"That's good to hear. We'll have some questions for him when he gets here." Brighton swigged the last of some coffee. "We'll let you know if we need anything else, Mrs. Vaughn." He turned to the others in the room. "Everyone, drop your stuff and head to the command room. Let's move!"

Brighton picked up his bag and hurried upstairs with his team members in tow. He used the passcode given him by the White House to enter the third room on the right. He threw his bag on the bed, then hurried with the team members back downstairs to the kitchen. Hidden in the wall of the kitchen pantry was a three-tiered security system programmed to scan fingerprints, eyes, and badges and open a door to the underground command center. Brighton slid open an access panel and traversed the three-tier system. Seconds later, a heavy discreet door opened.

"In here," he said to the team. He trailed everyone down the stairs to the command center for reconnaissance and intelligence gathering. The room was stereotypical—riddled with computers, digital screens, and every level of imaging system imaginable.

Brighton guided the team straightaway. "Dr. Forest, you take point on determining the rate of travel of those ships. We need to know how long until they arrive.

"Drs. Gupta and Sharp, isolate their communication mechanisms, characterize those ships, and assess their electromagnetic signals. Foremost is to determine if they're battle capable.

"Gen. Childress, we'll look to you for oversight, strategic decisions, and communication with the White House."

The team took their orders to heart and went straight to work. In less than six hours, the scientists had some answers. They gathered in a conference room to review.

Dr. Forest started. "At their current rate of travel, the ships will arrive in three months."

"Three months?!" Brighton asked. "Even our most advanced spacecrafts would take, what, seven *years* to reach Saturn? That means they're traveling at—"

"At about 435,000 miles per hour," Dr. Gupta finished.

"Perhaps the good news is, even though that's fast by our standards, three months gives us some time to prepare," Brighton said.

"Yes, but if their ships can sustain that level of speed on a planetary travel scale, that's indicative of highly advanced systems," Dr. Sharp pointed out. "And I'm not surprised, given the additional data we collected."

"Do share," Gen. Childress said with a raised eyebrow.

"Well, for starters the instrumentation available in this command center allowed us to refine the parameters of our detection equipment, and we were able to capture these higher-resolution images."

Dr. Sharp turned on a large screen in the command center to show the high-resolution images. Everyone's facial expressions intensified. The images provided a crystal-clear view of the three silver ships that flanked the larger black one.

The silver ships each had building-sized metallic rings that revolved vertically around spherical bodies. Esoteric machinery dotted their surfaces. Thousands of high-powered lights lit up their exteriors, which had hundreds of barrel-like protrusions. Each ship's spherical body contained transparent sections through which the team could see hundreds of man-sized aircraft resting on platforms.

The large black ship dwarfed the silver ones. Each of its four arms that extended horizontally away from the hexagonal body had transparent covers through which more advanced crafts and machinery could be seen. The ship's arms were somewhat elliptical with a tapered front and back. Large fluorescent tubes ran along the pitch of the arms and connected to three, mile-wide turbines equally spaced on the underside of each arm.

Dr. Sharp reported, "We then tweaked some equipment, which is typically utilized to characterize the chemical structure of planets, stars, or asteroids, and applied it to the ships."

"And ... what did it show?" Brighton wondered.

Dr. Sharp continued, "The black ship's surface is composed of a carbon-fused astatine amalgamate unlike anything on Earth. You can see those transparent regions on each craft. However, despite collecting hundreds of images, I couldn't capture any sharp enough to detect movement or chemical makeup within the ships."

"Anything else?" Brighton asked.

"Well, the data also show that each ship is putting off tremendous electromagnetic and heat signals consistent with a unique energy. I'm not sure if it's what science fiction would call a 'force field,' but the energy states are compelling."

Gen. Childress took a deep breath. He disliked all this information more and more, then addressed the elephant in the room, "And what about weaponry systems, Dr. Sharp? Any indication as to how much firepower they have?"

Dr. Sharp clicked a remote and cycled to another set of images. "From what we can determine, things don't look good from a peace-keeping perspective. If we look at the barrel-like structures on the exterior of the silver ships, they're indicative of artillery.

"And see these rugged edges of the vertical rings around the silver ships?" Dr. Sharp clicked to a slightly closer-up image and pointed to the region on the images. "These appear to be very large razor-sharp protrusions made of materials fused with palladium, platinum, silver, fluorine, and tungsten. That blend of metals could constitute a super strong, metalloid material. I can only fathom the level of damage they could do to a structure. All in all, Gen. Childress," Dr. Sharp paused, "we conclude that, yes, these ships are *intensely* battle capable."

Chapter 11

The Vaughn Home, San Antonio, TX

Ryker looked out the passenger window of his mom's crossover SUV and saw two large, black SUVs in the bed-and-breakfast driveway. "Huh, they really did come to me."

"Yes," Grace emphasized as she pulled into their driveway and parked the car, "and they really did ask when you were going to be here."

"I don't understand why they still need me. I gave the only information I had to Dr. Sharp." Ryker shrugged. "I guess I'll find out."

"Maybe the surgeon implanted something else inside your body, and he wants it back," Jack scoffed from the back seat.

"Ha, ha, what am I, Jason Bourne?" Ryker retorted as he opened the passenger side door. "Problem is I remember everything … a little too well. In fact," Ryker contemplated, "it'd be nice if I could forget a few things."

"All right, Ryker," Grace stressed in a motherly tone, "we're home now, and I want you to work on positive thinking. Your team would be proud of you. Your father gave all that he had, and he would want you to carry on."

Ryker nodded but struggled to agree with what everybody reiterated to him. He still couldn't shake the feeling that he was responsible for the deaths of his team members. "Could you bring my wheelchair over for me?"

"Of course," Grace said. She grabbed Ryker's wheelchair from the back of her car, unfolded it, and locked it in place outside his door.

Ryker slid into the seat and began to wheel himself toward the house.

"Jessie's here," Jack announced.

Jessie parked along the curb in her white sedan, having followed them to their house so she could drop off exercise and rehabilitation equipment for Ryker. Although she wasn't required to accompany them, she volunteered. Ryker knew she didn't mind the opportunity to spend some additional time with him; she wanted to help him through his rough patch. And he wanted her to. Their attraction was magnetic. But today, in his current mental state, he wouldn't be attempting any next steps.

"What an adorable home, Grace!" Jessie admired as she stepped out of her car. "I absolutely love your flowers. They're beautiful!" Jessie observed the hundreds of perennials—crocuses, tulips, hyacinths, delphiniums, and dianthuses–blossoming in Grace's flower beds, which were isolated from the crab grass lawn by a flowing cement barrier. The flowers contrasted nicely with the white siding that blended the Vaughn home with the bed-and-breakfast. "Those hyacinths are some of my absolute favorite flowers. Did you plant this all yourself?"

"I do most of it, yes, but of course I 'encourage' my boys to help. Speaking of, Jack, why don't you help Jessie bring in that equipment? I'll grab Ryker's bags."

Jack nodded, went to Jessie's car trunk, and hefted out a load of equipment.

"Okay," Ryker said dejectedly as the group reached the front porch stairs, "this is the first thing we'll have to modify for a wheelchair-bound guy."

"Well, maybe we just take it slow for a bit," Grace said. "Give it some time, in case you decide you do want to use the Ozzies."

Ryker looked back at Jessie who was holding his Ozzies in her arms. They all stood in silence for a moment.

"I'll just set these in a corner for now," Jessie offered. "We'll focus on wheelchair-based exercises and activities. Don't think about these for now. And if you decide ultimately that you don't want them, I'll come by and snag them."

"I, uh, yeah, I can agree to that," Ryker said.

"Ryker!" a voice called from the front yard of the bed-and-breakfast, cutting the current conversation short.

Ryker turned around and saw Brighton and Dr. Sharp approaching.

"Son, good to see you," Brighton panted. "I know you've just arrived, but we have some pressing questions to ask. Could you join us for a few moments, then we'll let you get settled?"

"Yes, sir. I'll answer what I can. Mom, Jessie, Jack, could you get my things into my room?"

"Of course," Jessie said and followed Grace and Jack inside.

"All right, Captain," Brighton said, "I'll wheel you over."

Ryker gripped his wheelchair arms as Brighton pushed him swiftly around the sidewalk and up to the entrance of the bed-and-breakfast. Ryker didn't hesitate to wrap an arm around Brighton's neck as he lifted him out of his chair and up the porch stairs. Dr. Sharp grabbed the wheelchair, and within moments they were all in the basement. Brighton set Ryker back in his wheelchair.

Ryker had never actually seen the completed reconnaissance facility despite living next to it for more than twenty years, yet it wasn't anything more than what he imagined; myriads of computer systems, a few small offices, a kitchenette, one bathroom, and equipment that would be familiar to scientists, but foreign to him.

Ryker shook hands with Dr. Gupta, Dr. Forest, and Gen. Childress.

"Welcome, soldier," Gen. Childress said as they shook hands.

"An honor, sir," Ryker replied.

"Typically, we'd bring you up to speed on some things," Brighton said, "but what we're working on is confidential."

"I understand. So, what can I help with?" Ryker asked.

The five-member team looked at each other. They had pulled him into the basement yet were unsure of how exactly to ask Ryker why his name had appeared on a screen of the Situation Room a day earlier.

Ryker broke the silence. "Is it something that happened in Afghanistan? I don't recall seeing any additional codes other than what I gave to Dr. Sharp."

"No, no, we have all the information we need from that," Brighton said. "We've received some ... *new* information that we want to ask you about."

Ryker waited, sensing that something bigger was at hand than the IED field tests in Afghanistan.

Brighton said, "Well, son, your name came up in a meeting at The White House."

"Did I do something wrong?"

"No, no, it's not that. It's—"

"For crying out loud, just show him!" Gen. Childress cut in with an annoyed voice. "Enough of this tiptoeing around!"

The group agreed.

Brighton nodded and cleared his throat. "Ryker, what we're about to show you doesn't even have a classification level, and fewer than a dozen people on Earth know about it. Consider yourself bound to Top-Secret status by The United States Military from this moment forward."

Ryker nodded.

"Dr. Sharp, pull it up," Brighton ordered.

Dr. Sharp powered on two screens. One displayed images of the extraterrestrial ships, the second showed the message: *Justice to Ryker Vaughn.*

Ryker was confused. He leaned forward and took a moment to process what he saw. He almost laughed at first; this had to be a joke. But he had to consider otherwise for multiple reasons: the secretary of defense was standing in front of him, demanding that he be shown highly confidential information without any military clearance; moreover, two people, Col. Brighton and Dr. Sharp, were flown from Afghanistan to meet with the POTUS—who had phoned him personally—and then they swooped him into a military reconnaissance facility without any authorization papers. The circumstance was unprecedented, and Ryker knew it.

"Justice," Ryker read aloud and paused for a moment. "Justice for what? And what does that have to do with these ... what *are* these? Spaceships?"

"It appears so," Gen. Childress said. "And our first question is: can you confirm you had nothing to do with coordinating this?"

Ryker was caught off guard, then felt incredulous. *How could someone suggest I coordinated an arrival of extraterrestrial ships?* "Sir, I assure you I have no knowledge whatsoever of this. I've been in Afghanistan for months. How would I even coordinate—" Ryker inhaled and exhaled a few times to control his anger. "And I've been in hospitals. I got these ... these *things* shoved into my legs," Ryker pointed at the metal posts in his legs, "without even *asking* for them! And frankly," Ryker nearly began to tell Gen. Childress and Brighton off, but remembered he was speaking to his superiors, "frankly, I haven't been in a right state of mind. I don't even know how to process this accusation or whatever those ships are all about."

Gen. Childress articulated, "And I respect all that, but I hope you can understand, soldier, we need to make sure this isn't a hack or a joke. If this isn't a coordinated con by you or someone else, that means these things we're looking at are real, and they pose a material threat to civilization.

Before we strategize hundreds of billions of dollars' worth of military resources to prepare for the arrival of these things, we need to make sure what we're looking at isn't man-made."

"Well, you can put me on a lie detector if you need to," Ryker said wearily, "but I promise you I have nothing to do with what you're looking at on those screens."

The deflated nature of Ryker's voice was notable. He wasn't doing well, and they could all tell.

"We believe you," Brighton consoled. "Perhaps what we need to understand is why, whatever is inside of those ships, has it out for you."

"I honestly don't have a clue," Ryker said. "All I did was dig up that cylinder. I never should have done that!"

"Ryker," Dr. Sharp said, "you may have saved the world by doing that. We likely never would have known about a second one of those cylinders, or the ships, if you hadn't found the first one."

"So, there's two? I—I—Whatever. But if I called those things here with that cylinder and they aren't looking for new friends, well, take me to prison! Because I'll be the one who destroyed Earth! It'll be no different than what I did to my team. I just ... I—"

Ryker felt another panic attack looming. He hyperventilated and put his head in his hands.

"Get him to his room," Gen. Childress whispered to Brighton and Dr. Sharp. "I think we all need a break. The two of you," he said pointing to Drs. Gupta and Forest, "finish up what you can, then take twenty."

Brighton and Dr. Sharp helped Ryker out of the reconnaissance facility. Brighton carried him to his house, and up to his room. Dr. Sharp pushed his wheelchair into their kitchen. Grace, Jessie, and Jack followed.

Ryker could tell that Grace, Jessie, and Jack sensed something was wrong as Brighton set him on his bed.

"He just needs some rest," Brighton said. "Maybe get him some food and a drink."

"What I *need* is to be alone for a bit," Ryker pleaded. "I appreciate you all, but I just ... if you could just leave me alone for now."

Grace hugged Ryker and said, "Take your time. Come on everyone," Grace shooed everyone out of the room. "Let's go downstairs."

Jessie obliged and set the Ozzies in the corner of Ryker's room before she left. She smiled at him and put her hand on his shoulder as she walked by. He almost grabbed her hand—he wanted to—but pulled back.

Ryker waited until everyone was out, then threw his pillow across the room and yelled to relieve his frustration. *What's happening?* He looked down at his legs. *These metal posts, that's one of my problems!* Then he looked at the Ozzies in the corner. *I don't deserve those.* He decided that he would call the doctor first thing tomorrow and demand that they remove the metal from his legs.

He looked out his bedroom window and saw Jessie walking to her car. She turned and waved with an encouraging look. *I'm here when you need me,* her face seemed to say. Ryker desperately wanted to wave back and ask her to stay; to be with him, to help him recover. Yet he turned away, threw himself on his bed, and rubbed his eyes with his fists. He laid there, thinking nothing, sensing nothing.

Without warning, an unexpected emotion began to course through his body. It was the same feeling he felt as a child whenever his dad hugged him. When his dad held him, he felt like he could overcome anything, that everything was going to be okay even if it wasn't at the moment.

"Dad?!" Ryker called aloud. He sat up. He didn't see or hear anyone, but a presence was palpable. "Man, Dad, I could use you right now. I'm not in good shape." He paused and wiped soft tears from his cheeks. He wished a voice would respond. None did. "What do I do? I mean, I don't think it's right that I walk or run when I got my team killed. And aside from that, I go into the bed-and-breakfast and see there's some ... *something* coming our way. And it knows my name and is ticked off at me. What's that all about? Did I seriously call space travelers here? I don't even know how to process it all!"

Ryker bowed his head and sat in silence, wanting only to bask in the warmth of his childhood senses. Yet as quickly as the feelings came, they drifted away, and Ryker felt empty again. He laid back and tried to forget everything.

He must have drifted off. A knock at his door startled him.

"Come in," he groaned.

Grace opened the door. "Say, is there any way I could get your mind off things for a bit and, uh, convince you to come eat a cinnamon roll?"

Ryker didn't want to smile, but he did. Grace always made cinnamon rolls for him and Jack when they needed comfort.

"Tell you what," Ryker said, giving in to his mom's prodding, "I'm not going to wear those Ozzies, but if you're telling me there are cinnamon rolls to eat, I can get behind that."

Grace waved for him to follow her.

Ryker slid off his bed, army-crawled backwards down the stairs and to the kitchen table with Grace's help and pulled himself into a chair. As he, Grace, and Jack made small talk late into the evening, he nearly forgot about the images he'd seen just hours prior. Their family time was more therapeutic than any medication could ever be. He came to a conclusion: cinnamon rolls are more effective than morphine.

Chapter 12

Bed-and-Breakfast, San Antonio, TX

No member of Project Galago could sleep. They laid awake in their beds, wondering what their world would soon behold. Only a handful of individuals knew of the potential threat. The information they held was paramount. Worry encompassed their thoughts, along with concern for their spouses, children, family, friends, and country.

Dr. Sharp was particularly uneasy. His was the only equipment that could detect signals from the ships. What if something happened to it? He was certain there was more information that could be gathered, information that could help protect the planet. His mind wouldn't stop racing.

At 3:03 a.m., he got out of bed, shuffled to his bedroom window, and observed the picturesque neighborhood. No homeowners of the ramblers across the street had any idea what was going on in the subterranean complex thirty feet beneath his feet. From his vantage point, he could see the bed-and-breakfast's well-manicured lawn and stone path that led to the front door, behind which guards were keeping watch. Each guard could view the front yard through a window, which was designed such that if someone looked in, they would see coats hanging in a closet because of an angled mirror.

Dr. Sharp gazed at the tranquil and innocent San Antonio suburb. It reminded him of his neighborhood in

Cambridge, Massachusetts, where his family was likely snoring heavily at home. He missed his wife and two teenage girls, but they had grown accustomed to him taking frequent trips. As a busy professor, he traveled to science conferences, consultations, and business meetings every other week. He chuckled to himself. *What would they think if I told them what I'm working on now?*

At 3:08 a.m., Dr. Sharp noticed lights coming on along the side street roughly half a block away. He heard the rumble of a pickup truck. Before coming into view, its headlights turned off. He heard a metal clang. Curious, he peered, trying to see if there was movement in the dark. Several minutes passed. Nothing.

Before turning around to lie back down, he saw a giant man, who must have been seven feet tall, round the street corner. Dr. Sharp had never seen a man that tall in person, only on TV during a sports event. He was intrigued. The man was dressed in a black-and-red trench coat and hid his face from the light of the streetlamps by holding a forearm in front of his eyes. His gait was choppy yet calculated. Dr. Sharp assumed his odd movement was due to his unusual height. When the man was about a hundred feet away from the bed-and-breakfast, he straightened his left arm and held it at a high angle. Dr. Sharp squinted. *What is he doing?*

A circle of blue light illuminated gradually on a device at the end of his hand. In an instant, three flashes of indigo zipped toward the streetlamps. The light bulbs sizzled, then died out. The hairs on the back of Dr. Sharp's neck prickled. He darted behind the curtains in his room, eyes riveted on the man in the street as he approached the bed-and-breakfast. The man shifted his arm toward the porch. Dr. Sharp thought he saw the blue ring weapon the man was holding morph into a hand. Blue orbs, the size of golf balls, shot from his fingertips through a guard post window. Seconds later, a security officer leaped out the window and scrambled on the grass. A blast rocked the ground, blew off the front door, started a fire in the entrance, and triggered a blaring alarm.

Within seconds, four guards bolted from their quarters and ran through the wreckage of the front door. Two of them were talking to their wrists.

Four blue tracers screamed from the fingertips of the tall man, connecting with each of the four officers. They collapsed instantly on the front lawn.

Dr. Sharp cowered below his windowpane and crawled toward his bedroom door. Fumbling, he opened it and entered the hallway.

He saw Brighton who was already crouching wide-eyed in the hallway.

"Dr. Sharp!" Brighton whispered loudly. "Get over here!"

Dr. Sharp watched Brighton put a clip in his 9mm. Flickers of light from the fire at the entrance below reflected off Brighton's gun. A second explosion rocked the house's foundation. Dr. Sharp and Brighton covered their heads and plastered their faces against the hardwood floor.

Gen. Childress threw open his door at the end of the hallway, as did Drs. Gupta and Forest. Gen. Childress, dressed only in boxers—revealing his leathered, yet surprisingly toned midsection—stood in his doorway clasping both hands around a .45 caliber.

"What's going on?" Dr. Gupta begged.

"Get down! Shut up!" Brighton ordered. The team slammed to their hands and knees simultaneously.

"There's a seven-foot-tall man out there!" Dr. Sharp trembled.

Dr. Gupta's face paled. "Please, let me get out of here."

"Stay where you are!" Brighton said.

Through the railings at the top of the stairs, Dr. Sharp saw two guards trample over the rubble. Before reaching the porch, blue tracers entered their chests. They fell in a heap.

Brighton held up a hand, signaling for Gen. Childress and the others to maintain their position. Dead silent, Dr. Sharp watched from the loft as the tall man entered the front door. His hand again had a blue ring mechanism at the end of his arm, which crossed the threshold first, then his trench coat sleeve. A machine gun blasted from the kitchen. Bullets ricocheted off the tall man's body. His blue ring device swiveled backward and rotated 180 degrees, exchanging for a set of four lights that clung to his fingertips.

His hand is modular! Dr. Sharp thought.

In an instant, the man returned fire from his fingertips toward the kitchen and dropped the last security officer.

The tall man stepped onto the smoldering rubble, keeping his body square with the kitchen.

Dr. Sharp could see what looked like metallic boots under the man's coat.

As the man entered the house, Brighton aimed his 9mm at his head.

Dr. Sharp tried to make out the man's face. It was covered by a sagging hood, the interior of which glowed a warm azure blue.

The man's shoulders were twice the breadth of a body builder, and he had to duck to avoid hitting his head on the doorway. After checking his surroundings, he pulled his left sleeve up and looked at a screen embedded in his forearm.

Dr. Sharp breathed heavily yet quietly as the man inched toward the kitchen pantry.

In shock and unable to handle the stress, Dr. Gupta ran down the hallway and jumped over the balcony, trying to make an exit out the front door. A streak of blue light raced from the kitchen and passed through his chest. Dr. Sharp watched him groan as he hit the floor.

"Dr. Gupta!" Dr. Forest screamed.

Gen. Childress covered her mouth and whispered, "Shut up!"

She spat on his hand as she exhaled through his fingers. Her hot tears poured over Gen. Childress' skin. He drew his hand away but put a finger up to his lips and whispered, "You *must* stay silent if you want to survive!" She nodded.

Gen. Childress gripped his .45 caliber and pulled Dr. Forest back into her bedroom. He cracked her door slightly and aimed his gun into the hallway. "Be quiet, everyone," he said.

Dr. Sharp trembled violently, unable to control his convulsing muscles. He had never experienced such terror. He watched Brighton narrow his eyes and grit his teeth, ready for battle.

The tall man obviously heard Dr. Forest's scream and changed course from the kitchen to the stairs. Brighton rolled back into his bedroom followed by Dr. Sharp. Dr. Sharp could still see Gen. Childress through the crack of the door.

Dr. Sharp and Brighton could see the tall man methodically climbing the stairs while assessing his surroundings. He paused on the landing to examine the screen in his forearm. It illuminated the hallway. He tapped it with his index finger.

Though none of them could see it, Dr. Sharp's laptop, which he had left powered on to crunch data, responded, and the screen lit up. The man raised his chin and moved toward Dr. Sharp's room.

Dr. Sharp and Brighton watched through the cracked door as the man passed. Gears in his left leg whirred with each step.

Dr. Sharp watched Gen. Childress breathe rhythmically as the giant pushed Dr. Sharp's door open just five feet away.

Dr. Sharp felt a tap on his shoulder. Brighton motioned for him to move over so he could slip out of the bedroom. Dr. Sharp obeyed and watched Brighton stealthily slide his back along the hallway wall.

Dr. Sharp watched Brighton peer inside his room. They both heard the big man rip the laptop plug out of the wall, then click the computer shut. Dr. Sharp poked his head out into the hallway and watched the invader slide his laptop into an oversized pocket in his trench coat.

He cringed. *All the data I collected will be gone without that laptop!* Dr. Sharp caught a glimpse of the man's enormous modular hand and fingers. He was otherworldly. *Not a man. A giant ... what?*

Dr. Sharp continued to spy. The invader stood resolute and worked on his arm-embedded computer screen.

What is he doing? Dr. Sharp thought, fuming that he was about to be a robbery victim.

Brighton laid on his back, aimed his gun at Dr. Sharp's doorway, and signaled to Gen. Childress that he was going to attack. For nearly a minute, nothing happened. The hiss of the fire below was intensifying and worked its way toward the stairs. In the background, sirens blared in the night air.

Footsteps from Dr. Sharp's room began to approach the hallway. Brighton held his breath and steadied his gun. The moment the giant's body emerged, Brighton unloaded his 9mm, sending bullets into his torso.

Gen. Childress then fired at the back of the intruder's head. The thief jolted under the pressure of the bullets, yet they ricocheted in every direction. On the defensive, the giant turned and blasted a plasma ball from his forearm into the door behind which Gen. Childress was hiding. It left a softball-sized hole in Gen. Childress' left leg, disintegrating his femur and muscle, and he fell to the floor, limp. Shrapnel pierced Dr. Forest's neck. She dropped in a hysterical scream, then stopped moving.

Dr. Sharp shoved his fist into his mouth to silence his outcry of horror. Dr. Forest had become a beloved colleague. He would never see her again.

~

The chaos awoke Ryker who had been sleeping in his bedroom, which shared a wall with the bed-and-breakfast's second story. *Gunfire!* Without thinking, Ryker jumped off his bed. He forgot he didn't have legs. He flailed his residual limbs back and forth, but there were no feet to catch him. He slammed to the floor in a heap.

"Ow!"

He rolled over, holding his torso in pain, but shook it off. He looked up and saw the Ozzies. Without second guessing, he snatched them and clicked them onto his metal posts. The Ozzies lit up, ready for action.

Ryker rushed outside, observed the growing blaze, and saw Grace and Jack holding each other, tears in their eyes. A host of neighbors were filming the burning bed-and-breakfast with their cell phones.

"Look," Jack said, pointing to flashes of blue that were filtering through the upstairs windows.

Grace cried, "the fire. It's going to reach our house!"

"Stay here," Ryker said. He ran and grabbed a garden hose and started spraying the flames that now encompassed the bed-and-breakfast entryway. As the flames dampened, Ryker saw a tower of a man inside standing at the top of the second-story stairs. Ryker couldn't see the top half of the man's face, covered by a dark hood, but he could make out a nose and mouth, both highlighted by a hue of blue, which appeared to be coming from his neck. The man's body and appearance were unearthly. Ryker watched the intruder pause and look straight at him with a hint of intrigue. The creature tilted his head as though he were analyzing Ryker's movements. Ryker backed away, sensing he was preparing to rush him.

Yet as the invader was analyzing Ryker, he failed to recognize the threat behind him.

~

Brighton jumped onto the enormous brute's back and lodged his bicep into his oversized esophagus. He used all the strength he had to lock the giant in a chokehold. He felt what he thought to be a solid metal flak jacket under the being's coat. The armor melded with the skin of his neck, as though it were part of his body. The beast—that was the word that came to Brighton's mind—squeezed its gigantic jaw, crushing Brighton's arm, but Brighton held on like a vice.

As they struggled, the brute slammed Brighton into the wall, leaving impressions of his body in drywall and two by fours.

Brighton struggled to maintain his grip. His forearm was throbbing, and he could feel his bone beginning to crack. Determined, he wrapped his legs around the giant's waist and squeezed harder. The creature grunted, apparently surprised at the strength of his opponent's legs. Brighton landed multiple punches to the invader's face.

It's like striking a rock! Brighton thought. Yet eight punches in, he finally broke skin, causing vibrant indigo-colored fluid to cover his hand.

The beast responded to Brighton's attack by reaching his arms back, grabbing Brighton's mid-section, peeling him off his back, and throwing him over the railing. Brighton smashed into a wall and fell to the first floor, cracking five ribs. He lay motionless just feet from the insatiable fire.

Staggering, the tall being got his bearings, then bolted down the stairs toward the kitchen pantry. He blew the security door open and entered the underground facility.

~

Dr. Sharp crawled to the top of the stairs and watched the tall creature reemerge from the underground area carrying the metal briefcase that contained his essential digital imaging equipment. Dr. Sharp ignored the increasing sense of loss gnawing in his gut and instead gazed at the being in amazement. His coat was torn in the middle, revealing a mesmerizing hybrid of metal and organic tissue in his upper body. His metal chest fused with his pulsating neck and a ten pack of stomach muscle. Blue sludge oozed from the bullet holes Brighton had blasted into his stomach. Light emanating from the back of his neck illuminated the interior of his hood.

The invader stood tall and walked toward Dr. Sharp. Dr. Sharp flinched and hurried back to Brighton's bedroom. His body shook wildly.

These could be my last moments, he thought.

Images of his family ran through his mind. He tried to find his phone. It was on the nightstand in his room. He agonized at the thought of never seeing his daughters marry. He couldn't bear to think of the devastation his wife would experience.

He heard the tall intruder ascend the stairs. It was quiet for a moment; the invader was probably listening for him. Dr. Sharp couldn't control his panting. The bedroom door flew off its hinges, and he screamed.

"No!"

The beast grabbed Dr. Sharp and carried him under his arm like a rag doll. He ran down the hallway, through Dr. Sharp's bedroom, and smashed the window as he jumped two stories down to the grass where he landed in front of Jack and Grace.

"Help!" Dr. Sharp yelled.

Jack threw his cell phone aside, dove to the ground, and grabbed the creature's lower legs, hoping to trip him.

Grace screamed as though her life were ending. The tall thug slipped out of Jack's grip with minimal effort and kicked him out of the way.

"Obnoxious fool," the barbarian groused in a deep, echoey voice.

The crowd screamed as they saw the immensity of the organic machine holding the silver case—and a middle-aged hostage squirming and screaming.

"Jack!" Ryker yelled.

Jack jumped up, fury coursing through his veins, and leapt for the man's legs again. "Let the guy go!" Jack yelled as he tried to take the giant down.

The beast hit Jack with the briefcase, knocking him out. As Jack started to sink to the ground, the creature caught him and wrapped him under his other arm, then started running down the street, carrying Jack and Dr. Sharp with ease.

"Nooooo!" Grace shrieked.

~

Ryker full-on sprinted and chased after the abductor, but the massive being was outpacing him easily. A split-second thought zipped through his mind: *Battle mode!* He bent down and rotated the dial on his Ozzies. The blue lights that coursed down the flanks of his Ozzies changed to a brilliant shade of red, indicating they were ready for whatever Ryker threw at them.

Ryker looked ahead; the invader was now halfway down the street.

How is it even possible he can move that fast, let alone with two people in his arms?

Ryker sprinted again. He could feel the gravel, grass, and asphalt under his feet as he flew past the fire engines and ambulances that were arriving on scene. He felt like he could have easily set a world record in the 100-meter dash.

The assailant looked back and slowed involuntarily. He stared at Ryker, seemingly mesmerized by the soldier. It appeared he didn't realize that Ryker was gaining on him. He shook his head and repositioned Jack and Dr. Sharp under his arms and started to flee again.

Ryker's pace now superseded that of his prey; battle mode gave the Ozzies bionic speed.

When they were fifteen feet apart, the brute turned the street corner and headed for a backyard. Ryker realized that he could catch him if he cut through the neighboring yard—after years of night games in the neighborhood, he knew all the shortcuts. Ryker took the shortcut and emerged from a row of trees just in time to see the creature rush through a gate.

The huge being headed toward a patch of tall grass in which an arrowhead-shaped, SUV-sized craft with a gold exterior and sharply bisected canopy was hidden.

What is that?! Ryker wondered. *Definitely not a military jet.*

He noticed a tall oak tree to his right. Suddenly, the Ozzies seemed to speak to him: *Use the oak tree as a springboard.* Ryker jumped and soared through the air with a force that he wasn't expecting. His feet nearly missed the tree trunk, but he was able to angle them just enough to connect. He catapulted off the tree, bent his leg, and kneed the abductor in the face.

The metallic man tumbled to the ground, dropping Dr. Sharp and Jack in the process. Dr. Sharp was in shock and didn't even attempt to move. Jack lay unconscious.

Indigo-colored ooze dripped from the tall being's face and onto his trench coat. He stood erect and looked toward Ryker with a hood-covered face. He smirked and said, "Justice to Ryker Vaughn. You're an idiot for compromising us."

How does he know my name, and what is he talking about?

He rushed toward Ryker.

Ryker dodged with unexpected swiftness and dealt a blow to his big head. Ryker's tendons strained as his fist connected with his skull. *Is that a metal plate in his head?!* The punch had no effect—except on Ryker's hand, which instantly swelled with fluid.

The invader pivoted in one swift motion and heaved a blow to Ryker's abdomen that sent him to the ground. He scooped up Dr. Sharp and Jack again before Ryker could recover, spoke a command into his left arm, and rushed to the hidden craft.

The bisected canopy of the craft melted back like ferromagnetic fluid, revealing an oval-shaped cockpit.

Ryker rolled over and caught a glance of the craft's interior. The cockpit was more spacious than he expected, yet it had far fewer dials than any man-made aircraft.

The beast threw both of his prizes behind the single seat in the flight deck, jumped in himself, and spoke another command, causing the gold canopy to resolidify into solid metal.

Ryker could no longer see inside; the craft had no windows. He watched as it lifted into the air without causing the grass to move underneath it. It bolted into the sky with breathtaking acceleration.

"Jack!" Ryker yelled as he slumped to his knees.

His consciousness gyrated. Moments later, he realized there was a group of people kneeling around him looking up at the sky, asking streams of questions. Ryker didn't process any of their queries. A piercing ringing drowned out his hearing. He thought the ringing was coming from his inner ear, but realized it emanated from incoming sirens.

Ryker saw his mom in the distance. She ran toward him and fell into his arms.

"Ryker! Where's Jack?" she begged.

"I—I—" Ryker shook his head and pointed to the sky as tears slowly slid down his cheeks. "There."

Grace wailed: "No, please, Father, no! My boy. My boy!"

Ryker collapsed to the ground as Grace sobbed on his shoulder then fell to her knees.

He sensed that although he had just returned from battle in Afghanistan, a war for Earth was about to begin.

But even more important to him was finding a way to save his brother.

He looked at his Ozzies. A surge of something deeper than anger catalyzed inside him. He knew that his deceased team and dad would want him to do anything necessary to save Jack. If he ever wanted to see his brother again, he would need his new legs. They were now an essential part of his body, no, his soul.

Ryker vowed to himself that very moment: "I'll never *not* walk again!"

Chapter 13

Bed-and-Breakfast, San Antonio, TX

Brighton startled as flames licked his cheek. His body was contorted, with his shoulders on the floor and his feet scaling the wall near the entryway of the covert house. Intense pain coursed through his ribs, neck, and bowels. The contusions on his back were deep, traumatizing his ribs, scapula, and vertebrae as a result of being incessantly thumped against the wall. The tall man, or whatever he had fought, was stronger than anything he had ever encountered.

"Anyone there?"

He heard Ryker yelling from outside.

"Yes!" Brighton coughed. He could barely speak louder than the crackling inferno. Smoke was starting to asphyxiate his lungs.

"Survivor!" Ryker yelled to the fire crew. Ryker and three firemen braved the burning wreckage and within seconds knelt at Brighton's side.

"Do you have feeling below your neck?" Ryker asked.

Brighton checked his senses. "Yeah."

Ryker signaled to pick him up.

"Just don't touch my left hand," Brighton warned.

They all looked at his hand. It was covered in indigo-colored ooze. They eased Brighton off the wall without disturbing his hand. A firefighter grabbed an industrial extinguisher from the kitchen and sprayed it to create a path through which two others could carry Brighton. Flames singed their arms as they passed through the firestorm.

"There may be ... two more ... people alive upstairs," Brighton stuttered as they reached the grass. Then he fell unconscious from pain and shock.

~

Ryker rushed upstairs with two firefighters.

"Hello?" he called. No response. They checked each bedroom. They found Gen. Childress and Dr. Forest in the second-to-last room they checked. Dr. Forest had obviously passed away, but Gen. Childress had a pulse. Ryker patted his face gently to see if he would respond.

Gen. Childress fluttered his eyes. He grimaced and put pressure on a lesion with one hand and reached for Ryker with his other.

"Let's get him to an ambulance," Ryker said.

Ryker watched Gen. Childress fade in and out of consciousness as they carried him across the lawn and into an ambulance. Even though the EMTs had seen nearly every form of traumatic injury, they gasped when they saw the hole in Gen. Childress' left leg. They didn't need to place a tourniquet; the wound was completely cauterized. Unable to fully comprehend what had happened, an EMT placed an IV in Gen. Childress' hand and banged on the cab barrier and yelled, "Get him to surgery!"

Ryker stepped out of the way, and the ambulance sped ahead toward BAMC.

Ryker walked over to Brighton, who had been laid on the lawn and was coming to. He saw that all emergency personnel were otherwise occupied, so he prodded, "Come on, we need to get you to an ambulance as well."

"Let me help," Grace said solemnly as she came up from behind.

Ryker knew his mom was trying to be strong, despite having just experienced a mother's worst nightmare. He nodded, and the two of them each put one of Brighton's arms around their neck and hobbled to another ambulance.

"Here's fine," Brighton said and flopped onto the back bumper and let go of Ryker and Grace, careful not to touch them with his left hand.

"What just happened?" Grace asked rhetorically.

"Well, one thing for sure," Ryker said. "I just got myself out of taking a lie detector test!"

Grace gave a puzzled look. "What are you talking about?"

"Mrs. Vaughn," Brighton said, "there's no secret anymore. We're not alone in the universe. And what just happened is: we received an invitation to interstellar war!"

Grace took a step back and put a hand on her heart, overcome.

Brighton shook his head. "Our scientists estimated that those things would take three months to get here. Well, that data was *crap*! We couldn't have known this would escalate so quickly, but we also shouldn't be surprised. We can't apply our science to their tech." Brighton raised his left hand and pointed into the empty ambulance. "Ryker, grab me that towel."

Ryker snapped a white towel from a shelf and handed it to him. Brighton wrapped his hand with it to protect the viscous blue material covering his fingers.

"Do you have a cell phone?" Brighton asked. "I'm sure mine was destroyed."

"Yes, but it's in the house," Ryker answered.

"Here, I have one." Grace pulled her phone out of her pocket and handed it to Brighton.

Brighton dialed a number with his right hand. "Get me the president and ready a plane. I need to get to Washington, D.C. Now!"

Chapter 14

Beyond the Thermosphere, Outer Space

Dr. Sharp covered his mouth—the universal signal for an upset stomach. The g-forces of the initial takeoff, mixed with his emotions, churned his gastrointestinal juices beyond the point of control. As the abductor's craft exited the thermosphere, he spewed the contents of his stomach dead center onto his captor's head. The organic machine flailed his arms, splattering gastric liquids onto the cockpit walls.

The hydrochloric acid-based ooze dripped on Jack's face, forcing him awake. He gagged at the sight and smell then followed Dr. Sharp's lead, tossing a second set of cookies onto the captor.

The machinish man spat and wiped away the acids, that apparently were stinging the wounds on his face. He glared at his prisoners, checking to see if they were attempting to attack him with vile fluids. They didn't appear to be a threat; they were pale, sweating, and introverted in the fetal position. He gave them a look of disgust and swore in a foreign tongue. He grabbed a nearby cloth, wiped his face, body, and the cockpit, and threw another rag back to Dr. Sharp and Jack to do the same. After they were done, the abductor took the cloths and tossed them into a hexagonal chamber to his right. He double tapped the wall and the chamber closed.

Dr. Sharp figured that was their version of a garbage can.

Once they were beyond Earth's atmosphere, and distanced from its gravitational pull, the g-forces subsided exponentially, and the craft accelerated with ease. Within a matter of minutes, they passed the moon at hundreds of thousands of miles per hour. Dr. Sharp opened his eyes. He was surprised that he could see out of the craft from every angle. The canopy wasn't made of glass, but it was transparent.

It's probably video displayed, Dr. Sharp thought.

His pains dulled as he watched the Moon, Earth, and Sun fade in the distance. For several moments, he forgot he was the prisoner of a completely novel life form. Nothing he had seen on Earth compared to the view of the unimpeded night sky.

"Young man, look at all that," Dr. Sharp said in awe as he shook Jack's shoulder.

Jack coughed. He blinked several times and wiped his eyes with a clean section of his shirt. Unlike Dr. Sharp, Jack started to cry as he looked at the vastness around them. He didn't share Dr. Sharp's intrigue of space's empty brilliance.

"Go to sleep, my boy," Dr. Sharp soothed and helped Jack rest.

Jack passed out again as soon as he laid back down.

Dr. Sharp realized they were only partially weightless. Some form of microgravity held them in place. The excitement of outer space faded as he remembered their dire situation; they were flying through the solar system with no chance of return, in the craft of a merciless brute. A foreboding sense of death encompassed him. He forced himself to breathe, trying to calm his nerves. Maybe he could find a way to survive.

But most likely not.

Dr. Sharp couldn't help but think that the being in front of him captured him purposefully. In many ways, he would have preferred to have been killed. If horror stories of extraterrestrial abductions contained any truth, he was in for a torturous experience. He rebuked himself internally for having crawled out of Brighton's bedroom. He should have stayed put and waited for it all to end.

What was I thinking?

He kicked the craft's black wall in anger. The organic machine ignored him and pushed the craft faster by sliding his fingers upward on a panel.

The creature breathed oxygen; that was apparent from the fact that all three of them were breathing in the craft, but Dr. Sharp couldn't determine much more. The flight deck had a single seat. The walls were obsidian colored with streaks of blue and insets of what he assumed were advanced communication devices. None of the data displayed on them were decipherable, except for a few glimpses of the quaternary code he had seen on his own instruments during the IED field test.

He gazed at the universe. Hundreds of thousands of stars illuminated its expanse. Despite his aeronautics and astronautics background, he'd never consciously considered that stars gleamed with more than white light. Reds, blues, oranges, and purples flickered wildly, piercing the blackness.

They flew in silence for hours before the craft jolted and the abductor began to communicate with someone, or something. Their communication reminded him of the complexity of the Finnish language. It was composite and sophisticated. And clearly their technology and travel capability far exceeded mankind's.

Dr. Sharp looked ahead and saw a set of piercing lights flicker in the deep distance. He began to make out three silver ships and a single black ship. He deduced that they had moved closer to Earth because he could barely make out Saturn and its shimmering rings in the distance. He wished they had stayed nearer to Saturn. It would have been incredible to see it up close!

But still he wondered, *how did we arrive so fast?!*

As they approached, Dr. Sharp's eyes widened; the size and prowess of the ships were drastically more looming in person than satellite images portrayed. The razor-like apparatuses on the three silver ships were enormous and powerful. The grandeur of the black ship was breathtaking. Seeing it in person intrigued a part of his brain he didn't know existed.

At their current speed, Dr. Sharp thought for sure they were going to run into one of them, but their craft slowed with physics-bending ability. And his stomach felt calm. *How ...?*

The captor angled the craft around the hexagonal core of the black ship and headed for an open chamber on the underside of one of the ship's long arms. The craft's canopy darkened before they entered. They could no longer see anything outside the ship.

Dr. Sharp shook Jack's shoulders until he was awake. "My boy. Jack, isn't it?"

Jack startled and nodded.

"Well, I'm Dr. Sharp in case you didn't know. We'd better get ready. We're here. Er, somewhere. At the mothership, I'd surmise."

Jack licked his lips and looked around. He nearly fainted again.

"Dang it," Jack lamented. "Why couldn't this all be a dream?"

Dr. Sharp nodded in agreement, then sensed his weight shifting. "Do you feel that? The big ship produces increased gravity."

Jack tried to stand.

"Wait a second!" Dr. Sharp warned and pulled Jack back to the floor. "I think this thing's going to jolt vigorously when we dock." Dr. Sharp was correct. The craft lurched before coming to a complete stop. "There, now we can stand."

Suddenly, the ceiling of the craft melted away, replaced by brilliant lights that illuminated their surroundings. Dr. Sharp and Jack gazed at the larger ship's interior. Far overhead, they could see stars through a transparent roof—an aspect of the ship Dr. Sharp had observed in satellite images. Whale-sized tubes ran the length of the ship's skeleton, connecting to turbines and a towering tank in the hexagonal core.

Dr. Sharp noticed rainbows on the ship's walls. "Oh, my goodness, Jack, that enormous tank, the tubes, the transparent roof ... they're all made of pure *diamond*."

The diamond structures scattered light in every direction, giving the ship an inspiring ambiance of color and brilliance.

"Is there even that much diamond on the whole planet?" Jack asked. "I mean, *our* planet."

"Probably not. And look at the plant life," Dr. Sharp said. "It's fascinating!"

Abstruse plant life scaled the walls. Many of the florae were transparent and glowed an intense purple. Tanks that held tens of millions of gallons of luminous turquoise water lined the atriums and were plastered with vines. The water's color reminded Dr. Sharp of coral reef seawaters, which can glow at night from bioluminescent microorganisms.

Other areas of the ship they could get a glimpse of resembled a complex manufacturing facility. Stairways led in every direction, and massive platforms held hundreds of single-seat crafts. From the walkways, hexagonal-shaped hallways sprouted in every direction. Hundreds of doors dotted the corridors. Dr. Sharp assumed they led to living quarters or other unknown areas. Several oversized machinish things were off in the distance on platforms checking systems, working on computers, and mending sections of the ship. Dr. Sharp couldn't quite see their faces, but he was surprised that none of them paid more attention to them. Maybe the presence of new captives was less novel than he thought it would be.

The machinish beast undid a harness and stepped out of the craft. He flipped the cloth hood off his head, revealing his face fully for the first time.

Dr. Sharp and Jack reeled and stumbled backwards. They saw metalloid components fused with a muscle-ridden biological face, a strong jaw, and piercing opal eyes with a black wolf's intensity. His face was chiseled and appeared threatening in every direction. Streaks of stagnant metallic liquid formed an amorphous pattern down his neck and body. There weren't any blue lights on the back of his neck, which surprised Dr. Sharp as the interior of his hood had glowed blue when he saw him in the house. Rather, the blue light originated from underneath their captor's skin.

It's emanating from his vasculature!

Dr. Sharp was equally intrigued by a dimmer green light that diffused through a noticeable protrusion of skin on the man's left temple.

I swear that's an implanted device in his head, Dr. Sharp thought.

"Get out," the invader ordered in English. "Maazi wants to speak with you."

Dr. Sharp and Jack hesitated and exchanged a look. They thought their time had come.

"Now!" he yelled, gesturing at a metal platform outside the craft.

Dr. Sharp and Jack startled to action and jumped onto the platform. They both stumbled; their legs weren't used to the transition from microgravity to full gravity. After securing their footing, they followed their captor.

The machine creature limped slightly and held his stomach as they walked; the bullet wounds were obviously bothering him. He guided them through a series of hallways until they reached a control room filled with computers.

When he turned his back to Dr. Sharp and Jack, Jack said quietly, "Why don't we make a run for it?"

Dr. Sharp looked at Jack sympathetically. "My boy, where would we go?"

Jack shrugged.

"I hate to say it, Jack, but all roads out of here more than likely lead to a bad outcome. We need to keep our heads down for now. Just do as they say." Dr. Sharp put his hand on Jack's shoulder. "Things will be okay." Dr. Sharp didn't actually believe that. He was simply trying to soothe the teary teenager.

Dr. Sharp could tell that Jack didn't believe him, either, but he nodded anyway, wishing he could.

The machinish man removed Dr. Sharp's laptop from his trench coat and handed it and Dr. Sharp's briefcase to another creature who was obviously female. While her hair was the same shoulder length as the male captor's, her chest was noticeably accentuated, her brow and chin were less prominent, and her eyes were softer. But none of that meant she wasn't intimidating.

Dr. Sharp noticed the same protrusion of skin on her left temple through which a dim green light glowed. The organic machine woman placed Dr. Sharp's devices on a metal pad. In less than a second, all the contents of his systems pulled up on several transparent panels in the room.

Dr. Sharp pointed. "Look at those computer systems! Their technology must be lightyears ahead of ours." His eyes widened as he scanned their systems. "It's terrifying, yet … remarkable at the same time."

The woman opened Dr. Sharp's IED-detection software and used it to access an innumerable number of networks on Earth. She tapped into satellite feeds, news reports,

Internet blogs, ATM cameras, FBI servers, and government reconnaissance. Dr. Sharp went pale as he gazed at the endless amounts of information they could access.

"Their decoding software must use super quantum algorithms," Dr. Sharp whispered.

On the opposite side of the room, several other machinish people worked on computers and examined footage. One of the screens in particular caught Dr. Sharp's eye.

That one shows, he squinted and leaned forward, *three other ships! Just like the one we're on. How many of these things are roaming around out there?* He analyzed the images further. *And they're certainly not in this solar system.*

The ships hovered over large bodies of water that looked like those on Earth, but the water color and land features were notably different.

Those are definitely different planets.

The ships started sucking water into turbines that were on the undersides of their arms.

"Ah! You scavenge for water," he spoke to those in the room. "You must need it to survive just like we do."

Several of them turned their heads and glared. He watched as the creature who had his computer toggled through images of the Pacific Ocean, the Gulf of Mexico, and the Indian Ocean.

"That *was* a water beacon we found!" he exclaimed. "That's how you know which planets have water. Are you here to take our water?"

No one paid attention.

"Do you take lives in the process intentionally or only out of necessity?"

Before he could say any more, his captor pulled him and Jack away and pushed them down a dark hallway with moist, fungal-smelling walls. At the end of the hallway, the abductor opened a concave door. It groaned as it opened and revealed an arena-sized room with an incalculable number of plant species. Two dozen humanoid but non-human creatures were sitting on a rocky, dirt floor in the middle of the room. Obviously hominid. Dr. Sharp knew immediately why the organic machines weren't curious about his and Jack's presence; they had encountered human-looking beings before—many of them!

Each person in the room had slightly differentiated features. One man had ears that were enlarged, another had a triangular head shape. Another had the appearance of a caveman with an enlarged forehead like early Earth dwellers.

"Wait here," the beast said and heaved the door shut.

Dr. Sharp and Jack looked around, taking in their strange new prison. Flowering trees, fruit trees, and trees they'd never seen the likes of on Earth lined the walls. Large-leafed vines dangled from their branches. A selection of vines were transparent with brilliant purple ooze in their shoots. Enormous water tanks, like the ones they saw in the main area of the ship, were perched high above, their waters a vibrant blue-turquoise hue. The floor was backfilled with sandy soil and a variety of large and medium-sized rocks scattered throughout. The walls were metal with sections of pipes that ran the length of the room. A pile of detached pipes was laid up against a tree in the far corner.

Those pipes are probably there for some repairs, Dr. Sharp thought.

Several captives began to walk toward them. So far, they appeared peaceful.

"What the heck is this place?" Jack asked Dr. Sharp nervously.

"It's a biosphere, Jack. They must collect people from across the universe and keep them here."

"What's a biosphere?"

"Well, Earth is a biosphere, for example—a very large one at that. But a biosphere can be as large or as small as the creature that lives in it. It's basically any defined area that houses or is occupied by living organisms."

"And what happens to things that are kept in a biosphere?"

"Well," Dr. Sharp contemplated and chose his words carefully, not wanting to scare Jack beyond his current state of terror, "I suppose that depends on *who's* keeping things in the biosphere."

They looked at each other.

"So, you think that Maazi dude the guy mentioned is the one in charge of this biosphere?" Jack asked.

"I don't know, but something tells me we'll soon find out."

Chapter 15

Brooke Army Medical Center, San Antonio, TX

Gen. Childress awoke from surgery.

"Good morning," a young male Asian surgeon who was degloving addressed him.

"You are?" Gen. Childress asked sluggishly, recognizing the dull pain in his left leg. He palpated it. There was a metal post protruding from his amputated leg.

"Dr. Chen Kwok. Director of orthopedic surgery here at BAMC. Gen. Childress, I wanted to be here when you awoke so we can discuss your surgery and next steps."

"You weren't sure how I'd handle the news that you had to cut off my leg?" Gen. Childress quipped. "You probably tried contacting my family, and they refused to have anything to do with me."

"I'm ... um, yes," the surgeon said. "We did everything we could to save your leg. I'm sorry. The trauma was too great. I had to amputate—"

"Save it!" Gen. Childress stopped him and sat up in his bed. "I don't need to be coddled. I've held shredded limbs in my arms, carried dead men's bodies for miles to get them home to their families. You think I don't know the risks involved every day of my life?!" He spoke sternly, not to the surgeon in particular, but to the ethers of war. "I've been willing to give limb and life to this country. Frankly, I'm glad I finally got the chance. Now, is that an Ozzie I see over there?" Gen. Childress pointed to the far side of the room where an Ozzie was resting against the wall.

"Yes, sir," the surgeon said, shifting his mindset completely; the explanatory dialogue he had expected to give was now irrelevant.

"Bring it to me."

The surgeon grabbed the Ozzie and handed it to Gen. Childress who clicked it in place. He slid off the bed and stood erect on both feet.

"Can I go ahead and walk now, son, or do I need to do something special?"

"No, nothing special, the Ozzie technology allows you to function normally right away," the surgeon answered, admiring the general's pluck.

"Good! We don't have time to waste," Gen. Childress spoke sternly as he walked across the room. He bent down to grab the TV remote, revealing his buttocks in the process. "I'm guessing it's already on the news?"

The surgeon cracked a smile; surely Gen. Childress didn't mean his buttocks was on the news. "What do you mean?" The surgeon had been scrubbed in surgery all night and hadn't watched any news reports.

Gen. Childress picked up the remote and turned on the TV. News report after report showed a clip of a massive organic machine dragging a middle-aged man and a teenage boy around like rag dolls, followed by a streak of light that sped upward in the night sky.

"That," Gen. Childress said.

The surgeon stood speechless.

"And so, the battle begins," Gen. Childress whispered to the human-like monster on the television. "You and I have unfinished business."

"What the—What *was* that?" the surgeon asked, still dumbfounded by the images on the TV.

"Nothing. Get me my things. I need to get on the next plane to D.C.!"

Chapter 16

The White House, Washington, D.C.

It was 0730. Brighton looked down through his helicopter window at a bare spot on the White House lawn where an iconic magnolia formerly swayed. He used to eat lunch under the tree as a young infantryman. Before it was cut down due to disease and age, the magnolia had been pictured in dozens of presidential inauguration photos for nearly 200 years. Andrew Jackson had it planted in 1829 in memory of his wife who had died just days after he was elected to office. The tree was derived from a sprout of a magnolia on his and his wife's farm. Its history was long and its absence noticeable. The void in the lawn symbolized change.

Change is inevitable, and often uncomfortable, Brighton mused with irony. The world would never be the same after the events of a few hours ago.

The Blackhawk helicopter landed on the back lawn of The White House. Brighton stepped out onto the grass and gripped the towel that covered his left hand so it wouldn't blow away under the force of the helicopter's downdraft.

The White House premises were abuzz. Brighton estimated that thousands of agents already were surrounding The White House's exterior and rooftop, while tens of thousands of military troops surrounded the federal lands and monuments nearby.

The president was on the lawn awaiting Brighton's arrival. He waved as he approached, then yelled over the noise, "Col. Brighton, I'll admit, I didn't hope to see you so soon. Certainly not under these circumstances. And I would offer to shake your hand, but ...."

Brighton didn't salute, a forgivable action given the need to keep a firm grip on the white towel covering his left hand. He lifted it in the air slightly. "I have to protect it. There's vital information on my fingers. I got in a fight with ... something ... and have its remnants on my hand. I'm assuming you've seen the videos?"

"You mean of the seven-foot-tall biological-looking machine you fought?" The president smirked. "I'm the president of the United States. Yes, it did come across my desk. But it's certainly no secret. YouTube is reporting more than 3 billion views already. Come on, let's get inside."

The two were escorted to the rear entrance of The White House by a slew of Secret Service agents. They navigated the halls until they reached the Oval Office. The historic room was overfilled with reporters, journalists, military representatives, and staff.

"Take a seat by the fireplace," the president said. "First things first, I'll call for a team of forensic scientists to take samples of your hand. But stay here afterward. We need to chat after I address the world."

Brighton sat down and held onto his toweled hand. He watched the president make a call, and, within minutes, a team of forensic scientists was in front of him, taking swabs and vials-full of the now-dried indigo juices on his hand. They also took a vial of Brighton's blood and a swab of the inside of his mouth.

"For a baseline control," a scientist said.

Brighton nodded; he knew they would need his DNA and biological makeup to differentiate it from whatever was on his hand.

Just as quickly as they arrived, the scientists left to process the samples at the FBI's nearby forensics labs.

"All right, folks, everyone quiet down," the president said. "We're live in three minutes, and I need a moment. You're welcome to pray with me."

All eyes turned to the president as he bowed his head and prayed in silence for over a minute. Then he lifted his head and breathed deeply. "Now, let's prepare the world for what's about to come."

Film crews adjusted their cameras and readied their feeds. The lead cameraman started a countdown, "We're live in five, four, three, two, one."

~

The backdrop of the Oval Office streamed onto billions of devices across the globe and opened with a somber-looking president of the United States sitting straight-backed at the Resolute Desk.

"My fellow Americans, my friends and neighbors across the globe, as billions of you have already observed, our planet experienced its first extraterrestrial visit last night in San Antonio, Texas. The long-awaited question of whether we are alone in the universe is now satisfied. Our military intelligence members and scientists collected evidence this week that confirms this visit was factual. The images you are about to see are real." Images of the ships near Saturn cycled through the feed. "We've shared what limited information we have on these ships with countries across the planet.

"Our experts estimate that the ships you see are on pace to arrive in approximately three months. At this point, these large ships are hundreds of millions of miles away. However, after last night, we believe that they have smaller, faster-moving crafts that can reach Earth at an expedited rate. We believe the visitor last night was a scout sent to collect military intelligence. Its actions indicate they are hostile.

"We ask that you go about your daily lives, but we are setting a national curfew of 8:30 p.m. for all non-essential functions to reduce the risk of additional events. Our National Guard, military personnel, and local law enforcements will work around the clock in all our cities and towns to manage the situation.

"Prepare your homes and gather sufficient food and water for at least a one-week period. We are working with the Red Cross, FEMA, humanitarian branches of numerous churches, temples, and mosques, and many relief organizations to disperse food and supplies to all our major cities in a timely and orderly fashion. We have no reason to panic, but wisdom dictates we should prepare. Please treat one another with respect as you do so.

"I assure our citizens and the world that we have protective measures in place to defend ourselves against this potential threat. *We will be safe!* Weekly updates will be sent from the White House to keep everyone informed. As we work together, let us remember our motto, In God We Trust, and pray for help to make it through this. Please be considerate. Never has a time required mankind to unite more than now. Thank you. God bless America, and God bless us all."

The feed faded.

~

The Oval Office's atmosphere was uncomfortably silent. It felt like a dream. The quintessential president's message-in-a-time-of-doom had been delivered. Brighton never had considered just how unprepared his mind would be for that experience.

No one wanted to respond or move.

The president broke the silence. "All right, everyone. There's no time for solemnity. We need the world to know we're ahead of this. Gather yourselves and your things. Let's get to work."

Attendees followed the order and burst into action.

The president cut through the crowd and walked to Brighton. "Come with me," he said.

Brighton hurried behind the president, a group of Secret Service agents, and several political figures as they made their way to the president's personal office.

The workplace smelled rich—adorned with wood and linens that only a world leader could afford—and was decorated accordingly with items that only a world leader could have: signed letters from the Queen of England, rare historical documents, an original pen from the era of the Founding Fathers, and a custom-cast bobble head of the president's wife.

Brighton eyed the trinket and smirked. The sight distracted the serious scene for a moment. "A bobble head next to a letter from the queen? Not what I would have expected."

"My daughter put it there," the president grinned and shrugged. "What can I say? No world leader is more important than their family."

Brighton half smiled and walked past the agents who took equidistant positions around the room. Several important governmental figures took seats around the room, some silently somber, some speaking in hushed tones.

"How you holding up?" the president asked as he took a seat in a cherrywood chair with a plush cushion and motioned for Brighton to sit in an adjacent twin seat.

"I've been worse," Brighton answered honestly as he sat.

The president leaned in. "Attention, everyone. Col. Brighton is here to give us his confidential firsthand account. We know about most of what happened last night. But the footage is limited, and we don't have a good idea of what we're dealing with. Anything more you can tell us? Do we know what these things are, or how one of them got past our detection systems?"

Brighton shook his head. "As for how it got through our detection systems, I'm not sure. Maybe we were overly focused on the main ships near Saturn. None of our systems detected smaller crafts in the region. They could have cloaking abilities.

"And we've only encountered one ... I guess 'thing' is what I'll call it for now ... at this point, so we don't know fully what we're dealing with. However, I caught glimpses of its body as I wrestled it." Brighton lifted his sleeve, revealing a massive contusion on his right forearm. "It resembled an oversized man, but its eyes ... they were ..." Brighton considered his words. "They had the intensity of a predatory animal. The videos confirm that."

The president nodded, concurring with Brighton's description.

"Its right hand was modular and fired more than one type of weapon. A blue ring device had the ability to convert into individual discharge units. That said, it did have five fingers on each hand, at least at some point. I saw its fingers when it grabbed Dr. Sharp's laptop. It also had a type of tracking system embedded in its left forearm. It knew what it was looking for. It was intelligent and could communicate with our computer systems. Most of all, it was extremely powerful."

"And what about its appearance?" the president asked.

"It looked biological in nature, but metal in its chest and head was incorporated into its body."

"Was it a machine, then?" one political leader asked.

"In a sense, I suppose, but it was certainly more man than machine. I wouldn't even say the metal parts of its body were mechanically distinct per say, they were *fused* to its body. Perhaps the best way to describe it would be a fused machine."

"Or … a fused *organic* machine," the president added.

"Yes, more along those lines. Hmmm. If we follow military tradition, an acronym for that could be F. O. R. M. The FORM."

"I like that," the president stated. "We'll call them the FORM. But let me get back to the weaponry. Do we know what this … *FORM* was shooting out of its hand?"

"Some idea at least," Brighton said. "It looked like hot energy. The bullets, or whatever they were, were dynamic, not solid like metal. For lack of a better description, they looked like miniature suns. The reason I say that is they had this vivid appearance like the sun's surface but were blue instead of yellow and orange."

"Any idea what they want or why they're coming?" the president asked.

"If Dr. Sharp was right about their signaling device, we should assume that they want water. That would make good sense if they *are* biological in nature."

"I agree," the president said. "If they do want water, we have to assume they'll stop at nothing to get it. They've already shown us they're hostile. One of them killed nine people and took Dr. Sharp and the brother of one of our soldiers just to get a laptop and instruments. What I need to know is: when and how do we engage them? By 2100 tonight, I want a full proposal from each of our military branches as to how we defend ourselves, and—if negotiation isn't possible—how we attack."

Before the president could say any more, his desk phone rang. He picked it up and listened carefully. "What?" he said and raised an eyebrow. "We'll be right there." He hung up. "Brighton, well-done saving the blue material on your hand." The president stood from his chair. "They discovered some things at the FBI's forensics labs. You and me, let's go."

~

The FBI's forensics satellite lab was less than a mile away from the White House, yet it took Brighton and the president twenty minutes to arrive by car; the crowds in the already-clogged D.C. streets were growing unruly. News reporters attempted to stop the motorcade and shouted at the president, begging for details of the impending threat. People cared little about traffic as they ran from work and home to gather supplies or leave the city. The overall sense and scene was that of controlled chaos.

"Here we are," the president said as he pointed to the gray building ahead. "When you step out of the limo, let the Secret Service agents surround you. It's protocol."

Brighton swiveled out the passenger side of the limo and inspected the concrete façade and rectangular windows of the forensics labs building. There were no signs of danger. He stood erect as a group of Secret Service agents surrounded him and the president. They approached the entrance and entered the lobby together.

A gray-haired Indian male scientist with an overt amount of wrinkles, paunch belly, crooked teeth, and a blue lab coat greeted them. "Welcome, Mr. President, agents. Please, right this way." The scientist directed them down a hallway and updated them as they walked. "We've been able to use several rapid screening methods to determine a few of the phenotypic characteristics of the blue material that was on Col. Brighton's hand. Specific genotypic testing will take us a bit longer, but I think you're going to find this interesting."

"I'm sure that was all English, but, uh, did we catch your name?" the president asked.

"Oh, my apologies. My name is Dr. Jag Krupa. I'm the head scientist of the forensics labs."

"Dr. Krupa," the president probed, "I don't think any of us understood a word you just said. Could you put it in simpler terms?"

"Sorry, sometimes I tend to ramble away when I get excited about my findings. We've never seen anything like this! But instead of me talking your ear off, why don't I just show you what we've found?"

"Wonderful."

The group entered Dr. Krupa's 7,000-square-foot lab, in which a dozen technicians were abuzz. The floor in his office, immediately to the right, was covered with scientific articles, magazines, and pipets. His U-shaped desk contained three brands of computers and half a dozen spectrophotometric instruments. A variety of 3D printers sat on his elongated windowsill. The lab itself contained multiple PCR machines, genetic sequencers, analyzers, mass spectrometers, crystallographers, UV light sources, centrifuges, incubators, vortexers, test tube racks, a negative eighty-degree freezer, microscopes, and every research-relevant chemical one could imagine, no shortage of which was phosphate-buffered saline.

"Welcome to my discovery world," Dr. Krupa said as he invited them into the lab. "If you'll go to the back wall where the TV screens are, I'll show you our results."

The group made their way to the back. Dr. Krupa uploaded several images to the screens. "I'll begin by showing you what the blue material is made of. On the screen to your right is an image of the material components. It's only slightly more viscous than water. We thought this material was going to be something completely unique that we had never seen before, but we were very surprised to find that it is in fact a form of hydrogel that is primarily composed of water."

"And a hydrogel is?" Brighton asked.

"A hydrogel is a polymeric material that can hold many times its weight in water. We use a wide variety of hydrogels for medical applications like wound dressings or knee injections. As opposed to having blood like we have, whatever that was you encountered, Col. Brighton, has a slightly viscous hydrogel material running throughout its, or his or her, body."

"I imagine the FORM I fought is male," Brighton noted.

"The what?" Dr. Krupa questioned.

"The FORM," Brighton answered. "Short for fused organic machine. It's what we're calling them."

Dr. Krupa looked at him, intrigued. "Sounds appropriate. Okay. As fascinating as that is, there's even more to the hydrogel than we initially considered."

"Go on," the president prodded.

"Well, the fact that their blood is hydrogel-based is interesting enough, but it's what *gives* the hydrogel its intense color that is equally fantastic."

Brighton said, "We could all see it glowing vibrant blue in the dark when it came into the facility in San Antonio."

"Right." Dr. Krupa nodded. "It might remind you of ocean waters off the coast of tropical areas that often glow. That's because the glow comes from the same source: cyanobacteria! Their hydrogel is teeming with them."

Brighton retorted, "Cyanobacteria? You mean phytoplankton found in the ocean?"

"Precisely," Dr. Krupa said. "Their hydrogel material appears to contain a variant of photosynthetic bacteria similar to those that make our ocean waters glow blue at night and produce the vast amount of Earth's usable oxygen."

"But wouldn't bacteria in one's vasculature cause septicemia?" the president asked.

Everyone looked at him curiously. They wondered why, as a politician, the president would have that kind of medical knowledge in his back pocket.

"What?" The president shrugged. "I watch Nova when I can't sleep."

Dr. Krupa smiled and answered his question. "Typically, yes, bacteria in the bloodstream would cause infection, but for whatever reason, the … *FORM* … have this particular organism thriving in their blood."

"Astounding," Brighton said under his breath.

"I agree!" Dr. Krupa beamed. It was as though all his scientific senses were satisfied at once. "I think this is all indicative of a highly intelligent life form. But there's another reason why I think they are highly intelligent."

"Continue," the president encouraged him, intrigued.

Dr. Krupa pulled up an image of microscopic cells on the middle screen.

"What are we looking at?" Brighton asked.

"These are images of white blood cells from your blood." Dr. Krupa clicked a button on a computer and pulled up several more images of different cells, half the size of Brighton's and spherical in shape. "These were also in the blue material. I haven't determined exactly what they are, but I think they're *synthetic* immune cells. They're responding to all our tests similarly to how our own cells would respond."

"Hmm. What makes you think these come from an intelligent life form?" Brighton asked.

"Well, they're made of titanium. To be more precise, they're made of titanium nanoparticles fused with biological components. From the data I've collected so far, they seem to express surface antigens much like our own cells, but with a metal shell. I have no idea how it works. I can only imagine that with this type of system, you could selectively deliver drugs, growth factors, nutrients, or an endless array of molecules. These are things that only a highly intelligent life form could produce."

"So, what are you getting at, Dr. Krupa?" the president begged.

"Well, Mr. President, we also found that their DNA has almost exact homology to our own."

"What does that mean?" Brighton wondered.

Dr. Krupa lowered his head and thought about his response for a moment. He shifted his eyes toward Brighton. "Col. Brighton, based on the information I have so far, I think what you fought last night was as human as we are, but for whatever reason we don't know yet, it purposefully altered its biology."

Chapter 17

FORM Ship

Jack watched Dr. Sharp attempt to communicate with other humanoids in the biosphere, but his words were useless. In fact, they had the opposite effect; the others seemed to grow agitated the more Dr. Sharp spoke. He finally gave up and returned to Jack.

"And I thought international language barriers were challenging!" Dr. Sharp said.

"Maybe they don't communicate with words," Jack said.

"Then why do they have mouths?"

"To eat, maybe. Or kiss, I guess." Jack chuckled.

Dr. Sharp pulled his head back and thought for a moment. "What an astute observation. You would make a good scientist."

Jack smiled. "I'll probably stick with basketball, but sure, I'll think about science." Jack paused. "What the heck am I saying? We're sitting on a ship a billion miles away from home. I'm not going to be anything! I don't know, I was just thinking with my stomach. Man, I'm getting hungry. If I was home, Mom would cook—" Jack teared up.

Dr. Sharp put his arm around him, recognizing he was struggling on many levels, and justifiably so. "Come, my boy. Take a breath. We're going to make it."

"How do you know that?"

"I guess—I guess I don't, to be honest."

Jack shook his head. "You know, you *can* just *lie* sometimes to help me feel better."

"Ah, Jack, lying won't help us survive. As we face our truth, we'll have a better chance of finding our way home."

Jack shrugged and wiped his eyes. "Whatever, I guess."

The thud of metal footsteps outside the biosphere entrance cut their conversation short.

"Perhaps our truth is coming sooner than we thought," Dr. Sharp cautioned.

Jack and Dr. Sharp startled as the concave door to the biosphere entrance clanked. The latch rotated, and the metal hinges creaked. They both stepped back when they saw a commanding male personage step through the doorway.

The enormous man opened his arms wide, proudly displaying a mind-bending nearly eight-foot-wide arm span and spoke with a booming yet surprisingly pleasant voice. "Dr. Steven Sharp! Jack Vaughn! What a pleasure to have you aboard!"

"How ..." Dr. Sharp stammered as he looked the enormous man up and down.

The man's figure was breathtaking both in size and appearance. His eyes were a brilliant azure opalescence with stunning limbal rings—circumferential rings of black around the outside of his irises. The distinctiveness of his eyes matched the uniqueness of his face. Dr. Sharp was surprised his expression looked so handsome given the fusion of metal in his brow and right cheek. The man's nearly eight-foot-tall frame rippled with muscle and commanded respect; the fusion of liquid-appearing titanium and biology in his body was exquisite and intimidating.

His left bicep was biological whereas the top half of his right bicep was metallic. The physique of his legs was inimitable, with multiple muscle groups made of fluid-like steel that flexed like a stallion's hind quarters as he walked.

His unruly, wavy dark hair reached his shoulders. He wore a metalloid cloak that revealed his ten-pack abs and broad chest. Heavy cloth pant-looking coverings protected his groin and thighs. Dr. Sharp marveled at how welcoming the massive man's smile was; he wasn't expecting to be endeared by his appearance, but he was.

"How ... do I know your names?" the man finished Dr. Sharp's question. "Well, lest you think we are complete imbeciles, not only is your name written on your laptop, but we used your computer to gain a pretty decent understanding of your world. You can probably imagine what you can do with computer systems when you have a few thousand years to optimize them!" He laughed warmly. "But before I get into that, allow me to introduce myself. I'm Maazi. In your tongue, my name is interpreted 'Water Hunter!'" Maazi involuntarily flexed his oversized right bicep as he declared his title. "It's a pleasure to host you both."

Maazi strolled into the biosphere and looked around before coming face to face with Dr. Sharp and Jack. "You probably noticed *this* little thing." Maazi touched his left temple—the skin of which was glowing a mild green—and leaned his head down close to Jack.

Jack took an involuntary step back as his body prepared a fight-or-flight response. He tripped over a rock in the process and flopped to the sandy floor.

"Oh, Jack," Maazi said, "don't hurt yourself. Here, let me help you up." Maazi reached a gorilla-sized hand out to Jack and helped him off the ground. "All right?"

Jack nodded and swallowed hard.

"As I was saying, what you see under the skin of my head is a neurochip. It allows me to upload gigabytes-worth of information directly to my senses. I invented it over 2,000 Earth years ago, which," Maazi tilted his head back and ran a quick mental calculation, "would be about 3,000 of our circuits. Of course, I've made some improvements over time. I can learn almost anything as fast as I can generate a thought with this thing. Speaking of ... English, we *like* this language."

Dr. Sharp's eyes widened with wonder. *What fantastic technology!*

"I thought you would find that interesting. So, Dr. Sharp, you're a scientist."

Dr. Sharp nodded and gulped.

"You seem intrigued by the plants in our ship. We've collected them from planets all across the universe. Fascinating botany. But the plants aren't the real heroes on our ship. Do you know what is, Jack?"

"I, I guess I don't. Sorry. What is it?"

"No need to be sorry, Jack. It's the bacteria! We grow what your planet refers to as cyanobacteria in our water systems. Cyanobacteria are evolutionary geniuses! Have you ever heard of them?"

Jack shook his head and held a blank face. He was in near shock, terrified that Maazi was going to hurt him at any moment if he gave a wrong answer.

Maazi paced around him, leaving deep and broad footprints in the soil.

"You see the turquoise waters, don't you?" Maazi paused, looked at the tanks overhead, then at Dr. Sharp.

"We do, they're ... um, very beautiful," Dr. Sharp said.

"We've optimized the growth formulation of cyanobacteria so they produce oxygen ten times faster than they do on your planet. Our bodies need oxygen just like yours. Of course, our bodies are larger and far superior." Maazi gave a smart-aleck grin and sat down on a large rock. "We infuse cyanobacteria into our upgraded vasculature to provide oxygen to our bodies. They provide the necessary balance to our self-contained ecosystems."

Dr. Sharp marveled at the biology Maazi described.

"Cyanobacteria are the most basic and essential form of life for oxygenated planets, but you already knew that, didn't you, Dr. Sharp?"

Dr. Sharp shook his head. "No, I, er, I hadn't considered that."

"Well, now you know. But let me tell you something else you may find interesting; about 2,400 circuits ago, we found a planet made entirely of diamond. When you need to transport water across the universe like we do, you don't want corrosion to occur, but you knew *that* didn't you?" Maazi's questions were becoming noticeably condescending. "Well, when we found all that diamond, we wondered, what the heck are we going to do with it? *Buy* something?" Maazi laughed at his own comment and stood to walk again. "No, Dr. Sharp, money has no value to us. We used the diamond for more practical purposes; to make the tubes and ceiling canopies of our ships corrosion resistant. I mean, if you're going to store water, you gotta control corrosion! Granted, diamond provides a dual benefit; it serves its function and gives a nice ambiance. The best of both worlds, Dr. Sharp."

Dr. Sharp shifted his weight and patted Jack's shoulder. Jack was fidgeting with his fingers, and Dr. Sharp could tell he was struggling.

"And don't even get me started on why we use astatine! Let me just say that I found a way to functionalize astatine's radioactive properties to support our transmission signals. Brilliant if I do say so myself.

"But enough about me! You," Maazi put his hands on his hips, "your people ... once I learned about your world, I *had* to come and meet you in person. I'm *fascinated* by your technology and social system. You are one-of-a-kind, Dr. Sharp." Maazi continued to pace casually, vibrating the ground with each step. "I see you met the others that look similar to you. They're everywhere in this universe. Your scientists are way behind the game; they're still only *hypothesizing* the presence of single-celled life forms."

Dr. Sharp swallowed hard and nodded.

"You think there are a few thousand planets like Earth. Well, there are *billions*, but humans aren't what matter." Maazi slowed his pace and glared at Dr. Sharp and Jack. "Water ... *water* is what matters, you two. Usable water is scarce out there. You just have to know how to find it! Our beacons do a nice job, as you discovered quite quickly.

"A years-old signal from those beacons led us to this solar system. But by the time we arrived, we lost the signals and thought the beacons were lost. But we did find millions of pounds of ice in Saturn's rings! So, we started scavenging. But do you have any idea how much energy it takes to *melt* ice and subsequently collect the water in the frigidness of outer space, Dr. Sharp?"

Dr. Sharp cleared his throat. "No, but I imagine the exothermic energy expense requirements must be high."

"Ah, there's my scientist! You're right. Capturing liquid water requires much less energy expenditure. But then ... then, Dr. Sharp, a couple of you Earth dwellers helped us out! Imagine that, a completely inferior species that we could crush in an instant helped *us* out!"

Dr. Sharp's face paled. Maazi may have been the most intentionally passive aggressive individual he had ever met. He seemed to display a cordial, even friendly mannerism, but made no qualms about reminding them repeatedly that he could inflict harm.

"Ah, yes, Dr. Sharp. Thank you, by the way, for activating that second beacon. When the first awakened, then died, and the second one did the same, we thought we were out of luck! But then you came along and reactivated that second one. Dang! You led us on to one of the most abundant sources of liquid water we've ever discovered!

"But make no mistake, that captain in your army will pay for what he did. Somehow, he commandeered our signals. His name came through when he connected some system with ours. *He* is the one who ultimately divulged our location. I don't take kindly to those who uncover our secrets. That Ryker Vaughn will receive justice!"

Dr. Sharp could tell that chills were running up and down Jack's spine. He had to have been asking himself how they knew about his brother.

Dr. Sharp nearly vomited. *What did I do?*

Maazi watched both of their faces contort uncontrollably. Dr. Sharp could tell their pain brought Maazi deep pleasure.

"We were hesitant to travel any closer to your Sun. We typically avoid getting close to stars because it increases the risk of having our water sources evaporate. But Earth, my goodness, its atmosphere is so unique, it can hold water indefinitely! I'm not so sure your people will thank you for guiding us their way. Remember," Maazi put a hand to the side of his mouth "you're kind of the reason we'll commandeer Earth soon. But perhaps … do you think your people will welcome us kindly, Dr. Sharp?"

"I'm sure they will come to, uh, an agreeable arrangement," Dr. Sharp said hesitantly.

Maazi smiled shrilly. His face shifted from pleasant to conniving. "You … your people are on the right track. We've never met anyone as intelligent as you. There are few in the universe with advanced technology like you have. But you had the ability to detect our presence. That was impressive! We typically annihilate a species before they even know we've arrived."

Jack's eyes reddened and filled with water.

Maazi walked deeper into the biosphere and paused, then turned to Dr. Sharp and measured him up visually. "You have weapons that kill one another on a scale that is unparalleled in this universe. None of these people here lived on planets where people tried to kill their own kind." He pointed to the other human-like beings in the room.

"Not that it mattered, because we took care of the rest of their kind but it's not a good method of long-term survival. Think about it Dr. Sharp—killing one another is ... unwise." Maazi nonchalantly paced back to Dr. Sharp and unexpectedly grabbed his throat, causing him to gasp horribly. The once-appealing look of Maazi's face morphed into a venomous expression. "Do you know how I know that?"

Dr. Sharp was silent.

"Answer me!" Maazi got in his face.

"No! No, I don't," Dr. Sharp struggled.

"Because my people did the same." Maazi let go of Dr. Sharp's throat, but his handprint remained. "Once we started destroying one another ... once *he* tried to overtake me, I had to ruin our planet."

Dr. Sharp wondered who "*he*" was.

"Our water became our only source of survival. My closest ally, my trusted friend, deceived me—and my people—and tried to *kill* us when all we had left was water. You know of treachery, hatred, Dr. Sharp? Ah, you know it well on your planet. It made me who I am.

"So we had to find alternative sources of survival, new planets on which we could dwell and thrive. But most planets have minimal water. Within a few ten thousands of years after human life evolves, most planets are depleted of sustainable resources. Mars, the planet in your solar system, is an example. Nothing is more essential in this universe than water if you want to live. There are others in this universe, seekers of water. They will do anything for it! Would you kill for water, Dr. Sharp?"

Maazi stared at Dr. Sharp, sizing up the very valor that lay in his heart. He looked at him long enough to make the silence uncomfortable.

"I can't say that I have had to consider that," Dr. Sharp finally muttered.

Maazi continued to walk the area. His massive feet snapped twigs on the floor beneath him. "Your planet doesn't yet know what it means to fight for water. Well … we'll change that."

Dr. Sharp reeled internally. *This man is a legitimate menace.*

"But water doesn't just fall out of the sky when you're a space traveler. You have to seek the right *kind* of water. Some planets have acidified water, some have toxic components. This Earth, your Earth, has more varieties of useful water types, and greater amounts of salinized water, than we've ever encountered. Most planets can only sustain a few thousand humans with minimal amounts of water. Earth has nearly eight billion survivors, according to your estimates, yes?"

"Yes," Dr. Sharp said softly.

"An optimized planet! It's fascinating to consider, Dr. Sharp. So exciting in fact, that we may have to do more than just take *some* water. We may need to become permanent citizens."

Dr. Sharp and Jack gulped as beads of sweat began to trickle down their faces.

"I learned something interesting from your president and Col. Samuel Brighton. Speaking of, I'm intrigued by that man, Brighton. We picked up some of their communication from a wiretap in your president's office. Remarkable, actually. Your government thinks they keep so many secrets, yet other countries listen to almost everything they say. I wouldn't make that mistake as a leader, but that's neither here nor there.

"It's a marvelous experience, I tell you, having so much power in a society." Maazi gave a threatening glare. "It sounds like your military is going to call us 'fused organic machines.' The *FORM!*" He let the word hang in the air for a moment. "Dang, I actually like it! It fits us well. I'll call myself, FORM Commander Maazi. You like that, Dr. Sharp?"

"I, uh, I suppose," Dr. Sharp answered.

"Well, we *FORM* are a superior people. We have long since replaced our blood with what you call hydrogel material." Maazi took a sharp object and cut his forearm, causing blue material to ooze outward. He wiped some on Dr. Sharp's face. "This hydrogel circulates throughout our bodies. I developed it. It gives us so much more versatility for survival than typical ... no ... *inferior* human blood. We extract it from a plant we encountered eons ago, the one that you saw in our corridor, transparent with a blue glow to it? It consists of very specific organic products so only cyanobacteria, and no other pathogenic bacteria grow in it. That way, our bodies stay free from infection. Bacteria are the ultimate survivors. They're *everywhere* in this universe. If you want to live, you need to resist pathogenic bacteria!

"With this hydrogel, we can tailor each FORM to function in a specific manner. Hydrogel also synergizes wonderfully with metal. We can survive indefinitely by fusing bacteria-resistant biological components with metal. Something of a break-through, wouldn't you say?"

"I ... yes, yes, I guess so," Dr. Sharp stumbled.

"You guess so." Maazi sneered. "You're still not convinced of our superiority. Well, that'll come in time. I'll never again allow myself to be inferior in this universe. Being weak will get you killed, and death is so unwelcome when you've lived as long as I have.

"We were once like you—you know, weak. But now, Dr. Sharp, now we're so much more. 'Super human,' your comic books might call us. I prefer Superior Human." Maazi bent his massive body down, got in Dr. Sharp's face and breathed heavily. "No human species has been able to survive us. What do you think about yours? Will you survive?" Maazi's voice was deep and threatening.

Dr. Sharp gulped dryly. He looked at Jack who appeared on the brink of blacking out.

"Well, if your people are anything like you, the fight will not be difficult. I'm told that you cowered in a room as my scout searched for you. And yet here, Jack, a teenage boy, was willing to fight my servant to save you!"

Dr. Sharp's face turned crimson red as he held back tears.

"That's why he took you. We always keep the weaker ones in a human species. It's a reminder of our dominance in this universe. Old Jack here, well, he was a bonus. He may end up being the perfect *bait*."

Dr. Sharp watched Jack grab his stomach. He could hear his stomach acid churning. He imagined how his soul longed for home.

"Are you feeling weak, Dr. Sharp?" Maazi asked.

Dr. Sharp's slender face trembled violently, causing Maazi to smile wickedly.

"I hope the fight with your people will be, you know, exciting. It's been *way* too long since we've had a worthwhile battle! You saw some of my FORM out there working in the ship, didn't you?"

"I did," Dr. Sharp answered shakily.

"If your militaries weren't so extensive, we'd approach your planet much faster, but I'm having my people prepare. Why rush, I say. We're not in a hurry to get anywhere. Maybe that's the reason I've sat here talking so long!" He laughed out loud. "No, living is all we have to do." Maazi stroked his chin. "We used to have more than a million people living on our ships. Too many weak people ... it takes its toll. Your people know about that. My army is now a fraction of what it used to be, which would perhaps not be enough in hand-to-hand combat, but there are alternate methods to destroy armies. I'm thrilled you have weapons, the likes of which we've never encountered. We'll cripple them, I'm not worried, and show water seekers throughout the universe that we will not be challenged.

"Of course, it's not just about water, there's an aspect of fun to be had. It's rewarding to watch people run in fear, with nowhere to go. What's the farthest your people have traveled so far?"

Maazi waited for an answer, though he already knew the response.

"To the moon," Jack whispered.

"To your own moon? Good heavens, you're hopeless. Your people will never survive long-term in this universe. Some guy wants to colonize Mars from what I gather in your news reports. Your Sun will dehydrate people on that planet in no time! Perhaps that's why you've developed such powerful weapons. You can't travel beyond your own planet, so you must protect the one you have."

Maazi licked his lips, circled his prisoners once more, and stopped in front of Jack. He raised an eyebrow. "There *is* one thing I'm certain of." He paused and grabbed Dr. Sharp's face.

Maazi's enormous fingers swallowed his fragile bones and forced his middle-aged wrinkles to compress together. "I'm willing to do whatever it takes to get my hands on a planet's-worth of water!"

Maazi slid his fingers off Dr. Sharp's face and dusted off his hands. He smiled, morphing his face back from evil-ridden to pleasant and welcoming. "Dr. Sharp, this was a nice conversation. I hope you enjoy this place we've prepared for you. Oh, uh, feel free to eat any fruit you can find in here. But, as you might expect, we'll provide water … sparingly." Maazi grabbed a small jug of water from a pocket in his cloak and tossed it on the ground. He laughed briefly and said, "Oh gosh, I can't help myself, I just have to use one of your cliches, because it's so truth-filled: Dr. Sharp, this will be like taking candy from a baby!" Maazi laughed again then sauntered out of the biosphere.

The heavy clang of the concave door signaled that Jack and Dr. Sharp were once again captive in an undesirable place. It wasn't until Maazi was gone that they realized all the other beings in the biosphere were huddled in a corner. They avoided Maazi, perhaps wisely.

Dr. Sharp reached his hand to his face and wiped off the blue ooze Maazi wiped on him. He sank to one knee. "What have I done? How can I possibly go on knowing that I'm the one who caused this?"

"Come on, Dr. Sharp, you just told me a minute ago that we're going to get home. I need you. The world needs you. We—You gotta figure something out. He just said I'm freaking bait! We gotta get out of here!"

Dr. Sharp breathed heavily for a few moments, then lifted his head. "You're right. By golly, you're right! We *can't* give up. Humanity is worth fighting for. If there's any bright side to look at, it's that we're on our way *toward* Earth and not traveling away from it. There must be something we can do!" Dr. Sharp punched the ground for effect but didn't recognize an unforgiving rock just below the soil surface. He heard a pop and howled in pain.

Not only would Dr. Sharp have to figure something out while living in a distant jungle-like prison; now he would have to figure it out with a sprained wrist.

Chapter 18

San Antonio, TX

Ryker studied the obstacle course in front of him. He smirked. It was odd that it felt like home. Day in and day out, he'd traversed obstacle courses in basic and advanced training as a newly enlisted private, then as captain. But he couldn't think of a better place to learn what his Ozzies were capable of.

This obstacle course was a privately owned, custom-designed challenge known for its world-class level of difficulty, in particular after being featured on multiple international reality TV programs. Its structure consisted of more than one hundred tons of steel, thousands of webbings, and myriads of ninja steps, bumper pads, rope swings, cushioned landings, all creating unique obstacles. Elite athletes across the globe came daily to practice on it but only a handful ever made it through.

First thing the morning after Jack was taken, Ryker had contacted the owner and explained his situation: he needed to know what his Ozzies could handle so he could save his brother. The owner told him to come any time, free of charge.

Ryker went within an hour; there was no time to waste. No one knew what was coming next with the FORM—the name for Earth's anticipated invasion force that was now airing over the Internet.

He was surprised at how many people were at the obstacle facility. Given the FORM's imminent arrival, he thought more of society would be cowering in their houses.

"If they're going to show up, I'll be in shape to fight," one guy gave as the reason he was there.

A woman said, "Getting a good workout is more therapeutic for me than sitting in my house worrying about the end of the world, so I figured I'd get out and do this."

Ryker couldn't disagree. He approached the starting line of the obstacle course with a dozen other people and took in a breath of blossom-scented spring air. The smell reminded him of spring days he used to spend playing ball with Jack. His heart was still agonizing. *Is Jack okay? What is he doing right now? How will I even be able to save him?* Ryker wished he had answers, but all he knew was that he needed to challenge his Ozzies.

"What did you say the course record was?" Ryker asked a facility employee at the starting line.

"Three minutes, seventeen seconds," the employee said.

"You thinking you gonna break the record?" a mid-twenties, fit black lady next to him asked.

"Well, you're about to find out," Ryker said confidently.

The lady looked at Ryker's legs, contorted her face, then raised her eyebrows. "Whatever you say."

Ryker reached down and turned the dial on his Ozzies to "sport" mode, then wiped his sweaty hands on his shorts.

"Welcome, everybody," an announcer said through the speaker system. "You'll hear a countdown and then a gunshot to get you started. You each have twenty minutes to complete the course. If you fall off an obstacle and into a safety net, you need to get off the course and wait for the next round to try again."

The athletes nodded their heads and did their final stretches.

"Here we go. Five, four, three, two."

Bang!

Ryker ran toward the first obstacle: a rotating three-foot diameter foam barrel set on a horizontal plane. He pushed off one Ozzie leg hard to jump over the barrel. The Ozzies responded without hesitation, and Ryker cleared the first challenge with ease.

Next was the seven-mile-per-hour uphill treadmill. His Ozzies whirred seamlessly as he ran to the top and jumped onto a padded landing. Four other athletes were neck-and-neck with him.

Each jumped onto the next obstacle: a rope course. They swung like agile apes from rope to rope, challenging their upper and lower body muscles to keep pace. One of the lead contestants fell, leaving Ryker and three others in the lead.

They reached the next obstacle: parallel transparent panels followed by angled springing footboards—the first of which they had to traverse by plastering their hands and feet flat against the walls and crab crawl through a bottomless cavern of plastic walls, then jump from board to board without falling. Ryker knew this would be an interesting challenge for his Ozzies. *Can they handle an angled force like this?* The question was short-lived as Ryker flattened the feet of his Ozzies against the walls. They responded without flaw, yet the springboard portion took more effort than he expected; his mind still had to process the balance of the Ozzies.

One of the frontrunner contestants began to fall behind, failing to find a decent foothold on the plastic panels, leaving Ryker and two other racers in the lead.

Next came another rotating padded barrel on top of which the contestants had to run without falling. Ryker danced over the barrel, but halfway through, his left foot slipped. He caught himself just before going over and jumped onto another padded landing. He was safe, yet his mistake cost him. Two contestants were now seconds ahead.

Ryker ran through a mid-length maze and reached a springboard off which he had to jump to a twenty-foot-tall webbing tower. He soared off the springboard and worked the web, exchanging hand over hand, foot over foot. He struggled at first to find the right connection with his Ozzies. When he finally found a rhythm, his arms reminded him they were getting weak. Nevertheless, just as he had done in hundreds of workouts before, he pushed through the discomfort and kept climbing. His lungs were on fire when he reached the top landing. He nearly lost his grip.

The two challengers in front of him already had cleared the web and were onto a dangling field of Olympic rings. Ryker hefted his body over the last section of webbing and rolled onto the landing. He jumped up and grabbed the first ring.

He swung synchronously but had to take a quick break midway through to wipe sweat from both hands on his T-shirt. One of the two leaders ahead of him dropped onto the net below. Only one challenger was now ahead. Ryker blinked the sweat out of his eyes and gritted his teeth. He grabbed the closest ring and shifted his weight to reach the next one. When he was close to the end, he heaved his body weight forward and jumped onto a landing.

Sweat dripped from his forehead onto the plastic platform below. Ryker exhaled heavily and stood for the next challenge: a slanted rock-climbing-inspired wall with barely there footholds. He watched the contestant in front of him traverse the obstacle. They were nearing the final two challenges of the course: a reverse ascending and descending staircase, and a tower of parallel walls that required tremendous leg strength to summit.

Ryker peeked at the timer suspended in the rafters above him. He only had thirty seconds to set the course record.

"Oh!" the crowd below him hollered in unison as they watched several contestants drop from an obstacle behind him.

Ryker refocused and started making his way across the wall. Halfway in, he observed the pattern of the footholds. *Aha. I just need to get to that upper section*, he thought. But the split-second he used to observe the pattern cost him his current foothold, and without warning, he slipped and fell to the safety net below.

Ryker hit the netting in frustration. *It's going to take more than that*, he thought.

"Okay, off the course," a voice from the ground below said.

Ryker rolled off the netting and made his way to the ground. The lady who had stood next to him at the starting line was near the exit and looking at him with taunting eyes.

"Don't. Say. Anything," Ryker huffed sarcastically with a hint of irritation.

The lady raised her eyebrows. "I *didn't* say anything, but apparently I don't need to."

"Just keep watching." Ryker smirked and exited the course.

"Oh!" the crowd's holler roared as the final contestant who had been just ahead of Ryker fell off the course. There was no one else remaining.

"All right, contestants," the announcer projected. "It looks like we don't have a finisher this round. For those who would like to try again, we'll give you a ten-minute breather."

Ryker walked over to his duffel bag and grabbed a swig of sport drink.

"Hey, stranger," he heard a woman's voice say.

Ryker looked up and saw Jessie. She was dressed in yoga pants and an exercise top with her hair in a ponytail. His heart leapt.

"Hey." Ryker smiled. "What brings you this way?"

"I went by to see how you and your mom were doing. Your mom said you were here, and I thought you might like some company. I heard about last night. I'm so, so sorry about Jack. I, I don't actually even know how to put it into words. I just feel so empty, and I can only imagine what you're going through." She fidgeted her fingers. "After the president's message this morning, it's like, weird. The world is about to experience something completely unknown, but we still need to go on living normally. I don't know, it's just … I can't even really process it. I'm just so sorry about Jack."

"Thank you," Ryker said. "After we got home last night, I went to Jack's room with my mom, and we looked at his pictures and stuff. It's the emptiest I've ever felt. I'm still numb. You know, I've lost my buddies in battle, but it's different when you watch someone you love get taken. I sat and thought about everything for hours. I felt like I wanted to get revenge at first, and I'm not gonna lie, I still do, but I know revenge never satisfies in the end. It's justice that matters, returning balance to things, and that's what I've fought for all my life. I decided last night, so long as those things are coming toward us, I'm gonna be ready for anything. It may be a mix of revenge and justice, but no matter what, I'm gonna do all I can to get Jack!"

Jessie smiled.

"So, you decided to use the Ozzies."

Ryker half-smiled. "Yeah, I know what you might be thinking. But after last night, I decided I can't *not* walk, or fight as the case may be. My team, my brother, my dad, they deserve everything I can offer. And they would want me to keep going. The first step is to learn how to use these things to their fullest extent. It's ultimately my duty to pay something forward. In fact, I'm going to call the president after this and tell him I'm ready to return to duty."

Jessie smiled and gave Ryker an impulsive kiss on the cheek. She pulled away and covered her mouth with her hands. "Oh my gosh, I'm so sorry. I don't know why I just did that." She blushed.

"Nah, you're okay. We're in strange times. Random kisses, you know, aren't the *worst* thing that could happen."

They looked at each other for a moment. Both could tell deeper feelings were developing.

Ryker wiped his face with a towel and said, "Just so you're aware, that first run was a warmup."

"Oh, *really?*" Jessie teased. "I guess you'll have to prove that."

He bent down and turned the dial on his Ozzies from "sport" to "battle" mode. The lights on the Ozzies changed from blue to red. "Now we're going to see what these things can *really* do!"

Ryker did a few arm stretches and jogged in place. The Ozzies' mechanics were fluid and strong.

"Let me know how they handle," Jessie said.

"Oh, I'm about to show you that." Ryker winked, then ran toward the starting line.

"Back again?" the lady who didn't believe he could break the record asked.

"Yes. I'll never back down," *again*, he thought.

A minute later, the countdown began. "Five, four, three, two."

Bang!

Ryker raced toward the six-foot diameter foam barrel and hurdled it with ease, then sprinted the uphill treadmill. The Ozzies responded like lightning. As Ryker pushed harder, the Ozzies seemed to ask for more. He used the Ozzies to balance and synchronize the rope swings. The internal artificial intelligence of the Ozzies counterbalanced and balanced without hesitation as Ryker thrust them back and forth. He then traversed the plastic panels; rather than use his hands, he bounded off each plastic panel with his feet—just as he had catapulted off the tree trunk the night before. He bounded over the springboard pads and reached the rotating barrel tube.

The Ozzies gave him cheetah-like reflexes and speed as he ran across the rotating tube. He stood on the landing pad and took a split second to size up the leap to the tower of webbing, then sprinted, jumped, and soared through the air. The Ozzies launched him farther than he anticipated, and he grabbed the mesh more than halfway up the web. His arms and Ozzies worked fluidly together as he wrangled the mesh. This was a major test for the Ozzies; Ryker wondered if the connection between his bone and the metal posts protruding from his legs would hurt as he climbed. He was pleased that they were painless. He climbed harder, trying to push the Ozzies to their limit. He crested the landing. The Ozzies felt great.

He continued to push them and jumped deep into the field of Olympic rings. His arms and Ozzies worked together to optimize his momentum as he swung back and forth like a forward moving pendulum.

"Keep it up!" someone in the crowd yelled.

"Look at him!" another exclaimed.

The crowd was energized about something. Ryker figured it was because someone was gaining on him. He pushed himself and the Ozzies harder.

Next was the angled wall with barely there footholds. Ryker didn't hesitate. He grabbed two grips with his fingers and placed both feet in the upper section of the wall where he knew he had his best chance of getting across. The Ozzies again used their internal AI components to put his balance right where he needed it. He climbed across the rock-climbing wall slightly too fast. Midway across, his fingers slipped, and he fell but snagged two fingerholds on the lower section.

He used his upper body strength to pull himself back to position, ignoring the burning in his arms and fingers. He swung his Ozzies up and continued climbing the wall. He jumped onto a landing pad and assessed the final two obstacles. He used his tremendous upper body strength to climb up and down the reverse staircase obstacle, then turned backwards and looked up the tower of parallel walls.

The Ozzies seemed to tell him, *Jump already!*

He bounded up one section, then the next and the next, using the power of the Ozzies to lift him to the top of the tower. When he got to the peak, he took a deep breath and threw his hands in the air.

Ryker enjoyed the sense of pride that swept through his soul. The Ozzies not only did their job, they surpassed his expectations.

These bionics would change his life.

"Smash the button!" the crowd below yelled.

Amidst his thoughts, Ryker had forgotten to hit the red button at the top of the obstacle. He obeyed the crowd and slammed it. Sirens blared and the crowd cheered.

Ryker looked down. There wasn't a single other contestant on the course. In fact, no other contestant had even started the second race. They'd all stood in awe as they watched Ryker maneuver his way through the obstacle course.

Ryker looked at the clock: one minute and fifty-three seconds. He had smashed the old course record. He knew the Ozzies gave him an advantage, and the record wouldn't stand. Yet he wasn't there for the record. He was there for Jack. He now knew what the Ozzies could do; everything he needed them to do to save Jack if ... no ... *when* the time came.

Ryker climbed down the tower and met the obstacle course owner.

"Thanks for letting me do that," Ryker said.

"No, man, thank *you*. I never knew prosthetic legs could move like that!"

"Neither did I, to be honest," Ryker smirked.

They high fived, and Ryker made his way to the exit.

The lady who had been next to him at the starting line looked him up and down. She conceded, "I don't mind being proved wrong sometimes, but dang, man! You sure made a point! Respect."

"I told you to keep watching. You never know what you might miss!"

She laughed and shook her head as she walked over to her family.

Ryker wiped the sweat off his forehead and made his way to Jessie.

"So. They work better than I imagined," Ryker said.

"I should say so, soldier," Jessie agreed. "You may even get yourself some airtime with that performance."

Ryker looked up. Several TV cameras were filming him and probably had recorded everything he'd done.

"Credit to the rehab folks who designed these things, I'm just the user," Ryker said as he reached into his bag and grabbed another bottle of hydration. He drank the whole of it and exhaled. "OK, now it's time to call the president."

Ryker grabbed his cell phone out of his bag and dialed the number from which the president had called him previously. It chimed, signaling someone picked up.

"Mr. President?" he asked.

"No, but this is the president's office. May I ask who's calling?"

"This is Capt. Ryker Vaughn. I'm wondering if the president still needs my services."

"Just a moment."

Ryker waited patiently then heard the president come on the line. "Ryker, it's good to hear from you, son. I'm terribly sorry about your brother."

"Thank you, sir. But, uh, with him being taken, I'm ready now … for anything you need."

"That's great to hear. I appreciate you reaching out. I'll get right to it. The first order of business is to determine why we received a message saying, 'Justice to Ryker Vaughn.'"

"Right. Col. Brighton and Dr. Sharp showed me that message. Mr. President, the FORM last night said something to me about me divulging them. They must just be angry that I found that cylinder thing."

"Probably. And now you're a target. We already have a task force close by watching out for you."

Ryker looked around. He nearly slapped his forehead. He thought there was something off about the half dozen men dressed in suits who were outside the training facility watching him. "Ah. Thank you, sir."

"I think it's best you stay in San Antonio for now," the president said. "We're going to monitor the situation and see how things progress. We need more information before we strategize a defense ... or an offense."

"Yes, Mr. President. I'm ready when you need me."

"Stay well, soldier."

The call ended, and Ryker slid his cell phone into his pocket.

"I don't think anyone really knows what's going on yet," Ryker said to Jessie. "He just told me to wait for now." Ryker sighed. "I just feel so helpless. My brother's out there. I want to *do* something, but there's just nothing to do."

"You did what you could today," Jessie consoled as she squeezed his arm.

"Yeah, I gotta accept the wins. Today was a big step forward for me."

"One small step for Ozzies, one giant leap for mankind," Jessie teased.

Ryker laughed. "Good one."

Jessie smiled. "Well, I need to head out. Apparently, we have a curfew to abide by now. I have a lot to do at work before then. I mean, I guess we're all just going to work normally still."

"Yeah, I guess so," Ryker said. "So, uh, assuming the world doesn't end tonight, I'll catch you later."

Jessie winked, brushed Ryker's hand with hers, waved bye, and pulled her keys out of her purse as she walked away.

Ryker admired her curves as she walked toward her car. He watched her pass a basketball standard near the training facility exit. It reminded him of Jack.

Just get here safe, brother. Ryker looked at his Ozzies. *We'll be ready!*

Chapter 19

The Pentagon, Washington, D.C.

Brighton poured himself a cup of cold water from a dispenser in the Pentagon's bunker room. The bunker was arguably the safest room on Earth. It was part of the underground War Room complex and had oversized screens that dwarfed even the largest Imax theaters. The rationale for such large screens was for a viewer to readily see all of Earth's geographies. The bunker also housed the most expansive communications systems with endless computer technologies, the highest level of security, and concrete walls lined with the most damage-inducing firearms and explosives available—in the event The War Room complex needed to be defended.

The president, Brighton, and military commanders chose to meet at the Pentagon instead of at The White House—as it was a prime target for attack—while they waited for Gen. Childress, who, as the secretary of defense, was authorized to finalize a strategic military effort. Gen. Childress had surgery yesterday and was en route to the Pentagon.

Brighton drank his water fast and exhaled with his eyes closed. He needed a moment to reset. His mind kept dwelling on events of the past few days.

Ryker was hit by an IED, became a double amputee, and received state-of-the-art Ozzies. We saw UAPs near Saturn hours later, team members and I on Project Galago rushed to

San Antonio and characterized the UAPs, then Earth's first confirmed extraterrestrial visitor arrived, and I fought the miscreant. Now I'm in the Pentagon strategizing an extraplanetary attack plan!

It was a lot to take in. Brighton thought about how the world was changing exponentially.

Humanity is reeling. Conflicting crowds are gathering on the streets. Some groups welcome the incoming visitors, others draw their weapons and dare them to trespass on their property. Millions are avoiding work—including White House staff—banks are closed, stock markets are plummeting, and economies are already suffering. Social media feeds are filled with end-of-the-world dialogue and solemn tributes. Few engender hope. People who claim to have been abducted are offering words of advice on how to handle extraterrestrial interrogations.

Brighton gulped down another cup of water and washed his thoughts to the side. He couldn't solve all the problems at hand, but he *could* try and sway Gen. Childress to agree with the official narrative that he, the president, and two dozen other military commanders had discussed in the bunker over the last several hours. They'd determined that Earth's military forces would need the most advanced, no, *revolutionary* weapons systems in order to defend their nation and their world.

"He's here," the president said from the head of the bunker room table and pulled his reading glasses off.

"Good, let's bring him up to speed," Brighton said as he threw his cup in a recycling bin and walked to the bunker's entrance. He put an eye up to an iris scanner on the cement wall to activate the heavy entrance door, which groaned as it slid open.

Gen. Childress strode in without a limp despite having had an Ozzie implanted just a day prior. "Sorry I'm late, I ran into an alien."

Brighton smiled at the unexpected joke. "Me too."

"And you don't look so bad yourself," Gen. Childress said.

"Glad to see you're walking already," said Brighton.

"This Ozzie technology supersedes its expectations," Gen. Childress said. "I never would have imagined just how functional an Ozzie could be if I hadn't gotten one myself." He adjusted his pant leg so the metal components of his Ozzie didn't catch his pant material as he sat in a leather chair between two other generals at the table. "It's no wonder we put hundreds of millions of dollars into the development of this technology. It serves its purpose. But enough chitchat. Where are we? I have an especially dull axe to grind with these FORM."

Brighton scanned his iris again to close the bunker door. He sat across from Gen. Childress and a dozen other military commanders, then said, "We've completed an initial plan. In addition to standard military defense protocols, we have two strategies that we're ready to put into motion."

"Go on," Gen. Childress said.

"First, we propose to launch the nuclear H bombs surrounding the moon. The FORM are already in range. We don't see any reason to delay an attack. They initiated warfare by assaulting and abducting civilians. We believe we should take an offensive approach as soon as possible. Let them know we're ready for a fight."

"I fully agree," Gen. Childress stated.

The president and other leaders nodded their heads, seconding the comment.

Brighton continued. "Our second strategy is ...." Brighton knew Gen. Childress wouldn't like this, "to deploy the CZ-51 disruptors."

Brighton was right.

Gen. Childress jumped out of his chair. "Have we lost our minds, ladies and gentlemen? Apparently, it's a good thing I arrived when I did. There's no *way* we should consider deploying those disruptors when we're planning the most esoteric attack strategy in history! We all know that."

"General, please," the president implored as he put his hands out to calm him. "If we don't deploy them now, they may never even be ... *deployable.*"

Gen. Childress' wrinkled face turned red, but he followed orders and sat down. "How many times have I warned military leaders and politicians against deploying *untested* weaponry systems? It leads to troops being killed, and battles lost. Listen, I understand the motivation, even the temptation to use the disruptors. These times are unprecedented. But the disruptors aren't even close to battle ready. We haven't field tested them, we haven't validated them, and we have no data to suggest they *actually* will do what the scientists and engineers say they will. For all we know, if we deploy them in battle without knowing exactly how they work, they could have the opposite effect and cripple our defenses."

Brighton reflected on what he knew about the disruptors. They'd been developed by a physicist out of California who had promised to create the most powerful weapon since the B-41 hydrogen bomb, not in terms of explosive capacity but in terms of strategic properties. The military wanted to know if the outcome matched her claim, so the Defense Advanced Research Projects Agency—commonly referred to as DARPA—had dumped over three billion dollars into disruptor development. Early prototypes were fraught with problems. Newer versions, however, were improved and made of a four-foot diameter concave disc with an electromagnetic coil connected at the focal point that functioned like a miniature Hadron Collider, which excited subatomic particles into electromagnetic and reactive energy by heating neutral gases. The coils released the energy at a desired target with the hypothesis that the materials, even metal, would become superheated and vaporize into an alternate energy phase. *Very powerful stuff, but unproven,* he mused. *But we have no choice.*

"Gen. Childress," the president said, "DARPA ran tests last month, and the disruptors are performing better than expected." He leaned forward and raised his voice. "They can *vaporize* armored vehicles more than a mile away without any collateral effect on nearby armaments—or generating reactive chemicals in the air."

Gen. Childress raised his eyebrows. "What?" He leaned back in his chair. "Why wasn't I aware of this?"

"I was going to brief you this week, but … *something* came up."

"How many tests did they run?"

The president hesitated and cleared his throat. "One."

Gen. Childress harumphed. "And we're going to base their battle readiness on *one* test?"

"We have no other options," Brighton said. "To protect ourselves, we need every ounce of weaponry available. We've already prepped our military units," Brighton motioned to the leaders in the room, "mobilized railguns, nuclear bombs, Black Hawks, Raptors, smart bombs, anti-tank missiles, miniguns, Bastion-Ps, thermobaric rockets, SAMs, and more. But the FORM weapons could be hundreds of times stronger than anything we have. We're not saying the disruptors would replace any of these strategies. They would be additive."

Gen. Childress pursed his lips and put his hands behind his head. Before he could add anything else, alarms in the Pentagon blared.

Everyone looked at each other, unsure of what was happening.

"Pull up the live video feeds," Gen. Childress ordered.

A military commander stood from her chair and hurried to the computer systems. She clicked several buttons and brought up five separate video feeds of the

Pentagon's exterior and surrounding city regions. She searched the Lincoln Memorial, Jefferson Memorial, Martin Luther King Jr. Memorial, the National Mall, the Arlington Cemetery, the Washington Monument, the Capitol. Nothing seemed out of the ordinary.

"What triggered the alarms?" the president asked.

"There! In the river!" Gen. Childress yelled, pointing at one of the screens.

About three miles away from the Pentagon, more than a dozen faint streaks of blue light began to develop under the waters of the Potomac.

"They're coming subsurface," Brighton said with chilling undertone.

The commander focused multiple cameras on the Potomac, and they all watched in horror as ultra-aerodynamic, polished gold FORM craft glided through the river waters. They surfaced all at once, leaving minimal wakes.

"They must have triggered the water sensors," Gen. Childress said. "And they can *move* in water!"

That proved to be an understatement as more than four dozen FORM craft increased their speed exponentially until they reached the east region of the Pentagon where they rocketed out of the river and soared through the air, throwing blue-lit streams of water in every direction and illuminating the darkening evening sky. The crafts circled the city, as though assessing their surroundings, reflecting sapphire light on a host of federal buildings as they maneuvered. They unified their course until they settled in an equidistant circle around the Pentagon where they hovered, motionless ... and fearless.

Everyone stared at them, awestruck. They were mesmerizing, their formation majestic.

Why aren't they firing? Brighton wondered.

Gen. Childress yelled at everyone in the room as they gawked at the scene. "What are we stalling for? They're in our air space in attack formation! We fire first!"

"Wait ...." Brighton said, thinking through the situation. Just moments ago, he'd been the one suggesting they take the offensive and attack. Now, he second-guessed his own initial comments as he observed the craft hanging in the sky. *Why aren't they firing the first shots?* "What if it's a trap?" Brighton asked. "Why are they just sitting there? Maybe they *want* us to attack first."

"Or want to communicate," the president added.

The military commanders looked at one another, considering.

"There's no way we should be willing to find that out," Gen. Childress warned, unwilling to risk one of their most powerful strongholds—the Pentagon, which had been extensively renovated to be a battle-capable facility after 9/11. "Get the Black Hawks in the air and launch the F-22 Raptors—weapons ready!"

A commander in the room looked at the president for approval. The president nodded, and the commander grabbed a radio and ordered his subordinates at Andrews Air Force Base to mobilize the Black Hawks and F-22s. Within minutes, the whip of helicopter blades and the blare of fighter jet engines echoed through the streets of Washington, D.C.

Brighton watched people onscreen scatter in terror and dive into the nearest available building for protection.

The FORM craft floated static above the Pentagon.

"Do we wait at least one minute before firing to see if they try to communicate?" the president asked.

"We may not have a minute!" Gen. Childress screamed, becoming unhinged. He was ready to jump across the table and order an attack himself.

Nerves were on edge, but the deliberation was short lived as the FORM craft made the first move. They simultaneously rotated out of formation, zipped away from the Pentagon, and angled their noses toward buildings and monuments in the city.

Brighton wondered why the FORM drifted away from the Pentagon. *They clearly identified the Pentagon; they formed a circle around it. Are they avoiding this building's firepower? Do they know it's the military command center?* Brighton grabbed one of the controls, directed a camera at one of the craft and followed it as it approached the Jefferson Memorial. Brighton zoomed in.

A dozen elderly tourists were hiding behind the Greek-inspired columns. A FORM craft lowered its body over the Tidal Basin and aimed its nose at the Memorial.

He shifted the camera to another craft, which lowered itself over the Lincoln Memorial Reflecting Pool and brought its cockpit parallel with Lincoln's throne. Brighton zoomed in again and saw more than a hundred children taking cover inside the Lincoln Memorial. *No!*

Brighton yelled, "Gen. Childress, order the attack! They're targeting civilians! There are children out there!"

Faces in the room went pale.

"I knew it!" Gen. Childress growled and grabbed the microphone of a comm system to execute an attack. "Fire the SAMs, unload the Black Hawk minis, and activate the Raptors. Take every one of those vagrants out, *now!*"

The response was immediate. Surface-to-air-missiles blasted from hidden locations around the Pentagon and rocked the bunker walls with earthquake-force shockwaves. Brighton and nearby commanders steadied their balance as they watched SAMs and orange tracers from mini guns zip toward their targets.

The FORM craft remained stationary as the armaments approached them.

Why are they still not firing, or dodging what's approaching? Brighton pondered, but only briefly. He soon had his answer: as each SAM, mini gun bullet, and F-22 missile approached its extraterrestrial target, each FORM craft produced a purple energetic orb around its exterior. The orbs phase shifted and danced with dark and light hues of magenta energy. Brighton remembered: *That matter looks like the blue balls of energy that shot out of the FORM's hand in San Antonio!* Their exterior flowed like the superheated structure of the Sun's photosphere. He eyed the orbs carefully. Their energy state and color also reminded him of something more, something from his past.

Everyone watched and few breathed as military artillery slammed into the orbs. But instead of exploding into millions of damage-inducing particles, the SAMs, bullets, and F-22 missiles disintegrated on contact—and were incorporated *into* the energy state of the orbs.

The president put a hand to his face and wiped his clammy skin. "Their shields, they aren't reflecting our weapons, they're ...." His mind drifted.

"They're *swallowing* them," Brighton finished. "Our weapons aren't even exploding against their targets. Those orbs aren't a *reflective* shield, they're an energy sink!"

All sense of exhilaration in the room morphed into horror.

Brighton's neck hairs stood erect as his previous fear was being fulfilled. Earth's weaponry may very well be ineffective against the FORM.

"Maintain the sequence!" Gen. Childress commanded. "Let's blow through those balls!"

Tracers from SAMs, mini gun bullets, smart bombs, and Raptor missiles irradiated the sky yet resulted in explosionless effect as each one was swallowed by the FORM's orbs of alien energy.

Brighton watched the *lack* of carnage carefully. The FORM still hadn't fired a single weapon. He noticed an anomaly developing. "The orbs around their crafts, does everyone see that?" he asked.

The group eyed the orbs.

"Yes ... they're ... they're *growing* in size," the president answered. "They're swelling with each weapon they absorb."

Brighton raised his eyebrows. "Of course! I know where I've seen that energy state before." He shook a finger at the screen. "That's *plasma* energy. That's the same purple hue a gold sputter coater generates when preparing a sample for electron microscopy."

Everyone in the room looked at Brighton blankly. The esoteric science note was lost on the group.

"Well, when we have time, we'll ask for an explanation," the president said. "But for now, what about plasma? Is that why they're swallowing our weapons?"

"Most likely. Companies are researching this type of technology with military funds. Plasma shields are designed to *absorb* energy and prevent shockwaves and explosions. I'm not sure how the FORM are producing it around hovering crafts, but I'm sure it's plasma. Their crafts must be made of gold so they can super-energize gas. It's a highly reactive energy state. Plasma molecules stick to anything they touch."

"So, let's blow up the highly reactive crap!" Gen. Childress cried. "We have a planet to defend."

"Quite the opposite. We need to stop the attack!" Brighton said.

"Are you out of your mind?" Gen. Childress bellowed. "You called it, then uncalled it, then called it again!"

"I know. Look, the FORM haven't fired a single weapon in nearly five minutes of being attacked. If those orbs are *absorbing* the energy from each munition, where's the energy going? They must be holding on to it. Imagine if they can reverse the effect and release it! A single orb would contain the equivalent explosive power of all the armaments it absorbs. We're strengthening our enemy."

The president's eyes opened wide. "I agree, we should stop the attack. The damage could be insurmountable."

Before anyone could respond, a commander in the room yelled, "Something's happening!" He pointed to the craft hovering near the Jefferson Memorial.

Brighton's hypothesis became acutely prophetic.

The purple orb around the craft formed into a teardrop shape, gathering a bulb of energy near the back of the craft that elongated to a point near its nose. The energy ball flashed a bright mauve, then zipped away from the craft and toward the Jefferson Memorial. In less than a second, the majestic statue of Thomas Jefferson and its surrounding Memorial exploded, sending bronze and marble shards in every direction and creating a quarter-mile-wide cavern of earth underneath it.

Recognizing that the elderly tourists had met their end, Brighton grimaced, and a hot surge of anger coursed through his veins.

The FORM craft reformed a second oval orb around its exterior and returned to swallowing waves of military armaments.

"There's another one!" the president yelled.

A second craft's orb repeated the process and fired at the Martin Luther King Jr. Memorial, near which a group of runners were passing. The white granite held up no more than clay could against a sledgehammer. The Memorial and the runners were dust.

"Stop the attacks!" Brighton yelled as the group watched a third craft's orb form the teardrop-shaped accumulation of energy. It ripped away from the FORM craft, tore straight through the most iconic obelisk in Washington, D.C.—the Washington Monument—and continued to soar over the city until it lit up The White House.

"My family! My staff!" the president wailed. He jumped out of his seat. His pupils dilated and his eyes adopted a distant look.

The orb left a path of destruction in its wake: the pyramidal cap of The Washington Monument groaned as it broke away from the four-sided obelisk and plummeted to the ground, plastering a dozen buildings in the National Mall. The White House likewise erupted, sparing no level of catastrophe to the building or grounds.

The destruction was incalculable. The city was ripping at its seams.

"We have to stop the attacks!" Brighton pleaded.

Gen. Childress slammed his fist on the table, less out of anger that Brighton challenged his orders and more because he was probably right. But Gen. Childress was resolved. "Do that and we die!"

"I agree with Brighton," the president yelled hoarsely. He shook his head. He was noticeably fighting emotions. "St—st—stop the attacks!" But his words were muffled by a series of loud crashes.

A blast rocked the building. Iron beams behind the cement walls groaned. Everyone cowered and covered their heads as cement around them began to crumble.

Brighton shook his head and grabbed the camera controls again to view the FORM craft above the Lincoln Memorial Reflecting Pool. The craft's orb was pulsating through a series of light and dark purple waves. "It's priming to fire. *There are children in there!*" Brighton looked at the president. "We have to deploy the disruptors."

"The disruptors?" Gen. Childress questioned. "I thought they were still at the testing grounds."

The president stated, "I was going to tell you before we were cut off. I had DARPA assemble two dozen disruptors the moment we learned about the FORM. They were installed in Black Hawks and on the roof of the Pentagon while you were in San Antonio."

Brighton could sense that Gen. Childress wanted to lunge at the president. He barely controlled his fury as he gritted his teeth.

Gen. Childress griped, "All these surprises, Mr. President. Nukes around the moon, disruptors deployed without military supervision. Next time, let us *know* what you're doing!"

"Leave the whizzing contest for later!" Brighton shouted. "We need to deploy the disruptors. Now!"

Gen. Childress and the president began to argue.

Brighton shook his head and looked at the crowd inside the Lincoln Memorial. They screamed in horror as the orb around the FORM craft began to shift into a teardrop shape. There was no time. Brighton had to act.

He jumped across the table and hollered into Gen. Childress' mic: "Deploy the disruptors. Aim at the craft above the Reflecting Pool!"

Gen. Childress flailed his hands in the air out of frustration, feeling undermined again, but he decided not to stop the disruptor deployment. He subconsciously knew the military forces were trending in the wrong direction and like it or not, they needed an out-of-the-box counterattack.

The group watched on screen as three Black Hawks rotated to fire disruptors from the flanks of their four-blade, twin-engine machinery. The mini Hadron Collider-like units whirred and released a swath of energy that shook each Black Hawk. The chopper pilots controlled the recoil, allowing the troops to aim the disruptors at the craft above the memorial's Reflecting Pool.

As the craft prepared to launch its devastating attack on The Lincoln Memorial, three disruptor energy streams met its flexing orb with precision and disrupted the energy field, causing a gaping hole to form in the fluctuating plasma.

Brighton noticed the opening and yelled into the mic, "The disruptors opened a hole in the plasma. Shoot everything you've got through that opening!"

A nearby Raptor screamed toward the craft and unleashed its fury: two AIM-120 and two AIM-9 missiles, followed by M61A2 20mm Gatling rounds. The FORM craft didn't make a counter maneuver. It didn't know what was coming. One hundred 20mm bullets and two of the Raptor missiles whistled through the opening and connected with the craft. It exploded into a golden glitter bomb. The remains turned the Lincoln Memorial Reflecting Pool into a pond of sparkling flecks.

Everyone in the room cheered. There was hope!

"All right, I can accept when I've been wrong," Gen. Childress conceded. He grabbed his mic and gave another order. "Launch the remaining disruptors! Cease fire on all crafts until a disruptor sensitizes its orb. If an opening arises, resume fire through the opening."

Before the command was relayed to all the troops and pilots, two more FORM crafts swallowed a volley of missiles and released the energy, leaving a gaping cavern where the International Spy Museum stood, and a crater on the east side of the Capitol.

Yet multiple disruptors soon did their job and crippled a dozen more orbs, allowing military forces to eliminate one craft after another.

Two FORM craft, noticeably larger than the rest, dodged the disruptor energy streams and shifted their course toward the Pentagon. As they approached, their speed increased. They both disengaged their orbs, outmaneuvered incoming weaponry, and opened a panel on their underside through which an advanced weapon emerged. They shot elongated ellipses of energy at the Pentagon walls, breaching the area directly over the War Room.

Everyone in the bunker room braced themselves as it shook violently. The bunker, along with the War Room, was built deep underground to withstand multiple nuclear warheads, yet shockwaves coursed through the cement walls as the building overhead exploded.

"Did you see that?" the president asked in a whisper. No one heard him. "That's the first time I've seen them fire their own weapons. They disintegrated the Pentagon wall … like it was nothing."

The group lost sight of the two FORM craft as they entered a plume of smoke billowing out of the Pentagon's façade. From high above their heads, they heard two heavy thuds.

"They've landed," Brighton said.

The group listened carefully. They gasped as the power went out. The oversized screens before them went black. All they could monitor now was the faint noise of explosions and gunfire outside. Emergency power turned a few lights on in the bunker, but the comm systems were cut off. They were isolated, the sound of strained breathing their only companion.

Clangs of heavy footsteps reverberated through the air vents.

"Quick, everyone grab a weapon!" Gen. Childress ordered.

Commanding officers, Brighton, and the president hurried to the concrete wall lined with weapons, grabbed one or more along with preloaded magazines, and hunkered behind whatever barrier they could find: a large table, a concrete wall, a computer panel.

They waited in silence. A metallic bang on the bunker room's entrance door signaled someone—or something—sizeable was trying to enter.

Though he portrayed a stance of confidence and was always battle-ready, deep inside, Brighton was nervous. With relatively minimal effort, the FORM had initiated warfare on the cerebral cortex of Earth's most powerful force—the United States Military. *Now we fight for survival.*

"Be ready," Brighton said. "It's time to make some blue blood splatter."

Chapter 20

The Pentagon, Washington, D.C.

FORM leader Maazi threw aside debris from a section of reinforced concrete deep in the Pentagon's belly so he could access the main power panel of the War Room and connected bunker. He punched the power source repeatedly. He was livid. Never had a human species found a way to penetrate the protective barriers of his army's crafts, let alone so quickly. For the first time in over 600 circuits, he watched his people get killed in battle. These humans were more astute than he had anticipated.

After pummeling the power box, Maazi said, "There, the power's out," to Taahiya, his second-in-command. "Now let's cripple their command center and send an undeniable message to this planet."

Taahiya smiled and tapped her left shoulder twice with her right index finger—the universal FORM signal of agreement.

Maazi wiped his forehead and tapped the rectangular computer screen embedded in his left forearm. If the blueprints he'd hacked from the humans' black web were correct, the digital readout on his arm indicated that the corridor leading to the Pentagon's deep-seated bunker, where they believed some of America's highest-ranking military leaders were, was behind the angled cement wall in front of him.

"That one." He pointed for Taahiya to blast through.

Taahiya—who had fewer metallic components than almost any other FORM and retained the natural rugged beauty of her people, especially throughout her facial features—always obeyed Maazi without question and would give her life for him. She had once loved Maazi romantically but chose to be his servant after he had figured out a way to make them live indefinitely and commanded his people to stop having children and intimate relationships approximately 1,500 circuits ago. That allowed them to focus more on world domination and water acquisition. She obeyed his command as always, raised her arm, swiveled the five small weapons on her fingertips in exchange for the larger circular cannon that each FORM had integrated into their right forearm, and blasted the wall, exposing the Pentagon's main basement artery.

Maazi hesitated before charging through, expecting that several enemies would be in the corridor guarding the bunker entrance. He was right. Hundreds of bullets ricocheted past his and Taahiya's heads followed by a sequence of grenade blasts. "Wait for it," Maazi said as they remained behind a massive cement structure. He knew that after the initial volley of attacks, their enemy would hesitate to see if they had destroyed their target. After centuries in battle, he had learned that universal pattern of attack.

Exactly two seconds after a lull in explosions, Maazi emerged into the corridor. He saw several of his enemies' eyes widen. He didn't even have to fire a weapon to exude fear in them; his size alone was enough to terrify their senses. Yet he didn't hesitate long enough to gloat. From his fingertips, he unleashed a dozen miniature blue fireballs that zipped into the chests of his enemies while Taahiya launched large blue tracers from her cannon and eliminated any semblance of their stronghold. Within seconds, the bodies of over a dozen enemies laid motionless on the ground.

"That was easy," Taahiya mocked.

"Don't underestimate them," Maazi warned. "We saw how quickly they adapted and adjusted their battle methods against our meliks."

"Of course, Bohanna," Taahiya said, using the FORM's endearing and respectful term for "leader."

Maazi trudged his heavy legs on the ground with extra flare as he walked toward his destination: the enormous and complex entrance door to the War Room's bunker at the end of the corridor. He wanted whoever was behind the thick metal barrier to know he was coming. As he approached the entrance, it was obvious that Earth's inhabitants had placed this specific room deep in the subterranean location of the Pentagon with a specific intent: to keep things out—both organic and inorganic.

The entrance was purposefully over-engineered with composite fluoride steel and a triple-reinforced frame embedded deep in multiple layers of metal. *They're good engineers, I'll give them that,* Maazi grudgingly admitted.

He analyzed the bunker room's innards using the integrated computer in his left arm. "I can faintly detect about two dozen people inside. Likely in battle position," he said.

Taahiya double tapped her left shoulder in acknowledgment, then raised her weapon.

Maazi touched several spots on his computer screen so it could survey the door's mechanics. "Electromechanical locks backed up by mortise pin inspiration and a tiered bioaccess component. Is this the best they got?" Maazi derided with oozing ego.

Taahiya smirked. "They have a long way to go."

Maazi pressed a few more times on his computer and decoded the redundant safety mechanisms. The gears in the door clanked and started to release.

"Ready," Maazi grunted. He tapped his left leg three times, causing a metal compartment in his lateral thigh to open. He pulled his most powerful and preferred firearm out of the compartment—an over-under double-barrel handgun that fired hybrid bullets made of fused diamond and platinum, coated with a chemical similar to what humans called graphene, engineered to create maximum penetration through a primary material followed by obliteration of a secondary target. Maazi wrapped his left fingers around the handle, then raised his right arm, readying his five small, yet versatile pure energy-wielding weapons. Taahiya retained the larger circular device—her preferred weapon for creating massive destruction—of her right hand and likewise pulled a firearm from her left thigh.

The moment the bunker door creaked an opening, Maazi and Taahiya opened fire, sending incendiary balls of energy and diamond-based bullets whizzing into the bunker. They annihilated tables and barricades.

The destruction was quick and unforgiving, yet they were countered with innumerable assault rifle and machine gun bullets, one of which sliced the flesh of Maazi's left arm, sending spatters of blue hydrogel on the walls.

Maazi grimaced but otherwise ignored the pain. He dove through the now-open bunker door and slid behind the tallest stone barrier he could find; the humans hadn't built the room to provide protection for a person that was over seven feet tall.

"Get them!" Maazi heard someone yell from behind a plume of smoke.

Taahiya aimed her cannon at the voice and fired. The enemy was instantly voiceless.

Maazi rolled his massive body on the ground and aimed his over-under at a large, overturned conference table. He fired straight through the four-inch-thick cherry wood and eliminated the three enemies hiding behind it, then kicked the table with his horse-like muscles. The table slid across the floor, connected with a cement step, and launched in the air. Maazi fired four blue tracers at it, causing it to splinter and release wood shrapnel in the direction of five enemies. They all sank to the floor. Their green military outerwear turned a deep red, symbolizing the bleeding hope of the humans in the room. Maazi felt a growing satisfaction.

He heard a commanding officer, who was hunkering behind a ledge on an upper balcony of the room, yell, "Brighton, target the blue ring!"

Maazi looked at Taahiya. She was creating incalculable destruction in the room with her unforgiving O-shaped electromagnetic cannon. He smiled, unafraid of whether they targeted the blue ring at the end of her arm; it would vaporize any bullet that came in contact.

Maazi looked at the man who gave the order. The microchip connected to Maazi's brain deciphered that it was Gen. Childress. He then eyed the man to whom Gen. Childress had given the order. Brighton, hiding behind a four-foot-thick cement barricade in the back corner of the room.

Keep those two alive, he told Taahiya telepathically.

Taahiya double tapped her shoulder.

As well as the president, if he's not already dead.

Taahiya obeyed and didn't flinch as she unleashed blast after blast toward her assailants.

Maazi saw two assault rifles aim toward him. He dove forward, grabbed the weapons out of the wielders' hands, then tossed both attackers against the wall. Their bones cracked, and they fell lifeless to the floor.

The number of bullets flying in the room had lessened exponentially. Only five humans remained.

Maazi took cover behind a protrusion in a wall and yelled, "Do you want to surrender, or should we finish you *all* off?"

The gunfire came to an unexpected halt. Did the humans know they had no chance?

"Drop the weapons, then," Maazi said.

He heard two clanks signaling two guns dropped to the ground. There should have been five, assuming all five remaining enemies had a weapon. Maazi didn't trust the situation. He briefly jutted his head out from behind a cement column, then retreated it. Just as he thought, a swath of bullets sank into the stone wall next to him.

"Fools," Maazi said, then lifted his firearm over his head, angled it downward to position its trajectory just right and fired twice. Two more assailants screamed.

"Okay, okay! We surrender!" a voice pleaded.

"Drop your weapons and show your hands, then!" Maazi demanded.

Brighton, Gen. Childress, and the president dropped their weapons and raised their hands in the air.

"They're clean," Taahiya said and kicked the weapons aside.

Maazi clicked his firearm back into the chamber in his left leg and stepped into the open. He watched the president's eyes widen. He recognized the president was paralyzed, obviously struggling to grapple with how enormous, authoritative, and commanding Maazi's size was.

"Mr. President," Maazi said jovially. "My goodness, what a pleasure to meet you. Although, I wish it could have been under better circumstances."

The president grimaced but didn't say anything.

"Col. Brighton, Gen. Childress, I've been anxious to meet the two of you. You coordinated a decent attack against us out there. It's been several hundred years since any one of my people have died!" Maazi, demonstrating his tinderbox like temper, smashed the cement wall next to him. Crumbled stones and rebar shards fell at his feet. "And rest assured, you'll pay for that!"

Brighton and Gen. Childress both gritted their teeth yet maintained composure.

"Longevity, gentlemen ... longevity means *everything* to me and my people, and when you take my people away from me," Maazi growled heavily, "I don't play nice. I mean, you should've thought it through or something. We could've come to some agreement, an arrangement, if you will, to share what you have on this planet. But you chose to engage us, so we had no choice."

"What are you talking about?" the president asked. "One of your people accosted two of our civilians, then you entered our air space, failed to divulge your intentions— and you expect *us* to work out an agreement? Have you learned about two-way communication?"

Maazi leaped toward the president and landed with a thud. His metal-shodden feet snapped the concrete next to him. "Moron! Dare you question my rationale?"

Maazi squeezed the president's head. Gen. Childress started for the president but held back and kept his ground, knowing Maazi was like a bulging volcano and could erupt at any moment. He also knew he'd be powerless against the beast before him.

Maazi glimpsed Gen. Childress' movement out of the corner of his eye and released the president's head. "My gosh, what a disappointment, Mr. President!" Maazi's voice was textured with a low rumble that jolted the president's heart. "Your most prominent soldier's like a crippled chicken. How can you ever expect to overtake us?!"

Brighton reached for his sidearm. Maazi rushed him and crushed the handgun, then pinned Brighton against a wall.

"Brighton ...." Maazi's trenchant voice trailed. "Allow me to introduce myself. I'm Maazi, Commander of the FORM—I like that name you gave us, by the way—we're the most powerful people in the universe, not that you would comprehend its vastness.

"But never mind that, I've been excited to meet you!" Maazi breathed deeply and examined Brighton's face. It was red and grimacing. "Something lives inside of you. A pride for life that's unparalleled in other humanoids. Gosh, your passion is mesmerizing to observe. Yet, sadly, it's dwindling in most of your people.

"Ah, but when I heard of *your* power, this force inside of you that my scout experienced in San Antonio, I knew I couldn't destroy this civilization without seeing it for myself. I like to savor these kinds of things. Thank you in advance for that pleasure."

Suddenly, Brighton kneed Maazi in the torso and grappled his enormous forearms. Maazi held him firm. The president rushed to help, angered at Maazi's condescending comments. Maazi knocked the president over as though he were a weightless toy. Gen. Childress slowed the president's fall, then reached for his .45 caliber.

Maazi saw what Gen. Childress was doing and energized a protective purple orb that encompassed both him and Brighton. The plasma-like sphere melted the five bullets that Gen. Childress shot at him.

"Seriously? Didn't you just see that your weapons are useless? I thought you were a quick study. Tsk, tsk." Maazi dropped Brighton, deactivated the purple sphere, and lunged for Gen. Childress. With one heave, he launched him into a chair that slid across the floor. Gen. Childress grunted in pain. Maazi leaped again, landing directly over him. Prideful, he gazed at the scene around him. He and Taahiya had decimated some of the world's most powerful commanding figures.

"I mean, isn't it just a *little* bit worrisome, gentlemen, that your most sophisticated troops and weapons can't even handle *two* of us?" He picked up Gen. Childress and held him like a hamster by the back of his camouflage jacket near his neck. "So, Mr. President, *this* is your fearless director of military supremacy—the secretary of defense?"

"Why are you *doing* this?" the president begged as he scrambled to his feet. "We've done nothing to you!"

"How can you lie so easily?" Maazi shouted hatefully. "You spent the entire day planning a nuclear attack against us with weapons, the power of which are unmatched in this world. You threaten to destroy me and my people!"

"How did you know—?" The fear in the president's face was noticeable.

"Seriously, it really takes you this long to see?" Maazi taunted. "We know everything about you. It's okay to be second best. Or as you like to say: 'reality check.'" He grinned.

Brighton stood, holding freshly created wounds on his neck. For the first time, his will to fight was shaken. This FORM was magnitudes more powerful than the FORM he had put in a chokehold in San Antonio.

"Come on," Maazi said, "enough of this. I need you to call off your attack outside, then I need to make an announcement to your world. We'll broadcast it far and wide. A live YouTube channel, perhaps? Better yet why not put it on all your platforms? That sounds more exciting! Are we able to broadcast from this room?"

"No, you destroyed the communications systems in here," the president sneered.

"Ah, silly me. Guess I should've thought of that. All right, then, where else can we broadcast from?"

The three of them hesitated.

Maazi pulled out his over under handgun and fired it next to the president.

The president flinched, held his ear, and screamed, "All right, all right, I'll tell you."

Maazi flared his nostrils, awaiting the answer.

"Two floors up, we have a communications room that can patch into a global emergency system."

Maazi smiled and motioned for the three of them to lead the way. "Oh, and lest you get any ideas, call off *all* the troops that are preparing to protect you. Unless you want to see them all killed, of course, then by all means, let them come."

"Our communication systems are down, remember?" the president chided.

"Oh, right," Maazi laughed, "I guess we'll just have to kill them." Maazi watched the president shake his head. He knew the president thought he was evil. Maazi disagreed internally; he was simply posturing—and of course, protecting his longevity, which he was always willing to do at any cost. "Come now, your country invades other countries at will and polices this world. I'm simply the policeman of the universe. And I'm the only one who can sustain life indefinitely. That comes at a cost sometimes. Now let's get to this alternate communications center."

~

Brighton led the group down the main corridor and called out, "Hold your fire!" as they approached a stairwell that would take them to the floor with the communications center.

They walked past dozens of soldiers who obeyed, recognizing the president, Brighton, and Gen. Childress were at risk of being killed if they didn't. The soldiers gawked at the monstrosity of Maazi and Taahiya's bodies as their hybridized leg muscles rippled, and their enormous torsos swayed.

As the group walked through the upper halls, they passed by the gaping hole that Maazi and Taahiya had created in the Pentagon's structure so they could access the War Room. Through the rubble, they could see the battle between the United States military and the FORM continuing to rage in the nation's capital.

Brighton hesitated. From one vantage point, he could see the American flag whipping in the winds of explosion-induced shockwaves. The flag's borders were singed and tattered from fireballs erupting around it, and bullet holes exchanged places with several of its stars, yet it stood erect, majestic, and stalwart. *And the rocket's red glare ... our flag was still there*, he reminisced internally.

"Move!" Maazi ordered as he shoved Brighton in the back.

Brighton kept walking and noticed that Maazi stumbled slightly after shoving him, as though his body were aching or weak. He looked back at Taahiya. She likewise seemed drained, even stopping for a moment to wipe her brow and take a deep breath. He squinted and pondered; something was off in them.

As Brighton looked forward, he noticed that a protected room from which the nuclear weapons orbiting the moon could be launched was still accessible. Maazi apparently hadn't noticed the area; the blueprints or whatever he had used to access the Pentagon wouldn't have shown that room because it recently had been renovated and wasn't updated in the Pentagon's system due to a breakdown in the bureaucratic nightmare of the government. *For once it's good that the government was slow to process something*, Brighton harrumphed. *What an irony.* A surge of hope coursed through his veins. *I've got to find a way to get in there. Can I make a run for it and reach the room?* He couldn't take the risk, at least ... not yet.

Maazi noticed Brighton's pensive look. "Something you want to share, Brighton?"

"Yeah, yeah, I'll have you over for dinner one night, and we can talk about it," Brighton snarked.

Maazi shoved him once again. "Don't get cocky!"

The five-member group reached the upper communications area that was furnished with multiple cameras, equipment for audio-visual connections, and a large screen for videoconferencing. Several military technicians were inside and startled as they entered, pausing instinctively with eyes wide as Maazi emerged.

"Cat got your tongues?" Maazi teased. "Stop staring for crying out loud and get these men some communications equipment so they can call off the attacks."

They looked at the president with questioning looks. The president nodded.

The technicians scrambled, and, within seconds, a comm system was ready.

"Now, Gen. Childress. Call off the attacks, and I'll do the same."

Gen. Childress stood still. He was willing to give his life in that very moment if necessary. He refused to obey.

"No need to be a hero, Gen. Childress," Maazi said.

Gen. Childress was resolute. When Maazi and Taahiya had entered the Pentagon, the military troops outside were gaining an upper hand with the disruptors.

Brighton could tell what Gen. Childress was thinking. If he stalled long enough, perhaps it would give them time to overtake the FORM.

"Stop stalling," Maazi prodded.

Gen. Childress didn't budge.

"All right," Maazi said, "need some persuasion?" He pulled out his over under and shot one of the military technicians dead.

"No!" the president yelled.

Gen. Childress hardly flinched. He knew that every soldier in that room was willing to sacrifice their life for the protection of their brothers and sisters in arms, and the betterment of mankind. "You can kill all of us in this room. I'm not going to tell my people to stop fighting the tyrants you brought to Earth."

~

Maazi's eyes narrowed. His fury was integrated with an unexpected intrigue. These humans were willing to sacrifice life with a selflessness that he had never experienced.

Fascinating, he said telepathically to Taahiya. *They're willing to die for their cause and their people without a second thought.*

Taahiya acknowledged the thought and was likewise interested. *They need a different persuasion. Tell our people to attack children in the schools in the area. That's who they protect most.*

"A different form of persuasion then," Maazi said. He watched the president give a worried look to Gen. Childress and Brighton. He smirked, then lifted his left arm and spoke into the computer system embedded in his flesh. He gave a command in an indecipherable tongue, then smiled. "Would you like to see where my people will attack next?" Maazi turned his long torso toward the communications technicians. "Turn on that screen and use a camera to follow my meliks."

The large screen in the room illuminated and showed a series of meliks angling toward several schools in the city.

"Are you willing to sacrifice *these* citizens?" Maazi asked.

"Enough!" the president pleaded. "Everyone, please. There's no reason we should go on like this."

"Your president speaks truth. Do we have a deal?"

Gen. Childress cursed under his breath and grabbed a receiver. "All fighters, troops, commanders." He paused for a moment. "Stand down! We're breached. We're compromising with the enemy. Stand down, disengage, and end the attack."

One by one, fighter jets withdrew and distanced themselves from the city. Anti-aircraft missiles ceased their barrage, and Black Hawk helicopters halted the disruptors.

Maazi took his turn and spoke into his arm once again. The FORM meliks responded by shifting away from the schools and flew into the stratosphere where they hovered, awaiting their commander's next order.

"See, we can work together," Maazi snorted.

Gen. Childress shook his head. "Funny what you consider a mutual agreement."

"Take a seat, Gen. Childress. I have a message ...." Maazi stumbled slightly and caught himself with a chair.

Taahiya rushed to his side and whispered in his ear, "Our bodies don't have sustenance much longer."

~

Brighton watched their interchange. He couldn't hear what Taahiya said, but he sensed again that something was off. He looked at the exit door, which Maazi had left open, then glanced at Gen. Childress. Brighton raised an eyebrow and motioned his head toward the door, signaling he was developing a plan. Gen. Childress nodded. At some point, Brighton would have to make a move.

~

"I'm fine!" Maazi snapped and secured his footing. "I have a message to share with this world. Move over!" He yelled at the technicians in the room and marched to their communications systems. He pulled a half-circle-looking device out of a pocket in his metallic cloak and clicked it onto the main panel. "Now we can connect with the world. Roll those cameras," he ordered the technicians.

The technicians looked at the president who nodded.

Within moments, a global emergency network displayed footage of Maazi's threatening persona. He stood tall and showed off his domineering frame. He didn't need to flex to intimidate his viewers; his hybridized metallic and biological muscles were defined and self-promoting. He focused his piercing blue eyes toward the cameras and spoke in a booming voice.

"Hello, everyone out there!" Maazi said with a fake sense of personal connection. "It's such a pleasure to be here." His voice was low, oddly pleasant, yet unignorable as it penetrated screens across the globe. Maazi connected the circuitry in his brain to news station feeds around the world. He saw people stopping in their tracks, looking at their phones, televisions, and computers, surprised by the being onscreen. Maazi beamed inside—his was the only voice that mattered on this planet right now.

He went on. "I'm sure you'd all like to get to know me a bit but I'm not sure you'll be around long, so, what's the point?!" Maazi laughed. "Okay, I'll just get right to business here. I hate to be the one to tell you, but you're all taking something pretty spectacular for granted here on Earth. A life source that is unparalleled. I'm not gonna lie, you're all kind of nuts. Despite having one of the most fantastic living circumstances in the universe, you sit here and fight, argue, bicker, and dismantle one another. I mean, I've got one guy in here," Maazi motioned toward Gen. Childress, "who's willing to give his own life for others, then there are bunches of you on this planet wanting to *take* the lives of others. It makes no sense! But it's no loss to me, honestly. What it does is justify everything I'm about to do. Because frankly, I'm not sure you deserve what you have. You can't take care of yourselves or your planet, so I have to do it for you. Oh, but I'm getting ahead of myself. I guess I should introduce us before I start explaining how aimless you all are.

"From this very city," Maazi spread his arms wide, "the president of the United States announced our presence. That was, of course, very kind of him, but if you'll allow me, I'll *properly* introduce us. I'm Maazi, leader of the FORM, as you so … creatively … call us. We are the longest-tenured and most superior beings in the universe."

As Maazi spoke, Brighton pretended to adjust his weight and took a step toward the exit. Taahiya noticed his movement. She wasn't sure if he was making a move, but just in case, she stepped in front of the doorway. Her enormous body would be impossible to get around. Brighton pretended to pay no attention to her maneuver and waited patiently.

"I'm a master warrior and unparalleled leader," Maazi went on. "More than *2,000* Earth years ago, I led my people in the greatest battle of our planet, a planet where citizens likewise foolishly killed one another, never considering the outcomes. We were on the brink of destruction. I oversaw the final source of water on our planet. My closest friend and ally," Maazi gritted his teeth, "conspired against me in an attempt to kill me, my people, and to steal our remaining water—the fundamental source of life, the commodity you hardly appreciate!"

Maazi paused and breathed in and out. "Well … I committed then to treat water with the respect it deserves, and we became the most sophisticated water scavengers in existence. Over thousands of years, we've found that aqueous water sources are running low in the universe. Sure, there's loads of frozen water out there in asteroids and cold planets, but the frozen stuff isn't easy to collect and support life in the harshness of space. And what is this universe without life? A bunch of nothing! Your scientists are starting to figure this out. Only planets with liquid water and a suitable star can sustain life! I mean, you sit here with a huge supply of water, enough to support billions of lives for hundreds of thousands of years, and … and you take it for *granted*. What a waste. You have no respect for what you have. Let's be honest, you're straight up idiots!"

Maazi started to laugh but stopped unexpectedly. He hurried and paused the video feed as he felt his legs begin to shake. His body needed sustenance, which could only be found in a concoction of organic material designed to infiltrate his nanotitanium cells.

With so many centuries since he and his people had last fought in battle, he'd failed to anticipate how much energy he would expend in a crossfire fight, especially after being shot in the arm. He didn't want the world to see his weakness as he stumbled again and caught himself on a chair.

Taahiya instinctively raced to his side, leaving the room's exit unattended without thinking. She pulled out a vial of organic material and injected it into Maazi's arm.

~

Brighton looked at Gen. Childress, who opened his eyes wide. *Now!* his glare screamed.

Brighton's heart rate surged, and he scuttled his feet backwards as fast as he could with as little noise as possible. He made it to the doorway and slipped into the hallway. He pressed his body up against a wall. Was he safe? He thought so; there weren't any footsteps coming. He took off his boots so he could run quietly. He tip-toed down the hallway for several feet, then opened into a full-on sprint toward the access area where the nuke controls were located. He didn't look back. It was either run, or die trying.

~

Gen. Childress kept his eyes locked on Maazi, pretending that he didn't see what just happened. The president and technicians were oblivious to it. Gen. Childress chose not to attack Maazi in his state of weakness. *I have no weapon, and the female seems to still be functioning at a high level.*

~

"I said I'm fine!" Maazi fumed at Taahiya and pushed her away, showing not one ounce of gratitude that she'd just provided him with what he needed to function. He was mad. In the very moment when he was supposed to be posturing in front of a weaker species, he had nearly shown his own frailty.

Taahiya backed away but stayed close enough to help him again if needed. Neither she nor Maazi paid attention to the exit, nor the absence of a person in the room.

Although he would need much more sustenance and recovery time, Maazi had enough for a short while. As the organics took effect, Maazi stood tall and looked sternly at the camera, then resumed the feed and spoke as though nothing had happened. "My people are going to secure your water. We'll make it our own. For a thousand years we've sought such a wellspring. But listen, we're really not terrible people. We like to give those we attack a chance to fight for what they want. I'm not like that guy who tried to overtake me in the dark of night without warning. Nah, come on. We shouldn't do that kind of thing to each other. We give everyone a *fighting* chance.

"So, here's what we're going to do. We're going to give this world three days to prepare for a battle of battles! That'll give you all time to say goodbye to your families, children, and people because, I guess I'll be honest, there's something enjoyable about watching captives fight for their possession. It makes the water ...." Maazi paused and reached over to grab a glass of water on a nearby desk. He held it in the air, then took a long drink. "Oh, wow! That's better than I expected! But here's the thing, when you mix that with *earning* the water that you find, it just ... boy ... it just makes the water taste that much better."

Maazi shattered the glass on the desk. "Aha, and *that's* why we'll have an epic battle, folks. Because there's more to life than just drinking water—there's *fighting* for it!

"All right, so with this battle, we'll have you gather all the forces you can at Port Aransas, Texas, where our second water beacon was originally discovered. In three days, we'll engage in a battle, the likes of which this universe has never experienced! Of course, I can't promise that we won't have a bit of fun with you from now until then. That's simply my people's nature." Maazi laughed and grabbed the president. Maazi side hugged him mockingly with an exaggerated squeeze, making him squirm uncomfortably. "See what I mean? That's fun.

"Okay, okay, enough of my rambling. I'm always verbose. It's one of my most endearing qualities!" Maazi shoved the president aside. "I imagine you have stuff to do. We'll leave these three men I have here with me in charge. The president of the United States," Maazi pointed toward the president, "Gen. Van Childress," he pointed at him, "and Col. Samuel Brighton ...." As Maazi moved his arm to point toward Brighton, his face went expressionless. He scanned the room. There was no sign of Brighton. "Where's Brighton?"

Taahiya looked toward the exit.

"Where's Brighton?!" Maazi yelled. He threw a chair across the room and growled. "Fools!" He cut the video feed, leaving the world with an unexpected ending to an ominous message. "You second-class soldier, Taahiya, how could you let him escape?"

Taahiya flared her nostrils and bowed her head. "I have no excuse, Bohanna."

Maazi rolled his eyes and slammed his fist on a table. "Stay here, and don't let *these* ones go! I'll get that slippery prick myself!" He rushed out the door and looked up and down the hallway. No one. He saw Brighton's boots and moist footprints on the ground. "Oh, ho, you sly devil, you!" He pulled out his over under and started in the direction of the footprints, speaking to himself in a low voice as he ran, "Brighton, we could have done great things together. I was really hoping I wouldn't have to kill you. Welp, some things don't always work out the way you expect! You're a dead man once I find you."

Chapter 21

The Pentagon, Washington, D.C.

Brighton sprinted madly down the hall en route to the nuke launch room access point, ignoring the fact that his soggy socks were leaving a sweaty trail behind him. He was running, not only for *his* life but the life of mankind. He slipped and caught himself, then paused to listen. *Footsteps. Heavy. Maazi is coming.*

Brighton pressed his hand against a wall and pushed off to continue his sprint. Three doors down on the right, a discrete placard read, "Authorized Personnel Only." Brighton pushed his hand into his left pocket. *Phew.* His access badge was still there. He pulled the badge out and slapped it against the scanner on the wall.

The scanner light was red. If access was granted, it would turn green.

Brighton watched the light intently. "Come on!" he said quietly.

The light stayed red.

"I knew it!" he said in frustration, referencing the decision that Pentagon officials recently had made to accept the lowest bidder for the installation of the new security access system. He had voted against the decision, saying they needed to go with the pricier, more reliable system. But government defaults were to always select the lowest bidder—a short-term demonstration of using taxpayer dollars wisely, but that invariably led to inferior performance and long-term problems that cost more money and safety concerns. *And how about the unforeseen circumstance of needing to access this room in a timely manner when an extraterrestrial visitor is chasing you?* Brighton wished he could throw this circumstance in the face of the committee who refused to listen to him.

He pulled the badge away, gave the scanner a second to reset, and slapped the badge against the scanner again.

Red light.

He looked up and down the hallway. *Is there another way to access the launch room?* There wasn't.

Third time's a charm! He pushed the badge against the scanner a third time.

Red light.

"No!"

Brighton looked down the hallway again. Heavy footsteps were getting closer. His heart began to despair. Maazi was no more than twenty seconds away. He would have to fight. But with what? Maazi was clearly impossible to kill in hand-to-hand combat.

Brighton closed his eyes and hit his head against the wall, shaking beads of sweat loose from his forehead. As the sweat splashed on his hand, several drops seeped into the security scanner's circuitry.

Click!

The light turned green.

"Seriously?" Brighton shook his head and threw open the door.

The sound of suctioning air should have warned Brighton that something was off in the room, but his brain failed to process the warning; he was focused on the ominous being chasing him.

As Brighton stepped into the room, his feet failed to find any footing. A massive hole had been created in the floor of the nuke launch room from explosion after explosion that compromised the building's moorings. The cavern reached four stories down.

Brighton fell forward and started to involuntarily dive into the hole. He thrust his massive forearms outward. One of a dozen rebar rods protruding from the cement floor poked his left arm, making him bleed, but his right hand gripped a second rod. His body swung like a pendulum. He ignored the stinging cut in his left arm and grabbed a second piece of metal with his left hand. With both hands affixed to metal rods, he controlled his pendulum swing. He repositioned each hand to strengthen his grip.

He looked down. That way led to certain death. He looked behind him. He could see HVAC ductwork in the ceiling of the floor below. It was sliced in half, revealing an enormous circular tube that was inset slightly from the perimeter of the hole and still pushing air.

Brighton looked up and breathed deeply, assessing his situation. *Maazi had to be in the hallway by now.* He couldn't hear any footsteps; the rush of forced air drowned out anything else.

What do I do?

~

Maazi broke a guardrail as he stopped his body from sliding past the hallway where Brighton's moist footsteps led. He pressed a hand against a wall to steady himself. He was struggling physically. The bullet wound in his left arm was throbbing, and he was losing too much hydrogel-based blood. The infusion of organic material that Taahiya had given him wouldn't last much longer. He would need more sustenance and a decent recovery period soon.

Push through! he ordered himself. He looked down the hallway. Three doors down, a room was open, and an obvious rush of air was coming through. He gritted his teeth. "So, help me, Brighton, if you're trying to get away with something ...."

He breathed deeply and slowed his pace as he walked down the hallway with caution. Brighton could have accessed some weaponry he wasn't aware of. He couldn't chance anything that would threaten his existence.

The sound of forced air grew louder.

"Authorized Personnel Only." Maazi read the placard outside the door. He eased his head across the threshold and looked into the room. Besides the massive hole in the ground and broken rebar protrusions, there wasn't anything worth getting excited over. The room was nothing more than an oversized janitor's closet: mops and brooms dangling along one wall, a wash bucket and in-floor sink for rinsing things on the other side of the hole in the floor, closets lining the opposite side, and a computer on the back wall with a note on the monitor that said, "Log your daily cleaning chores here."

Maazi eased forward and looked down the hole. It was dark at the bottom. He positioned his fingertips downward and shot five rounds of blue plasma-like energy into the grotto. The cavern lit up a bright blue, highlighting the hallways of various floors beneath him. The plasma balls exploded at the bottom. Nothing was down there.

Maazi waited for several moments to see if any movement occurred. Nothing. He looked up and down the hallway, then jutted his head deeper into the janitor's closet. Nothing ... except ....

"There!" he said to himself.

A pair of moist socks were hanging on a section of rebar two floors down. *He jumped to a lower floor.*

Maazi leapt into the hole. As he plummeted toward the landing of the second floor down, he glimpsed the silhouette of a man huddling in a large HVAC tube. Brighton!

Maazi tried to change his trajectory and stop his descent, but his body and velocity were committed. He couldn't find anything to grab onto.

"Fool!" Maazi yelled as he dropped one floor beneath Brighton. He landed hard and lost his footing, causing him to fall yet another floor down. Normally, he would have been able to simply jump back up from floor to floor without a second thought. But he didn't have the energy; his organic sustenance was depleting. He watched as a barefoot Brighton shimmied to the edge of the HVAC tube.

Maazi pulled out his over under and aimed it at Brighton.

"Not another move, Brighton! You're in my sights."

~

Brighton's plan worked, mostly. He had tossed his moist socks to the floor below as a decoy, hoping that Maazi would jump down and start running through the hallways of the lower floor. But he'd failed to anticipate that the blue hue from Maazi's body would provide enough light to divulge his hiding spot in the HVAC tube.

Now he had two choices: either carry on with his plan and jump from the HVAC tubing back up into the nuke launch room—which was covertly decorated as a janitor's closet with a computer actually connected to the moon's nuclear launch system—and likely get shot by Maazi who had his over under aimed directly at him, or follow Maazi's order and surrender.

Brighton looked at Maazi. He was noticeably weak, but still deadly.

"Well, what's it gonna be, *colonel*?" Maazi sneered. "Why don't you make your way down here?"

Brighton hesitated and looked into the nuke launch room.

"There something special in that janitor's closet?" Maazi asked. "Obviously, it fooled me. Must be something pretty pivotal for you to risk your life."

Brighton breathed in and out, still trying to decide. A bullet zipped past his head and into the concrete above.

"I don't do well with people who waste my time," Maazi yelled.

Brighton looked down and assessed Maazi's surroundings. *He's standing on the weakest part of that floor*, he thought, *I might be able to work with that.* Brighton knew the floor was compromised because he was on the Space Committee of the Pentagon. They had just hired a group of engineers to shore up some sections of the building. That particular floor was scheduled to undergo redesign and asbestos abatement. The temporary supports had been demoed two weeks prior.

Brighton had an idea.

"Okay, okay, I'll come down."

"I figured I could convince you," Maazi said.

"Please, just ... just give me a minute. I don't have very good footing. I'm going to turn around and back my way out."

"Whatever floats your boat," Maazi said.

Brighton steadied his feet and turned his body backward ever so slowly. He slipped his right hand toward the inside of his camouflage jacket and unclipped an M67 hand grenade, which he still had from the bunker room battle. He pulled the pin, released the lever, waited two seconds, and pretended to slip on the HVAC tubing.

"Oops!" Brighton yelled, and dropped the grenade, expecting its explosion to weaken the floor under Maazi's feet just enough to make him fall farther.

Maazi noticed that an object was falling. The circuitry in his brain identified the threat. He raised his blue blaster straight in the air and launched a fireball of disintegrating energy that dissolved the grenade before it could cause any damage.

"Brighton!" Maazi yelled. "I'm offended. What is this? You trying to kill me?"

Brighton's heart sank. He was officially out of ideas, and surely Maazi, who was continuously proving that he could flare up at the tiniest spark, and couldn't be easily fooled, wouldn't be willing to take any more of this.

Maazi yelled, "You sorry excuse for a—"

But before Maazi could finish, the flooring under his feet cracked. The cement crumpled, and he flailed as the floor began to give way completely. Maazi dropped his over under and grasped at the walls, trying to find something to grip. He couldn't.

Brighton watched as Maazi fell into the cavernous ruin. He couldn't see where he landed, but he couldn't wait around to find out.

Brighton jumped to action. He positioned his body forward and leapt from the HVAC tube. He grabbed two rods of rebar and heaved his muscular body onto the floor of the nuke launch room, er, janitor's closet, and rushed to the computer. He slid his badge into an access slot.

"Welcome, Col. Brighton," the computer read.

"Yeah, yeah," Brighton said. "Just fire up."

The computer clicked for a moment then pulled up a selection screen. Brighton moved the mouse cursor over the selection box that read, "Activate defense strategies." He clicked it and entered in an accompanying code. Normally, for nuclear weapons, the president's codes would have been the only acceptable ones. However, the Extraplanetary Committee for Nuclear Weapons in Outer Space had provided approval for a handful of military personnel to activate the sequence—Brighton being one of them because he was spearheading the FORM initiative.

The computer accepted Brighton's code and opened a software program. He typed in a series of command sequences that he and the military body of commanders had established earlier that morning.

"Here we go!" Brighton said to himself. He tapped "Enter."

A software replica of the firing sequence pulled up on the screen. A dozen nuclear warhead systems orbiting the moon angled their launch devices toward the four FORM ships.

The first two warheads launched successfully. Brighton watched intently.

"Don't fail us now," he encouraged the system flatly.

Thirty seconds later, two more warheads launched successfully. Brighton stood and almost began to clap, but instead startled at the sound of the nuke launch room entrance door being ripped off its hinges.

"Stop the sequence!" Maazi yelled from the doorway. "Now!"

"You'll have to kill me. I'm not stopping it!"

"Stop now, or they're dead." Maazi angled the computer in his left arm for Brighton to see and showed a video of Brighton's wife and sons.

"You son of a—They're children!"

"What do I care about your children? They'll just use up more of my water. Now stop the sequence!"

Brighton hesitated. He wondered why Maazi didn't just stop the sequence himself. His computer system had demonstrated its ability to connect into the government's mainframe computers.

Maazi shot Brighton through and through the outer thigh of his right leg. Brighton screamed in pain.

"Now, Brighton!"

Brighton spat as he breathed in and out furiously. "All right, all right, I'll cancel it."

He reached up to the keyboard and canceled the remaining eight warhead launches.

"And the ones that already launched!" Maazi demanded.

"I can't cancel the ones that already launched. Not from here. It's a failsafe."

"Fool!"

~

Maazi left Brighton behind and ran back down the corridor and through the Pentagon hallways to the communications room. Taahiya was there, keeping the president and Gen. Childress guarded.

"Bohanna, what is it?" Taahiya asked.

"Nuclear warheads. Brighton launched them toward our ships."

Gen. Childress looked at the president. Maazi saw them both smile but didn't have time to chide them for it.

Maazi turned on the large screen in the room and connected the Pentagon's system to a satellite near the moon. Video feed of four nuclear warheads zipping toward his ships appeared. Maazi worked vigorously on the computer in his arm.

"Just intercept their systems and blow them up," Taahiya said.

"These peons' disruptor weapons scrambled our computers, and now we can't communicate with their weaponry systems."

"Can we communicate with *our* people? Have them destroy them." Taahiya began to work on the computer in her arm as well.

"What do you think I'm trying to do?!" Maazi fumed with scathing condescension.

As the FORM worked on their computers, Gen. Childress and the president noticed Brighton hobble into the room. He had a tourniquet on his leg. He nodded, indicating to the two of them that he was all right. The three watched in silence as nuclear warheads ripped through space.

"I have them!" Taahiya hollered.

"Get over here," Maazi commanded and grabbed her arm. He yelled into her comm system, "Defense team, do you see four missiles approaching?"

"We do, Bohanna."

"Counter them! They're nuclear warheads, the most destructive weaponry these good-for-nothing humans have."

"We're on it, Bohanna."

~

The president looked slyly at Gen. Childress and Brighton. They all knew what the president was thinking.

The nuclear weapons surrounding the moon were outfitted with a system that sent a preemptive signal, known as an ante-signal, in front of the missile itself to prevent defense systems from locking onto it and rendering a counterattack less effective.

Now we'll see how the ante-signaling system on the warheads works, the president thought.

~

Everyone watched as the missiles raced toward the four FORM ships: one silver craft leading in front, the large black mothership in the middle, and two craft in the back of the triangular formation.

The FORM ships launched a counterattack. Their weapons missed the leading warhead yet exploded the trailing missile.

"What? No, no! You missed the leading one. What are you doing?" Maazi yelled into Taahiya's computer.

"Adjusting, Bohanna! They have some kind of scrambling technology."

The three remaining warheads continued their trajectory.

The FORM launched a second counterattack. Once again, they missed the front missile but prevented a second from reaching them.

"Take them out!" Maazi yelled.

"We identified the pattern, Bohanna. We'll get the remaining two."

The president, Gen. Childress, and Brighton smiled. They knew what was coming.

700 miles ... 600 ...

The missiles approached with increasing speed, free from the drag of winds or air.

As the FORM's third counterattack approached, their weaponry exploded the leading warhead, this time right on target.

Maazi looked at the president and Gen. Childress, then he noticed that Brighton had arrived.

"Oh, looks like you hurt your leg," Maazi mocked Brighton. "Your little stunt isn't going to pan out."

Brighton smiled at Maazi.

Maazi squinted. *Why would this infidel be smiling? Something is up.* He looked at the large screen. A single missile was left.

400 miles ...

"Bohanna," one of Maazi's crewmembers said, "we're engaging the fourth missile."

Maazi looked at the president, Gen. Childress, and Brighton. They seemed too calm. "Stop the counterattack!" Maazi screamed into Taahiya's comm unit.

Taahiya flared her nostrils. "What?"

"Something's wrong! Don't send the counterattack. Engage your shield instead!"

The message reached them too late. The FORM volleyed a fourth counterattack, but before their armament reached its target, the lagging nuclear warhead disconnected into fifteen separate missiles. The leading two nukes sacrificed themselves and absorbed the FORM's counter offensive. The remaining missiles breezed through the final one-hundred-mile distance and connected with the FORM's leading silver ship.

"No!" Maazi and Taahiya yelled together. Despair filled their faces. Never had they lost so many at once—not in 3,000 circuits! Longevity, which meant more to them than anything, was stripped away in an instant for thousands of their people.

Maazi teetered back and forth. Taahiya tried to catch him, but he crumpled to the floor. Suddenly, the enormous and powerful FORM commander looked vulnerable.

Taahiya scooped Maazi up in her arms. She rushed toward the exit and punched Gen. Childress in the chest on her way out, making him collide with a camera in the back of the room.

~

Brighton hobbled to the communications system and connected to the cameras on the exterior of the Pentagon. They watched as a melik flew out of a plume of smoke in the Pentagon's walls. Taahiya was taking Maazi back to their ship.

"Smart work, Brighton," Gen. Childress complimented as he stood up and held his chest.

"Agreed," the president praised.

A wave of pride surged through Brighton. He had successfully taken down one of the FORM's major strongholds. They now knew it was possible to fight against the FORM.

"Hurry," Brighton ordered one of the communications technicians in the room. "Help me reconnect the Pentagon's communications systems to the satellite around the moon and display the footage on the worldwide feed Maazi was using. The world needs to know we can defend ourselves against them."

"Of course." The technician worked with the computer system. In moments, the live feed of a FORM ship exploding in space was broadcast globally.

Brighton, the president, and Gen. Childress cheered in unison, high fiving each other. Their glee matched that of a million others watching across Earth. Hope was on the horizon.

Yet the celebrations were short lived.

The camera feed from the satellite shifted and showed a dozen nuclear warhead systems orbiting the moon.

"What's happening?" the president asked.

"I don't know," a technician said. "I didn't move the satellite camera."

The president jerked when one of the warhead systems exploded.

"No! Did it malfunction?" the president begged.

A second warhead system burst apart.

"Someone tell me what's happening!"

"It's the FORM," Brighton said. "They must have hacked the software controls. They're initiating the nukes' self-destruct function."

They all watched with the world as the remaining warhead systems blew up on camera. Brighton's heart went through a roller coaster of emotions.

"Mr. President," Gen. Childress said sternly, "we need to get every last troop, military vehicle, tank, weapon, and whatever else we have to Corpus Christi. Now there's nothing between us and them. They're coming!"

Chapter 22

FORM Ship

Dr. Sharp grimaced. His wrist was throbbing. Two of his human counterparts in the biosphere—who obviously were experienced at mending injuries as it seemed to be second nature to them—had bandaged his ailing wrist, but no meds were available to assuage the pain.

"Jack, my boy," Dr. Sharp asked, "could you get me some water?"

Jack wiped a few tears, still trying to cope with everything, and said, "Yeah, yeah." He got up, grabbed the small water jug that Maazi had thrown on the ground, and handed it to Dr. Sharp. "Here. You can have all of it. I'm good for now."

"That's kind of you, but listen, we *both* need to take care of ourselves. We're going to get out of here."

Jack nodded flatly, failing to signal any belief in Dr. Sharp's statement.

Dr. Sharp sipped some water, shifted his weight, and wiped his soiled brow. Panting, he set down the jug and held his hand. He rocked his head back and forth, trying to cope with the pain. "That *must* have been a rock I punched."

"Probably. Let's see," Jack said as he got down on one knee and started sweeping the ground. As he moved dirt back and forth, he uncovered a rose-colored trapezoidal rock.

As Dr. Sharp watched Jack uncover the rock, a surge of excitement pinged his mind. "Wait a minute, Jack, do you recognize what that is?"

"Yeah. A rock."

"Yes, of course, of course, but not just *any* rock. It's a sedimentary iron-ore-based rock!"

Jack looked at Dr. Sharp blankly and said with a touch of sarcasm, "Wow, I guess that's better than one of those *other* types of rocks."

"Rocks may look the same, but what they hold inside can make a world of difference! This rock has *iron* in it." Dr. Sharp looked around the biosphere. "I have an idea. If we can find enough of those rocks, we may just be able to make something that could help us out."

"How about those ones?" Jack jumped up and lifted a spot of greenery that was covering a pile of rocks next to the back wall of the biosphere.

"Yes!" Dr. Sharp said.

They heard heavy footsteps approaching from the corridor outside.

"Hurry, Jack! Cover those back up."

Jack dropped the greenery and made his way back to Dr. Sharp's side just as the biosphere door flew open. The door hit the wall with such force, its ricochet caused the single camera that was keeping an eye on the inhabitants to loosen and smash on the ground.

"Dr. Sharp! Jack! Did you miss me?" Maazi hollered.

Maazi looked frailer than their last meeting. He was adjusting some bandaging wrapped around his upper left arm and the elbow of his right arm.

"You missed quite the initiatory battle down there. Dang, your people know how to fight!" Maazi punched a wall and yelled, startling Dr. Sharp and Jack in the process. "Your military killed thousands of my people, Dr. Sharp!" Maazi hobbled farther in and looked back and forth at Dr. Sharp and Jack. His brilliant blue eyes were aflame. "Who's going to pay for that? Huh? Are you two going to pay for it? *Someone* is going to die. *Someone* is going to die a painful death."

Maazi worked the bandage on his elbow. He caught Jack looking at his arm. "It's how I get most of my sustenance. If it weren't for my comrade, Taahiya, I'm not sure I would have made it back. You would have liked that, wouldn't you? If I were dead?"

Jack swallowed hard. He didn't like Maazi.

"Your leaders were lucky I wasn't at full capacity down there. Otherwise, your planet would have been ... let's just say ... uninhabitable right now. Ah, but *boy* was it great to fight again!" Maazi stopped adjusting his bandaging and braced himself against a rock. "All right, you two. How is this room treating you?"

Dr. Sharp and Jack stared at Maazi but didn't answer.

"I'm serious. That wasn't a rhetorical question. How is it treating you?"

"Uh," Jack hesitated.

"Speak up, Jack!" Maazi ordered.

"I mean, we need some food and water."

"Hmm. You need some food and water." Maazi grabbed Jack by the neck of his shirt and got in his face.

Jack was noticeably shaking.

Dr. Sharp worried for his safety.

"Figures," Maazi said. "I didn't think you'd be able to provide for yourselves."

"We could if you treated us like people and not prisoners," Dr. Sharp said under his breath.

Maazi's eyes widened and he let go of Jack's shirt. "What did you say?"

"I said, maybe you should treat us with a little more respect!"

Maazi tried to lunge for Dr. Sharp, but stumbled in the process, then steadied himself and continued forward. Dr. Sharp rushed to the back wall of the biosphere where the leaves were covering the pile of rocks and cowered on his knees as he leaned against the wall.

"Please, please! Commander Maazi, I didn't mean to offend you. I don't know why I said that."

"You moron!" Maazi panted as he approached Dr. Sharp and pressed his nose against his cheek. "You should know your place by now!" he growled through gritted teeth.

Hot tears ran down Dr. Sharp's cheeks.

"Please, please, I'm so sorry. Don't hit me."

Maazi stood tall, took a deep breath, and laughed with a wheeze. "Seriously, Dr. Sharp, have some self-respect. Look at yourself. You're like a whimpering child." Without warning, Maazi swung a fist in front of Dr. Sharp's face and punched a hole in the back wall of the biosphere. Sparks spurted from the wall and fizzled on the dirt below. Maazi had punctured a box of electronics.

"Now look what you made me do!" Maazi struggled to hold himself up and shook his head. "Maybe you're not who I thought you were." Maazi grabbed Dr. Sharp, dragged him sluggishly back to Jack, and threw him on the ground.

Dr. Sharp slumped to the sand and dirt floor and sobbed.

"Like a child!" Maazi said. "Jack, maybe you can teach this elderly man how to behave. I'm honestly a bit disappointed. Your people down there showed a resiliency that isn't common in the universe, and here this *doctor* sits, like a child on the ground—sobbing. I thought your American pride and courage would have instilled some strength in you.

"Whatever. Judgment day is near. I look forward to showing your people what else we have in store. And, oh, I'll be sure to give some extra special attention to your dear brother." Maazi chuckled evilly. "Have no doubt about that."

Maazi gaited slowly toward the exit. He turned and smiled at Jack. "Oh, and Jack. I'll think about that food and water."

Maazi slammed the door closed, leaving Dr. Sharp and Jack alone with their despair.

Once again, the other humanoids in the room were huddled in the corner, avoiding conflict with Maazi.

Dr. Sharp broke the heavy silence and said in a chipper voice, "I don't know what to make of how weak he looked just now, but do you think he's gone for a while?"

Jack turned and looked at Dr. Sharp who was wiping his eyes and dusting off his clothes.

Jack asked, "Wait, were you faking that?"

"Of course I was! I didn't take three years of drama in high school for nothing! I saw an opportunity to trigger that foul creature's anger and get him to do just what I needed. I also needed him to think that we're going to hunker down and do nothing. Look at that!" Dr. Sharp pointed to the hole in the wall with sparks bursting sporadically through. "That may just be our ticket out of here, Jack!"

"What do you mean?"

"You just discovered a pile of iron-infused rocks right next to that hole. And I imagined they had some kind of electrical apparatus behind these walls because electricity is the essence of function. With that electricity now exposed, we can turn those rocks into magnets! And what do magnets do?"

"I mean, all kinds of things I guess, but ... they stick to each other?"

"Indeed, they do—and they also disrupt computer systems! Come on, we need to turn those rocks into magnets."

Dr. Sharp led Jack to the rock pile. He grabbed a broad, waxy leaf from one of the nearby plants. "Watch this." He reached into the wall using the waxy leaf and grabbed a set of wires. "Ah!" he screamed as his body shook.

"Dr. Sharp!" Jack yelled, fearing he was being electrocuted.

Dr. Sharp stopped shaking and smiled. "Gotcha."

Jack shook his head and huffed. "Dr. Sharp, for real, this probably isn't the best time to be joking around."

"All right, all right. Just trying to lighten this dreadful mood, my boy. But let's get to work. Here's what I need you to do. Move some of that dirt aside so we can bury these wires in the sand by the rocks."

Jack jumped right to it and dug a small hole in the sand next to the pile of rocks.

"Okay, now we need to complete the circuit." Dr. Sharp snagged one of the metal pipes he had eyed earlier that was leaning against a tree. He stuck it on the opposite side of the rock pile and touched it to a metal wall, then grabbed the electrical wires again. "Now stand back. This may electrify the ground, and I don't want you to get hurt."

"Well, what about you?" Jack asked.

"The current should course through the rocks, not me. I'll be fine."

Jack wasn't so sure but took a step back anyway and watched nervously as Dr. Sharp dragged the set of wires out from the wall and shoved them into the hole. A flash of sparks shot several feet in the air, then dissipated. They could hear the electricity hum.

"Ha, ha!" Dr. Sharp cheered. "There we have it, Jack. Electricity is now coursing through those rocks. They'll become magnets in no time. Now," Dr. Sharp stroked his chin and looked at the hole in the wall, "there may actually be more that we can do with that hole in the wall. Are you thinking what I'm thinking?"

Jack laughed. "Somehow I doubt it."

"Well, let's just say you're going to have a story to tell one day." Dr. Sharp picked up a rock from another area of the biosphere and went to the wall. He smashed it into the façade repeatedly, creating a gaping hole next to the exposed electrical components. Through the broken wall, they began to see an opening to a section of hexagonal ductwork. "That's what I was hoping for. Now come on. We're going to get in there, crawl around a bit, and see what we can find."

Jack breathed deep. "I don't like any of this, but given the circumstance, I'm not sure what else to do." He breathed again and looked at the looming portal. He shook his head.

"Jack, we don't know how much time we have. We have no other options. We need to do something, maybe even a bit drastic. Now, hop on in there and let's see what we can find."

Jack exhaled through rounded lips. "All right, I guess ... here goes nothin'!"

Chapter 23

The Vaughn Home, San Antonio, TX

When chaos becomes commonplace, people surrender to fear.

The words of Ryker's commanding officer in Afghanistan rang in his ears. She was a wise woman who had shared many life lessons.

Hope is dissolving, Ryker thought as he looked out his front window and watched people loading their cars, scrambling to secure personal possessions, and attempting to flee as far away as possible from the battle zone. Though San Antonio was 180 miles away from Port Aransas, people knew the FORM craft could easily travel that distance in minutes, and with multiple military bases located in the city, battle spillover and collateral damage in San Antonio was not only anticipated but expected.

Within hours of Maazi's "introduction" to the world yesterday, worldwide military forces had collaborated and begun sending aircraft, sea vessels, and every imaginable piece of military weaponry to Texas. San Antonio was a prime bridge point with dozens of military bases—perfect for readying weaponry, machines, vehicles, and equipment before shoring up Port Aransas and the surrounding regions of Corpus Christi.

"Hold onto hope. It's the catalyst for victory," Ryker said out loud. "And for Jack's return." He was a veteran of holding onto hope; that kept him alive during his firefight with al Qaeda enemies.

"What was that, honey?" Grace asked as she poked her head out of their living room coat closet. She was assessing their stock of emergency supplies and food. Despite the unexpected battle, the FORM had initiated a few nights earlier, their house was still intact; the same couldn't be said for the attached bed-and-breakfast.

"Oh, I was just talking to myself. How are we looking on batteries?"

Grace stood and exhaled slowly. Keeping busy helped keep her mind off of the atmosphere of impending doom, not to mention the void in her heart that an absent Jack left. "Batteries are good. We have enough to last us well over a month. But what has me more worried is our food reserve. Most of the extra was in the bed-and-breakfast." She fought back tears, cleared her throat, and forced herself to talk. "I guess I should have listened when those missionaries from that one church came by and talked about having enough food storage. Who would've thought? Anyway," Grace put her hands on her thin hips, "if those *things* hanging out in space really are going to be here in two more days, we should see what else we can get our hands on. But I refuse to leave the city. If there's any chance Jack is on one of those ships, I'm jumping on it to get him when it arrives!"

Ryker smiled. He knew she wasn't kidding. "I'll be right there with you, Mom. And I agree we should stay here. I mean, we have half a dozen Black Hawks coming every few minutes." Ryker pointed to the sky just as a Black Hawk flew overhead. He continued, "If these FORM or whatever have an entire army that are as strong as the one I fought, we'll want to be where the firepower is. And the reality is, if they win *this* stronghold, there won't be anywhere *to* hide. Best thing we can do is stand up and fight. Speaking of, how's our ammo looking?"

"Well, this *is* Texas!" Grace looked at Ryker and smiled. "But most of what you and your dad had was also in the bed-and-breakfast, so we could use more."

Ryker nodded. "All right, so what we need most is food and ammo. That's what Jessie and I will focus on."

"When is she coming?" Grace asked.

"Um." Ryker checked the smartwatch on his wrist. It was 10:13 a.m. "When we texted last night, she said she didn't have much of anything in the way of emergency supplies and she wanted to meet up here at about ten so we could get some stuff together." Ryker looked out the window and saw Jessie pull up. "And that answers that. Here she is."

Ryker turned around and double checked that his Ozzies were securely latched and fully charged.

When the doorbell rang, Grace dropped what she was holding and answered the door. "Jessie, welcome, welcome. Please, come in."

Jessie stepped inside. "Thank you, Mrs. Vaughn. Is Ryker here?"

"Right here," Ryker called as he finished tying his shoes and stood up from the couch. The gears in his Ozzies whirred smoothly.

Jessie entered the living room and smiled at Ryker. "Hey, thanks for being willing to help. I, uh ... you know, it's good to have someone to get supplies with, especially when times are crazy like this."

Ryker knew that Jessie was fully capable of handling herself, but he also knew they both liked the thought of being together—impending aliens or not.

"I'm glad you texted." Ryker smiled back. He patted his Ozzies, which were easily visible because he was wearing shorts. "All right, these are ready. *I'm* ready. What do you say we head over to HEB and the ammo shop? They're within walking distance. There's no way we'll be able to drive around with the chaos out there."

"Sounds great. Food is what I need most, too."

"I'm guessing you'll want to bring this?" Grace asked as she handed Ryker his favorite Glock.

Ryker looked at the weapon and shook his head. "I never thought the day would come when my hometown would be a battle zone."

"Sadly, it is," Jessie said as she lifted the side of her T-shirt slightly to reveal her concealed carry.

"Nice, then that means I don't need mine," Ryker joked.

"You can be my backup," Jessie half teased.

Ryker chuckled and grabbed his Glock from Grace, found a loaded clip, slid it in place, and holstered the gun on his shorts. "Okay, let's get some supplies." He leaned down, grabbed an oversized backpack that was on the couch, and put it onto his back.

"Do you have a backpack or something to carry food in?" Grace asked Jessie.

"Oh my gosh, I didn't even think about that. With all that's been going on …."

"Just a second," Grace said and went into their coat closet. She reemerged with a heavy-duty camouflage backpack. "You can use this one." She handed it to Jessie. "It was my husband's. He used it in Iraq."

"Thank you," Jessie offered with true gratitude and swung it onto her shoulders. "Ready!"

~

Ryker led the way down their street. The panic in the suburb was palpable; people were rushing in and out of their houses, arguing about what they considered to be essential, and begging family members to hurry into the car so they could flee the city.

Ryker paused in front of the yard where Jack and Dr. Sharp were taken. "It's kind of crazy to think this will be considered Ground Zero."

Jessie looked up and down the street and shook her head. Words weren't enough to express how she felt. She took a deep breath and said, "Yeah. Best thing we can do is prepare for what's coming. Let's keep going."

Ryker adjusted his Ozzies to sport mode and hopped several fences and helped Jessie do the same to shorten their journey to the nearest HEB grocery store. One guy ran them off his lawn while holding a shotgun.

"Y'all get out of here! No one's gonna get *my* possessions!" he warned.

"We're not here to take anything," Jessie soothed. "Just passing through."

The man lowered his weapon and let them pass.

Just under a mile later, they reached a limestone precipice that overlooked the HEB storefront and parking lot. The parking lot was filled with packing materials, waste, and debris—remnants of looted things.

"Whoa!" Jessie said. "It looks like a hurricane hit this place!"

"Seriously," Ryker said. "Let's see if there's anything good left."

They weaved their way down the rocky terrain and jumped onto the asphalt of the parking lot, then made their way to the front doors. The atmosphere was dreary: lights in the store were out, shelves were mostly empty, the floors were a mess, and empty cash registers were wide open.

"Hello?" Ryker hollered, assessing whether anyone was inside. "Hello?"

No one responded.

"Over there," Jessie said as she pointed to the left side of the store. Several vegetable and fruit bins still had food in them.

"Nice!"

They wanted to run, but instead walked cautiously to the bins. Ryker's military training intuitively kicked in:

assess for danger, be on the lookout, stay calm yet ready. They analyzed each of the store aisles, confirming danger wasn't afoot.

As they reached the food bins, Ryker slipped the backpack off his shoulders and pulled out two duffel bags.

"Let's fill that one up with fresh food," Jessie suggested as she motioned to one of the duffels, "then let's see if we can find canned or packaged food for the other one and our backpacks. That will last longer."

"Agreed."

They collected foods with sturdier composition and that were unripened so they would last longer than a few days: cantaloupes, mangos, apples, onions, potatoes, and beets—of which there was an abundance.

Ryker chuckled as he stuffed a handful of beets in the duffel. "Apparently beets are the food that last in an apocalypse!"

"Well, now we know." Jessie shrugged. She shimmied the duffel so things would settle and make room.

After the duffel was filled with a transportable number of fruits and vegetables, Ryker zipped it closed.

"All right, let's see if any canned foods are left," Jessie said.

Ryker nodded and picked up the second duffel. He left the full duffel by the food bins and followed Jessie.

"Aisle 13, canned foods," Ryker said as he pointed to a sign.

They turned down the aisle to assess what was left but didn't get far before a thunderous boom from outside startled them. They looked toward the front doors of the store.

"That was close," Jessie said.

"Feels like I'm back in Afghanistan," Ryker said. "It's most likely a practice exercise out of Lackland or Randolph. They've been prepping planes and tanks all night."

Jessie pulled out her sidearm and checked the clip unnecessarily; the bullets wouldn't have dissolved from the last time she checked the magazine, but her mind needed reassurance in the moment of stress.

A second blast echoed off the surrounding hills, followed by an explosion about a mile away.

"Practice runs don't typically happen in the city," Jessie said.

"True. Probably not a practice run."

They watched the front doors for another moment. There was a faint rustle that morphed into footsteps. Ryker drew his weapon and readied his mind for combat.

Two teenage kids emerged through the front doors, panic in their eyes. The moment they saw a woman and man holding guns, they turned on a dime and ran away.

Ryker slumped his shoulders and loosened his grip. "Glad that didn't turn into anything."

"I think they're gladder," Jessie added.

They holstered their weapons.

Ryker took a deep breath. "All right, what's left of the canned foods?"

Jessie ran her hand up and down the shelves. "Looks like we've got kidney beans, black beans, pinto beans, chili beans, green beans, and oh ... corn."

"Wow, those are some remarkable options," Ryker teased. "Well at least now we also know an apocalypse isn't short on methane!"

"Ew!" Jessie blurted.

"What?" Ryker shrugged. "Jack would have liked that joke."

His mood grew somber.

"He's coming back," Jessie assured. "You're going to find him."

Ryker nodded. Words were difficult to come by.

"Hey, we need to stay in the game here," Jessie said. "We need to take care of ourselves before we can even think of helping others. Let's get ready for what's coming. You know what it takes."

"Right," Ryker agreed. He turned his back to the front of the store and started selecting cans. "Hope. It all goes back to hope." Ryker closed his eyes and reminded himself of what hope had done for him in the past. "All right, let's keep filling this bag and see about batteries as well."

Ryker looked at Jessie. She didn't make eye contact; quite the opposite. The whites of her eyes were glaring as she stood statue-like with her view fixed on the front doors of the store.

"What?" Ryker asked.

Jessie didn't respond.

Ryker twisted his body around and looked at the doors. An oversized being—fused with biological and metallic components—raced toward him and leapt in the air. The blue hue from lights on the FORM's body illuminated the store shelves.

"Jessie, move!"

Ryker jumped to his feet and shoved Jessie toward the store's back aisle, then he braced himself for impact.

"Ryker!" Jessie shrieked.

Ryker's adrenaline poured into every organ of his body. He didn't have time to draw his weapon. He stepped back with his right leg to brace himself. Lifting his powerful arms in the air, he locked hands with the terrorizing FORM. He managed to offset the FORM's trajectory, causing them to tumble to the ground and knock over a shelving unit. Ryker stood faster than he thought he could and readied himself for an intense blow to his stomach. The FORM's fist was like steel and cracked two of his ribs. Ryker exhaled heavily but returned the attack with three rapid jabs to its head, causing viscous blue gel to splatter from his cheek.

The FORM was caught off guard and stumbled momentarily. He seemed surprised by Ryker's strength. Innervated, the FORM regained his composure and continued to swing at Ryker. Ryker's forearm almost broke under the force of the FORM's metallically fused components as he blocked several swings.

Ryker yelled and laid into his torso with punch after punch. Eight punches in, the FORM's muscular frame began to give way and bruise. The FORM grabbed his midsection momentarily. Ryker took the window of opportunity and heaved a tremendous uppercut to the FORM's head, causing him to fall backward into another store shelf.

Angered at the willpower of the human, the FORM shouted in a deep, grumbly voice, "You worthless piece of—"

The FORM couldn't finish his sentence as he jolted under the force of a crowbar smashing his head; a massive divot formed in the left lobe of his cranium.

Ryker looked to the side and saw Jessie holding a crowbar.

"*Don't touch* my boyfriend!" she shrieked at the motionless creature and smashed his head again.

"Nice! Come on!" Ryker yelled with an outstretched hand.

The two of them raced to the front of the store.

"Where the heck did you get a crowbar?" Ryker asked as they ran.

"Apparently, they're thirty percent off right now. Thank you, HEB!"

They raced into the sunlight bathing the stony hills outside. Ryker shook his head in amazement; a 125-pound woman had just bashed in the head of a FORM many times her weight.

Yet their triumph was temporary. The FORM teetered to his feet, somewhat discombobulated, anger raging in his eyes. Jessie had unknowingly hit him near his temple where a neurochip was implanted. The FORM collected himself and rushed toward them. His speed was mind bending, allowing him to catch up with minimal effort.

The FORM jumped at Ryker's legs and knocked him off balance. Ryker tumbled to the ground and attempted to tuck and roll, hoping to protect his Ozzies, but to no avail. His body flipped head over Ozzie.

The skin regions where the metal posts protruded through his amputated legs were scraped and bleeding. He slid into a puddle of mud on the outskirts of the parking lot. Muck contaminated his new wounds along with the connected Ozzies. The blue lights that ran down the Ozzies' flanks went out, and the hinges popped out of rotation; his Ozzies were mangled, bent, and wrecked beyond repair.

The FORM scrambled to his feet and pinned Ryker.

He growled, "I've been waiting for this moment, Ryker!" then spat blue blood to the side. "*You're* the reason our location was compromised, and karma's gonna come full circle! You'll be the first official casualty of this war." The FORM lifted his right hand and energized all five blue-lit weapons on the tips of his fingers. "You're a sorry excuse for a solider."

But before the FORM could fire, his body rocked back and forth. Some repetitive force was pelting him. He looked at his shoulder and torso. Bullet holes.

Ryker and the FORM both looked over and saw Jessie, wielding a handgun. She fired three more rounds at the FORM, aiming high to miss Ryker. The bullets sank into a metal region of the FORM's head, resulting in minimal damage.

The FORM jumped off Ryker and aimed at Jessie—the one thing standing between him and sweet revenge.

Ryker punched the FORM's legs, knocking him off balance. Blue tracers fired off kilter, yet grazed Jessie's left thigh.

Ryker snatched his sidearm in a fluid motion and fired seven bullets into the FORM's torso, groin, arm, and chest before it could do any more damage. The FORM crumpled in pain and rolled over. Blue ooze covered his body. His blue-lit weapon went dark.

The FORM looked at himself. Ryker noticed the perplexed look in his eyes. It was as though the FORM couldn't comprehend what was happening.

"For 3,000 circuits," the FORM said with a distant tone. "I haven't felt pain ... 3,000 circuits." The FORM seemed intrigued by his circumstance. He looked at Ryker. "You!" With one last surge of energy, he kicked Ryker's right Ozzie and snapped it in half.

Ryker hit the ground.

The FORM hobbled on top of him. "We'll kill you, that stupid scientist, *and* your annoying brother!"

A surge of anger, beyond what Ryker had ever experienced, throttled his senses. With Herculean force, he grabbed the FORM's throat, his fingers vice-like. The FORM choked madly. Ryker could feel his esophagus throbbing.

"If you ever *touch* my family, I'll dissect your morbid face with the very metal from your oversized body."

The FORM flailed and punched Ryker to break free.

Ryker sensed the FORM was increasingly impressed by his strength. He yelled and shoved the FORM off him, then rolled to his side, steadied his Glock, and connected three more bullets on the opposite side of the FORM's head where there was no more metallic shield. The FORM finally went limp.

Ryker dropped his gun, grabbed his decimated Ozzie, and grunted. His upper leg hurt, but he was lucky; the metal bionic had broken at the hinge and hadn't ripped out the metal post attached to his femur.

Jessie hurried to Ryker and held him close. She was shaking, close to shock. She noticed his bionics: bent, mangled, and non-functional.

"You okay?" Jessie implored.

Ryker nodded weakly, grabbed his stomach, and took a deep breath, which made him wince. "Kinda, just glad we killed that thing."

"That thing came for *you*!"

"I guess I ticked them off pretty good or something. Sounds like they wanted to come in the night and not be divulged."

A tank and military truck pulled into the parking lot. Several personnel jumped out.

"You two all right?" an officer asked.

"Yeah, yeah, we're okay," Jessie answered, and motioned toward Ryker, "but he's beat up pretty good."

"Um," Ryker said, pointing to the dead FORM, "I'd say *that's* in worse shape!"

"Medic!" the officer called and waved his hand for help to come to Ryker.

"So, you killed one?" the medic asked. "We all wondered if that was even possible. Gives us all a little more hope."

"It wasn't easy," Ryker confided. "If it hadn't been for a crowbar, I'm sure neither of us would be alive right now."

Jessie smiled at Ryker. "I mean, it *was* thirty percent off."

Ryker laughed, but stopped himself and grabbed his stomach.

"Tell you what," the officer said, "we'll take the body of that ... thing for someone to look at. Let us help you get to where you're going."

"Thanks," Jessie obliged. She pointed inside the store. "Our stuff's in there. Two big duffel bags."

"And now we need even more ammo," Ryker added. "And we *were* going to leave cash. We weren't looking to steal anything."

A private ran inside to get their supplies.

"There's no one here to *take* the cash right now anyway, you guys," the officer said.

"Thanks, we appreciate your understanding. But the worse thing is ...." Jessie held back tears. It suddenly dawned on her what all had transpired; Ryker no longer had his Ozzies. "Now he can't walk."

"Come on, we got you," the officer said and helped Jessie get Ryker into the back of the truck.

The private returned from the store and tossed their supply bags next to them in the truck. "I put ammo in this one," he said as he patted one of the bags. "And it's just these two bags, right?"

"Yeah, we have our backpacks," Ryker said as he grabbed at his backpack straps.

"All right, let's go. We have work to do. These things think they can just come and terrorize us any time they want now. I promise you this, we're going to stand our ground and beat the blue crap out of 'em."

"Well, I won't be doing much beating anymore," Ryker noted, eyeing his lower limbs.

They all looked at his leg stumps.

"Oh my gosh!" Jessie screamed. She hadn't recognized Ryker's legs were bloodied and mud-covered. Her first aid training took over. She looked at the private. "Hurry! Get me some rags and do you have any sanitizing solution? We have to clean that interface between his skin and those metal posts. Infection would—"

Jessie stopped herself. She didn't want to scare Ryker. Yet she knew that infection was the Achilles heel of the Ozzie technology. If infection developed, it could track up the skin and into his bone to which the metal post components of the Ozzies were attached. If Ryker's bone became infected, he would never be able to use Ozzies again. He could even die.

"Here!" a medic said as she handed Jessie a medical kit with betadine solution. The medic didn't try to take over; she had never seen an Ozzie implant and it was obvious Jessie knew what she was doing.

Jessie ripped open the pack and cleaned Ryker's Ozzie posts. Once they were clean and the bleeding stopped, she wrapped his legs with gauze.

"Do you have any antibiotics?" she asked.

"Yeah, but only one dose of some basic broad-spectrum," the medic said.

"That'll have to do. We'll just hope they didn't get contaminated with a resistant superbug."

The medic handed Ryker two antibiotic pills, which he swallowed.

"Okay," Jessie sighed. "Could we hitch a ride back to his place? His mom is waiting for us."

"Yeah, of course."

Jessie helped Ryker into the back then climbed in behind him.

"Hit it!" the officer called to the driver.

The truck rumbled out of the parking lot.

Jessie looked over and noticed Ryker was smiling. She was curious. "Um, I'm not sure I'd be smiling after all that."

"I know I should be mad as anything right now," Ryker said. "Not gonna lie, I kind of want to kill another one, but I just got to thinking, do you realize what we just learned?"

"I mean, I can probably think of a number of things," Jessie said sarcastically.

"Jessie, that FORM just told us that *Jack and Dr. Sharp are still alive!*"

Jessie thought for a moment and looked out the back of the truck to the flat San Antonio landscape. It dawned on her. "Oh my gosh, you're right! It said they *would* kill Dr. Sharp and your brother."

"Exactly! I can't wait to tell—Oh man, Mom is going to freak. In a good way."

"Seriously!" Jessie yelled.

The military personnel in the back of the truck could tell something exciting was developing.

"Hope, Jessie. We gotta keep *hope* alive."

"You've convinced me, that's for sure." Jessie rubbed her fingers over the mangled mechanics of Ryker's Ozzie. "I'm going to see if—*hope* that there's a way we can get new ones of these." Jessie wiped developing tears in her eyes. "We have to get you back on your feet. Just like on that obstacle course. It's amazing what you can do with these."

"I know. I never thought I'd be able to move like that." He paused for a moment. "But what's crazy is, I'm not even really thinking about the Ozzies right now. Something else really caught me off guard in the store back there."

"Really?" Jessie mused. "Did it have something to do with a *FORM* attacking you?"

"Yeah, but there was this—something about a ... boyfriend."

Jessie smiled awkwardly. "Oh. You heard that?"

"Yeah. And to be honest ... I kinda liked it."

Jessie grabbed Ryker's hand and smiled through glistening eyes. "I kinda liked it too."

Chapter 24

Corpus Christi, TX

Brighton, the president, and Gen. Childress stepped out of Marine One after it landed in the middle of the Whataburger Baseball Field—home of the AA Minor League Corpus Christi Hooks.

The president yelled over the whip of the helicopter blades. "Follow me! We'll take my transport."

They kept their heads down to protect them from the downdrafts of three other helicopters landing in left field and hurried to The Beast 3—one of the president's armored limousines that had been shipped the night before in anticipation of his arrival.

"Let's go!" the president ordered the Secret Service agent driving the limo.

The agent hesitated a moment and asked the president the same question he had been asked a dozen times over the past twelve hours. "Mr. President, are you sure you shouldn't stay back in D.C.?"

"I'm sure," the president responded. "What kind of leader would I be if I tried to hunker down in a 'safe' place while everyone else puts themselves in danger? I'm not going to be the president who hides at Camp David while the world fights for survival. D.C. isn't even safe! We learned that already. And none of us are sure *anywhere* is safe right now."

The agent couldn't argue with that. He nodded, then floored the gas, traversing the stadium tunnels and squealing onto the palm-tree-lined streets of Corpus Christi.

Gen. Childress pointed at a road to the southeast. "Take that road to the American Bank Center. We've blocked off other routes so only military personnel can reach it. It's less than a mile away."

"Why the Corpus Christi Convention Center?" the agent asked. "Didn't they say Port Aransas?"

"There isn't enough infrastructure in Port Aransas itself," Gen. Childress said. "Fighting will likely go on there, but we're setting up an international military all around."

"In that case wouldn't the Shoreline Plaza have been a better option?" the agent asked. "You can see the horizon better."

"The Shoreline Plaza is 28 stories tall. The taller the building, the bigger the target, the harder the fall," Brighton answered.

The agent nodded. "Ah."

"And also, the Convention Center gives us a deeper foundation to protect our communications systems," Brighton said, rubbing his injured leg. "It's the base of operations for all incoming world-wide military forces. Nearly every nation in the world has sent troops and artillery. It's the best building in the region to protect our ability to communicate. That will be crucial for the disruptors."

"The disruptors? Oh, you mean those new-age weapons that everyone saw on TV in D.C.," the agent remarked.

Brighton harrumphed. "Yeah, they were *supposed* to be Top-Secret."

"They're not anymore," the agent smirked.

"Guess not. So far, the disruptors have proven to be our saving grace against the FORM. They may be our key to success."

The agent furrowed his brow. "Are you saying this won't be a war of nukes? But a different kind of weapon?"

"We all hope that Earth-bound nukes won't be needed. But we *do* have them for a reason," Brighton answered.

"You sound like you've been in battle a time or two," the agent commented as he swerved to miss a pothole.

"Maybe two too many, son," Brighton said. "Two too many." Brighton sat back and took in his own comment. He *had* been in many battles, and wars. And he hoped this was the one and only with the FORM. He thought, *thanks to God and modern medicine for painkillers or I couldn't keep up with everything, and my country needs me right now.*

He assessed the scene and situation around them as they drove. The alleys were ransacked. Remnants of looting were everywhere. The sound of heavy military aircraft rippled across the Gulf as dozens of cargo planes and fighter jets zipped overhead, making their way to San Antonio's Airforce tarmacs, or Corpus Christi's International Airport. As they drew closer to the American Bank Center, the level of military activity increased exponentially. Within the half-mile radius of the newly formed base, military personnel lined the streets, readying gear, armor, weapons, and provisions. Corpus Christi was now a battlefield.

"We're here!" Gen. Childress hollered.

The three of them hurried out of The Beast 3 and strode up the front steps of the Convention Center. They walked in sync underneath the oversized and distinct S design of the building's front façade, shielding their eyes from the Sun's blinding rays that reflected off its massive glass windows.

They pushed the front doors open and entered the lobby, which was filled wall-to-wall with armaments, fatigues, and pallets of military equipment. Not ten steps inside, they heard the screech of an airplane crash outside, rocking the Convention Center's moorings.

Brighton got his balance and looked at Gen. Childress. "What was that?" he asked rhetorically.

"Outside!" the president yelled.

The trio ran back out the lobby doors and gasped. A Lockheed Martin C-5M Super Galaxy cargo plane was crumpled on Shoreline Boulevard. Its body and one wing were mangled beyond repair but not on fire—yet.

"Is that ...?" the president's question trailed.

"It is," Gen. Childress said, "the transport carrying the disruptors!"

Their faces paled.

"Everybody down!" a staff sergeant yelled. "We have company!"

Brighton grabbed his sidearm and slammed his body to the ground, pulling Gen. Childress down with him. A group of Secret Service agents ran by them and encircled the president.

A line of explosions erupted along the beach, narrowly missing the cargo plane.

"Where's that firepower coming from?" Gen. Childress asked.

A swath of meliks blasted out from behind the American Bank Center.

"There's your answer," Brighton yelled.

A group of F-16 fighter jets trailed behind and started a dog fight. The meliks circled the bay, routed their bodies upward, arched behind the F-16 jets, and within moments gained the advantage. They unleashed a merciless attack that resulted in remnants of F-16s falling into the Corpus Christ Bay.

The meliks angled their way toward the cargo plane.

"They're going for the disruptors!" Gen. Childress yelled.

Brighton assessed the situation. He had an idea. "You, all of you," he motioned to the Secret Service agents, Gen.

Childress, and the president, "follow me!" Brighton rushed them back into the lobby. "Everyone grab a MANPAD."

Brighton ripped a tarp off a pallet holding a stack of man-portable air-defense systems—referred to as MANPADS by the military—that were locked and loaded with three spare missiles. They each snatched one and raced back outside and took cover behind an armored tank in the street.

Brighton yelled, "Aim at the meliks, let it lock on the target, trigger is right here." Brighton pointed to the trigger. "Shoot in sequence, down the line, then reload when it's not your turn. I'll shoot first, then go to the cargo plane. You all keep firing. Try to divert them away from that plane. I'll compromise their shields with a disruptor, then you shoot through the hole I create. Just like in D.C."

Everyone nodded. There wasn't a better short-term gameplan.

Brighton heaved a MANPAD onto his shoulder, leaned around the tanks' metal tracks, aimed, and fired.

The missile zipped toward a melik and melted into its fluid-like purple shield. Yet it had the desired effect; the melik shifted its course. Brighton dropped the MANPAD and sprinted to the plane less than a hundred yards away. When he reached it, he turned around and saw the president firing his MANPAD.

Well, he thought, *the pen may be mightier than the sword, but not a MANPAD!*

Brighton hurried through the plane's cargo door. "Anyone in here?"

"Here!" a soldier with a bloodied head said. "We're fine. Bloody, but fine. This plane could blow any second, though."

"We'll have to take our chances. I need a disruptor, now. You know how to use one?"

The soldier pointed to two rows of disruptors. "Take your pick, and yeah, we're the ones who designed their software."

"Come on, unstrap one and follow me."

Brighton and several soldiers unstrapped five disruptors and heaved them to the street. Brighton pointed his at a melik. "We need to expose their shields. Then our crew back there will send a missile through an opening. Just like in D.C."

"Ready," the soldiers said.

They aimed the disruptors at an individual melik, opening several holes in its shield. Two missiles soared toward it. The melik exploded.

"Yeah!" the bloodied soldier yelled. "Get some!"

"Focus, soldier!" Brighton said. "Hit the next."

They aimed the disruptors at a second melik.

The melik pilots didn't know which way to turn to avoid the disruptors' firepower; because their beams of energy were invisible, only their effect could be detected, which gave a pivotal advantage to the disruptor technology.

The second melik erupted into a plume of flames.

"Three more!" Brighton yelled.

Brighton maintained the pattern and soon, a third melik crashed into the Shoreline Plaza, which collapsed on itself.

"Just like I said," Brighton hollered, "too big a target!"

They aimed at the fourth melik, but there was no effect.

"That fourth one's getting smart!" Brighton yelled. "It's keeping its shields down and staying at a higher altitude. Missiles aren't going to reach him up there. Hold your fire."

Brighton and the soldiers gripped the disruptors but withheld their energy. The two remaining meliks suddenly beelined out over the ocean.

"What's that all about?" a soldier asked.

The air was silent. They monitored the horizon for several seconds but couldn't see anything.

Brighton wiped his brow and waited. "I don't know, but—"

He was interrupted by a male FORM emerging from the Corpus Christi Bay waters. "What?!" The FORM zipped three blue light tracers straight through the chests of the soldiers next to Brighton. Each sank to the ground.

Brighton dove under the cargo plane's bay door. Streaks of blue mixed with sparks of reactive metal sprayed his face as the FORM tried to kill him. Brighton saw a puddle of fuel. He rolled past it, knowing the FORM's tracers would catch it on fire, yet the flames would provide a layer of protection between him and his attacker.

The plan worked.

As flames erupted, Brighton rolled deeper underneath the plane's belly. He heard gunfire in the distance. He peeked through an opening and saw the FORM shift his attack to a different set of assailants who were laying down cover.

Brighton took advantage of the opening and shimmied out from under the plane. The flames were chasing him; his clothes had absorbed some jet fuel and left a trail of liquid that merged with a leaking fuel line. He ripped his pants off and left them behind as he ran toward Gen. Childress.

"It's going to blow! Take cover!"

The FORM heard Brighton but didn't go after him. Instead, he signaled for two other FORM that had emerged from the water to follow him elsewhere.

Brighton, Gen. Childress, and the president watched from behind the tank as each FORM wrapped a disruptor under an arm and carried it into the Bay waters. Seconds later, the cargo plane erupted, vaporizing the remaining disruptors.

Brighton protected his face from the fireball's heatwave. He and the group looked on in disbelief. The pivotal weapons in the battle against the FORM were gone.

"What do we do now?" the president asked.

Brighton looked at Gen. Childress who was shaking his head.

For the first time in his military career, Gen. Childress said, "I don't know."

Chapter 25

FORM Ship

Dr. Sharp put his hand up, signaling for Jack to stop. For nearly two hours, he and Jack had been weaving through mazes of ductwork in the FORM ship, getting to know its innards, its workings, its pathways. They'd climbed through a vented grate in the ceiling of what appeared to be a lab, with metal beams and sporadic plant life running their length. The room contained medical-looking equipment, an old weapons cache on a side wall, and an elephant-sized set of sharpened fan blades inset in a large cylinder in the far corner. They heard the entrance door open and looked down. An oversized FORM stepped in.

"Maazi," Dr. Sharp whispered, stating the obvious.

Jack nodded.

Maazi was carrying a dead elk over his shoulder. He struggled under the weight of the animal's body; his own body was obviously still weak.

"What the ..." Jack hesitated, "why is he carrying an elk?"

Dr. Sharp shrugged.

Maazi hefted the elk to the cylinder and threw it in. The blades ground the elk to pieces in seconds, flinging tissue and bone along the cylinder walls.

Jack nearly threw up.

"Look away, Jack. Don't give away our position."

Jack looked away and composed himself.

"What is that grinding thing?" Jack whispered.

Dr. Sharp watched Maazi approach a wall with computer-like screens. He couldn't see what they showed, but he saw Maazi trudge to the opposite end of the wall, open a compartment, and grab an enormous syringe that had just been filled with a purified bioluminescent substance that glowed a brilliant blue. Maazi injected the fluid into his arm and sighed heavily, as though the injection were satisfying.

"It's an organics processor," Dr. Sharp breathed with intrigue.

"A what now?"

"An organics processor. That must be how they 'eat.' They grind up organics, purify them, and inject the processed product into their body. And I'm guessing they combine it with cyanobacteria like he said because that solution glows blue just like ocean waters with bioluminescent organisms."

"Wow, not really an appetizing way to eat."

"Sophisticated though," Dr. Sharp mused quietly. "They can probably control their nutrients with precision."

Maazi hobbled to a table just underneath their position. The blue hue from his body illuminated their faces through the grate. If Maazi looked up, he would see them.

Dr. Sharp put his finger to his lips and widened his eyes, suggesting he and Jack be extra quiet.

Maazi grabbed a wristband from the table. It looked like an advanced archer's brace. He slipped it on his right arm and pressed a series of icons on a small screen embedded in the device. A purple shield instantly encircled his body. He admired the energized plasma for several moments, then pressed the buttons again, making the shield disappear.

"Ha!" Maazi laughed to himself. "My first prototype. Still works. Dang, Maazi, you're a masterful creator! You deserve everything you get from this planet."

No ego in that man, is there? Dr. Sharp thought.

Another FORM entered the lab, startling Maazi.

"Don't you knock?" Maazi yelled as he took the wristband off and set it on the table.

"Apologies, Bohanna, but we retrieved three of their military's disruptors, and destroyed the rest."

"Now *that's* what I wanted to hear!" Maazi shouted. "Are they here?"

"Yes, in the Control Room."

"Let's see what they do," Maazi ordered and followed the messenger out of the lab.

As soon as the door closed, Dr. Sharp and Jack took deep breaths.

Dr. Sharp said, "We need to get to that Control Room and see what they're up to with those disruptors they're talking about. It sounds like they got them from our military!"

"Yeah, but first we gotta get that wristband thing. Imagine what we could do with that. We might be able to get out of this place!"

"Jack, that's a tremendous amount of risk. You go in that room, and you're exposed."

"We have to. *I* have to. I've got to see my mom—" Jack teared up.

Dr. Sharp put his hand on Jack's shoulder. "All right, all right. Look, if we open that grate," he pointed to the next grate down, "there's a pipe you could shimmy down, but it's got to be thirty feet to the floor. Question is, how will you get back up?"

"I have enough arm strength. I can do it."

Dr. Sharp breathed deeply. "You really think you can?"

"I can."

Dr. Sharp pursed his lips, then nodded. "I trust you, my boy."

They crawled to the next grate in the ducting and pushed it open. Jack slipped through, grabbed the pipe, and slid down to the floor. He crouched for a second to make sure he was alone, then eased over to the table.

He grabbed the wristband. It was black with two straps that could be tightened, and it had a thin flexible smart-phone-like screen that displayed a series of numbers and icons. It was heavier than it looked. Jack slipped it in his back pocket and hurried to the pipe.

Dr. Sharp could tell the climb was more difficult than Jack anticipated.

Just over halfway up, Jack said, "My arms are burning. I need a break."

"Come on, Jack. You can do it!" Dr. Sharp whispered.

Jack nodded. "Just need a second."

Without proper nutrition, Jack's body didn't have the strength he was used to. He climbed another five feet, then paused to breathe. He nearly slipped when he heard the lab door click.

Dr. Sharp's eyes widened. *Someone's coming!* "Don't move!" he whispered.

Jack held his position—clinging helplessly to a pole twenty feet in the air—as the door groaned open.

Maazi walked in and said, "Bring it over here. We'll connect it to the decoding system."

Dr. Sharp watched a FORM carry a medium-sized piece of equipment to a table in the middle of the lab. The device had a satellite-dish-looking face with a scope and two handles for maneuvering.

Maazi pulled an oversized hexagonal stool over and plopped his tired body on it, then grabbed a decoding unit, slapped it onto the satellite-dish-looking piece, and powered on the disruptor.

"All right, let's find out how these things affect our shields," Maazi said.

Dr. Sharp watched Maazi power on the disruptor. The connected computer began to decode the disruptor's software.

As the program cycled through parameters, Maazi hollered, "There it is!" and pointed to the screen. He vigorously worked a set of sequences on the computer. "Well, well, would you look at that? Who would have thought, they created the essence of a disruptor for plasma-based energy: a combination of electromagnetism with a dash of radiation. Just the thing that would affect our shield systems. I doubt they even knew what they were doing." Maazi was unwilling to give humankind a shred of credit for the innovation.

The other FORM in the room snorted, signaling his distaste for those they were about to take over.

Maazi worked some more sequences. "You know what else they probably didn't know?"

"What, Bohanna?"

"If we alter the bond strength in our shields, their disruptor technology might make our shields more powerful as opposed to destabilized. In fact, we can test it out! Hurry, grab my mobile shield generator over there on that table."

Jack shot Dr. Sharp a terrified look. They both knew that if the FORM looked for the shield generator, he wouldn't find it; it was in Jack's pocket.

Dr. Sharp looked at the shield device. *No!* he thought. The device was dangling precariously out of Jack's pocket; he hadn't stuffed it all the way in; all the shimmying up the pole made it wriggle halfway out.

Jack was sweating profusely. Dr. Sharp could tell his arms were burning. His fingers looked like they were starting to slip, but he couldn't readjust his grip, and he couldn't push the device further into his pocket; the movements would potentially give away his position.

Dr. Sharp watched Jack grip the pole tighter and let the sweat develop, but he knew he couldn't hold on much longer. Dr. Sharp couldn't do anything to help. He could only pray. *Just don't let go, Jack!*

"Bohanna," the subservient FORM said, "we shouldn't test it on a first-generation shield. We should test it on the current generation. That's the version their disruptors disable."

"Ah, I knew there was a reason I keep you around. But I would have thought of that soon enough," Maazi said, his ego never too small to be on display.

Maazi stood slowly from his stool and pressed a set of icons on the computer embedded in his left arm. A purple shield encompassed his body.

"All right, aim the disruptor at my shield. It should enhance its circumference with the parameters I put in."

"Yes, Bohanna."

The FORM aimed the disruptor at the top of Maazi's personal, plasma-based shield and powered it on. As it absorbed the disruptor's energy, the shield swelled an inch.

Maazi took out his over under handgun and fired a bullet at the spot where the disruptor was aimed.

The blast of the handgun startled Jack. He slipped, causing the shield device to fling out of his pocket and begin a freefall toward the floor. He held onto the pole with every molecule of ATP in his cells; the burning in his arms was more intense than anything he had experienced during a basketball or weightlifting workout.

Dr. Sharp put his hand to his mouth to stop himself from yelling.

Maazi's shield absorbed the bullet faster than it normally would have.

"Aha! Look what we found!" Maazi yelled and hit a nearby metal table at the same moment the shield device slapped the ground, so he failed to notice its landing.

"It worked!" the subservient FORM emphasized.

Jack sighed. Luck was with him, but his fingers started to slip.

"Hurry," Maazi said as he disengaged his shield, "this is a game changer! We're going to use these disruptors to our advantage. Take them back to Earth. Put them in a warehouse or something so their military *thinks* they had some extras they didn't know about. We'll adjust our shield parameters, and when they start using the disruptors, they'll get an unwelcome surprise."

"I like the way you think, Bohanna."

"I know. That's what makes me better than you."

"Of course, Bohanna."

Maazi removed the decoder, and the subservient FORM carried the disruptor out of the lab. Maazi stood and took a deep breath. He put his hands on his muscular hips and grinned. "We're going to have some fun with this."

Jack couldn't hold on any longer.

Maazi flipped his cloak to the side and strode slowly to the door.

Jack's grip failed. He slid down the pipe and hit the floor just as the lab door clicked closed.

"Oh my gosh!" Jack whispered. "Sorry, Dr. Sharp. I couldn't hold on any longer."

"Jack," Dr. Sharp said, "that was too close a call. Get up here as fast as you can. They might come back."

"Right!"

Jack snatched the shield device and stuffed it all the way in his pocket this time. He wiped his hands and waved them in the air to dry them off and shook out his muscles.

"Okay, here we go."

Jack began his ascent. The last five feet were difficult, but his adrenaline helped him make it to the grate. He reached for the lip of the ductwork and swung his body over.

They heard footsteps outside, and the latch to the lab door began to twist.

"Now, Jack!" Dr. Sharp ordered.

Jack heaved his right leg up into the ductwork, then pulled his left leg through.

As the lab door opened, Dr. Sharp softly closed the grate.

A FORM carrying a dead alligator walked in and threw it in the organics processor, which did its job straight away. The FORM left the lab with no indication that it noticed Jack and Dr. Sharp.

Jack held up the wristband shield device. "This better have been worth that!"

"It had better," Dr. Sharp agreed. "And we'd better find a way to communicate with Earth. Our military, our whole planet, is in significant danger!"

Chapter 26

San Antonio, TX

"Ryker, they're here!" Jessie said excitedly, getting up from the Vaughns' front room couch. She opened the door.

She and Ryker had been back for nearly an hour with supplies in hand—and the wonderful news that Jack was still alive. Grace had nearly fainted when they told her. A sliver of hope existed!

"Here you go, Jessie," a CFI comrade in camo said as she handed Jessie a new pair of Ozzies.

"This is amazing. Thank you for bringing them," Jessie said.

"Anything for a fellow soldier," the woman said. "Good luck to you all." The woman waved and walked back to a Humvee.

Jessie closed the front door and hurried to hand Ryker the replacement Ozzies.

"Thanks," Ryker offered as he clipped them in place. He stood up and took a jog across the living room. "Ouch!" he said and sat down on the couch.

"What is it?" Jessie asked.

"A, uh, burning pain or something where the metal posts stick out of my legs."

Jessie's face paled. *No! That's a tell-tale sign that infection is developing.* "Stay there, let me wash your legs up a bit better." Jessie filled a bowl with warm water and gentle soap, set it on the end table by the couch, then knelt next to Ryker and looked at his legs. The skin around his metal posts was growing red and inflamed. *Not good*, she thought. She washed his skin and the metal posts.

Jessie knew that washing the site was the equivalent of putting a bandage on a bullet hole. She whispered under her breath. "We're going to need stronger antibiotics."

"Stronger antibiotics?" Ryker repeated.

"Where can you find those?" Grace asked.

"At the hospital. But I'm not sure they'll have any to spare," Jessie speculated.

"What do we do, then?" Grace wondered.

"Let me reach out to some colleagues. In the meantime, let's slather the site with some antibiotic gel. That could slow the infection. Do you have a first-aid kit?"

"Yes, I'll be right back." Grace went to the bathroom and returned with a white box filled with medical contents.

Jessie rummaged through it, found an antibiotic gel, and rubbed it on Ryker's legs.

"Thank you, doctor," Ryker said, trying to lighten the tense mood.

"Ha, I'm no doctor, but I've treated a few wounds in my day," Jessie said. She sat back and assessed her treatment. "All right, that will have to do for now. Let me see what I can do about some antibiotics." Jessie got her phone and started texting.

Ryker looked at Grace. Her eyes were filled with motherly worry.

"It's going to be okay, Mom."

Grace nodded.

Jessie gave Grace a reassuring smile, but she wasn't sure she believed Ryker.

Chapter 27

FORM Ship

Dr. Sharp wiggled back through the biosphere wall opening that Maazi had created. Jack reached down and helped him onto the dirt.

"Thank you, my boy," Dr. Sharp said. He bent over and brushed his knees. "These old bones don't handle things like they used to."

"Feeling old all of a sudden?" Maazi's voice blared through the biosphere.

Dr. Sharp and Jack both startled. They looked at each other. *Where was the voice coming from?*

Neither of them had noticed that the biosphere door was cracked open. Maazi pulled it all the way open and stepped through. He laughed so hard Dr. Sharp knew he was forcing it.

"Look at you two," Maazi said. He coughed; the laughing made him overwork his lungs. He was still in need of rest and additional sustenance to recover his enormous body from all the fighting and flying he had done. "Vigilantes!" Maazi laughed more and walked toward them. "You found a way through our ductwork. Wow, I guess now we should make you a couple of heroes!"

Dr. Sharp and Jack were at a loss for words. They thought they had gone undetected.

"Did you find anything interesting?" Maazi queried calmly.

Neither of them spoke. They didn't know if Maazi was aware they had taken his personal shield device.

"Our nutrient source, I assume. I mean, I'm sure Jack had to have seen something while dangling in the air like that."

Jack swallowed.

"Jack, I gotta hand it to you. You have some epic arm strength, kid! All that basketball and training stuff. Boy, it sure saved your life back there. I kept hoping you were going to fall and break something." Maazi chuckled as he reached down and picked up a handful of sand. He let it sieve through his fingers, from one hand to the other, and stared at them. "We have a problem, gentlemen. Seems Jack's brother, Ryker, killed one of my people."

Jack avoided eye contact with Maazi.

"You know, there's one thing we FORM value more than anything else, Jack. Do you remember what that is?"

Jack was silent.

"Answer me!" Maazi screamed. His voice reverberated through the biosphere.

"Water. I think it's water," Jack mumbled with his eyes fixed to the ground.

"Decent guess. Longevity, Jack. Water is the means. But longevity is the reason!" Maazi raised his arm and threw the handful of sand in Jack's eyes.

Jack gasped and screamed as the sand pierced his eyeballs.

Maazi yelled like a maniac, "And when someone kills my people, Jack, *I kill theirs!*"

Maazi darted for Jack and shoved him into Dr. Sharp.

Dr. Sharp absorbed Jack's fall. They tumbled to the ground. Dr. Sharp knew something bad was about to happen. Amidst the turmoil, he snatched Maazi's shield device from Jack's back pocket and shoved it under his butt as he lay on the ground.

Maazi picked Jack up by his T-shirt and screamed, "And don't think for a *second* that I make a revenge-filled death quick. You, my young man, are about to suffer the *full* wrath of my fury! I'm going to make you pay for what your brother did—and for my people's suffering!

"And as for you, Dr. Sharp," Maazi glared at him, "since you like experiments, we're going to run one on *you*. I'm not going to provide any more food or water for your decrepit old body. We're about to enter Earth's atmosphere. If you want to eat or drink ever again, we're going to see if you can find your way off this ship and back onto Earth: I mean, that shouldn't be too difficult now that you know how to walk through our ductwork and all."

Maazi spat on Dr. Sharp's face and yanked Jack's shirt. Jack screamed at the top of his lungs as Maazi dragged him toward the exit.

"Dr. Sharp, help!"

Dr. Sharp had no recourse. He could only yell, "Jack!" with outstretched arms.

The biosphere door slammed shut. As quickly as the scene had developed, it disintegrated. Dr. Sharp listened to Jack's screams in the corridor.

His pleas grew distant, then faded altogether.

Dr. Sharp looked around. The other biosphere inhabitants looked on, wide-eyed. Deeply trauma-stricken, they wanted nothing to do with Dr. Sharp. He seemed to bring nothing but trouble.

Dr. Sharp started to cry and let out a howl. *How could this get any worse?* He slapped his leg and yelled at himself, "You moron! How could you let this happen? You've led an innocent boy to immeasurable suffering."

He sulked with his head in his knees, then inhaled and exhaled deeply and tried to gather himself. "All right, all right. There's no time for this. Sobbing won't help Jack. I have to figure something out."

He wiped his eyes, pulled his emotions together, and crawled to where he and Jack had covered up the iron-ore infused rocks. He used a waxy leaf to pull the electrical cables out of the way, then unburied the rocks. He selected two large rocks. He set one on the ground, grabbed the second, then stood five feet away from the first. He set the second rock on the ground and started to slide it toward the first. Once he was about a foot away, the first rock zipped across the dirt and slammed into the second one. "Eureka!" Dr. Sharp hollered. "That's a powerful magnet!"

One of the other humanoids looked vaguely curious, and repeated, "Yeeka?"

Dr. Sharp ignored him. He grabbed several leaves and stripped them into thin sections, which he wrapped together to make a series of strings. He tied the strings in a web design around six rocks and hung each of them more than a foot apart, dangling over the biosphere's entryway.

"There we go," he whispered to himself, hoping no one would hear what he said. "Now, when the next one of you comes in, those should scramble the processor in your robohead."

Dr. Sharp went back to the spot where he'd left Maazi's personal shield device. He picked it up and blew on it to dust it off. He touched the screen to assess its function. "Interesting," he emphasized. "I knew it. They use quaternary code!" He pressed several digital icons to get a feel for how the device worked.

He accidentally opened the shield function. As the purple orb encompassed him, it blew another hole open in the wall next to him. "*That* could be dangerous." He closed the shield and saw what appeared to be the main screen.

"Wait a minute! I bet anything that the code Ryker discovered has some unique capabilities." He took a moment to recall the code then punched it in.

His eyes stretched wide. "Well now ... *that's* more than I bargained for!"

Chapter 28

FORM Ship

Jack gagged as he came to. His vision cycled in and out of color. *How long have I been out?* He didn't know. He felt a cloth wrapped around his head and mouth. It not only muffled his screams, it messed with his head. The terror he felt trumped any fear he had ever experienced in life or dreams. His arms were throbbing; Maazi's grip had been like a metal vice on steroids. Fingerprints were still embedded in Jack's forearms. He couldn't tell if the liquid coming out of his nose was tears or snot. *Or is it blood?* Using a tissue was the last thing on his mind: his life was on the verge of ending.

Jack breathed in and out to the point of hyperventilation. There was no way out. What could anyone do with hands tied to a metal bench, in the back corner of an alien's reconnaissance room filled with plants and enormous bioluminescent tanks of cyanobacteria soup? He screamed again even though he knew Maazi wouldn't do anything about it.

He was forced to look on as Maazi and a female FORM analyzed an oblong, transparent screen that showed footage of Corpus Christi, Texas. They didn't care that Jack listened to their conversation.

"Taahiya, how many troops have they gathered?" Maazi asked.

"Over 50,000 so far. More are rolling in every hour," Taahiya said.

Maazi laughed. "They're going to need *so* many more! But you know what?"

"What, Bohanna?"

"It doesn't matter *how* many they gather, we'll wreck every one of them. And it's comical. I said three days, but they're straight up idiots! If they took me seriously, shame on them. We're taking their life source, for crying out loud. Why would I make some set of rules to fight by? Gosh, I'm not sure I've ever met a species that's easier to con than this one. There's nothing like giving someone false hope, then snatching it away!" Maazi sighed in delight. "There's no freaking reason for us to wait any longer." Maazi turned to Jack. "Especially now that they're *killing* my people, Jack! Let's just take out every one of you sorry excuses for higher life forms. What do you say? Should we get back to Earth?"

Barely conscious, Jack inhaled and exhaled repeatedly. He hardly comprehended what the FORM were saying.

Maazi laughed. "Wow. You can put a ball in a hoop, but you got nothing when it comes to torture. All I did was slap you a few times. You're certainly not built to take a beating."

Taahiya cut in. "Bohanna, should we begin the descent?"

Jack watched Maazi ponder. He didn't know that Maazi had a lot to consider.

The massive bodies of the FORM required tremendous amounts of nutrients. Before and after battle, that requirement nearly tripled. Although the FORM had found ways to increase their lifespan and maintain premier physical condition, it came at a cost; nutrients and energy diffused more slowly through a hydrogel-based blood transport system than what evolution had organized, and nutrient diffusion across titanium nanocells was slower than lipid-based cells. As a result, it took their bodies longer to recover after significant exertion.

They'd need an extra dose of sustenance before resuming battle, and then at least three days to fully recover.

"Yes," Maazi answered Taahiya, "we'll begin a descent, but let's wait to breach their atmosphere until first thing in their morning. We'll arrive a day early, give them a little leash, then catch them off guard."

"I'll make it happen," Taahiya said.

"And as for you." Maazi walked toward Jack. "Let's start Round Two!"

Jack braced himself. Maazi's next punch may as well have been a sledgehammer hitting his face. His eye burned; he knew it was bleeding. He also knew Maazi was right; he wasn't built to take a beating. Jack felt himself passing out. If ever he needed Ryker's protective hand, it was now.

Chapter 29

The Vaughn Home, San Antonio, TX

Grace looked out her front window. Dawn was breaking. Under any other circumstance, she would have taken the time to appreciate the morning light as it illuminated the treetops, then the street. But this morning, she didn't. She was too tired—not physically, emotionally. Neither she, Ryker, nor Jessie had slept a minute through the night. Not only because Ryker's status had worsened, making sleep unwelcome, but because every news network displayed image after image of the impending visitor ships. Myriads of news anchors offered their opinions about the visitors, now also arriving a day earlier than Maazi had indicated.

Ryker's ringtone startled all of them.

Who could be calling at this hour? Grace wondered. She looked at Ryker. He gave a weakened look of approval for her to answer.

"Hello?" Grace said.

A middle-aged man's voice came through with a choppy message. "Yes, ye— ... Doc— Sharp— I'm try— Capt— Ryk— Vau—"

"I'm sorry, you're coming through choppy. You're trying to reach Ryker Vaughn?"

"Ye—"

"This is his mother. Ryker's not feeling well at the moment."

Grace looked at Ryker. His forehead was moist; fever was setting in—a telltale sign that infection was raging. Jessie had been unsuccessful—so far—at finding anyone who could get them stronger antibiotics.

"Must speak— This— a matt— of life or dea—"

Grace's ears perked up. She thought she heard *life or death*. "Sir, who did you say this was?"

"Doc— —arp."

"Dr. Sharp!" Grace put her hand to her mouth. "You mean, *the* Dr. Sharp—taken by the FORM?"

Ryker and Jessie, who were both sitting on the living room couch, sat straight up.

"Dr. Sharp?" Ryker repeated. "What?"

"Ye—" his voice crackled.

Grace switched it to speaker phone. "You're on speaker. Can you speak slower so we can understand you better?" As much as she wanted to ask how Dr. Sharp was able to call them and where he was, she knew there wasn't time for that. She sensed his urgency.

"Not much time—Maazi leader … FORM—hurting Jack."

They heard enough to understand what Dr. Sharp was trying to say: one of the FORM was hurting Jack. What the intent was? They didn't know. How they were hurting him? Their guess was as good as anyone's.

Ryker punched the couch and growled. "We have to get to him!"

"Ryker, please," Grace pleaded, "let Dr. Sharp finish." She moved the phone's microphone closer to her mouth. "Dr. Sharp, what can we do?"

"Whatever you ca— Ryk— get on this shi— as soo— Have to warn— military. Disrup— not work. They reverse —shield!"

Ryker spoke in the phone. "Are you saying that I need to get on the ship?"

"Yes."

"We don't understand the other thing. What about the shields? Disruptors?" Grace asked.

The phone was silent.

"Dr. Sharp?" Grace pleaded.

Silence.

"Dr. Sharp!"

The connection was lost.

Ryker wiped his brow and shook his head. "I have to help Jack." He swung his legs off the couch and tried to stand. He crumpled to the ground instead; the infection in his legs burned so badly, it hurt to walk with the Ozzies. He dragged himself toward his wheelchair.

"Ryker, stop!" Jessie begged and tried to get Ryker back on the couch.

"No, Jessie. No! Let me go." Ryker broke free and dragged himself to his wheelchair.

Grace cupped her head in her hands and cried. It was a rare moment in her life; she didn't have the will to do anything. Jack being hurt. Ryker suffering. The stress was compounding.

Ryker pulled himself into his wheelchair and wheeled himself to the porch. He slid out of the seat, crawled down the porch stairs, onto the front lawn, and yelled toward the sky, "Bring him back and take me! You worthless beings! I'm the one you want, you know that. Get your sorry butts back here and *take me!*"

"Ryker!" Grace shouted from the porch. "What are you doing?"

"What I should have done a long time ago!"

"This is *not* the way to handle this."

"There aren't any other options at this point, Mom!"

Flashing lights from a police car rounded the corner. Ryker watched as a policeman approached.

"Sir," an officer spoke as he pulled alongside Ryker, "everything all right?"

Ryker looked blankly at the pulsating LEDs on the cop car. "No," he sank his head. "Everything's *not* all right."

"Come on, son," the officer said, "you should get back in your house. There's nothing you can do out here."

Ryker avoided the officer's stare and looked skyward. "You're right. There's nothing I can do out here. But I *have* to do something up there!"

Chapter 30

Corpus Christi, TX

Brighton had just finished taping fresh gauze on the largest gash of his wounded leg when he heard subwoofer-like hums of air percussions outside the American Bank Center. The rumbles vibrated the deepest innards of the building.

It was the sound—the moment—every soldier in Corpus Christi, Port Aransas, and all the surrounding regions expected to hear, only it came a day early.

"Brighton," the president hollered from outside the convention center doors, "you better get out here!"

Brighton rushed outside and stopped on the front steps. He listened to the warning cry of sirens as he observed the chaotic battle setup: tens of thousands of military trucks, tanks, helicopters, battleships, aircraft carriers in the Gulf of Mexico, and hundreds of thousands of soldiers from over one hundred nations, with assault rifles at the ready—then shielded his eyes and looked up in the sky along with Gen. Childress and the president. "It's time," Brighton said to no one in particular.

"They're a day early!" the president yelled.

"We never actually believed they would do what they claimed," Gen. Childress said. "We assembled what we could. We have twice as many armaments in San Antonio ready for battle."

"We may need every last ounce of it," the president warned.

The first two FORM ships entered the troposphere with enormity and prowess. Their silver surfaces alone were blinding enough, but the two rotating conveyors with building-sized razor protrusions on either side of each middle ring structure scattered the morning Sun's rays in every direction. The ships angled toward Earth and hovered within feet of the ocean surface.

"Dr. Sharp's images certainly didn't do *that* justice," Brighton stated.

"They're far more looming than I, than I anticipated," the president stuttered.

"We need to ready every weapon," Gen. Childress said with a fist in the air. "No use gawking. Time to fight!"

Before he could reach his comm system to bark an order, every onlooker was distracted by the snap of a thousand lightning bolts and accompanying thunder.

"What the ... look!" the president said, pointing to the sky.

The FORM's third and largest ship approached. The city-sized black behemoth with four-mile-long arms extending from the hexagonal core caused mini cyclones and billowing clouds to form as it entered Earth's atmosphere. The astatine material on the giant ship's surface caught fire as it interacted with the troposphere where high concentrations of double-bonded oxygen ignited. Flames enveloped its exterior and formed billows of gray smoke that generated intrinsic lightning storms along the ship's surface. Thunderclaps boomed endlessly over the ocean.

"My gosh. It's like how a volcano self-produces lightning," Brighton gawked and watched the president shake his head slowly.

Disbelief mixed with reality and confused all their emotions.

The electrical storm illuminated the gray clouds surrounding the ship. It took several minutes for the full shape of the ship to emerge through the rolling supercell. As the lightning and supercell storms receded, the ship's long, branched arms extended across the Corpus Christi Bay. The center of the craft stopped directly over Port Aransas. Its surface glowed a brilliant red; the flames had forged its metal.

Soldiers, generals, leaders, and onlookers stood paralyzed in silence; war was upon them, but they were unable to do anything else.

"Sir! Sir!" Brighton heard the voice of a female officer calling for him as she ran toward him from a tented warehouse to the south.

"What is it?" Brighton asked.

The officer caught her breath. "The disruptors!"

"What about them? They were destroyed and accosted."

"No, no. I found three more. In a warehouse." The officer pointed to the large tent.

Brighton, Gen. Childress, and the president looked at each other. The hairs on their necks stood erect.

"We may have a fighting chance!" Brighton yelled. He turned to the officer and asked, "Are they damaged?"

"No, they appear ready for use."

Gen. Childress chimed in. "Get each one of those on a Humvee, now! And put a micro army of protection around each one. Those may be our most valuable possessions! And listen, these freaks aren't going to wait around for us to prepare any further. You!" Gen. Childress pointed to a group of soldiers. "Help her!"

"Yes, sir!" They all saluted and ran to execute the order.

"What's the next move?" the president asked as they all looked at the three FORM ships hovering motionless over the waters of Corpus Christi Bay and the Gulf of Mexico.

"We fight. Like every human life depends on it, because it does," Gen. Childress said. He grabbed a flask from his camouflage coat and took a swig—an act against protocol, but no one cared given the circumstance—then reached for his comm unit. His voice boomed through comm systems in mobile barracks, dozens of which were positioned up and down the beaches of Corpus Christi. "Listen up, everyone. Let your training guide you. Your life, and the life of everyone on Earth, is in your hands. If *ever* there was anything worth fighting for, this is it!"

Gen. Childress planned to say more, but just then he and everyone else in a fifty-mile radius were knocked off their feet by a series of crippling explosions that emanated from Port Aransas. The black FORM ship was unleashing a sequence of annihilating shockwave blasts that moved heaven and Earth beneath it.

Brighton got to his feet as fast as he had fallen. He assessed the surroundings. Buildings were crumbling. Tanks were overturned. Every major stronghold was damaged.

Gen. Childress didn't have to give the command to attack. Earth's military forces knew precisely how to respond.

Surface-to-air missiles lit up the morning sky; the sum of firework shows across the nation on the 4th of July would have paled in comparison to the amount of black powder that soared through the air and rained down on its targets.

Thousands of FORM meliks launched from the lateral areas of their silver ships.

Brighton dove behind a barricade and grabbed a MANPAD. He launched two missiles as fast as possible. As he reloaded a third missile, his eye caught a glimpse of the Corpus Christi Bay waters. Something was wrong; the warm waters slurped and started to recede.

"Tsunami!" He yelled. "Everybody, run!"

A water swell developed in the distance. Barges closest to the outlet of the Bay rode the initial hump with minimal damage. Boats a half mile closer weren't so lucky; they couldn't maneuver their hulls fast enough to avoid the thirty-five-foot wave. It spun them like kites in the wind.

Brighton, Gen. Childress, and the president raced to Marine One, which had been readied in case the president needed a quick escape.

Brighton ignored the pain in his injured leg and kept pace with the president.

Gen. Childress yelled into his comm as they ran. "Get every jet off the ground. Black Hawks up! Prep the inland tanks and trucks. Everything by the shore is about to be under water!"

Brighton watched the wave rush toward land as they sprinted to the helicopter. Like any other gargantuan wave, this tsunami was merciless.

Meliks rode the wave like surfboards and used it as a catapult to eliminate nearby ships and troops. Human vessels weren't so capable; neither gunners, battleships, nor sailboats were equipped to wrestle Mother Nature.

"We're not going to make it!" Brighton warned.

"We have to!" the president yelled and increased his pace.

Two dozen soldiers came up behind them, hoping to catch a ride on Marine One.

"It can only handle twenty passengers, twenty-five max!" the president screamed.

Four Secret Service agents looked at each other. They knew they would have to sacrifice themselves to allow the president and soldiers to board safely. They stopped in their tracks, one saluted him, and they bravely faced the incoming wave.

The president looked at them as he ran past. There wasn't time to thank them. All he could do was offer a glance of gratitude.

"Get ready!" the president yelled to Marine One's pilot as soon as he and Brighton were within thirty feet of the helicopter.

Neither Brighton nor the president were sure Gen. Childress would make it. Due to his less-than-peak physical condition and stamina, he was lagging behind despite his Ozzie.

The tsunami peaked at forty feet when it reached the shore and began its destruction on land.

Brighton grabbed the president's jacket and forced him faster toward the helicopter. The salty foam was no more than a hundred feet away, locked and loaded with untold amounts of potential damage-inducing energy. "Jump!" Brighton yelled as they reached the stairs that led to the fuselage.

The president jumped to the stairs and made it on.

Brighton turned around and yelled at Gen. Childress who was thirty feet behind. "RUN!"

Gen. Childress switched his Ozzie to battle mode. The power of the Ozzie jolted him. His head nearly whiplashed as he sprinted forward; unfortunately, the world wasn't able to witness the speed of a middle-aged man who could have won the 100-meter dash. His newfound power brought him to the helicopter as it was lifting off.

Still on the ground, just below the copter, Brighton swiveled the shoulder strap of the MANPAD he was carrying so it rested on his back, put his hands in a cupping shape, and braced his body to create a catapult for Gen. Childress.

Gen. Childress connected his Ozzie foot with Brighton's hands and leaped with unexpected ability. He grabbed Marine One's stair cables and pulled himself toward the fuselage. Two soldiers pulled him the rest of the way in and squeezed him between the other human sardines in the metal canister.

The helicopter whirred twenty feet into the air.

"Where's Brighton?" the president begged.

Gen. Childress shook his head; the universal signal for, *he didn't make it.*

"Throw a ladder!" the president ordered. "We have to at least try!"

A marine in the back of the fuselage tossed a rope ladder out the rear door.

Brighton grabbed a rung just as the roar of unforgiving ocean waters reached his feet.

Everyone in the chopper looked at the marine with hopeful eyes; awaiting a signal if Brighton made it. The marine watched out the door as seawaters crashed over Brighton's head and rose at the same rate as the helicopter. The waters carpeted the American Bank Center, swallowing it from view. The ladder jostled back and forth wildly, causing the helicopter to shake violently and nearly lose control.

"There's no way he hung onto that," the marine said under her breath.

"Look out!" Gen. Childress yelled.

Everyone's attention diverted to the front of Marine One. A melik had maneuvered directly in front of the helicopter and stopped its forward motion. The melik hovered in tandem with the helicopter as it rose— saltwater nipping at its wheels—but didn't fire, seemingly taunting the passengers to either attack or get ready for an assault.

"Blow that thing out of the air!" Gen. Childress ordered.

"I can't, we only have defensives on this helicopter!" the pilot said.

The melik opened a carriage on its underbelly that revealed a powerful weapon.

"Incoming!" Gen. Childress yelled.

The pilots and passengers readied themselves for a volley of firepower but were met with surprise as a missile tracer, source unknown, zipped past Marine One's armored windshield and connected with the melik's weapon, dissecting it into a thousand pieces. The melik craft rocketed backward and ruptured in two. A FORM flailed out the bottom and crashed into the tortuous waters below.

Gen. Childress looked out the window to see where the missile had come from. "Ha ha!" he hollered. "Once a soldier, always a soldier!"

Those that could looked out the window and saw Brighton gripping precariously to Marine One's rope ladder with one hand—and holding a smoking MANPAD in the other.

Brighton smiled and yelled, "No way I'm letting them take us out that easy!"

The passengers cheered. Brighton climbed the rest of the way up the ladder and entered the fuselage, and everyone cheered even louder.

But the celebrations were fleeting. Below Marine One, the FORM ships were ripping the battlefield apart. Port Aransas and Corpus Christi already were unrecognizable.

Everything was buried under water, mobile artilleries were ruined, and the majority of armaments and barracks were rendered useless. Air-to-air combat was tilted in the FORM's favor; their purple orbs absorbed and discharged blast after blast of annihilating energy that crippled their human counterparts with ease. And global central command, the American Bank Center, was destroyed.

Within minutes, Earth's forces fell flat in the face of the FORM's fury. What they'd expected to be a valiant battle was a clear slaughter.

Brighton took a deep breath. "Our last hope may be that the disruptors made it through," he said. "You," Brighton pointed to a soldier who had the most wiggle room, "patch into the comms and see if anyone knows where they're at."

The soldier went to work. Within moments, he reported, "Two of them are viable on Humvees making their way inland!"

Brighton looked out the cockpit windshield. He could see the Humvees speeding in tandem up the streets of Corpus Christi, escaping the incoming waters and careening through fireballs of destruction. "There!" he yelled to the pilot and pointed to their position, "follow them to a landing spot. We need those disruptors!"

The pilot tipped Marine One forward and followed the Humvees to a Whataburger parking lot. As the pilot began to lower Marine One to the ground, a melik flanked it and sent an unforgiving series of blasts to its tail boom. The rear of the chopper exploded, flinging two soldiers out the rear. The helicopter spun out of control.

"Hang on!" Brighton yelled to everyone yet no one as he gripped a bar in preparation for a crash landing.

The pilot implemented the crash-landing sequence. He ignored the controls for the rear rotor since it no longer existed, and tipped and turned the main rotor blades to reduce the helicopter's spin. He knew if he could control the torsional forces just enough, the armored body of Marine One would lessen the blow of the crash.

The helicopter thumped the ground once, heaved into the air, flipped like a sausage roll, and slammed into the Whataburger drive-thru sign. Its armored metal yielded like a boxer's face after a hundred punches. It ripped the ground and slid a hundred feet before losing the battle with physics.

~

Brighton's cheek was warm and wet. He wiped it. Blood. He didn't know if it was his. He pulled his face off Marine One's floor and spat. He examined his body. *Minimal trauma.* The bitter blood wasn't his; it was the marine's next to him. He wiped his mouth, forced himself to stand, and looked around. *How many dead?* He counted. *At least fifteen.* And *who* was dead? Not Gen. Childress; he was breathing. And not the president; he was already wrapping his head with a torn sleeve of his jacket.

The chopper gurgled. Its fuel line spat jet fuel on the pavement immediately below a cluster of flames rising from the rotor.

"We have to get out of here before it blows!" Brighton yelled.

He pulled Gen. Childress to his feet and forced him and the president out of the fuselage. A few others straggled behind, and they all ran like dogs on the loose. They reached the end of the restaurant parking lot and realized the risk of an exploding helicopter suddenly seemed safer than the danger they met; a melik rose from behind a shopping center and angled its nose downward, ready to finish its prey.

"The disruptor!" Gen. Childress yelled. "We'll provide cover!"

Gen. Childress pulled a handgun from his belt and another from a strap on his calf and tossed one to the president. A handful of soldiers likewise cocked their handguns. Everyone armed fired at the melik while Brighton ran to the Humvee, leapt into its truck bed, and powered up the disruptor.

The melik was encircled in purple, swallowing the hordes of bullets sent its way.

Brighton aimed the disruptor directly at the undulating waves of energy and fired their last hope of protection. "Eat it, you sack of trash!" he demanded. "Everyone fire into the hole I create!"

As Brighton fired, a portion of the melik's shield disintegrated, allowing a brief window of opportunity for firepower to pierce its golden surface. Bullet after bullet pockmarked its smooth lines. The damage was minimal but the attack effective. The melik thrust upward to avoid further damage and raced toward one of the FORM's silver ships, which, until now, the group hadn't realized was approaching their position.

They didn't know that the melik had been a distraction.

"Get a crew of jets over here so we can use the disruptors on one of the big ones!" Brighton ordered.

A soldier in the Humvee reached for a comm and requested jetfighter support. Within seconds, a V shape of F-22s approached.

"Gen. Childress, man the second disruptor," Brighton said and pointed to the second Humvee with a still-intact disruptor.

Brighton looked for a landmark on the silver ship. "Tell the pilots to fire at the top left side. We'll aim the disruptors there."

Brighton and Gen. Childress gripped the triggers of the disruptors and aimed them synergistically. The cluster of jets released five dozen missiles—enough to level a small city—anticipating the hole Brighton and Gen. Childress would create.

Yet as Brighton and Gen. Childress fired the disruptors, no hole developed.

The FORM ship's enormous purple ball of plasma metabolized the missiles.

"Kick up the energy!" Brighton yelled.

Gen. Childress dialed up the disruptor and squeezed the triggers with fury. Brighton mirrored the action.

A second set of twice as many missiles flew toward the target where a hole should have been created. Yet as the missiles contacted the FORM ship's shield, they melded seamlessly with its energy, molding into its curvature and not only became part of the shield construct, but inflamed it.

"What's happening?" Gen. Childress asked.

Brighton shook his head.

"Give it one more go!"

The two of them fired the disruptors again. Attack after attack, missile after missile, made contact with the shield to no effect.

No! Brighton thought. *The disruptors are having the opposite effect on the big ship!*

"You seeing what I'm seeing?" Brighton asked Gen. Childress and the president.

The FORM ship's purple orb was enlarging rapidly.

"Kill the disruptors!" the president ordered. "They're not working this time."

Brighton and Gen. Childress released the disruptor triggers.

They all watched breathlessly as the silver ship's energetic envelope began to pulsate. The FORM ship, or at least its pilots, seemed to recognize the disruptors had stopped. It maneuvered away from what was left of the battle zone and careened twenty miles inland where depots of trucks, tanks, and troops were being held in reserve.

"Corpus Christi!" Gen. Childress yelled.

He, Brighton, and the president scaled a ladder on the side of a tall building. They watched as the FORM ship formed the imminent teardrop shape and released its deadly volatile energy onto the depot's vehicles.

The damage was blinding. The discharge launched the waters of Corpus Christi Bay skyward over two miles high. Not one ounce of cement from any building within five miles of the blast center remained. The destruction was all-encompassing.

As the shockwave reached them, Brighton thudded onto his back and was dogpiled by Gen. Childress and the president. They gasped; the air in their lungs was sucked dry by the implosion/explosion sequence. They shielded their eyes and watched as what was once Corpus Christi became the FORM's dominion.

The second silver ship engaged its rotating blades and tilled miles upon miles of Earth's crust in minutes, creating canyons, new bays of water, and valleys of death to anything close by.

Battleships sank. Tanks were flattened. Troops were decimated.

Brighton heard an unexpected voice on his comm.

"Col. Brighton," the voice said with tangible sadness.

"What is it?"

"It's San Antonio, sir. The FORM. They sent a thousand troops, compromised everything."

Brighton ripped a pipe off the rooftop and threw it down in anger. "Our fortifications in San Antonio are," Brighton struggled for the word, "*smothered!*"

The president looked at Brighton and Gen. Childress and asked, "What if we can adjust the settings on the disruptors?"

"It's no use," Brighton yelled. "The communications building is where the main activation controls are for the disruptors. They're dead now."

They all stared in the distance, watching the destruction play out before them.

Hope—the quintessential component of survival—was extinguished.

In less than an hour since their arrival, the FORM had immobilized, no, incapacitated the lifeblood of Earth. And the global army that had converged upon Corpus Christi was ruined.

The disruptors—once thought to be Earth's saving grace—had proven to be its kryptonite. Any expectation that mankind had of protecting their home, let alone the life-giving substance of water, vanished.

They had lost.

Earth's water—and by default humankind—now belonged to the FORM.

Chapter 31

The Vaughn Home, San Antonio, TX

Ryker startled from a comatose state. A thud reverberated in his head. The slobber on his chin didn't bother him; his headache did. He touched his forehead. It was hot! *Ugh,* he moaned internally, *the fever is even worse.* The monotony of news channels in the background blurred his mind. He heard something about annihilation in Corpus Christi, but it didn't sink in fully. His head was hurting too much to think.

He wiped his eyes, blinked a half dozen times, and scanned his surroundings. "Mom? Jessie?" *They must be outside.* It was dark. He checked his cell phone for the time. *It's the middle of the day!*

Ryker cracked the blinds and looked out the front window. Grace and Jessie were talking on the front lawn. Jessie was holding her phone in the air, trying to get reception. Her voice was muffled by the window. He heard her mention something about letting Brighton or Gen. Childress know about Dr. Sharp's phone call, but she hadn't been able to get through.

A thud in the kitchen diverted his attention. It was the same sound that had awakened him. He slipped his cell phone into his basketball shorts pocket and sat up slowly.

He reached for the new Ozzies Jessie had given him and clipped them on.

Another thud.

He grabbed the Glock on the end table next to him and inched his body forward to look down the hallway. He couldn't see into the kitchen from that vantage point. He listened.

Silence.

He shimmied his backside to the edge of the couch and grimaced as he stood. The pain in his legs was nearly unbearable. His leg stumps were swollen, and puss was starting to ooze from the skin regions around his metal posts. But he had to push through; he could sense someone, or some*thing*, was in the house.

His forearm muscles rippled as he gripped the handle of the Glock. The contour of his chest flexed with each breath. To stay quiet, he breathed slowly through his mouth, but he couldn't limit the sound of the gears in his legs. He peered around the landing wall of the staircase into the family room.

Empty.

Cautiously, he moved toward the kitchen, sliding along the hallway wall that led from the front door to the kitchen. As he approached the opening, he saw a hue of blue light. His heart tried to push through his sternum. He knew what was waiting, rather, *who* was waiting.

"So, you want to be brave, Ryker Vaughn?" Maazi growled from the kitchen. "Become a *hero*. Well," he laughed, "I'll let you be brave. There's nothing left to save here."

Ryker stood in paralysis. *What do I do?* He wasn't capable of fighting, he knew that. Yet adrenaline coursed through his body, numbing the pain in his head and legs.

"Is my brother alive?" he asked from the hallway without yet seeing Maazi.

"What does it matter? We've already done what we had to do. No one is going to survive much longer."

"If he's alive, you can take me to the ship in his place. If he's dead, I'll kill you."

Maazi spat out the water he was drinking. "Wow, you're an overconfident prick. That could get you in trouble, you know." He snorted. "Would you trust the answer I gave you anyway?"

"If you've already done what you came for, why are you here?"

"Aww, Ryker, the never-ending soldier! There's more to taking over a planet than just getting what you *need*. Sometimes, you have to take what you *want*. And despite what your empathetic folk teach, revenge is sweet! It's simple, really. I want to kill you, personally. And I want your brother to watch. Or vice versa. But first things first, I want you to suffer. You know, 'tenderize' you a bit.

"And I don't mean physically. No, no. There's more to torture. I want you to suffer *emotionally*, you freaking drudge! I lost *thousands* of my people because of you! And in case you didn't get the *memo*, we like to live a long time! So, I'm going to make you watch me *kill* your brother just like I watched your people kill mine, *then* I'll kill you and polish off the rest of this miserable species!"

Maazi threw the kitchen table through the back wall of their house, overturned the fridge, and emerged from around the corner. As quickly as he started, he stopped. Awe-struck, he stared at Ryker standing in the hallway.

"Holy crap, Ryker!"

Maazi admired Ryker's muscular body, chiseled like a statue with titanium components fused to his legs, like his own extremities.

"What the—" Maazi started. "*Ryker*," he spoke with surprise, "a *god* in the making." His voice was filled with amazement. "You patterned your body after mine! Inferior, of course, I mean look at that infection, but wow! You look incredible."

Maazi dragged his fingers along the metal components of his legs as he compared Ryker and himself.

"Don't flatter yourself!" Ryker said. He wanted to shoot Maazi, but the size of his body alone let him know it was useless. Ryker's subconscious marveled at Maazi. He looked twice the size of the FORM he'd fought at the HEB store. His body was like a steroid-pumped water buffalo with penetrating eyes, made even more intense by the bright blue hue of his skin.

Maazi inhaled eerily. "*Breaking* you will be more rewarding than I originally imagined! This will be fun! Shall we begin?"

~

Grace and Jessie heard crashes in the kitchen from the front yard. Before they could run into the house, Maazi emerged through the front door, defacing the threshold in the process. He held Ryker in his arms; his body bobbed like a slinky.

Grace and Jessie screamed in horror.

Maazi raced past them and jumped into the golden craft that they had been examining.

They watched as the craft accelerated at a mind-bending pace into the darkened sky clouded by ash and smoke.

Grace hyperventilated and sank into Jessie's arms. They both collapsed to the ground. Grace's vision went blurry. Jessie sobbed uncontrollably and punched the ground. Both their worlds were now empty.

Chapter 32

FORM Ship

Ryker grunted. His body was already weak. Maazi throwing him against a wall didn't help. Ryker stumbled as he braced himself and held onto a bundle of ... vines.

Is this some sort of greenhouse? he wondered.

The room had the most fantastic vegetation he'd ever seen. The enormous turquoise-glowing water tank mounted onto two juxtaposed walls of the cell was also something he never would have expected on an alien ship. The room was otherworldly, but his mind was too foggy to analyze it, let alone appreciate it. Especially given the circumstance. He didn't know how long it would be—minutes, hours, weeks—but he was already starting to prepare himself mentally to watch Jack's execution.

Maazi spat on Ryker. Ryker wanted to jump up in a rage and attack in return, but his body was too pain-filled. He looked at his captor through cloudy eyes. His vision was blurred by illness, but he could recognize that Maazi appeared weak; he was supporting his weight with the doorway and breathing heavily.

"I have a battle to finish," Maazi wheezed as he stood in the doorway. "Stay here." He laughed, which made him choke. "Not that you have anywhere to go! Oh gosh, I seriously need to stop having so much fun with all this. But what's not to love about a day of reckoning!?" He heaved the door closed and walked away. The sound of his heavy yet sluggish footsteps faded through the door.

Ryker closed his eyes and put his head in his hands. His cerebrum was throbbing. His vision worsened. He couldn't remember ever feeling sicker. He strained to breathe, but forced himself to: fast at first, then slower as he tried to calm his body.

"I have to save Jack," he ordered himself. But his body wouldn't respond. Even weeping took too much energy.

He laid on the ground and punched the floor repeatedly. His arms felt like dumbbells. Each punch he threw lessened in force. His body started to give out. It was the second time in as many weeks he'd experienced this level of exhaustion. He was strong, but human. Last time a team of medics had come to his rescue. This time, no one would be around to help.

Ryker groaned and slumped his face to the floor. His body felt like a cement bag. He couldn't move.

"Jack!" he whispered. "Dang it, Jack, I'm so sorry."

Chapter 33

The Vaughn Home, San Antonio, TX

Grace and Jessie huddled on the couch. Their eyes were bloodshot; not solely from lack of sleep—they hadn't slept in over forty-eight hours—but from tears. Ryker was gone. Jack was gone. Their world as they knew it was gone. Hope was a memory.

They watched whatever news networks were still running. What was once Corpus Christi was now a new shoreline. Buildings were powder, military forces were crippled, and those that survived had surrendered.

The FORM announced that they would give Earth's inhabitants three days to say their goodbyes, then those who desired could either become slaves, or be killed.

Grace sobbed. "Three days? Pft! There's no way I'll be a slave to these ... these *things*!"

Jessie agreed.

"I'll *die* fighting." Grace wiped her eyes and blew her nose. "It's what my husband did, what Ryker was willing to do, and what Jack—" She choked. "He's fighting with all he's got! I know he is."

Jessie wrapped Grace in her arms. She didn't have any words of comfort to offer. She simply promised, "I'll fight, Grace, right beside you!"

Chapter 34

FORM Ship

Ryker awoke. He didn't realize he'd fallen asleep and was unsure of how long he'd been out. The sound of metal-on-metal clicks—or was it rock-on-rock—must have been what woke him. They seemed to be coming from the ceiling. He looked up. There was a foreign-looking air vent with triangular shapes on the hatch. It was definitely the source of the noise, but he couldn't see anything through the grate.

He shook his head to try and focus. He was surprised; shaking his head didn't hurt. He sat up. His lungs didn't hurt like they did hours ago, er, however long ago it was he was awake. He breathed deeply. It felt good. He put his hands to his face. It wasn't clammy.

He got his cellphone from his pocket. There was no service, but it was fully charged, which made no sense. It had been nearly dead last he checked.

He palpated his legs. "What the—" he said aloud. The swelling was completely gone, and the skin of his amputated stumps was no longer red. Pus that had been oozing freely before he fell asleep was completely cleared. His legs were no longer infected.

"Am I in heaven?" he asked himself. He looked around. It was the same esoteric plant-filled room with turquoise lighting. *Hopefully not!*

"It's the ship's electromagnetic energy," a voice from the air vent said.

Ryker hopped up and peered at the vent. He couldn't see anyone, but he knew exactly who it was. "Dr. Sharp!"

"Ryker! It's so wonderful to see you! It seems you got my message."

"I did! How's Jack? Is he OK?"

"Yes and no. He's alive. Maazi's been using him as a punching bag. But he won't kill him unless—" Dr. Sharp winced.

"Unless what?"

Dr. Sharp inhaled slowly. "Unless *you're* watching."

Ryker kicked the wall with an Ozzie, leaving a deep impression in the wall's metal. "We have to get him!"

"We will. We will."

"Let's do it, then. My legs work now." Ryker looked down at his Ozzies. "I *did* have a massive infection in my legs but somehow it seems to have healed."

"Yes, it's the electromagnetic energy from this ship combined with the metal posts in your legs that healed you. The FORM discovered the same thing scientists have on Earth: if you expose metal in the body to alternating magnetic forces, it heats the metal up. The heat, mixed with antibiotics, kills bacteria, and heals infection. I'm guessing you have some antibiotics in your system as well?"

"Uh, yeah, I probably do, actually. I took some like a day or so ago."

"Just as I suspected. The FORM have designed many ways to stay alive longer: they changed their blood type, their cell type, fused their bodies with metal to replace tissue and maintain function, and they use electromagnetic energy to kill bacteria. Infection apparently isn't just an Earth problem. *Fascinating* creatures, to be honest."

"I don't consider them fascinating," Ryker said. "They just decimated our military! And they're trying to kill my family!"

"Right, right. I mean fascinating from a scientific perspective. But let's not give up yet! They have to recover after battles. That's why they're giving Earth's people three days to 'say their goodbyes.' It has nothing to do with them having any semblance of compassion. The only reason they're not all down there now finishing the takeover is because they have to rejuvenate. They've been going non-stop against us for so many days, they need to recover. They use organic material to fuel their bodies just like we do. They have an amazing organics processor that chews animals up so they can inject the byproduct into their body. We may have a window of opportunity to do something."

"Well, why don't we go blow that processor thing up?"

"No chance; there are bound to be thousands of them around it."

"Thousands? How many FORM are there, anyway?"

"About 20,000 in total on the ships from what I can estimate."

"Huh, I would have thought there would be more."

"Time has a way of decreasing a population."

"True," Ryker agreed. "So, if we can't blow up the processor thing, what can we do?"

"Use magnets!"

Ryker raised his eyebrows. "Say what now?"

"Magnets! Jack and I made some. But we need a distraction. There's no way we'll get to him with so many FORM hanging around. First things first, though, let's get you out of this room."

Dr. Sharp undid a set of connectors on the grate and threw it open. The turquoise light from the large tank illuminated his face.

"Holy crud, you look terrible," Ryker said when he saw Dr. Sharp's sunken face.

Dr. Sharp hadn't eaten in days. His body was already showing signs of malnourishment.

"Um, I'm not sure if I should say 'thank you' to that," Dr. Sharp responded.

"No, no, sorry, here you are focusing on everyone else. We need to get you some food!"

"I'm fine, my boy. We'll eat when there's time. Now grab about twelve of those rocks," Dr. Sharp pointed to a pile of rocks in Ryker's cell, "and line them up such that they're in two lines like if your legs were spread out on the ground. They're ore-based rocks and will make the FORM think you're still in here because they'll give off a similar electromagnetic signal as your metal legs. It should fool them for a while."

Ryker snagged the rocks and placed them in two lines near a wall the same distance away as his legs would be if he were leaning against it.

"Well-done. All right, now grab these," Dr. Sharp said and threw down a bundle of vines. "Can you use them to crawl up here?"

Ryker gripped the bundle and lifted himself hand-over-hand with minimal effort.

"Seems you've done that before," Dr. Sharp said.

"Yeah. The military *loves* their rope challenges!"

"Interesting. I thought it was genetic. Jack has tremendous upper body strength as well. He hung on a pole twenty feet in the air for several minutes without falling while two FORM were walking around below him. Probably saved his life, to be honest."

Ryker smiled as he climbed, thinking of all the days he'd forced his little brother to climb ropes in the gym. *They paid off!* He reached the air vent, pulled himself through, and looked around. "Amazing, this ductwork looks just like what you'd find on Earth."

The walls were metal, hexagonal, and meandered through the ship to diffuse air throughout the system.

"That's right," Dr. Sharp beamed. "Some engineering principles are so straightforward, they appear to be universal."

"Cool," Ryker said as he stood. He had to hunch his head slightly to avoid the ceiling. "All right." Ryker breathed deep. "I guess we're in the *innards* of an alien ship. Where to?"

"This way."

Dr. Sharp held his bandaged hand and limped as he led Ryker through a maze of metal.

"How do you know where you're going? And come to think of it, how do you not get caught? And how do you know so much about the FORM?"

"This." Dr. Sharp held up his arm around which Maazi's device was wrapped. "Do you remember that code you gave me?"

"How could I forget?"

"Well, Maazi designed this thing as a personalized shield device, but it works with a computer-like system." Dr. Sharp showed Ryker the screen in the device. "That code you saw is like a cipher and unlocks an unimaginable number of systems. I used that code and fused it with my own to hack their software. It's how I prevent them from finding me, how I listen to what they're saying, and how I was able to call you."

"That's incredible. We were lucky we could hear you. It came through pretty choppy."

"If only I'd had a cell phone to channel through, it wouldn't be choppy."

"I have mine if we need to make another call." Ryker patted his shorts pocket that carried his cell.

"That may come in handy," Dr. Sharp noted as he stepped over a bundle of wires. "Amazing as this technology is, it's also how they tapped into the tablet you were holding in Afghanistan, and why you weren't able to detect those IEDs soon enough."

"And why my friends were killed."

They both paused.

"I'm sorry about that, Ryker."

"Me too. But there's nothing they would want more than for us to undo what these tyrants are doing. Let's keep moving. Oh, wait." Ryker bent down and rotated the dial on his Ozzies. "*Battle mode*, just in case." The Ozzies' LEDs glowed red.

"That's the spirit, my boy!"

Dr. Sharp made a right turn and motioned for Ryker to follow.

Ryker's first step around the turn felt funny. The floor started to bend. "No!"

"I feel it," Dr. Sharp blurted. "Too much weight."

Before they could jump back to the previous section, the ducting gave way. They both fell through the yielded ductwork, slid down a wall, and crashed onto metal flooring.

Ryker got up immediately and ran to Dr. Sharp.

"You okay?" Ryker asked.

"I think so. No blood that I can see."

Ryker helped Dr. Sharp to his feet and noticed two rocks by his side. "What are those?"

"Oh, these are the magnets I was telling you about." Dr. Sharp picked them up and slipped them into two separate satchels he was carrying.

Ryker paused. "Do they by any chance have the ability to destroy a FORM?"

"In a way perhaps. Why?"

"Because that would be really useful right now."

Ryker looked at Dr. Sharp with eyes ablaze. He motioned his head toward the end of the hallway where two FORM were standing motionless, watching.

The FORM smiled evilly and started approaching.

"Stand still!" Dr. Sharp demanded.

"Are you nuts?!" Ryker shouted.

"Trust me. It's now or never."

Ryker shook his head. "Let's go! At least *try* and escape."

"There's no escape, Ryker. We have to take a stand against them."

The FORM drew closer.

"This is insane." Ryker scanned his surroundings, searching for an out. There was none. He would have to fight.

Ryker heard one of the FORM growling with a low purr as it approached.

"Did it really just growl?" Ryker quavered. "Tell me it's not growling right now."

"Yeah, *that's* a growl," Dr. Sharp confirmed. "Like uh … a cat. A big, *hungry* cat. Come to think of it, they used to be my favorite at the zoo when I was a kid."

"Why would you say that right now? Big cats in zoos *eat* things!"

"Well, you asked."

"Okay, enough about growling cats. If we're supposed to stand here, what's your plan?"

The FORM didn't give them time to discuss a plan. They jumped from nearly thirty feet away, aiming straight for Ryker.

Ryker's Ozzies went to work. He moved like a cheetah and dodged his enemies. They landed and immediately rushed him. Ryker used the Ozzies to shimmy and punch wildly at their stomachs and faces. The FORM flinched at the unexpected force of the human. Blue ooze coursed down one of the FORM's metal cheeks. It grappled Ryker's arms and threw him down, then readied its foot to smash his head.

Ryker rolled out of the way and kicked it in the groin.

The FORM bent over in pain.

Nice, Ryker thought, *their groin is a sensitive spot, just like for us.*

The second FORM started for Ryker.

"Stop!" Dr. Sharp yelled.

The second FORM was taken aback and looked at Dr. Sharp with slithering eyes. She put her face close to Dr. Sharp's, pulled at the whiskers in his beard, and asked, "You dare speak to me that way?"

Dr. Sharp slowly reached into his satchel. "An offering," he said. He pulled out an iron ore-based sedimentary rock the size of his palm.

"A rock?" the FORM scoffed and swiveled her fingertip weapons to the blue ring weapon on the end of her arm. She pressed the weapon against Dr. Sharp's head.

Dr. Sharp identified the slight bulge in the FORM's left temple; the spot where a neurochip was located immediately underneath her skin. The processor's faint green light flashed, indicating it was working. He thrust the magnetized rock upward and held it directly over the neurochip.

The FORM shook involuntarily and fell to her hands and knees in a daze.

Dr. Sharp grabbed the second rock from his other satchel and did the same to the FORM that was bent over in pain. He responded the same way; his body jerked and flailed as his brain was being zapped. He slumped to the ground.

Ryker looked at the injured beasts in disbelief.

"It worked! Ha, ha! It worked!" Dr. Sharp gushed like an exuberant child.

Ryker looked at Dr. Sharp, then at the stunned FORM. "What just happened?"

"You know how a strong magnet can destroy a computer's CPU? These things have neurochips in their heads. Our military's been working on something similar. It's called a direct neural interface. It's a microprocessor implanted in the brain and links to computers that transmit information. Their neural interfaces are far more advanced than anything we have. It's what allows them to learn our language instantaneously and integrate with so many of our computers and weapons. But I imagined they were similarly sensitive to a powerful, focal magnetic force. So, I made these magnets to scramble their neurochips!"

"Sick!" Ryker exclaimed. "What will that do to them? I mean, once they come around after being frazzled."

"Well." Dr. Sharp gave a pensive look. "I'm not quite sure. I hadn't thought that far ahead."

"Okay, so that means we need to get the *heck* out of here before they get up!"

"That sounds about right."

They both started to jog down the hallway.

"You there!" one of the FORM yelled from behind them.

Ryker and Dr. Sharp stopped, paralyzed. Their celebration was premature. They turned around, ready for another attack.

The FORM staggered to his feet followed by the second.

Ryker and Dr. Sharp's breathing intensified. They couldn't run; there was nowhere *to* run.

The FORM teetered toward them. As they neared, the first one asked Ryker, "Is this one with you?" as he pointed to Dr. Sharp.

Ryker stood in silence. He was confused.

"*Hello!* I asked, is this one with you? Or do I need to take it to processing?"

The second FORM stood by the first FORM's side, awaiting a response.

Ryker stammered, "I. Um."

"You're one of the forerunners, aren't you? An original?" the FORM asked.

It scanned Ryker's body up and down. Ryker noticed it observe his muscular frame showing through his mostly torn short-sleeve shirt. His sculpted body looked very similar to their own. Yet the FORM seemed less intrigued by Ryker's muscles; his legs were what grabbed his attention. His eyes dwelled on the hybrid-like structure of Ryker's limbs; solid metallic components fused with biological stumps.

"Your legs are from the first generation," the FORM said matter of fact.

Ryker looked at his amputated stumps and connected Ozzies. Dr. Sharp did the same.

Wait a second. It dawned on Ryker. *I look like a FORM! With their neurochips fried, they must think I'm one of them!*

Ryker relaxed and played the part. "Oh, yeah, yeah, that's right, *this* one's with me." He grabbed Dr. Sharp's arm. "I'm supposed to bring him to the, uh ...." He glanced at Dr. Sharp with a look that said, *Where am I supposed to take you?*

"The habitat," Dr. Sharp said.

"Ah," the FORM said. "Okay then, get to it. Don't be late for the arrival."

Ryker had no idea what that meant but agreed to it.

The FORM kept walking and passed them by like nothing moments prior ever had transpired.

Ryker and Dr. Sharp let out a heavy sigh as soon as the FORM were out of sight.

"Did you see that?!" Ryker said rhetorically.

"Of course! You apparently just became the newest member of this ship."

"They think I'm one of them! I, I mean, that's awesome, but what do we do with it? How is it going to help us?"

"I have an idea," Dr. Sharp said. "It involves calling Brighton. Does he have a personal cell number you know of?"

"I don't know, but I know he has a military-issued one."

"Perfect. Do you know his number?"

"Nobody memorizes numbers these days."

"True. It's not like when I was a kid; I still remember my best friend's number from childhood," Dr. Sharp mused.

"Can't you just hack into a system and get it? Is that how you called me?"

"For civilians, yes, but not military personnel. Those numbers are more difficult to hack. Do you know anyone who *has* his number?"

Ryker thought for a moment. "Oh my gosh, I do! My mom."

"Why does she have Brighton's number?"

"When I was recovering, she hosted them at our bed-and-breakfast. She got it then."

"All right. Let's make some calls," Dr. Sharp declared. "We may have found a way to turn this battle around!"

Chapter 35

The Vaughn Home, San Antonio, TX

Grace heard her hip buzz. Jessie heard it, too; the distinct noise of a cell phone vibrating. Grace fumbled and pulled her cell phone out of her pocket. Her heart fluttered when she saw Ryker's name on her smartphone screen.

"Who is it?" Jessie asked.

"Ryker?" Grace answered questioningly.

"What!"

Grace didn't get her hopes up; it had to be a scam. She answered. "Hello?"

"Mom!"

"Ryker?!" Grace sank to her knees.

"Yes, I can't talk long. Dr. Sharp and I are on the FORM ship over, well, wherever we are. Jack is alive. We're safe … for now."

Grace struggled to comprehend what was happening. Ryker was talking so fast, she feared she would miss what he was saying. She spoke through her sobs, "Ryker, tell me this isn't a joke." Her heart nearly burst hearing that both her boys were alive, but she didn't want to believe it if this was somehow a scam. She put the phone on speaker so Jessie could also hear.

"Mom, it's me. Double amputee; I wear Ozzies; used to play basketball; soldier in the Army; love your cherry cheesecake. And I miss you and Jessie more than I can describe."

Grace wiped her nose and tried to control her emotions.

Jessie cupped her hands over her mouth.

They had so many questions. They had given up hope.

Grace asked, "Wh— How— Can I get to you?"

"Not now, we need to outsmart these things. We need to contact Brighton, assuming he's alive. Dr. Sharp and I think we know how to beat these things! Do you have Brighton's number?"

"I—uh—Yes, I do."

"Can you give it to us?"

"Just a second." Grace scrolled through her phone until she found the number. She said it over the phone slowly enough for Ryker to put it in his phone directory.

"Thanks! I wish we had time to talk, but trust us. We're going to do everything we can to fight these things."

"Wait, Ryker, Jessie couldn't reach Brighton when she tried."

"I know. It's okay. Dr. Sharp's system doesn't require standard cell service."

"Good. Good. I guess all we can do then is wish you luck."

"Thanks. And Mom …." Ryker paused.

"What is it?"

"I'll bring him home, Mom. I'll bring Jack home. I promise."

"Thank you—" she struggled. "I love you. Please come home soon!"

The phone went silent.

"Ryker?"

No response.

Grace and Jessie looked at each other and hugged.

Jessie's heart leaped. "He's alive!"

Grace nodded unabashedly. "Yes. He's alive. And somehow … somehow, he's going to *beat* these things!"

Chapter 36

What Was Once Corpus Christi, TX

"Col. Brighton!" a soldier yelled. "Your cell phone, sir."

Brighton faintly heard the soldier's voice from the ground below. He was still on top of the building near the Whataburger parking lot, observing the destruction around him. His mind was numb as he viewed the smoke-filled skies, the fires with flames a hundred feet high dotting the landscape, the blood-red sun, the emaciated warzone.

"Col. Brighton!" the soldier yelled again. "Your cell phone, sir!"

Brighton didn't respond. Shock was meddling with his mind.

"Brighton," the president repeated as he shook Brighton's shoulder. "Someone's calling for you."

"What?" Brighton turned around and looked at the president whose face was bloodied and bruised. *Not even the world's most powerful leader can escape war wounds,* Brighton thought.

"The soldier down there," the president pointed down the ladder, "he's calling your name. He says someone's calling your cell phone."

Brighton cleared his throat and wiped blood from his cheek. "My phone? What's the point of a phone call? How is cell service even working?"

The president shrugged and shook his head.

Brighton went to the ladder and met the soldier who was now standing atop the roof.

"Sir ... you may want to take this call," the soldier urged.

Brighton took his cell phone from the soldier. "Hello?"

"Col. Brighton, this is Capt. Ryker Vaughn calling from the FORM's black ship."

"What?! Is this a joke?"

"Sir, you met with me right after my surgery in Afghanistan. I'm a double amputee. I wear Ozzies. My mother is Grace Vaughn."

Brighton knew that no one else would have known those details. It was Ryker.

"Ryker! How the ... how did you get this number? You're on their ship?" He pushed speakerphone.

Gen. Childress and the president leaned in.

"Yes, sir," Ryker answered. "Dr. Sharp is with me and has been able to patch into their systems, which is allowing us to call through my phone. My brother, Jack, is hurt, needs help soon. Dr. Sharp has learned how to ... manipulate, I guess is the word, several systems in their ships. And we've discovered something very unique. We have a plan. If we execute it properly, we may have a window of opportunity to fight back."

Brighton snapped his fingers and wrote in the air, signaling he wanted something to write on. The president pulled out a pen and a half-burnt notepad that survived the helicopter crash and handed it to Brighton.

"Go on, Ryker," Brighton said.

"Do you still have access to the disruptors?"

"Well, yes, but they don't do what we thought they would. They had the *opposite* effect than we expected. And besides, the controls are—Well, their remote functions are compromised in San Antonio."

"We know. Is there a way to restore communications and get some men on the disruptors?"

"We have, wait, how did you even know about the disruptors?"

"Dr. Sharp learned about them."

"Okay, I'm sure we can talk about that later. There are only two of them left."

"Good. Is there a team who can restore the system?"

"Yes, I'm sure we can find a team in San Antonio that can restore it. It may just require plugging satellites back in. At worst, the communication system needs to be rebooted."

"Great. And are there soldiers who know how to use them once they're restored?"

"Yes, even I know how to use them. A team is here with us as well."

"Perfect. The second thing we need is to surgically implant Ozzies in as many amputees as possible within the next thirty-six hours. The FORM gave people on Earth three days to 'say their goodbyes.' But it has nothing to do with compassion. Their frontline warriors need time to rejuvenate before they can 'finish' the job."

"So, they're not lying about their arrival date this time?" Brighton asked.

"No, everything Dr. Sharp can decipher is that it's legit," Ryker confirmed. "We have three days to get ready for them again. That's just enough time to implant Ozzies, give those soldiers a bit to prepare, and establish an amputee force."

Brighton considered what Ryker was saying. "The logistics of all this are difficult to even consider, but let's assume we can pull together enough amputees and get Ozzies in them. What are you getting at?"

Ryker continued. "Every FORM has a neurochip in their left temple: a direct neural interface in their head. It's like the one our military has been working on for years. Theirs is far more advanced, but it also makes them susceptible. Just like a CPU in a computer gets ruined by a strong magnet next to it, Dr. Sharp found that when we put a powerful magnet next to their neurochip, it disrupts their circuitry. They forget crucial information or lose a good portion of their cognitive abilities. It seems that the information they've gained for the past several hundred years or so scrambles. Their brains reset, so to speak."

"Interesting. And what does that have to do with amputees?"

Ryker answered with a hope-filled tone. "We just found that when we mess their brains up, the FORM recognize *me* as one of their own! My Ozzies are made of metal and connect to me via metal posts that are *fused* to my bones. When the FORM's neurochips are compromised, they recognize someone with Ozzies as a FORM!"

Brighton harrumphed. "Soldier, I don't know how you figured all this out, but well-done. So, what are you proposing?"

"Stealth, mixed with a little bit of crazy ... and some luck."

"Luck doesn't win wars, Ryker," Brighton warned.

"In this case, we can nudge it a bit, tip the scales," Ryker prodded. "Dr. Sharp and I can't get to all the FORM with our magnets. We can probably disable the neurochips of some on this ship, but there are upwards of 20,000 of them. We can't compromise them all. We have a plan, but it'll require the use of the disruptors and as many Veteran amputees as we can round up and get Ozzies into. Veteran amputees because they've been in battle and will have the shallowest learning curve.

"Dr. Sharp knows why the disruptors didn't work as expected. The FORM modified their shield parameters so the disruptors had the opposite effect. But we can still use them to allow an Ozzie amputee force to infiltrate the FORM and take them down from the inside out. Dr. Sharp can scramble the FORM's communications so they can't overhear us while we coordinate our defense, just like he's doing for this call."

Brighton looked at Gen. Childress and the president. They all knew there weren't any other options.

The president put his mouth close to the phone. "Ryker, this is the president. We're going to follow your lead. Give us every detail of your plan."

Ryker laid out the details. Gen. Childress offered a few tweaks, which the group accepted.

"Ryker, we'll do everything we can to make this work," Brighton said. "We'll coordinate the amputee Ozzie force. But are you sure you can overtake their ship's controls?"

"This is Dr. Sharp. I'll take care of that," he assured. "I've learned a thing or two about how they manage their mainframe. I'm scrambling their communications now."

"We'll have to trust you know what you're doing," Brighton said. "Let's get to work. Godspeed, you two!"

Brighton ended the call and breathed deeply. "Well, it's nontraditional," he said to Gen. Childress and the president. "Nothing like this has been done before."

"It may be just what we need, something unexpected," Gen. Childress said.

"Make it happen," the president ordered.

Gen. Childress snatched a comm and spoke to whoever could hear. "How many soldiers out there still have communications?" he asked.

He held the receiver in the air for everyone on the roof to hear.

"Here," one unit responded.

"We're ready for the next round," another said.

"Put us to work!" said another.

"We're up for another fight!"

Hundreds more responses came through.

"All right, listen up everyone, and spread the word to as many soldiers as you can—fast! Starting now, we begin Operation: Covert Amputee Strike Team, or Operation:

CAST! I want every available truck, helicopter, van, car, airplane, aircraft, hovercraft, Humvee, motorcycle, any transportation device to gather as many Veteran amputees as possible, yes, I said *amputees* across the country and bring them to San Antonio within the next eighteen hours.

"Send messages by Internet, mouth, text, fax, email, news stations, phone, pigeon, whatever means to reach *every* available, high-functioning and willing amputee. They'll undergo a surgical procedure at the San Antonio Military Medical Center.

"For any amputee across the globe who was ever removed from active duty because of an amputation, it's time.... It's *time* for you to *return* to duty!"

Brighton, Gen. Childress, and the president heard ripples of hoots and hollers emanate from the surrounding regions. The hairs on their necks prickled, and they all got full-body chills.

Gen. Childress provided a detailed overview of Operation: CAST through the comm. As soon as he finished his instructions, soldiers from every corner of the globe hurried to action.

Gen. Childress turned to Brighton and the president. "Well, gentlemen, I'm an amputee and I'll be joining this force."

"Gen. Childress," Brighton said as he lifted his pant leg to show an Ozzie, "had my tibia blown off in Desert Storm. I was one of the test soldiers who received an original prototype Ozzie when they came out. I'll be right behind you!"

"It'll be a pleasure!" Gen. Childress declared as he patted Brighton's shoulder. "Mr. President, you'll be eyes on the ground while Brighton and I cover the ship."

The president nodded. "I trust the plan."

Brighton smiled as a sliver of hope resurrected in his heart. He examined the fires, the smoke, the destruction. Earth had lost the battle and was hanging by a thread, but he, the president, Gen. Childress, and tens of thousands of soldiers weren't dead yet. And there was still a planet to defend.

"Gen. Childress," he said as he looked out at the horizon, "let's get some magnets!"

Chapter 37

FORM Ship

Maazi shoved his people aside so he could reach the front of the crowd gathering at the organics processor. The majority of the FORM had congregated from their silver ships onto the main ship and were accumulating around their food source to inject themselves with life-sustaining nutrients. They were depleted after multiple battles and minimal recovery time.

Maazi muscled his way to the front of the throng and ripped three oversized syringes out of Taahiya's hand. "Give me those!" he demanded and injected himself with a triple dose of life-sustaining substance.

He put his back against a wall and slumped to the floor.

That was close. He had gone far too long without sufficient sustenance and nearly died because of it. Although he had been in minimal hand-to-hand combat, the accumulation of battles over the past week, along with the mental toll it took to coordinate and execute the annihilation of Earth's stronghold, combined with the flights in his melik, had sucked the available energy out of him. He, and the rest of the FORM, would need at least three more doses and three more Earth days before they could function normally and complete their takeover. Battle wasn't the only requirement to overtake a planet. With nearly eight billion people to manage, planning and preparation also were required.

"Get me water!" Maazi ordered.

Taahiya grabbed another syringe and injected herself; she was likewise weary and drained. She pushed through her weakness and shakily filled a large diamond-cut vessel with water and handed it to Maazi.

Maazi poured the water down his throat, gasped, and wiped his mouth. "Is that Earth water?"

"It is, Bohanna."

"It's rich! I knew I made the right decision to come here!"

Taahiya snorted softly. It had been *her* idea to send a water beacon to this solar system and *her* idea to wait near Saturn even though the signal had been lost. Maazi never respected her input or gave her credit for her accomplishments. But after a thousand years of abuse, his narcissism was expected.

"How many did we lose?" Maazi asked.

"Not many," Taahiya said. "Our attack was effective. They had no idea their disruptors would be so self-destructive."

"Good! Do they have any military strongholds remaining?"

"No, Bohanna," Taahiya said. "Militaries across their world sent major provisions to Corpus Christi. We depleted the majority of what they had to defend themselves. Anything they have remaining can easily be eliminated. We took their legs out from under them."

"Just as we planned." Maazi snorted. "They're more like other races than I anticipated. Weak. I was expecting a more difficult challenge."

Taahiya tapped her left shoulder. "I'll monitor things while we recover."

"As you should," Maazi said condescendingly. "We should all be willing to do whatever it takes to make sure we capture this world. Its resources could sustain us for a million years!"

Maazi got up and went to his quarters. He fell on his resting place and breathed heavily. He would never admit it to anyone, but he was exhausted. Yet he had a lot to look forward to; in three days, he would be recovered and have a world's worth of high-quality, life-rich water. The very thought was more than he ever could have imagined.

Chapter 38

San Antonio, TX

Over 30,000 amputees arrived in San Antonio within eighteen hours. They came from all ends of the world—in trucks, jeeps, tanks, airplanes, private jets, boats, and helicopters. The response was immediate and overwhelming. Soldiers who had been injured and suffered amputations of legs, arms, and hands in Vietnam, the Gulf War, Iraq, Afghanistan, training exercises, and small conflicts were now in San Antonio. Each amputee had one or more missing limbs, feet, or hands.

The San Antonio Military Medical Center had long been preparing for potential wars with other countries and had been scaling up Ozzie manufacturing for two years. Ryker had been the first soldier to receive an Ozzie in the battlefield. The military wanted broader-scale testing, but given the dire circumstance, and after seeing the technology put to use by Ryker, they knew it was time, even necessary, to implement the Ozzie technology in a much bigger way.

For each dozen amputees that arrived, a quarter as many trauma and specialized orthopedic surgeons likewise traveled. They came from every walk of practice—Level 1 trauma units, general hospitals, private clinics—to implant metallic Ozzies into the amputees. Every room within the San Antonio Military Medical Center became a makeshift operating room. Each surgery required two hours per soldier. The brilliance of the Ozzie technology was that it rapidly integrated with the body, requiring minimal healing time before a soldier was ready for battle. Ryker had experienced that when he first stood on his Ozzies; he could have sprinted within moments after surgery.

Surgeons worked round the clock, and within forty-eight hours of the announcement, the CAST—the military's first Covert Amputee Strike Team—was born.

CAST soldiers gathered in the AT&T Center—home of the San Antonio Spurs—for their initial briefing, just twelve hours before the FORM would be returning.

Brighton, Gen. Childress, and the president entered the arena and assessed the newly formed army. The excitement and energy of CAST soldiers was contagious. Humility, determination, willingness, sacrifice; all were words Brighton thought of as he looked at them.

"Listen up, everyone!" a major in the Army said to start the briefing. "Turn off any electronic device you have, and—this is important—take out the batteries. We have Dr. Sharp up there scrambling our communications so the FORM don't hear us, but we need to take every precaution." The major waited for everyone to comply then continued, "All right, if we're going to take these evil things out once and for all, we need to follow some instructions. The president of United States would like to address us before we receive those instructions."

The CAST applauded as the president took the podium. He put his hands in the air to settle everyone down. "Nothing unites a clan," he began, "and nothing binds soldiers more fully than experiences shared in combat. I don't have the pleasure of calling myself a soldier, but after these past several days, standing side by side in combat with Gen. Childress and Col. Brighton, I can begin to appreciate what you have. In this arena sits a unique set of individuals, soldiers, wounded warriors. You all have a common thread: amputation. For Col. Brighton, it came at the hands of a malfunctioning Tomahawk missile in the Gulf War that took the lower half of his right leg. For Gen. Childress," the president pointed to him, "the loss of his left leg came at the hand of a FORM militant, bent on our destruction."

Cackles emanated from the CAST. "Let's get 'em!" A thousand voices cheered in unison.

"Men, women, Veterans, amputees, soldiers: we've brought you here to fill a need that cannot be filled in any other way."

The crowd erupted with applause and cheers.

The president leaned into the microphone. "The FORM are planning to finish us off tomorrow. They think we're crippled, defeated. *You* are going to show them otherwise! *You* will now be our most powerful artillery!"

"Yeah!" the soldiers hollered.

"This war is unparalleled in history. The human family depends on you."

"Bring it on!" a soldier in the back shouted, followed by whistles and hoorahs.

The president continued, "A double amputee, Capt. Ryker Vaughn, is currently surviving on the FORM's main ship with MIT Professor, Dr. Steven Sharp. Together, they determined a method by which the FORM can be sensitized for destruction. The goal right now is to outline a five-phase plan that will allow you to take advantage of this discovery and eliminate our enemy. *You* can *protect* this planet!"

The crowd erupted with cheers and thumped their Ozzies.

The president waited for the clanks and thumps to die down. "Soldiers, there is no time to repeat what you are about to learn, so listen closely and God bless every one of you!"

After a thunderous cheer, the air fell silent. Every CAST member was riveted.

Gen. Childress took the podium. He paused and measured the faces of those sitting before him. Many were worn and older like himself, some homeless, others fresh from combat in Iraq and Afghanistan, bulging with anticipation to get back into action. It was the most diverse and unexpected force of soldiers he had ever addressed.

He got right to business and spoke sternly as he pointed to the jumbotron video display in the arena on which the five-phase plan was displayed. "Our five-phase plan is as follows. Phase One is to form the CAST. That's complete and here you are!"

"Hoorah!" a soldier cheered, followed by a dozen more.

Gen. Childress smiled and gave a thumbs up. "Phase Two is to desensitize each FORM's neurochip." Gen. Childress briefly explained what the neurochip was. "Ryker and Dr. Sharp have found that once their neurochip is desensitized, the FORM recognize an amputee with an Ozzie as one of their own. Dr. Sharp tells us that the majority of the FORM are congregated on their main ship. We're going to desensitize their neurochips using the disruptors, which will create a ship-wide electromagnetic pulse, like an EMP. The pulse will frazzle their neurochips and make them susceptible to attack. This phase will take place at dawn.

"Phase Three is infiltration. Dr. Sharp will lower the enemy ship to Corpus Christi's waters. When we give the mark, we all get on at once.

"Phase Four is annihilation. We'll engage the FORM and incapacitate them from the inside out. We'll need to time it so we all attack at once and take out as many FORM as possible simultaneously and quickly. We'll annihilate them exactly thirty minutes from the time we give the announcement to board the ship. Timing our attack to happen at the same time across the ship will reduce the risk of them sending a message to other FORM that an attack is coming, or for them to get too suspicious. Each of you will have your Ozzies showing; you must make sure that they are visible to increase the odds that the FORM consider you as one of their own. When the thirty minutes is up, we attack!

"Phase Five is extraction. After the FORM are eliminated, you'll have thirty minutes to get off the ship so we can incapacitate it. We don't want any chance of some of them getting away or wreaking more havoc!

"Each of you will be given two hand-to-hand combat weapons, a sidearm, and two powerful yet lightweight magnets in case the electromagnetic pulse doesn't affect all of them. These will be your sources of protection and survival on the ship."

Gen. Childress looked at Brighton and asked him to provide a concluding statement.

Brighton stood at the podium and looked in awe as he considered that in just over twelve hours, the fate of the world would be decided by the army of amputee soldiers in front of him.

He spoke low. "Soldiers ... the world has never been in greater need. You are the face of survival. You will be the ones hoisted on the shoulders of citizens across the planet. To commandeer the words of Winston Churchill, this moment in history will be kind to you, for you will be the ones to write it!"

Hoots and stomps resounded.

"Now, get out there and outmaneuver, outwit, outpower these ... egotistical guerillas who think we are an inferior species. Let's show them what it means to be a soldier," applause erupted, "a human," yet louder, "and a protector—of this planet, our loved ones, our people and all that we hold sacred. Though you may have been previously relieved from active duty in sacrifice of this great world, today ... today the battle for Earth is in the hands of each and every one of you *amputees*!"

Ovations rumbled through the bellows of the arena as each soldier stood on their feet and clanked their Ozzies. They yelled at the top of their lungs and cheered wildly.

The CAST exited the arena with adrenaline thumping through their veins. They boarded dozens of transport vehicles and began the trek south.

The final battle for Earth's water was about to begin.

Chapter 39

FORM Ship

Ryker held his breath. He and Dr. Sharp were only three air vents away from the entrance to the room where Jack was being held. This was their window of opportunity to get Jack while the majority of the FORM were recovering.

Ryker followed Dr. Sharp through the ductwork. They eased their feet forward, taking each step as gently as possible. The air rushing through the ventilation system was loud enough to cover the noise of their soft footsteps, but not much more. They rounded a corner and saw what they expected to see: three FORM standing guard by Jack's holding room, not unlike the one Ryker had been in. Ryker bent down and switched his Ozzies to walk mode—their quietest setting—to reduce the risk of being detected.

The ductwork through which they were walking didn't traverse the room where Jack was being held, so they would have to go through the door, which also meant they would have to get past those FORM.

Ryker looked at Dr. Sharp. He appeared sickly and sweating.

"Dr. Sharp," Ryker whispered, "you don't look well."

"Well, I've hardly eaten in four days. I've been busy trudging through the ship. But I'm fine. Don't worry."

With no other options, Ryker agreed to continue with the rescue mission but worried about Dr. Sharp.

Ryker whispered, "Those ones don't look sick like the others."

"That's because they're not. They didn't fight in the battle. They're fresh."

Ryker nodded; that made sense.

Dr. Sharp held a hand up.

Ryker paused and watched as Dr. Sharp eased two magnets out of his satchels. He tied strips of vines around each one.

"Do you have yours?" Dr. Sharp asked quietly.

Ryker pulled out the magnet he was carrying. Its magnetism was strong; he could already feel it pulling toward the other magnets. They kept their arms far apart and swapped magnets. Dr. Sharp wrapped another vine around the third magnet.

"When we get closer, we need to lower these within about a foot of their heads to disrupt their neurochips. We can't talk lest we signal our presence."

"One question before we go: why aren't the magnets trying to stick to the walls of the ductwork?"

"Because the walls are aluminum. You mostly need iron for magnets to attract."

"What you're saying is, I should have listened in physics class?"

"That certainly would have been on one of my tests," Dr. Sharp smiled.

"Lead the way," Ryker said, "I'll work on my magnetics expertise later."

Dr. Sharp moved stealthily forward. When they reached the two grates over the guards, they each opened one just wide enough to slip their magnets through. Dr. Sharp eased two through. Ryker one.

Ryker monitored the FORM beneath him. All three had their backs to the wall and were in a half-sleepy state; they were obviously bored.

As he lowered the magnet, Ryker prevented it from swinging to reduce the risk of its movement catching the guards' eyes. He steadied it roughly two feet above their heads. He looked over at Dr. Sharp. He had his magnets roughly two feet above the other two FORM.

"On the count of three, lower it," Dr. Sharp mouthed.

Ryker eyed his magnet to make sure it was situated and started counting silently. "One. Two." He looked at Dr. Sharp before saying, "three."

Dr. Sharp's face suddenly paled.

Oh no! Ryker thought. *He's going to faint!*

Dr. Sharp fell forward, and his whole body slipped through the grate before Ryker could do anything. The FORM stood in surprise as the body of a middle-aged human thudded onto the floor in front of them.

As the FORM beneath Ryker stood, her head came within the electromagnetic field of his magnet, frying her neurochip. The FORM fell to her knees and grabbed her head. Ryker pulled his magnet up through the grate just as the other two FORM turned to look at what was happening to their compatriot.

One FORM approached Dr. Sharp, and the other went for their struggling partner. Ryker knew he had to do something quick. While the FORM near Dr. Sharp wasn't looking, he dropped his magnet once again through the grate. The magnet came within inches of his impact radius, but the FORM jerked his head out of reach as he helped his friend, writhing on the ground.

Ryker swung the magnet like a pendulum. He couldn't hit the FORM in the head, but he had to get it closer to the target.

The FORM near Dr. Sharp picked up one of the magnets that had fallen on the floor. He lifted it toward his head, puzzled. Then his neurochip frazzled, and he stumbled to the ground.

The third FORM knew something wasn't right. She readied her weapon, ignored her comrades, and looked around. She couldn't see a threat; Ryker had pulled his magnet up through the grate just in time.

The FORM observed Dr. Sharp. She noticed the wrist device on his arm and started toward him.

Oh no! Ryker screamed internally. *If the FORM get that device ... it's all over! I need a distraction, like when I was fighting the al Qaeda.* He looked around. There wasn't much to work with. *Aha!*

He unclicked one of his Ozzies, slipped open the grate, and pushed the Ozzie through.

The FORM saw a metal leg poking through the ventilation.

She yelled something in FORM language and lunged for the leg.

The leg slipped out of the opening as the FORM grabbed it. She looked up in confusion and saw a rock racing toward her face. Before she could dodge, she grabbed her head in agony and sank to the ground.

Ryker hurried through the grate and jumped to the floor. Standing on one Ozzie, he picked up his fallen Ozzie and clicked it back in place.

He shifted to Dr. Sharp's side and slapped his face lightly. "Dr. Sharp, are you okay?"

Dr. Sharp started to come to—and so did the three FORM.

Ryker heard a knock on the door behind him.

"Hello?" Jack's muffled voice came from behind the door. "Is someone there? Please help!"

Ryker had to make a choice; he could either save Jack or Dr. Sharp.

Dr. Sharp coughed. "Ryker, I need—I need ... food and water." He passed out again.

"I know, I know."

The FORM got to their feet and analyzed Ryker.

Painful as it was, Ryker knew he had to save Dr. Sharp first. Maazi wouldn't kill Jack without him watching, but without Dr. Sharp, he wouldn't be able to save mankind. There was also no way he could bash in the door between him and Jack with three FORM watching. "This is one of mine," he said to the FORM. "He needs a medic. He was injured during testing. I'll take him."

The FORM all agreed and acted as though Ryker was authorized.

Ryker scooped Dr. Sharp up in his arms, walked down the corridor and around a corner where he found a ladder that led into the ventilation system.

"Let's get you some food," Ryker whispered with tears forming. In his mind, he said, *Hold on, little brother. I'll be back to get you. I promise.*

Chapter 40

What Was Once Corpus Christi, TX

Brighton and Gen. Childress stood on a nascent shoreline near what was once Corpus Christi. Other than the lap of waning tide waves, the morning twilight was silent. A light sea breeze was just enough to chill the sweat on their faces. The absence of moonlight mixed with residual smoke catalyzed thick darkness, prompting them to wear headlamps to illuminate the warm waters.

"Ironic, isn't it?" Brighton remarked.

"What's that?" Gen. Childress asked.

"The silence. Just two days ago, the sound of war was raging."

Gen. Childress nodded and let the silence pervade momentarily. "Yeah, and in an hour's time, it'll rage again."

It was 0455; roughly an hour till dawn and the commencement of Phase Two. They had arrived with thousands of other soldiers eight hours earlier and set up a makeshift battle zone. Their heart rates were still above normal from moving gear, forcing sweat to seep through their pores and moisten their black clothing that overtly displayed their Ozzies. They synchronously sipped cups of over-caffeinated coffee, hoping to keep their senses alert. Sleep was urgently needed but unwelcome.

"It's time to check in with Ryker and Dr. Sharp," Brighton said.

"Good as any," Gen. Childress replied. "You know, they'd *better* be right about this."

"Alternative options aren't a luxury at the moment," Brighton said and took another drink.

Gen. Childress followed suit. "I can't argue with that. Let's do it."

Brighton grabbed his cell phone from his back right pocket and called Ryker's cell using speaker phone so Gen. Childress could hear.

Ryker answered. "Hello, Col. Brighton."

"Ryker, good to hear your voice. I assume you've continued to go undetected?"

"Yes. Dr. Sharp's figured out how to hack basically all their systems. We found a room to hide in. Things are going according to plan so far."

"Good. Do you know how your brother is doing?"

"He's okay. We haven't been able to, uh, rescue him. Yet. We were able to disable another set of FORM, but ... *other* circumstances arose. But at least Maazi hasn't hurt Jack anymore. All of this must have affected Maazi; he's been recovering in his quarters the entire past two days."

"Why don't you just go in and take him out while he's weak?"

"We thought of that, but there's only one access point to his room and, like most crucial areas, it's guarded heavily."

"Makes sense. Good your brother's doing okay. Let's take these things out so we can get him. We had a question come up for Dr. Sharp. Is he by you?"

"Yes. He's right here," Ryker said.

"Col. Brighton, what can I do for you?" Dr. Sharp asked with a mouthful of food.

Brighton was surprised to hear the sound of chomping. "Are you ... are you eating?"

"Oh, yes, my apologies. I was near starvation, but Ryker found some edible plants and a stock of water. Their plants are apparently remarkably nourishing to our body type. I'm recovering quickly."

"Plants? On a ship?"

"Yes, the ecosystem the FORM established on their ship is quite fascinating. How I wish we could learn how they created a nearly self-sufficient and regenerative environment. With the exception of water, of course. It's a shame we have to destroy these things. We could learn a lot from them, including interstellar travel."

"Sure, if they weren't trying to *end* our civilization," Brighton said.

"Well, I—Yes," Dr. Sharp conceded. "If they weren't constantly trying to *kill* us."

Brighton changed the subject. "Dr. Sharp, a question arose while we were en route to Corpus Christi. How will the FORM not detect that you're controlling their ship? More specifically, you plan to take over their controls and lower the ship so we can get the CAST on, but can't the FORM feel the movement, or see that they're changing position?"

"Good question," Dr. Sharp responded. "It's all about the hack. I locked their navigation system to where it will show them still hovering miles above the waters. I'll also lower it slowly enough to where, on this size of a machine, no one will notice. It doesn't have to move much distance or very quickly."

"But can't they just look out a window and see they're moving?"

"Their transparent canopy only faces upward. We're moving in the dark and their ship wobbles enough as it is. With how similar the sky looks overhead, there's not much change to notice."

Brighton inhaled and exhaled. He was anxious. There was a lot that could go wrong. "And you're certain you can control their ship without them finding out?"

"There's no guarantee, but so far, I have control."

"Where is the CAST going to board?"

"I have to get the center of the ship over your location. That's the only access point large enough to get tens of thousands of soldiers onboard in a ten-minute window."

"What about those huge turbine things on the underside of the ship's arms? Can they get in through one of those areas, farther away from the center, where I assume more of them will be?"

"Those turbines are what the FORM use to suck up billions of gallons of water and shuttle it to storage containers. If they turn the turbine on, we would lose every soldier."

"The middle it is, then," Brighton said.

Gen. Childress leaned toward Brighton to speak into the phone, "Dr. Sharp, how are you going to make the disruptors emanate their energy throughout the entire ship? The disruptors produce a relatively small beam of energy. So how will the energy disperse across the *entire* ship?"

"Great question. It's back to the hack. We're going to make their ship's technology do the work for us. The disruptors will provide electromagnetic energy, which can be amplified by the energy state of plasma, which is what their shields use. You know how they dissipated the energy they absorbed from the disruptors to destroy Corpus Christi?"

Brighton and Gen. Childress looked at the rubble around them.

"Oh, we're painfully aware, Dr. Sharp," Gen. Childress said.

"Right, I'm sorry about that. In essence, I'll do the same thing, just in reverse. As the disruptors' energy hits the ship's shield, I'll adjust it to where the electromagnetic energy is amplified by the plasma state energy in the shield, then I'll dissipate it backwards—*towards* the ship.

That should send a massive EMP throughout the entire ship."

"*Should?*" Gen. Childress implored.

"I mean, I haven't exactly had a chance to test this in a lab. Yes, it *should* work."

"And if it doesn't, we use the magnets as backup. Not ideal, much riskier—"

"Quite iffy, to be honest," Dr. Sharp cut in.

"But it's an option," Brighton added.

"A weak one given how many FORM there are, but yes," Dr. Sharp said. "Now, the thing we need to confirm is that the disruptors are ready. Were the communications repaired in San Antonio so they function?"

Brighton responded. "We have a team in San Antonio that repaired the connection. They just need to reset the system. My next call is going to be to them. I'll check now." Brighton grabbed a comm and spoke into it sternly. "Team Delta, is the communication system for the disruptors reset and ready?"

There was no response.

A spark of concern surfaced in everyone.

"Team Delta, I repeat, are the communications for the disruptors up and ready?"

No response.

Their concern deepened.

"Team Delta, respond!" Brighton demanded.

"Colonel!" a frantic voice came through. "Facility is compromised! The FORM—"

"Soldier, what's going on?"

The comm buzzed blankly for several seconds.

"FORM ... two ... I'm the only one left," the soldier muttered.

"Soldier, do you have backup?" Brighton asked.

They all waited. The response lag time was uncomfortable.

"No one else here," the soldier whispered. "... dead or left for Corpus Christi. I'm hiding in—"

The comm went quiet.

"Soldier!" Brighton yelled.

No one answered.

"We didn't leave anyone else in San Antonio?" Gen. Childress begged incredulously.

"We did," Brighton said, "but the FORM took them all out."

"Can we test the disruptors and see if they've reset the system?" Dr. Sharp asked.

Brighton angled his headlamp and rushed to where they were storing the disruptors. He flipped each of them on.

The screens read: *System disconnected*.

"It's not reset!" Brighton grunted.

"What do we do?" Ryker asked.

"If we don't get the disruptor system reset in San Antonio, we may have to consider surrendering ... again!" Dr. Sharp said.

"That's *not* an option!" Brighton yelled. "We're soldiers. We adapt. We modify our actions to the circumstance. There's no way to even get a chopper there in time. Who else do we have in San Antonio that can reset the system?"

Ryker's voice came through quietly. "There are at least two people in San Antonio still."

"Who?" Brighton begged.

"My mom ... and girlfriend."

"Give me their numbers," Brighton ordered. "They're about to become the military's newest volunteers."

Chapter 41

The Vaughn Home, San Antonio, TX

Grace and Jessie were asleep in the Vaughn's disheveled home. Not by choice, but by necessity. They hadn't slept enough in three days. They didn't expect to wake up at 5:05 a.m., but Grace's phone ring forced their groggy eyes open.

"Who's calling?" Jessie asked as she sat up in a chair and wiped her eyes. She pulled her unkempt hair into a ponytail.

"It's a blocked number," Grace answered.

"You should probably answer it."

Grace nodded and swiped the answer icon and put it on speaker. "Hello?"

"Mrs. Vaughn. Good, your phone still works."

"Col. Brighton?" She wiped her eyes, wondering if she was awake. "I can't tell ... Um, is this is a dream?"

"No. I wish it were. This isn't an ideal situation, but ... we need you. Your *sons* need you."

Grace sat straight up from her makeshift bed on the couch. "For what?"

Jessie's eyes opened wide. Adrenaline shunted to her muscles.

"Are you still in San Antonio?" Brighton asked.

"Yes. We heard the FORM had a couple of scouts around the city. Jessie and I didn't dare go out."

"How far are you from Lackland Air Force Base?"

"Maybe fifteen miles."

"Do you have a car or other transport?"

"I, um, actually, I guess I do."

"How fast could you make it there?"

"Well, I, I don't know for sure."

"Mrs. Vaughn, please listen carefully, this is very important. The FORM overtook several of our key troops at Lackland Air Force Base who were supposed to reset a system for some military equipment called disruptors."

"All right. Ryker actually had mentioned those to me."

"The disruptors are imperative to a, uh, *operation* that will be starting soon. We can't get to San Antonio in time. You and Jessie need to go to Lackland and access the Communications Building to restore our remote access to the disruptors within the next thirty minutes! I can guide you on how to reset it once you get there. And ... we believe the FORM have left the area."

A lump formed in Grace's throat. The thought of traveling in the dark, *toward* the location of where FORM had been, terrified her.

"Are there other soldiers in the city?" Grace asked.

"Unfortunately, no. We've shifted our remaining support to Corpus Christi."

Grace straightened her shoulders. She thought of her husband. When duty called, he went *toward* danger, not away. She thought of Ryker. He followed his father's footsteps in service of his country and now planet. She cleared her throat. "Col. Brighton, we—We'll do it!"

"Wonderful! Your country—Your *world* thanks you! Leave now. Once you arrive at the base, call me, and tell me what you find."

"Yes, colonel. We'll get there as fast as we can."

~

Grace put her shoes on as she explained the situation to Jessie. Jessie accepted the plan.

Grace grabbed her car keys off the table and worked her way through debris in her hallway.

"We'll take my car," Grace said as she pulled the garage door open.

She flicked the light on. She and Jessie stopped dead in their tracks.

"That's not good," Jessie said.

Grace's car was flattened under a metal beam.

"Must have happened when that brute ruined my house!" Grace said. "What about your car?" she asked.

"Good idea," Jessie said.

They made their way back through the hallway and went to the front yard.

"No!" Jessie yelled.

Her car was overturned.

"How did that happen?!" Grace asked.

"I don't know. Vandals or a bomb blast I'm guessing. What do we do?"

Grace bit her lip. "We may have one option left."

"What?"

"Follow me."

Grace went back inside, grabbed another set of keys from a drawer, and led Jessie to the side of the house.

"My husband, Paul, always said he was going to do a road trip one day."

Grace reached out and ripped a dust-covered canvas tarp off a motorcycle.

"Whoa!" Jessie said. "Now *that's* a bike!"

"The Harley-Davidson Road King. Paul's favorite."

Jessie smiled. The blacked-out bike was easy on the eyes. "Do you know how to ride it?"

"Is a pig pork?!" Grace asked. "I took lessons the week after Paul died. It was a small way for me to honor him.

Once a month or so, I've been going on a ride to keep my skills and the bike fresh. And, well, to remember him."

Grace raised the side stand, wheeled the motorcycle to the street, handed Jessie a helmet, and motioned. "Hop on!"

Grace straightened the wheel, flipped the run/stop switch, and pressed the starter. The engine growled, ready for action.

"Hold on tight!" Grace said. "We're gonna help my boys!"

Jessie wrapped her arms tightly around Grace. Grace turned on the headlight, twisted the handle, and maneuvered the Harley down the street. In less than a minute, they were dodging flotsam and jetsam on the freeway, hair whipping in the twilight, racing to Lackland.

~

Grace braked and downshifted as they approached a side gate. "We're here!" she said to Jessie. "How long did that take?"

Jessie looked at her smartwatch. "Eighteen minutes," she yelled through her helmet padding. "But how do we get in?"

Grace looked up and down the road. "There!" She pointed. "I see an opening, probably blown away in a blast. And we only have twelve minutes to reset that system!"

"You sure we can do it?" Jessie asked.

"We don't have a choice if we want to beat these things."

"Let's go!"

Grace angled the bike toward the opening and maneuvered it through. Soon, the bike was throwing grass from its rear wheel as they traversed Lackland's now-shredded landscape.

The scene was apocalyptic. The base was almost completely dark. Lights had been shot out, roads were ruined, and explosions had destroyed the once thriving military base.

"Do you see the Communications Building?" Jessie asked.

"Not yet."

"Did Brighton give any directions?"

"Not exactly. Why don't I call him to see if he can get us there?"

"Good idea."

Grace stopped the bike and called Brighton. He picked right up.

"Colonel," Grace said, "we made it. Can you guide us to the building?"

"Excellent. Head to the south of the base. It's a brown building, red trim, with several satellites on the roof. Toward the back, it has an entrance with stairs that lead underground. That's where you'll want to go in."

Grace didn't spend time with pleasantries. She hung up and drove.

"That must be it!" Jessie said, pointing to a building with satellites on top.

Grace nodded, pulled up to the building, turned off the bike, took off her helmet, and called Brighton again.

"OK, we found it. But it looks like most of the satellites are knocked down."

"That may be the problem," Brighton replied. "Can you get on the roof, see if the connections are all right?"

"Yes, um, looks like there's a ladder. The gate on the roof is knocked down, so I should be able to get to the satellites. Just a minute."

Grace turned to Jessie. "Can you help me up?" She pointed to the ladder.

"Here, step on my hand."

Jessie hoisted Grace to the ladder. Once on the roof, she looked at the jumbled mess of cables. "I just need to decipher all of this," she said to Brighton, "I'll need a flashlight."

"Here," Jessie offered, "use the flashlight on my phone." Jessie tossed her phone to Grace.

Grace worked through the cables, determining which led where. She plugged any unplugged cables into an outlet on a far wall. "Anything?" she asked Brighton.

"Not yet," he answered.

They all waited a few moments to see if the system would reboot.

"Still nothing. Looks like you'll have to access the computer in the building and reset the system."

Grace was horrified at the thought of going into the building. She began to pace and covered her eyes with a hand. She spoke quickly, "So, we're—You know—Just supposed ... I never really thought I'd have to go into a dark building where the FORM likely were just a few *minutes* ago. I mean, I'm not saying I *can't* do this, just saying that it could be dangerous. But I'm a brave, you know, modern age, independent woman. I can do this—"

"—Mrs. Vaughn," Brighton tried to cut in.

Grace paced along the roof and kept rambling. "I've done hard things. That's what I told my boys growing up. It's how I raised them. 'We can do hard things,' I'd tell them. And this is something hard that *I* can do to serve my country ... and I don't ramble, but this is ... Here I am rambling."

"Mrs. Vaughn, if you'll allow me."

"Yes, yes. Sorry, just a little distracted at the thought of FORM—"

"We're confident they've left the area, Mrs. Vaughn," Brighton consoled.

"On a scale of one to ten?"

"A nine."

"So, there's ... a *chance* they're still here."

"Mrs. Vaughn, you need to pull yourself together. The fate of Earth is hinging on what you do next."

"No, no ... I ... Um, sorry, just letting my fears get the best of me here. Okay, here we go." Grace exhaled heavily. "Where can we find the computer?"

Brighton gave directions to Grace and Jessie for reaching the terminal in the lower level of the Communications Building. Grace's phone was just about to die, so she gave Brighton Jessie's number just in case.

Jessie helped Grace off the roof and headed to the back of the building. The unsettling silence and lack of light in the pre-dawn air heightened their concern.

They circumvented a pile of landscape tools that were likely abandoned days prior.

When they reached the back stairwell, Grace said unnecessarily, "We need to hurry."

Jessie nodded and led the way down the stairs. The entrance resembled an uncharted abyss. Jessie felt her way through cobwebs, broken tree branches, and debris. She screamed when a mouse pounced on her hand. She flicked it away and exhaled, then cleared the remaining debris and unlatched the door. She illuminated the corridor entry with her cell phone flashlight. She checked her battery: 7%.

"My phone's only going to last about five minutes," she noted to Grace.

"Let's make this quick."

Huddled together, they sidestepped through. With darkness all around them, their ears were on high alert, every sound enhanced: their breathing, their footsteps, the rustle of their clothes. They didn't dare speak for fear that someone—or something—might hear them.

Grace swallowed hard. Jessie instinctively did the same. Sliding along the walls, they made their way into a series of hallways within the building. Several turns in, a set of fire doors blocked them from the area they needed to access. As they approached the doors, a motion detector triggered.

A metallic unit at the top of the door clicked, releasing a locking mechanism that was holding the door closed. They pushed the door open. In the beige brick-lined hallway, green lights from several EXIT signs gave minimal illumination.

"Is this the right area?" Jessie asked in a whisper.

"Check the signs on the wall. We should be in the C Wing, Level G," Grace answered shakily.

Jessie scanned the wall. A sign read *C Wing*. "Should be the right one."

"Okay. About seven doors down, there should be a door labeled *Control Unit*." Grace instinctively let go of the door behind them.

Jessie lifted her light. Just above the sign that indicated their location, she saw a black badge scanner. "No!" she gasped. "Don't let the door—"

She was too late. The door closed and locked behind them.

Jessie ran and pushed on the door. It didn't budge. "Shoot!"

"What?" Grace asked.

"We didn't prop the door open."

"It's not—"

"Yup. It's locked. We don't have a badge," Jessie said.

"Dang it. Let's just find the computer and find another way out."

"Agreed."

They quickened their step; both of them silently second-guessing their willingness to enter the Communications Building. They worked fast to find the door labeled *Control Unit*.

Halfway down the hallway, they heard a faint, repetitive clank reverberating through the corridors. Jessie held her flashlight forward, her heart flurrying.

Grace grabbed Jessie's sleeve. Her mouth dried instantly. She whispered, "Turn it off! Something's coming."

Jessie nodded rapidly and turned off her flashlight. Side by side, they put their backs to the wall and sank to the ground. An eternity passed before fringes of blue light began to appear at a hallway intersection sixty feet ahead.

Grace could hear her heartbeat. She eased air in through her nose and exhaled gently through her mouth, trying to stay calm. As the blue light approached, her thoughts flashed to Ryker. She couldn't help but imagine what he had been experiencing on the FORM ship. She felt like fainting but forced herself to stay alert.

The seven-foot-tall, brawny body of a female FORM came into view. From the blue light emanating from the back of her neck, right forearm and chest, they could make out the fused titanium componentry in her right leg, left forearm, upper torso, and one side of her face. Her long, black hair reached the middle of her back and contrasted with her olive complexion. She wore a cloak-like covering that concealed most of her body. Her piercing, cerulean eyes were wild. She stopped at the intersection and looked at the computer embedded in her left arm. Detecting a radiation signal, she started toward Jessie and Grace.

Grace assumed that if the FORM could detect them, she was likely detecting electronic signals from their cell phones. She quickly, yet silently slid the back of her cell phone off and pulled out the battery.

Jessie tried to do the same, but she couldn't keep her hands from shaking. The cover popped off and hit the ground. The sound of bouncing plastic amplified against the vinyl tiles.

The FORM perked up. She quickened her pace and started to raise a light. Grace and Jessie braced themselves. They were about to be exposed.

Suddenly, an explosion stopped time in its tracks. Rippling shockwaves from a distant blast flashed through the hallway, shuddering the ground. They both screamed. The blast drowned them out.

Two more FORM emerged in the intersection. They seemed hurried and called to the FORM in front of them. She responded and retreated with the other two down another hallway.

Jessie and Grace exhaled. They didn't—couldn't—move, unsure of what to do. The hallways were dark. Eerie silence had returned.

Grace said rhetorically, "So much for our nine-in-ten chance!"

"Where is—What do we do now?" Jessie asked.

"Let's find that room. The military needs the disruptors readied in less than *six* minutes!"

"Then what? We're stuck in here?"

"Let's find the room first, then worry about that."

Jessie nodded, believing the weight of the world hinged on the success of their mission. Wiping the mounting moisture on her clammy hands, she put the battery back in her phone and checked the power: 5%. "We've *got* to move fast." She reopened her flashlight app.

They helped one another stand and continued through the corridor. Scanning their surroundings, they searched for signs of other FORM. All clear.

Three more doors down, they found the *Control Unit*. They opened the door to a room the size of a walk-in closet. A control panel on the far side of the room that must have been more than thirty years old contrasted starkly with sleek and much-more-modern-looking monitors and panel hardware to their left. The instruments were dark. They needed electricity.

"Let's call Col. Brighton," Grace said. "We need some direction."

Jessie phoned him.

"Jessie," Brighton's burley voice penetrated through the phone, "did you make it?"

"Barely. At least three FORM are still here."

"Are you safe?"

"There was this—Like a huge explosion and the three of them took off running. We think ... I *hope* we're safe for now."

Brighton was silent. Jessie wondered why he wasn't responding.

"Colonel? You still there?"

"Jessie, you two need—You need to work *fast.*"

"Understood. Tell us what to do."

"Listen to me carefully! There should be a master control button on the older-looking control panel. Do you see it?"

She looked at the panel and nodded. "Yes," Jessie answered, "but these things aren't turned on."

"They probably surged in a power outage. The power button is on the back left of the panel. Tell me if you find it."

The intense tone of Brighton's voice made Jessie nervous. Something bad was about to happen, she could feel it. She and Grace both continuously looked over their shoulders to see if any FORM were coming.

Jessie fumbled around the side of the panel and found the power button, then pushed it. The instruments whirred to life. Dozens of red, green, and blue lights flickered on the panels of the old and new-looking hardware as several monitors turned on.

"Got it."

"Well-done. Once the instruments are warmed up, you'll need to uplink the remote systems. First, push the master control button. That will activate the newer systems to your left. The login for the computer is 'operationform,' all lower case. There will be an icon on the monitor. It's called RDS for Remote Disruptor Systems. Open that software, and tell me when you're there."

The moment the systems were ready, Grace pushed the master control button.

Jessie moved the mouse to maneuver the newer computer on her left. Her sweaty palms left heavy moisture on the mouse. She found the icon and opened the software.

"Okay. I'm there."

"Click on Actions in the Task Bar, then check the Remote selection. That should do it."

Jessie followed his instructions. After clicking on the Remote selection in the pull-down menu, a prompt appeared asking to confirm the action. She clicked OK.

"Let me know if that works," Jessie said.

Brighton was silent for a long moment, then said, "It worked! Now we can patch the software to our systems here. You should both be very proud. What you've done— We now have a chance!"

Jessie and Grace exhaled, relieved.

"An honor, sir, thank you," Jessie responded.

Grace nodded in agreement.

"Now listen close. The two of you need to get out of there and off that base as fast as you possibly can!"

"The fire doors locked behind us, is there another exit?" Jessie begged.

"You have six minutes ... arrives." Brighton's connection began to fade. "Get ... main floor. North corridors ...."

The phone went silent.

"Col. Brighton? You there?" Jessie couldn't see her phone in the lightless room. It had died. "No! Quick, call him on your phone," she begged Grace.

Grace swiped her phone and tried to call. A warning appeared, *No Network Coverage*. "Mine won't dial."

"He said, um," Jessie swallowed. Her voice shook. "We need to get out of here as fast as we can."

"North corridor, main floor. Is that what I heard?"

"I think so."

"Let's find our way out. Something doesn't feel right."

"I have the same feeling."

Together, they felt their way through the dark. They may as well have been in a maze. Finding the north corridor in this din would be impossible.

~

Brighton looked at his phone. He redialed Jessie's number ten times and tried Grace's just as many. His heart sank. He had failed to guide them to safety. The freedom, even survival of the world had been on the line. He'd had no other option than to send the two innocent civilian women into a deathtrap: the mother and girlfriend of Ryker no less.

"Sir," an officer called, "that explosion, it was the FORM blasting their way into the radio room of the Communications Building. They're preparing to decode Dr. Sharp's scrambling algorithm."

"No! If they decipher his code, Operation: CAST—*everything* will be compromised." He looked at the countdown clock on the computer in front of him. The drone air strike he ordered for Lackland Air Force Base would arrive in five minutes, immediately after they finished using the disruptors. He couldn't reverse the air strike, too much was at stake. Dawn was nearly breaking. Operation: CAST's Phase Two: Desensitization was soon to begin.

Brighton pursed his lips, gritted his teeth, and stared at the monitoring systems in front of him. He had to give Grace and Jessie a way out.

"Corporal!" he yelled to a female technician nearby, "can you unlock all the internal doors in the Communications Building on Lackland?"

"Could it wait five minutes, sir? Col. Sanchez asked me to—"

Brighton lowered his voice and spoke intensely, "Drop what you're doing and unlock them *now*! We don't *have* five minutes. Not five seconds!"

The corporal sprang into action. "Yes, sir!"

Brighton watched hawk-eyed as the corporal moved her wiry fingers across a computer keyboard to access a digital blueprint of the Communications Building on Lackland Air Force Base. The map of the ground floor showed the door locks highlighted in red.

"I should be able to ...." the corporal's voice tapered under her breath as she patched into the Communications Building systems. Her eyes were fixed, glossy, and determined.

"This area," Brighton pointed to where Grace and Jessie were. "Light a path that they can follow to the outside."

"Okay, I should have access," the corporal said. "Do you want the lights on in the hallways?"

"No!" Brighton hurried. "Don't attract attention to their location."

"If I may sir ... whose location are we—"

"Two civilian women are in that building with three FORM. You're giving the women a way out."

The corporal swallowed hard. The situation intensified. She exhaled and went to work.

Brighton watched the blueprint as multiple door statuses shifted from red to green. The corporal had been able to create a path to the outside.

"Good work," Brighton praised.

"Thank you, sir, but ... how are we going to let them know the doors are unlocked?"

Brighton looked at the countdown clock. T minus under five minutes till the airstrike arrived. The CAST was preparing for Phase Two to begin, and he was being summoned. "We've done all we can. I'm a praying man. That's all we have left."

Brighton turned on his heel. He closed his eyes briefly, asking whatever powers might be to give him the words necessary to tell Ryker what had happened when it came time. Filling his lungs to capacity and breathing heavy, Brighton stepped out of a makeshift tent and prepared himself mentally for Phase Two: Desensitization.

As he headed down a dirt path, the corporal called. "Sir!"

"What is it?"

"The airstrike ...."

Brighton rushed to the computer. The airstrike drones had crashed. "No! There must be interference with the satellites." He thought inwardly for several moments. "There's no other choice," he conceded. "We can't let the FORM in the Communications Building access the disruptor controls *or* the scrambling algorithm. If they do, this is all for naught." Brighton grimaced. "Corporal, we only have one option. Turn on *all* the hallway lights. Give away the civilians' position." He shook his head. "They need to be bait."

~

Jessie gripped Grace's arm as they slithered through the lower level of the Communications Building. The empty, silence-filled hallways were impending. Humid spring air was chilled in the underground corridors, making the bricks lifeless and dank. Nervous perspiration seeped through their T-shirts, forming sweat marks that would have been unwelcome in public. Jessie's ponytail was tussled and nearly undone. Grace's mind wouldn't stop reminiscing of Paul, her deceased husband, and what his final moments of life must have been like, scenes she had considered many times in her mind the past several days.

They felt along the walls, panting.

"We need to move faster," Grace whispered.

Jessie agreed and increased the rate of her shuffle, keeping in sync with Grace. After finding their way around a corner, they heard a loud click, followed by another.

"Was that—?" Jessie mused.

"The sound we heard when that door unlocked for us earlier."

"All of these doors are held shut by magnetic, uh, things. So, I'm guessing, hoping, that would be the sound of them unlocking?"

"Let's find out." Grace felt her way along the brick wall, picked up her pace and guided them in the direction of the sound.

Before making significant headway, their eyes were temporarily blinded as the hallway lights illuminated.

"Yes!" Jessie cheered. "Now we can get out of here."

"There," Grace motioned toward a set of doors at the end of the hallway.

They ran and slammed open the doors. Tearing through the halls, they searched wildly for the next exit point. Four turns later, they had come to the intersection that was close to the *Control Unit* room they had found originally.

"We're going in circles," Grace moaned and looked side to side.

"Let's take a left after that second set of doors," Jessie said. "I think that's where we were supposed to go."

"Sounds good," Grace agreed.

They ran full speed, adrenaline coursing through their nourishment-drained veins. When they reached the first set of doors that they had found unlocked, they heard the clank of metal footsteps.

"Stop!" Grace demanded.

Jessie nearly hyperventilated. The metal footsteps reverberated through the hallways. "It's them!"

"Go through the doors, quietly."

The hairs on their arms stood on end.

Jessie creaked open the doors so they could slide through. Closing them gently behind, they picked up their pace, hoping to outrun the menacing machines.

"Here, right here!" Jessie called at an intersection. "This is where we need to go left."

Grace didn't hesitate and followed her lead, running.

Several explosions erupted behind them. They screamed in unison but didn't stop running. Blue streaks of energetic matter raced toward them from the preceding hallway.

"Faster!" Grace shouted. "Run!"

With their lives in the balance, they mustered every joule of available energy and sprinted toward the next set of doors.

Grace crashed through and found a placard that gave directions to the outside. "Follow me!" she demanded.

Looking over their shoulders, they could see blast marks forming in the bricks behind them. Finding a flight of stairs, they rushed to the main level and found an exit to the outside.

"We're gonna make it, come on!" Grace cried.

~

Jessie screamed, unaware she was doing so. Her senses were jumbled. She had never felt so disoriented, lost, and threatened. The long night, lack of nutrients, sleep, and veins satiated with adrenaline made it difficult to function. She tripped just before the exit and twisted her ankle.

The FORM's footsteps were coming up the stairs.

"Grace!" she screamed.

Grace had made it outside.

Jessie dry heaved, then stood and kept running. Every step was excruciating. She threw open the doors to the outside, stumbled over the sidewalk, and flailed herself on a patch of unkempt crabgrass. She couldn't move any farther. No chance of escape.

She turned toward the building entrance and watched as three FORM emerged to meet her: two male, one female. Their faces were senseless, cold. Their bodies were enormous and commanding—fused with metallic components melded with their russet skin. Their eyes were wolf-like, focused, and penetrating. The blue hue from their arms and neck dimly lit the pre-dawn air.

Jessie noticed something: the blue hue from the FORM was just enough to illuminate metal portions of two garden tools seemingly hovering in the air, making their way toward the FORM. Jessie knew that garden tools don't float; someone approaching from behind was wielding a set of makeshift weapons. She needed to distract them, so they didn't notice.

Jessie cried, "What is *wrong* with you freaks?" She screamed uncontrollably. "Why won't you leave us alone?!" She stood, her body racking. She prepared to make the ultimate sacrifice, hoping to buy the incomer enough time to reach the FORM.

The female FORM smirked and lifted its hand to fire. "I can't wait for all this water," she mocked. The other two FORM stood on either side of her and smiled evilly.

They were so riveted on Jessie and her drama-filled movements, they failed to recognize the warning signal coming from the computers embedded in their left arms; a human was behind them.

Jessie shrieked violently. She pretended to hyperventilate and yelled louder as she got up and ran, dodging shots as she rushed the FORM.

Jessie heard a screech of metal mixed with a thud followed by a scream, which, she was somewhat surprised, did *not* come from her. The female FORM wailed, as though death had come upon her. She grabbed at the back of her neck and twisted around, allowing Jessie to glimpse an axe sunk deep into her cervical spine. The FORM gave one final groan, then fell lifeless to the ground. The now unobstructed view revealed Grace standing in the background, wielding a pickaxe in her hands.

Grace swung the pickaxe to the side and drove it deep into one of the male FORM's chests. Grace retracted the pickaxe as he fell to the ground. As he collapsed, he fired three rounds from his blue ring, bloodying and incapacitating Grace's right arm, forcing her to drop the pickaxe.

The final FORM stretched for Grace. She tried to get away but tripped and fell. The FORM started to bend down so he could attack her.

Jessie grabbed the pickaxe and sank it into the FORM's back as he was bent forward. The FORM stumbled backward and scratched at its back. Jessie removed the pickaxe and sank it into his oversized body again, this time in his chest, forming a death-filled hole. Blue hydrogel seeped out of his wounds.

The FORM stumbled, looked down at himself in disbelief, and fell to his knees. The thump of his body made the earth quake.

Grace limped her way to Jessie who was staring at the FORM. "It's done, it's done, it's done."

Jessie threw her crude weapon down and stood resolute. "Monsters!" She spat and wiped blue hydrogel off her mouth, breathed heavily, and shook her head, trying to take in what had just happened. She needed immediate closure.

"Your phone battery should have enough juice to text Col. Brighton," Jessie said. "Let him know we did it!"

Grace nodded with pride and grabbed her phone. She texted: *We're safe, and three FORM are dead!*

Brighton responded right away. Grace read the text aloud. *I'm thrilled beyond words to know that!! I can't wait to hear the full story. Your courage is appreciated!*

Grace put a hand on Jessie's shoulder. "That was for Ryker and Jack," she whispered. She looked toward the sky. "Now it's *their* turn."

Chapter 42

FORM Ship

Ryker and Dr. Sharp listened focus-eyed in a dust-filled room. They held their ears close to Ryker's cell phone awaiting Brighton's announcement; they didn't yet know if Grace and Jessie had been successful at getting the disruptors back online.

They waited anxiously until, finally, Brighton's voice pierced through.

"They're working!" Brighton cheered. "Grace and Jessie did it! They reset the disruptors system. Dr. Sharp, begin Phase Two!"

Ryker and Dr. Sharp both threw fists of celebration into the air.

"All right, commencing sequence," Dr. Sharp said. He tapped vigorously on his wristband computer. "Col. Brighton, I've activated the FORM shield. Without further ado, fire the disruptors!"

Ryker heard Brighton say, "Fire!" in the background. They waited.

"Can you confirm both disruptors are firing?" Dr. Sharp asked anxiously.

Brighton didn't respond right away.

Ryker looked at Dr. Sharp worriedly. They both gazed at Ryker's cell phone, as though it would somehow produce a response.

"Yes!" Brighton's voice finally came through.

Dr. Sharp breathed a sigh of relief.

Brighton said, "I can confirm both are firing. It looks like they're causing an effect on the shield at the point of contact. It's too far away to really notice. Can you tell?"

Dr. Sharp tapped on his wristband computer. "Ha, ha! It's working as expected. Keep firing, I'm going to amplify the electromagnetic effect now." He went back to work on the computer.

"I wish there were something I could do to help," Ryker said.

"Ryker, you saved my life. I should say that was plenty of help!"

Ryker swallowed and nodded.

Dr. Sharp paused what he was doing. "And don't think for a moment I won't do everything in my power to help you save Jack! It wasn't my life *or* his; you will have saved both of us!"

Ryker half smiled. "Let's make it happen."

"That's my boy. One more sequence," Dr. Sharp said, "and we're going to create the largest EMP burst these FORM have ever experienced!" Dr. Sharp bit his lip and fidgeted his mouth. "This is the tricky part," he said, "if I slip up, I'll send the EMP *toward* Earth, which would completely cripple every electronic device our military has left."

"Did I just hear you right?" Brighton asked.

"Oh, sorry, did I say that out loud?"

"Yeah, loud and clear," Brighton verified.

"Not to worry, I won't slip up."

Everyone held their breath.

Ryker watched Dr. Sharp work with wild eyes. He'd never seen him in his lab, but he imagined that if he did, this is what he would look like while performing his most esoteric experiment. He visualized his hair standing up like Einstein's, and Ryker smiled a little.

"Okay, we're going to go silent for a few moments. Ryker will need to protect his phone in an electromagnetic field. Otherwise, his cell phone will be incapacitated by the EMP. Ryker, place your cell phone in the middle of that rock pile," he pointed as he spoke.

Ryker sheltered his phone in between several rocks.

"Good, now, I'm beginning the burst sequence. Three ... two ... and ..." Dr. Sharp thumped his thumb down on the wristband computer, "one!"

Ryker's butt cheeks left the floor as the ship jolted under the force of the EMP. He flailed in the air and fell on top of the rock pile next to him. His ribs instantly ached. "Ah!" he yelled in pain.

Dr. Sharp scrambled to the wristband device, which had flown out of his hand during the turbulence. He analyzed the screen with wide eyes. "It worked!" he hurrahed. "Col. Brighton, what does the shield look like?"

Silence.

Dr. Sharp looked toward Ryker's cell phone in the rock pile. "Brighton?"

Ryker unburied his cell. The screen was shattered. "No! I broke it!"

"We're deaf, then."

"Can't you call him with the device like you did me?"

"Not while I'm controlling the ship. We'll have to trust the plan."

"Did we tell them which door to enter?" Ryker asked.

"No. I'll simply have to get the ship positioned right at their location. They'll have to improvise. But we can't put the cart before the horse. We have to confirm Phase Two: Desensitization worked."

Ryker took a deep breath. "And there's only one way to find that out. *I* become the experiment."

Dr. Sharp nodded.

Ryker stood. He went to a door with a long gray handle that swiveled up and down to open or close the latch. He pulled the handle up.

They heard an immediate chorus of chaos. That was odd because when they'd found the room they were hiding in, that particular area of the ship was deserted.

"Sounds like *something* happened," Ryker said. He opened the door wider, checked both directions of the hallway and stepped out. "I'll be right back." He closed the door behind him to reduce the risk of Dr. Sharp being discovered.

Ryker bent down and switched his Ozzies to battle mode. The LEDs glowed red. He walked to the end of the hallway and emerged onto a platform that overlooked a towering warehouse-like area of the ship where hundreds of FORM had gathered. Some were running to what he assumed was an intended destination, several were yelling at one another, many were fighting, others slumped against a wall. Several looked at him in passing and didn't think much of his presence.

"You!" a female FORM to Ryker's left said. "Why aren't you at the check in? Aren't you one of the originals?"

That was the second time Ryker had a FORM tell him he looked like an original. They must have modified their componentry over time.

Ryker knew if he hesitated to respond, it could be worse than a wrong answer. "I'm part of the medical team. I've been helping the injured," he said.

"Then what are you doing standing up here? Medics are down there." She pointed to a bay with what looked to contain medical equipment.

"My head, something happened. I must have gotten disoriented."

"Join the club," the FORM said. "Everyone senses something is wrong in their head. Just get to where you're supposed to be!"

The FORM supported her weight with a railing and staggered away.

"I guess that answers that," Ryker said to himself. Phase Two appeared to work.

Ryker started to turn around to return to the room with Dr. Sharp, but a specific FORM caught his eye. He paused and watched her enter from the far side of the room. She didn't seem to be disoriented. Rather, she was irritated. She started ordering other FORM around, and they listened.

"Oh my gosh," he whispered, "that's the FORM that was standing next to Maazi when they were in the Pentagon." Ryker remembered her appearance well; she was the FORM that had helped Maazi when he stumbled on global television.

The FORM looked up toward Ryker. Her eyes instantly glowered. Ryker sensed she knew who he was. He backed away from the platform slowly, hoping it was a fluke.

It wasn't.

The FORM yelled, "Ryker Vaughn!"

Ryker bolted off the platform and raced down the hallway. He could hear the FORM's footsteps thumping in the distance. His Ozzies pushed him faster. He reached the door and slid the handle up to open it. He stepped through the door, swiveled the handle, and pushed it over to lock it.

Dr. Sharp looked at him in surprise. "Did it work?"

"Mostly! One of them is coming! It doesn't look like she got desensitized. Hurry, can we lower the ship?"

Dr. Sharp didn't take time to respond. He wiggled his fingers across his wristband computer. "It'll take a minute!"

"We probably don't have a minute."

Ryker searched the room for a weapon or other form of protection. They wouldn't have time to escape.

"Is there a weapon or something?" Ryker asked rhetorically.

The ship jolted. Dr. Sharp had started its downward descent. Phase Three: Infiltration was primed, but unless they found something to stop the approaching FORM, it could be compromised.

The door clanged.

"What about that thing?" Ryker pointed to the wristband device. "Didn't you say it provides protection?"

"Yes!" Dr. Sharp said. "Hurry, get next to me."

The door crashed open. Dr. Sharp shuttered involuntarily at the bang and threw his hands upward, sending the wristband device into the air before he could engage the protective shield.

Taahiya caught the wristband device and scowled at them. "Are *you* the source of all the black magic going on on this ship?" she asked lividly. She breathed heavily and blinked her eyes.

Ryker could tell she was somewhat disoriented—the EMP must have partially disrupted her neurochip—but she was more angry than affected.

"First," she slurred her words, "an electrical attack disrupts half the ..." she mentally searched for the word, "*systems* on our ships, then I find my people thinking they're 3,000 circuits back in time, and when we go to get Ryker, he isn't in his holding place! How did you ...?" She stopped and looked at the wristband device. "You took his *sacred* one. Have you no regard whatsoever," she breathed laboredly, "for us or anything that belongs to us!?"

Dr. Sharp's cheeks turned crimson red. "*Sacred?*" he yelled. His middle-aged jowls shook. "*Sacred?!* You just annihilated entire cities on our planet. You leveled militaries, even citizens and children! And you want to sit and lecture *us* on taking things that are *sacred?*"

"You little piece of ... you know what?" She staggered and grabbed Dr. Sharp by the neck, making him gag wildly. As she lifted him in the air, a magnet in Dr. Sharp's satchel drew closer to her neurochip. "Why am I wasting my time? I'm going to kill—"

Taahiya dropped Dr. Sharp, grabbed her head, and growled in pain as she rocked back and forth. The magnet was affecting her.

Ryker noted the window of opportunity. He made eye contact with Dr. Sharp, pointed to his magnet-wielding satchel, clapped his hands, and held them out like he was calling for a pass in basketball.

Dr. Sharp had watched enough Boston Celtics games to read the signal. He grabbed the magnet and threw it toward Taahiya's head.

Ryker pushed off the floor with the full force of his Ozzies and snatched the magnet midair. He slapped it next to Taahiya's neurochip.

Taahiya's body and hands unexpectedly relaxed, causing the wristband device to fall to the floor. She didn't sink to her knees; she face planted onto the floor and laid motionless.

"Is she dead?" Dr. Sharp asked.

"I don't know," Ryker replied as he caught his breath.

Dr. Sharp was a pacifist at heart, but he wasn't stupid; these beings weren't trying to be friends. "We should, uh, make sure she is," he said.

"Don't watch," Ryker said.

Dr. Sharp turned his head.

Sounds of something being pulled from a sheath followed by the clank of metal on metal, then metal slicing through soft tissue, were muffled but distinguishable to the doctor's peace-loving ears.

"It's done," Ryker confirmed.

Dr. Sharp shivered. "Okay. Hurry, I can't imagine this location isn't compromised. We need to find another hiding spot to begin Phase Three. We have 30,000 soldiers to get onto this ship!"

"Lead the way," Ryker said as he wiped blue ooze off his hands.

They ran down several hallways. Six turns in, they heard a pain-filled scream. The howls echoed through the ship.

"That can't be good," Dr. Sharp said.

"I have a feeling Maazi just found what we left behind."

"And that probably means there's more than one FORM that wasn't successfully desensitized."

"And Maazi would be the worst one to still have functional," Ryker cautioned. "Hurry, we need to get the CAST on board, *ASAP!*"

"Wait," Dr. Sharp said. He grabbed Ryker's shoulder and stopped their forward motion. "If that's Maazi, and he's screaming about the FORM we just took out, Jack will be in grave danger. If Maazi wanted revenge before ...."

Ryker's face paled, then angered. "Dr. Sharp, can you lower the ship while running?"

"Of course."

"Do it. We need to get to Jack. He won't have much time!"

Chapter 43

What Was Once Corpus Christi, TX

Brighton stood with Gen. Childress and the president on a newly formed rise in the Earth's crust from which vantage point they could assess the CAST hiding in the surrounding region.

The three of them protected their faces from rough sprays of sea water. Brighton unshielded his face and stared at the black FORM ship a mile overhead.

The purple glow around its exterior still pulsated sporadically after sucking inward and dispensing its energy. The ship jolted as though an internal earthquake rocked its core. Shockwaves from the energy release ripped across the ocean waters, pushing violent waves of water ashore.

"Something seems to have worked, Dr. Sharp!" Brighton yelled into his cell phone. "Their shield is compromised, and the implosion affected the sea waters down here." Brighton waited for a response. There was none. "Dr. Sharp?" Brighton looked at Gen. Childress and the president. "Dr. Sharp!" He looked at his phone. There was no connection. "We're blind!"

Concern entered their hearts. Without a line of communication, they would be guessing at what to do next.

"That was the EMP," Brighton said. "We need to mobilize the CAST, now!"

They all observed the ship momentarily.

"That likely *was* the EMP, but we have no indication it worked!" the president said. He pushed his fingers through his hair, his telltale signal he was severely conflicted. He threw his arms in the air. "For all we know, the FORM are still up there readying a counterattack. What if they're stronger than ever? We saw what the disruptors did last time."

Gen. Childress squinted and rubbed his chin as he looked at the ship. He shook his head. "I have to agree with the president. It's too risky to make the call. If we show our next move too early, or at all if they're not desensitized ... this operation is over."

They had no way of knowing whether Phase Two: Desensitization worked, or whether they should begin Phase Three: Infiltration.

"The sun will rise soon. If we don't mobilize now, how long do we wait?" Brighton asked.

The president looked at Gen. Childress then back at Brighton.

"If we wait too long, we also risk compromising the mission," Brighton deliberated.

The president pointed at the ship. "Gentlemen!"

They all looked up. Through the breaking light of dawn, they could see the ship descending rapidly.

"It's Dr. Sharp, he's lowering the ship!" Brighton said. "That's the signal to begin Phase Three!"

"Or it's the FORM taking back over," Gen. Childress countered.

"The core of the ship is coming directly over our location," Brighton observed. "Just like Dr. Sharp said. It's him."

The three of them looked overhead. The ship was making its way toward them. The edge of the hexagonal-shaped core was nearly parallel with where they were standing.

"That's where Dr. Sharp said he was going to position it," Brighton said. "We *need* to mobilize!"

Gen. Childress inhaled and exhaled deeply, then nodded. "I don't see any other way. We don't have a military to fight with even if they are planning an attack. The CAST is our best hope." He nodded again. "All right, give the signal!"

Brighton raced to a Humvee ten feet away and grabbed a comm. "It's time! CAST! Return to duty! We have thirty minutes to infiltrate. Follow your commanding officer, don't rush each other, but move fast! Subvert the ship as deeply as you can. We're flying blind; we don't know for sure if Phase Two worked or how long the desensitization will last. If it didn't or it wears off ... well, *that's* why you have your magnets. Once you're aboard, use your best judgment and wait to execute Phase Four: Annihilation, from the inside out, until thirty minutes from my mark! Get ready!"

Brighton set a timer on his watch. As the ship teetered toward the shore, Brighton lifted his hand in the air. The CAST in the surrounding regions awaited his signal. The moment the ship rammed into the sand, Brighton dropped his arm giving the go-ahead and yelled into the comm, "Go!"

The 30,000-strong army of Ozzie-strengthened, battle-ready amputee soldiers poured out of collapsed buildings, tattered tents, broken homes, and still-smoldering rubble across the newfound beaches of what was once Corpus Christi Bay.

Those with Ozzie legs ran at world-record paces. Soldiers with Ozzie arms swung on poles to help them hurdle and clear wreckage in the streets.

The CAST rushed toward the black ship. Their silent approach reduced their risk of detection.

Brighton turned to the president and saluted him. "Mr. President, if we don't see you again ...." His words dangled.

He nodded in appreciation. The gratitude on his face spoke more than words.

Gen. Childress saluted as well with a similar expression of appreciation.

"Gentlemen," the president saluted, "the world couldn't ask for a better pair of protectors. It's been an honor!" He dropped his salute with vigor.

"Gen. Childress," Brighton remarked as he checked the timer on his watch, "T minus twenty-nine minutes till Phase Four. Let's move!"

Gen. Childress ripped his outer jacket off and ran. Brighton followed suit.

Brighton yelled as he sprinted toward the black ship, "Snipers, cover us. We're heading in!"

~

Sergeant First Class Jason Phillips was one of two dozen snipers along the shorelines. He squinted and peered through the reticle of his M24 from atop a hotel in the distance. He watched Brighton from a quarter mile away as he slammed several packs of C4 on a wall of the black ship, then saw him take cover behind a boulder. Brighton had to create another opening in the ship to get 30,000 soldiers on quickly. The reactive astatine in the ship's exterior doubled the force of the blast, creating an enormous entry point. Brighton checked his corners then disappeared into the hole with Gen. Childress and a handful of amputees behind him.

Phillips breathed shallowly, steadying his rifle. Soon after the explosion, eleven FORM emerged from the hole. They seemed disoriented. They appeared to notice they were in an unnatural environment. As they saw a swarm of soldiers who looked somewhat like them rushing toward them, they felt threatened and unleashed a barrage of plasma blasts that took out a dozen amputees. Phillips ripped three bullets into the chests of two FORM. Their blue hydrogel innards spattered on the surface of the black ship. They fell to the ground unresponsive.

"Two down," he announced through his mouthpiece.

"Got one," another sniper confirmed.

Within seconds, the sniper team had taken out all eleven FORM. No others emerged.

Phillips watched as the remainder of the CAST boarded the ship through C4-created entry points.

"We'll keep watch," Phillips said. "If any others come out, we'll be ready, but it looks like it's up to those on the ship now."

~

Brighton marveled at the plant-covered walls and brilliant turquoise water tanks perched in the rafters of the spacious opening. He suddenly understood why Dr. Sharp had said they had developed something fascinating. He wished there were time to observe things more closely. There wasn't. They were nearing a group of FORM who were noticeably dazed and confused. Two seemed to be arguing about who was in charge. Others were on one knee, or leaning against a wall, still trying to come to their senses.

"Don't draw your weapons," Brighton said to the group trailing him. "Act natural. We'll see what happens."

Brighton led the group forward. He walked confidently, to show that he belonged there.

A FORM noticed their approach. She narrowed her eyes, observing them carefully.

The fact that she didn't attack right away indicated to Brighton that the desensitization likely worked. They seemed to recognize the group as some of their own.

"I thought you were all dead!" the FORM said.

"We're not," Brighton responded. "We ..." he thought quickly about what he should say. "We survived the blast." He wasn't totally lying; they had survived many blasts the past two weeks.

"The blast!? No one could have survived that!" The FORM looked at Brighton speculatively.

"We had the shield technology," Brighton said.

The FORM was taken aback and opened her eyes wide.

Brighton swallowed. He couldn't tell if the FORM was shocked out of surprise or anger.

"So, *you* were the group that was chosen to test the energy formation!" the FORM said.

"We were," Brighton beamed.

"Then you should come with me. You'll need to share your report."

Brighton looked back at the group for approval. Gen. Childress nodded. They didn't have a choice.

"Lead on. We have much to report," Brighton said.

They followed a complex set of hallways with intersections, throughout which they saw extraordinary plant life and the ship's diamond-built canopy overhead. The ship was breathtaking, and magnitudes more valuable than Fort Knox.

They emerged onto a platform that overlooked a large gathering area. Brighton and those with him could see hundreds of CAST members infiltrating the FORM successfully. Brighton smiled at Gen. Childress who nodded back. The Ozzies were working!

Chapter 44

FORM Ship

"Is it working?" Ryker begged Dr. Sharp.

Dr. Sharp shook the wristband device. "It must have taken some damage from the EMP," he said. The device screen was failing. "I don't know which way to turn."

Ryker punched a wall. "How are we supposed to get Jack?"

"I, I don't know. I didn't memorize the hallways. I familiarized myself more with the ventilation systems."

"Then let's get up in them," Ryker suggested.

"But I don't know where we are in the ship right now. I wouldn't even know which way to go. We could very well head in a direction that gets us farther away from him."

Ryker put his head in his hands. He kicked the wall in frustration.

"Ryker, please, you may alert—"

"What's with all the banging!" a FORM yelled from the end of the hallway. As soon as he saw Ryker and Dr. Sharp he shouted, "I thought I heard humans!"

The FORM obviously had not been desensitized. He aimed his fingertipped weapons and fired multiple plasma bursts. Ryker dodged but not fast enough; one grazed his right arm.

"Run!" Ryker yelled.

They raced around a corner and took a left at an intersection that led to a large door at the end of a hallway.

Ryker shimmied the handle. It wouldn't budge. He looked around for a possible escape route.

Blue tracers zipped toward them from the intersection.

They froze. There was nowhere to go.

"Do you have a magnet?" Ryker asked.

"Yes!"

Dr. Sharp tossed a magnet into the air for Ryker to catch. It turned blue midair and exploded into plasma-like energy.

"Wow," the FORM said, holding his weapon upright. "I'll give you guys some credit. You move fast." The FORM laughed. "Gosh, you're something else. We've been trying to find you two all day. Seems like you've been up to some crap."

The large door behind Ryker clicked and groaned, then swung open.

A FORM emerged with Brighton and a few CAST soldiers in tow.

Ryker was somewhat surprised to see that Gen. Childress wasn't with Brighton.

The FORM with Brighton saw her counterpart holding a weapon toward Ryker and Dr. Sharp. "What's going on here?" she asked.

"We're being duped by these things," the weapon-wielding FORM said.

"What are you talking about? They're from the first generation."

"No, they're *not*. They *look* like them, but they're imposters from this planet who are trying to deceive us! They want to kill you, nothing more."

The FORM looked at each of the humans. She noticed Dr. Sharp and his lack of metallic componentry. "Where are *you* from?" The FORM didn't wait for a response. She looked at Brighton. "Is he telling the truth? Are you the blast survivors?"

Brighton replied, "We are," partially lying again.

"We come in peace!" Dr. Sharp yelled.

His comment caught the group off guard. They eyed him curiously.

"We truly want peace," Dr. Sharp pleaded.

"Oh, good. I happen to be a peacekeeper," the FORM aiming its weapon smirked. "All right folks, we're going to finish this charade."

The FORM raised his arm to fire a death shot, but a clang from a metal panel being ripped out of the ceiling above his head distracted him.

Suddenly, Gen. Childress swung out of the ceiling upside down and quickly exposed the FORM's head to a magnet. The FORM shivered briefly and slapped his head with his hand. He lowered his arm and took a few breaths like he was coming out of anesthesia, then stared at the group.

"What are you all doing up here?" he asked.

The FORM next to Brighton was taken aback. "What did you just do to him?" she begged. The FORM lifted her arm and prepared to fire at Ryker.

"Now!" Brighton yelled.

Gen. Childress pulled out his tactical knife and drove it into the heart of the FORM standing next to him.

Brighton attempted the same on the FORM near him, but she dodged the attack and flung Brighton back through the doorway. The FORM raised her arm toward Ryker and fired what she hoped would be a death blow.

The gears in Gen. Childress' Ozzie ground as he jumped through the air and angled his body to absorb the shot. "Run!" he yelled as his stomach swallowed plasma energy. He grabbed the remaining FORM and pulled her down to the floor with him. He used his last measure of strength and drove his knife into her heart. The FORM fell halfway onto Gen. Childress, lifeless.

"Finish this!" Gen. Childress whispered to Ryker and drooped his head awkwardly onto the chest of the FORM.

Gen. Childress and the two FORM laid motionless in the hallway.

Ryker's heart raced and his vision clouded. Gen. Childress' final act was a sacrifice for him. He could barely feel the several hands pulling him backward through the doorway as it closed, shutting Gen. Childress' body behind it.

Brighton locked the latch and checked their surroundings. They were safe—for the moment.

"What was that?!" Brighton yelled.

"Gen. Childress just got killed!" Dr. Sharp blubbered with a shaky voice.

"I saw that. A soldier of soldiers! We'll mourn when there's time. But that's not what I'm referring to. What was that with the FORM? Why did one want to kill us before Gen. Childress desensitized it and the other didn't?"

"Not all of them were fully desensitized," Dr. Sharp said. "I don't think it's many, but a few."

"Which means we really need to be on our toes," Brighton said. He pulled out a canteen and took a swig of water, then looked at his watch. "T minus fifteen minutes! We'd better keep moving."

"I have to get to Jack!" Ryker cried as he staggered to his feet. He coughed, trying to shake off emotions. "I, I know where we are now." He swallowed hard and pointed to a landmark he and Dr. Sharp had become familiar with. "Dr. Sharp, that's the hallway that leads to the organics processor. Jack is down the other way."

"You," Brighton pointed to a CAST soldier, "go with Ryker. Dr. Sharp, get us back to the place where the CAST is infiltrating successfully. We'll join the army for annihilation!"

"Will do," Dr. Sharp said. "Ryker, we'll meet you at the organics processor room for extraction."

Ryker nodded and took a breath to recover, then said, "Let's go!" to his new wingman.

"Wait!" Dr. Sharp stopped, halting the group. "Ryker, your—" He grabbed Ryker by the shoulders and nearly teared up. "Your father would have been proud, young man ... for all that you've done!"

Ryker smiled and nodded. "And your wife the same, doctor."

"Gentlemen, I appreciate your sentiments, but we only have *fourteen* minutes!" Brighton stressed. "No time for chit chat. Let's make it happen."

~

Ryker raced down the hall with his comrade while the rest of the group went in the opposite direction.

They turned a corner that led to the access point where Jack's cell was located. "This way!" Ryker directed and motioned his arm in the air.

They slowed before rounding the final corner. As they did, Ryker saw the same three FORM he had disabled earlier guarding Jack's cell.

The FORM looked at him with a tinge of curiosity.

"Is this another medic?" one of the FORM asked, motioning to Ryker's comrade.

"He is. The boy in that room is ill." Ryker pointed to the door behind which Jack was being kept. "We need to help him."

"What boy? We were told this room contained weapon reserves."

"Can we check?" Ryker asked.

The FORM hesitated. "Only if we go in first."

"Agreed," Ryker acknowledged.

The FORM opened the plant-draped door and stepped in the room. "I guess there *is* a boy in here," he mused.

Ryker saw Jack huddled under a swarm of plant leaves in the back of the room.

"Jack!" he cried.

Ryker could hardly bear to see what Maazi had done to his little brother: his body was bruised, an eye swollen, his face bloodied, his teenage innocence stripped.

"Jack!" he called again.

Jack looked up at Ryker with his non-swollen eye. "Ryker?" He got to his knees. "Ryker?" He tried to stand and stumbled. "Ryker, is this a dream?"

"No, buddy. It's me. It's me!" Ryker ran and scooped Jack up in his arms. He held him like his very life had hung in the balance.

It had.

"Ouch!" Jack blurted. "Well, apparently I have bruises where I didn't know a body part existed."

"And there's the Jack I know," Ryker rejoiced. He hugged Jack again. "Come on!"

Before Ryker could get another word out, he felt a thud of pressure on his head. His vision faded to blackness.

Chapter 45

FORM Ship

Brighton looked at his watch for the fourth time. *Ten minutes!* his mind yelled. Infiltration was running short. Brighton felt like they were wandering the halls aimlessly.

"Do you know where we're going?" Brighton asked Dr. Sharp.

"Yes, yes, this device," Dr. Sharp held up the wristband device, "seems to be malfunctioning slightly. But let me fix ..." His words trailed as he tweaked the device and tapped the screen. "Ha! That should do it. Maazi may be an egomaniac, but he sure did engineer a device with some serious power. This way."

Dr. Sharp turned them back around to a spot they already had traversed. They passed through several openings, which allowed Brighton to see CAST soldiers on platforms below interacting successfully with FORM enemies. Things still looked promising.

"Here, right here," Dr. Sharp pointed vigorously, "down this corridor is where we can enter the Grand Hall. You can hear them congregating."

Brighton listened. He heard what Dr. Sharp could: thunderous chatter emanating from a distant room. Brighton felt a rush of relief that was instantly trumped by anxiety; their destination also meant they were that much closer to the final battle for Earth.

He followed Dr. Sharp through clusters of draped vines in a corridor that led to an oversized set of doors. They heaved them open slightly and stepped into a scene of organized chaos. Thousands of FORM were mingling with CAST soldiers. *The infiltration is working on a broad scale!* Brighton thought. *Gen. Childress would have appreciated this.*

He assessed their surroundings. The hall was enormous. The ceiling had to have been more than 200 feet high, but not without reason. Trees the size of Sequoias tussled the rafters where bright lights provided photosynthetic effect. The trees' root systems must have been in a room below as the floor wrapped around the trees mid-trunk. Turquoise waters were contained in million-gallon tanks perched high above. Broad-leaf plants sprouted straight out of the walls. The room was otherwise empty, which meant only the tree trunks would provide a barricade of protection if needed during a fight.

"Dr. Sharp," Brighton cautioned, "it's going to get ugly in here. You need to take cover before someone recognizes you, or, *doesn't* recognize you."

Dr. Sharp looked around the room. "There." He pointed to an inset between two walls draped by plants. "I'll hide behind these plants." He hurried to the crevice and slipped behind a cluster of leaves.

Brighton led the group deeper into the crowd.

He brushed the arm of a FORM who looked down at Brighton's Ozzie.

"That's an odd one," the FORM noted.

"Yeah," Brighton said nonchalantly. "They only had prototypes available. I was one of the originals."

The FORM looked at Brighton skeptically. "An original! I thought you all died in the first war."

"We survived the blast. We just finished giving our report."

The FORM's eyes opened wide. "You're an enigma!" she emitted. "Is that where all of these have come from?" The FORM reached her arm out and motioned toward the CAST.

"The majority, yes," Brighton said, hoping the conversation would end soon. He looked at his watch. Seven minutes.

"Part of the reason we're here is to discuss *you*, apparently," the FORM said.

Brighton snapped his head to meet the FORM's gaze. "Us?"

"Well, yes. We all thought you originals were dead. And suddenly, tens of thousands of you are here. Seems odd, doesn't it?"

Brighton cleared his throat. "What can I say? We were supposed to go undetected ... we did our job."

"Ha, ha!" the FORM tipped her head back and laughed. "A true warrior! I should like to go into battle with you. And from the looks of it, we soon can; seems we just neared a planet with water the likes of which we've never encountered! Thing is, no one can remember how we got here! But that's a secondary concern Maazi and Taahiya will figure out. We're about to discuss our plan of attack to make this planet our own."

"Here, here!" several FORM near them cheered.

"I look forward to it!" Brighton added. "Now, I have to find someone from long ago."

"Whatever suits you," the FORM said and looked toward the front of the room.

Brighton went to a side wall, made sure no one was looking at him, and hoisted himself up using some vines to get a better idea of what they would be up against. From what he could estimate, there were slightly more CAST soldiers than FORM, but they looked so little by comparison. Their attack would have to be swift ... and deadly.

He saw a ramp that led to a raised landing at the front of the room. *That must be their version of a stage*, he thought. He was right. Seconds later, an authoritarian-looking FORM with a purple-colored cloak entered the room and made his way onto the raised platform.

"Settle down everyone," the FORM's voice boomed through the hall. He glared to quiet the group. "Two things are happening. First, we're trying to determine how we got where we are, but frankly, we don't much *care*. The planet beneath us is freaking incredible. It has more water than any planet we've ever discovered!"

The FORM cheered. CAST soldiers joined to blend in.

Brighton checked his watch. Four more minutes of infiltration. He wasn't sure how they were going to do it, but it was important they kept the annihilation timeline. CAST soldiers in other parts of the ship would soon begin Phase Four. If CAST soldiers in the Grand Hall didn't attack at the same time, FORM in other parts of the ship could send a message to those in the hall and compromise the mission. *We still have several minutes,* Brighton concluded. He waited to see how things panned out.

"And second," the FORM on stage continued, "we're trying to find out how it is that thousands of our originals, who we all thought were *dead*, suddenly appeared out of nowhere!" The FORM looked skeptically at the CAST soldiers in the crowd.

Thousands of FORM in the Grand Hall did the same. They analyzed the short, archaic looking versions of themselves.

"Yeah!" a FORM in the audience yelled. "What *is* going on around here? It's like some of us remember things from a thousand years ago, and some of us can't remember things from an hour ago."

"I can't remember my name, but I somehow remember this new, yet desirable language!" one FORM yelled.

The FORM onstage scowled again to settle the murmurings. "We know, we know. We're all in the same boat. We'll have answers soon, but our most pressing item is to take advantage of our situation and overtake the resources on the planet beneath us. It appears it's already been compromised on many levels. It shouldn't take much to commandeer."

"I disagree," another FORM said, "I think we have a different priority. I just received a message that one of our own is dead in a hallway with one of the originals laying on top of it. I don't like what's going on."

The room fell uncomfortably silent. Hundreds of FORM became restless and started to look suspiciously at the CAST.

The hairs on Brighton's neck raised. *Someone found Gen. Childress!* He looked at his watch. Three minutes. Things were headed south. He had to manage this.

"I have your answer!" Brighton hollered.

Every FORM and CAST soldier looked back at Brighton.

Brighton released the bundle of vines he was holding for support and strode to the front of the room. It was the longest walk of his life. Perspiration pushed through his forehead pores. Any of the FORM could have turned on him in a moment and taken his life. Yet he didn't let the fear faze him. He walked slowly, confidently, and strode up the ramp and made sure his Ozzie was on full display as he stood in front of the crowd.

"As you can see, I'm one of the originals. And I'll be happy to tell you where we came from and how we got here."

Every eye was on him.

"We survived the blast!"

Thousands of FORM gasped in unison. Doubt-filled chatter erupted in the hall. Several FORM waved Brighton off in disbelief.

"Our job was to go undetected. And ... we succeeded!"

Several FORM cheered, others shook their heads in disbelief.

Brighton glanced at his watch. Two minutes.

"And it's fair that you're wondering where it is we took refuge."

Brighton looked at the FORM onstage.

"Yes," the FORM said questioningly and flared his nostrils, "we *are* curious."

"Well, you need look no further than the planet beneath us. After we survived the blast, this is where we resided. And we're the ones who brought you here."

"What?!" the FORM onstage hollered in amazement. "But how did you get here?"

"A special ship, a forerunner to this one transported us. We found enough water to support all of us for eons to come. We've been awaiting your arrival."

The FORM onstage seemed floored at the response.

"But what's up with us forgetting so much?" a FORM in the audience asked.

"This planet," Brighton said, motioning his arm to the outer expanses, "has a powerful electromagnetic field. As you passed through it, your neurochips were fried, causing you to lose segments of memory."

The FORM onstage seemed to accept Brighton's responses even more.

"I'm not buying any of this crap!" a FORM yelled from the audience. "There's no way anyone could have survived that blast! I just—I just don't see how any of this is possible."

Several FORM agreed with their comrade.

"I think he's an imposter!" a FORM yelled and energized her personal shield, causing a purple orb of energy to emerge around her. "And until I remember who the heck I am, I won't trust *anything* he says."

Hundreds of FORM soon followed that FORM's lead; individualized orbs started sprouting around FORM throughout the crowd.

Brighton nearly panicked. With those shields engaged, the CAST would never have a chance. He glanced at his watch. *Forty-five seconds!* He had to get the shields deactivated. He scanned the room briefly and noticed Dr. Sharp peering through the leaves. He had an idea.

"Well, it's like a saying we've heard on this planet, 'The *proof* is in the pudding!' We even have a way to fix your neurochips and bring all your memory back."

The FORM onstage reared his head back and squinted as he looked at Brighton. He engaged his personalized shield. "Prove it," he ordered.

"Gladly. Uh, Dr. Sharp, would you be so kind as to help me out?"

Brighton looked at the crevice in the wall where Dr. Sharp was hiding. He noticed several CAST soldiers in the audience open their eyes in horror and look at each other. He knew they were worried he was about to compromise the entire mission.

Brighton motioned for Dr. Sharp to come out. Dr. Sharp hesitantly emerged from his hiding spot. He waved to the crowd, nodded his head, and smiled awkwardly.

"This is Dr. Steven Sharp," Brighton said. "He was one of the original scientists who worked with Maazi to develop our *first* personalized protection device. He found a way to survive without changing his body. Dr. Sharp, if my understanding is correct, you can *undo* what has just been done." Brighton gave Dr. Sharp a stern look. He hoped he understood that he wanted him to disarm each of the FORM's personalized shields. Phase Four was imminent!

"Oh, of course," Dr. Sharp obliged with a chuckle.

"I'll give the countdown," Brighton said. "We call this memory reversal procedure Phase Four!"

CAST soldiers knew exactly what Brighton meant. They all readied for what came next.

"Comrades, friends, we've been down on this planet for a long time, and we know *exactly* how to take over the people who live there. Let's get you all repaired so we can *annihilate* what's in our way and take this planet's water!"

Several FORM seemed to let their guard down and cheered, "Let's do this!"

"Here we go," Brighton said. "Three, two ...."

"Wait!" Dr. Sharp yelled. "Slight problem here." He fumbled with the wristband device. "Just need to adjust the algorithm."

Everyone in the room looked at Dr. Sharp curiously as he modified this and arranged that, then tapped here, then there on the wristband.

"Oh, okay, that should do it," Dr. Sharp said. He tapped his left shoulder and nodded toward Brighton.

Brighton raised his left hand and finished. "And ... one!"

Brighton watched Dr. Sharp thump his finger down on the screen of his wristband device. Each one of the FORM shields instantly disintegrated.

Brighton watched the CAST take immediate advantage. Ten thousand soldiers snatched long-bladed knives from their concealed locations and sank them deep in the chest of whatever FORM was standing next to them.

The unaccosted FORM keyed into the attack. But before most could react, they felt a sharp pierce in their chest. Then their world went dark.

The scene exploded into bedlam as screams, hollers, and growls erupted.

The final battle for Earth's water raged!

Unaffected FORM tried to reengage their shields, but their arm computers wouldn't respond. Their split-second hesitation cost them their lives. They were quickly annihilated.

FORM after FORM slumped to the ground.

"Traitors!" the FORM onstage yelled at Brighton. He raised his arm to fire a death blow, but before he could get a shot off, a bullet zipped through his head. The crash of his body on the metal stage rocked the floor.

Brighton looked into the crowd. One of the soldiers who had been with him had shot the FORM to protect him.

"Nice work, soldier!" Brighton yelled.

Brighton grabbed his knife and leaped off the stage toward a FORM that had its back turned. He drove the knife through the back of its neck. Blue ooze dripped down his hands and soiled his black shorts. He heaved the FORM to the floor and jumped up to attack another, but he was met by a fist to the face. The FORM's metal knuckles had no mercy. Brighton felt his cheekbone crack and his eye swell instantly. As he fell to the ground, he pulled out his sidearm and fired five rounds into the heart of the FORM. It grabbed its chest, blue ooze drizzling through its fingers.

"What are you doing?" the FORM begged. "We did nothing to you!"

"You annihilated our world, planned to take us over!" Brighton retorted.

The FORM teetered and fell to one knee. He stared at Brighton then smiled evilly. "I suppose that does sound like us. I guess we need to finish the job!" The FORM leapt for Brighton and grabbed his neck.

Brighton lifted his firearm, held it sideways to the FORM's head—and fired. Blue ooze splattered on Brighton's face, and the FORM sank to the ground.

Brighton spat and wiped his eyes. He didn't see the next FORM coming after him until her fist was next to his face. Instead of hitting him, the FORM's arm was sliced off and sank to the ground. Brighton wiped his eyes again and saw a purple orb of protection surrounding him. He looked to his side. Dr. Sharp was standing there. He had engaged a personal protective shield around them with Maazi's wristband device. The energy ball had cut the arm of the FORM clean off when Dr. Sharp engaged it.

The FORM were succumbing to the CAST.

"Thought you might need some help," Dr. Sharp said.

"Much appreciated, soldier!" Brighton rejoiced.

Dr. Sharp liked that. He nodded and smiled.

But the shield around them started to fizzle.

"Uh-oh, this thing keeps malfunctioning," Dr. Sharp said.

"And at the worst moments!" Brighton exclaimed.

As the shield disintegrated, Brighton pushed Dr. Sharp out of the way and readied his body for another blow from a FORM racing toward him. The FORM tackled him. As they tumbled, Brighton wrapped his arm around the FORM's neck in a chokehold.

"This feels familiar!" the FORM said as it tried to pull Brighton's arm away. "Have we met?"

Brighton realized it was the FORM he had fought in San Antonio, and he was performing the same move he'd tried before.

"I think so, and it's my turn this time!"

Brighton squeezed his bicep as hard as his muscles allowed. The FORM backed up against a tree and smashed Brighton's body against it, then compressed his jaw on Brighton's forearm, just as he had in San Antonio. Brighton wrapped his legs around the FORM's torso. He could feel the bones in his forearms beginning to crack. The FORM started to reach behind his head and grab Brighton so he could toss him away as he had in San Antonio.

Not again! Brighton told himself. *Don't lose your grip!* He squeezed his bicep harder and instead of punching the FORM's face like he had in San Antonio, he punched its temple repeatedly where the neurochip resided. The FORM howled under the force of the punches and staggered in pain. As the FORM stumbled, Brighton grabbed his knife and tried to drive it into his chest.

But he couldn't. The FORM's chest was metal.

"Forgot about that!" Brighton said. "Here, let's try another."

Brighton arched his back away from the FORM's body and drove his knife through his spinal column. No metal impeded the dagger. The FORM groaned in pain and fell to his knees, then his face. The FORM was eliminated.

Brighton got to his feet and looked around for another attacker. He was surprised to see 200 FORM standing with their arms in the air as thousands of CAST soldiers held their weapons at the ready.

"We surrender! We surrender!" a FORM hollered. "Give us our lives, that's what means most to us."

Brighton inhaled and exhaled to gather himself then asked, "How can we know others on the ship won't come and attack?"

"Because they're all dead!" the FORM yelled. "You killed the rest of us!"

Brighton wiped blue ooze from his mouth and looked over at Dr. Sharp who was laying on the ground. "Can you confirm that's true?" Brighton asked.

Dr. Sharp used the wristband device and scanned the system. He looked up at Brighton and nodded. "It's true. We did it!"

CAST soldiers cheered while maintaining their weapons in place.

Brighton took a deep breath. The adrenaline coursing through his veins pushed him to keep on fighting, but he didn't need to; the CAST had accomplished exactly what they intended—annihilation, with deadly quickness.

Brighton slid his knife into its sheath and approached Dr. Sharp.

"You okay?" he asked as he helped him up.

"I'm fine. For an old man, I'm just fine," Dr. Sharp said as he brushed dirt off his pants.

Brighton analyzed the battle scene. Hundreds of CAST members laid lifeless on the ground. He mourned for them. Yet he knew they had accomplished what was necessary.

Brighton smiled. A sense of unique pride surged through his body. He looked at the bloodied and beaten amputees in front of him. The ragtag CAST they had pulled together in two days' time had overtaken an army that not even the world's most powerful military weapons could defeat.

"Get 'em out of here!" Brighton ordered the CAST.

CAST soldiers led the FORM out of the room and toward the ship's exit points where the military could take them prisoner.

"Nice work, Dr. Sharp," Brighton commended. "I wasn't sure I was going to say this, but your crazy plan worked!"

"Well, we're not there yet," Dr. Sharp said. "I don't mean to deflate the situation, but ...."

"What is it?"

"It's Ryker. With at least one FORM who's not dead!"

Brighton's exuberance faded. "Where is he?"

Dr. Sharp tapped on the wristband device. "Not in a safe place, let's just say that."

"Can we get to him?"

"If we're lucky," Dr. Sharp said. "But I don't think this is over yet."

Brighton started for the exit in a full sprint. "Dr. Sharp, let's move!"

Chapter 46

FORM Ship

Ryker heard muffled noises. They were intermittent. He listened. Then he realized it wasn't the noises that were intermittent, it was his consciousness. He was slipping in and out.

~

He came to again. His head was throbbing. Something must have hit him, hard.

The muffles were growing louder.

"Help!"

It was a distinct cry, but he couldn't tell who was yelling.

He tried opening his eyes. The image was blurred. He couldn't maintain consciousness.

~

"Help!"

This time the cry was clearly discernible. Ryker tried to open his eyes again. He was upside down, or someone in front of him was. He tried to lift his arms to wipe his eyes for a clearer view, but he couldn't. His arms were as heavy as sledgehammers. He struggled to move.

He swallowed hard and tried to breathe. He couldn't breathe deeply. Something was compressing his chest.

"Wha—Who—Where—Up ... then ... ache ... around." Gibberish was all he could produce. He passed out again.

~

"Come on!" He heard a voice calling for him. "You're supposed to be a soldier!"

Are my legs gone? he thought to himself. He reminded himself that that trauma had already passed. He was beyond it. He remembered being on a new mission, with new legs.

He shook his head. His cheeks were wet. He was crying. His subconscious must have realized something emotional was happening.

He gritted his teeth and let out a groan.

Wake up! he commanded himself mentally.

He shook his head again. Then again. His vision started to clear.

He saw two people. One person must have been the embodiment of an ox. His body was enormous. And they were holding the second, much smaller person ... upside down.

Ryker listened more carefully. Between the muffled screams, he could hear the whir of blades. *Fan blades?* No. Much bigger, louder, more powerful. Blender blades. Industrial-sized blender blades.

Something felt off. He blinked vigorously. *Come on, brain!* he demanded.

He forced his eyes open. He saw a wall of computers to his left. To his right was lab-like equipment. In front of him, the two people. One of them was in distress; the one who was upside down.

"Ryker!"

He heard his name distinctly.

"Get up!"

A boyish voice was commanding him to get up.

Ryker vomited. The acid in his throat woke him up more fully. He spat and coughed, then looked at the kid hanging upside down.

Jack!

Jack was in distress. Someone, something, was holding him upside down. Over a massive cylinder. With oversized blades that were spinning.

"Jack!" Ryker mustered. "Jack!"

"Ryker, help!"

Ryker could finally move his arms. They were numb. He slid them out from behind his back and slithered them along the ground.

His brain started to recognize the emergency.

Maazi was holding Jack upside down over some kind of grinding equipment.

"Get away from him!" Ryker shouted.

"Ah," Maazi said, "there we go. Wakey, wakey soldier!"

Ryker coughed some more. He tried to stand but stumbled and hit his head on a table leg. He fell to the ground and grabbed his head. It hurt even worse now.

"Let him go!" Ryker yelled, his subconscious forcing him to say something.

"You sure you want me to do that?" Maazi taunted. "You don't even want to *try* and save him?"

Ryker sat up and held his head between hands. He half-dazedly looked at Maazi. His penetrating wolf-like eyes were fiery with rage, demonic even. His thick lips were compressed tight; his neck muscles were tense, forcing a dozen veins to bulge outward.

"Get up, you imbecilic piece of feculence!" Maazi taunted. "Get up and watch your brother die! You deserve this! *I* deserve this! Everything you've done, you sorry degenerate fiend, is beyond forgivable. You divulged my people." Maazi breathed violently. "Uncovered my plans.

You killed my people! Then you took my—" Maazi screamed. "The one who could, *could* have become my wife!"

Ryker put his hands on the ground to steady himself and got to his knees. He looked at Jack. His face was crimson red; he must have been hanging upside down for far longer than he should have. He could tell Jack was in severe agony.

"You didn't get desensitized?" Ryker didn't mean to ask out loud, but he did.

"Am I some kind of moron? Of course not. There's a reason I put my quarters in the center of the ship; to avoid radiation bursts. The three of us who were in there were spared from your and Dr. Sharp's conniving stunt to disarm our neurochips and make us think you were one of us. Smart. I'll give you that, but I won't let you take my remaining people hostage."

"Did it work?" Ryker asked.

"Did what work?"

"Our plan."

"I just told you it didn't!"

"Not that one."

Maazi squinted. "You connived a second plan—"

Ryker cut Maazi off by catching him off guard; he had faked the last few seconds of being sluggish; his body was ready for battle. He bolted from his position and jumped through the air while snagging a magnetized rock from his pocket. He reached his arm out and brushed the desensitizing rock next to Maazi's left temple.

Maazi let go of Jack's ankle and cradled his head in his hands, grunting in agony.

Ryker extended his other arm while still midair and pushed Jack out from over the churning blades of the organics processor, but Jack didn't get his feet under him all the way. He slipped and caught the railing surrounding the death trap. Jack dangled precariously over the unyielding blades. They devoured the tips of his favorite Nikes.

"Help!" Jack screamed.

Ryker knew Jack's body didn't have the strength to hold on long. But before Ryker could reach Jack, Maazi punched him into a wall. His ribs cracked instantly.

"It won't work on me!" Maazi yelled as he shook his head. The desensitization didn't take effect.

Adrenaline drenched every capillary in Ryker's bloodstream. The pain in his side vanished. He bounced to his feet and dodged the next swing that Maazi threw. He ran for cover.

Maazi lifted his arm and fired a burst of blue plasma toward Ryker. Ryker's fully capable Ozzies moved him like a cheetah. He averted the shot and slid behind a metal table.

Maazi hurtled his massive body through the air and smashed one side of the table, exposing Ryker.

Maazi tapped his left temple to indicate his neurochip was still working. "You see? I'm too advanced for your meaningless tricks."

Ryker saw a glass flask next to him. He snatched it, broke it in half on the ground and shoved the jagged remains toward Maazi's left side. It made a clanking noise.

Maazi laughed and pushed his cloak to the side. The left torso of his body was nothing but metal. The glass shard had no effect.

"Would have been a great move," Maazi taunted. "How about this?"

Maazi connected a punch to Ryker's shoulder, causing it to rip out of socket.

Ryker's muscular frame readily absorbed the blow. He grabbed his arm and popped it back in place, then swung a vicious uppercut to Maazi's chin.

It dazed Maazi momentarily.

"I *like* it!" Maazi proclaimed as he adjusted his jaw. "A decent challenge!"

Ryker was already halfway to Jack.

Maazi leapt and grabbed Ryker's ankles making him tumble to a heap on the ground.

"Run, Forest, run! I liked that movie," Maazi teased. "What's the matter? Gator got your legs?"

Maazi got up and stood over Ryker.

"Ryker, I'm slipping! Help!" Jack screamed.

Ryker used the strength of the alloy metal in his Ozzies and kicked Maazi in the kneecaps, hyperextending them both.

Maazi winced and fell backward, crushing two more tables.

Ryker raced to the railing Jack was holding. He had barely touched Jack's fingers before Maazi grabbed his ankles again and sent his body swirling centripetally through the air. Ryker crashed into a set of cabinets, flinging materials in every direction.

Maazi trudged to Ryker and picked him up by his shirt.

Ryker's Ozzies dangled precariously.

"It's over!" Maazi screamed hysterically.

"One thing first," Ryker said with his eyes half closed; he was once again struggling to maintain consciousness.

Maazi looked at him curiously.

Ryker uttered, "You've been saying I look like you, but I learned something; you're actually like *me*!"

Maazi scrunched his face, trying to process what Ryker was getting at. "Wha—?"

Ryker kneed Maazi in the groin with the tip of his right Ozzie patella.

Maazi grabbed his crotch and fell to his knees.

"Little trick I learned in a previous fight!" Ryker declared, then kneed Maazi in the face, sending him backward.

Maazi damaged his spine on the corner of a ceramic bench that scraped his flesh. Blue ooze drizzled onto the floor. Ryker watched Maazi get to his feet, tap his left leg, and open the chamber that held his favorite over-under double-barreled handgun.

Ryker raced toward Jack.

"Stop!" Maazi yelled as he got to his feet, yet had to stoop and hold his middle. "Enough of this!"

Ryker turned and watched as Maazi shifted his aim between him and Jack.

"We're not done here until you watch your brother die!" Maazi said as he hobbled toward Jack.

Ryker looked at Jack. His fingers were slipping. He wouldn't last much longer.

"Just let him go! It's me you want. You know it is. *I'm* the one who caused all your problems. He's an innocent kid. Had nothing to do with anything."

"You *made* it his problem when you killed my *family*. Seems only fair I return the favor."

Maazi hurried the rest of the way to Jack and grabbed his arm to yank him off the organics processor railing. The force of his mighty hand nearly ripped Jack's shoulder out of socket. Jack screamed in pain.

Maazi flipped Jack in the air and grabbed his ankle again and held him upside down over the churning blades, then aimed his gun at Ryker.

"No! No!" Jack pleaded.

"You watching?" Maazi asked Ryker. "It's time!"

"Pass fake, Ryker!" Jack yelled as he pointed toward the organics processor computer. "Pass fake!"

Ryker knew exactly what Jack was getting at. Their dad used to make them practice pass fakes in basketball for hours on end. The concept was to make an opponent look in an opposite direction so you could take advantage of them; you faked a pass to a teammate, making the opponent look toward the teammate, then took a shot instead while the opponent wasn't looking. Ryker had perfected the move.

Ryker looked at the organics processor computer system, the brains of Maazi's life source. Without it, his existence would be compromised.

Ryker snatched a massive metal canister from a table next to him. He pretended like he was going to throw it in the air.

Maazi's intense eyes involuntarily followed Ryker's arms.

Ryker shifted his weight and threw the canister toward what looked like the most sensitive component of the organics processor computer.

"No!" Maazi yelled. He dropped his gun so he could snatch the canister midair and prevent it from destroying his life-extending creation.

Ryker took advantage of Maazi's move in the opposite direction. He pushed his Ozzies to their limit and sprinted across the floor. He jumped into the air with every ounce of power the Ozzies could muster. He reached for Jack with one arm and pulled him close to his body. They held onto each other as they started sailing over the organics processor blades.

Maazi tried to hold onto Jack's ankle, but the force of Ryker pulling him away made him lose his grip and contort his body. Maazi lost his balance.

As Ryker's left knee soared past Maazi, he thrust it forward, connecting a massive blow to Maazi's Adam's apple, crushing his esophagus.

Maazi gagged and grabbed his throat with both hands. He lost his footing completely and slipped upside down— directly into the organics processor!!

The enormous blender blades struggled under the pressure of the metal from Maazi's body but did their job without mercy.

"Aaaaaaah! Aaaaaaah!" Maazi screamed in agony as his eons-old body and self-coveted life were annihilated.

Blue ooze spattered along the cylinder walls.

Ryker and Jack continued to sail over the organics processor. They grimaced at the carnage beneath them. Shredded debris was all that was left of Maazi.

Ryker wrapped Jack up in both arms to protect him as they ended their flight over the organics processor and smashed against the far wall of the room. Ryker felt the wind knock out of him. He groaned as he slumped to the floor. He let go of Jack and laid his head on the ground.

"There you go, buddy," Ryker muttered. "You're safe. I, I kept my promise." Ryker closed his eyes. He sensed his last moments approaching. He felt Jack grab his face.

"Ryker! Dude, don't fade on me now, bro!"

"I can't—I can't do any more," Ryker grunted. "Nothing left in me." Ryker's body was giving out. The penetrating cuts on his back, mixed with the double breaks in his ribs, and trauma to his entire body, were overwhelming. He was ready to die.

Ryker heard Jack sobbing.

"Help! Someone help!"

Ryker's mind faded.

~

Jack watched Ryker's head go limp. "Come on, Ryker!" he demanded as he cradled his head in his lap and patted his face. "You can't leave me now! We need to get back to Mom!"

Jack put an ear next to Ryker's heart. It wasn't beating. He screamed and let hot tears flow freely. "Heeeeeelllpp!" he screamed.

No one was coming.

He looked around the room. Through blurred vision, he noticed one of the enormous syringes that he had watched Maazi use to inject himself had just finished filling up.

"Oh my gosh!" he said to himself.

He jumped up, grabbed the syringe, and lifted it high.

"I hope this works!"

He jabbed it into Ryker's arm and injected the entirety of the brilliant blue substance into his brother.

He waited. Nothing happened.

Jack slumped to his knees and wept for what felt like an eternity. All sense of life drained out of his body and mind. He felt barren.

"Jack?"

Jack heard a voice behind him. He turned around and saw Dr. Sharp and a man with a lower leg like Ryker's rushing toward him.

"Dr. Sharp, I—" Jack started. He let out a convulsing sob. "I couldn't save him." He held his head in his hands.

"Looks like you did just fine to me," Dr. Sharp countered.

"What?" Jack begged.

He turned back around and saw Ryker lifting his head up. He pulled the syringe out of his arm.

"Dude, what size of needle is on that thing?" Ryker wondered as he held the syringe in the air and gazed at the blue hue underneath his skin.

"Ryker!" Jack screamed. "Ryker, you're alive!"

"I sure am, buddy."

They embraced each other for a long moment.

"I love you, man," Jack said.

"I love you, too." Ryker patted Jack on the back and eased to his feet. "Now come on. I promised Mom I would get you back home."

Chapter 47

San Antonio, TX

Ryker rolled his eyes. During the entire helicopter flight from Corpus Christi to San Antonio, Dr. Sharp hadn't stopped talking.

"I mean, it was wonderful we didn't have to execute Phase Five! We didn't have to blow up the ship because they agreed to surrender. Not only that, they agreed to share their technology with us, all in exchange for letting them live. And we'll be able to learn about the other humanoids that Jack and I were with. Imagine what we'll be able to learn about the FORM technologies!

"Ryker, can you give me an idea of what it felt like when the blue substance was coursing through your veins?" Dr. Sharp begged. "I mean, it must have some crazy life-giving properties! Imagine what we can do with that scientifically, medically! And what will it do for longevity?"

"Listen, Dr. Sharp," Brighton spoke through his helicopter headset, "let's get these guys home, then I'm sure Ryker will let us take blood samples, and you can do all the research you want."

Ryker nodded in agreement, hoping to stop the barrage of questions. *I can't even begin to explain how different I feel. I'm definitely still me, but more. Like when I got my Ozzies.*

"That sounds wonderful," Dr. Sharp conceded. "I mean, just imagine what we can learn!"

"Hopefully not how to take over planets," Jack quipped.

"Good call, Jack," the president said. "The FORM certainly won't be bothering us anymore."

"Yeah," Jack said, obviously having a hard time believing he was sitting in a helicopter next to the president of the United States. "Once they heard Maazi was dead, they seemed crazy willing to comply with being prisoners of war, or whatever you're calling them."

"Yes, and that's thanks to your brother here," the president added, pointing at Ryker.

"I never doubted our plan would work," Dr. Sharp said.

Ryker laughed. "Not even when you fainted and fell upside down in front of three FORM?"

"Well," Dr. Sharp faltered with a shake of his head, "maybe *after* that there was no doubt."

The group laughed, then glanced out the windows. They were coming up on the Vaughns' home street.

"Well, there's also no doubt that each one of you *must* be thanked for all that you did to save our country," the president said.

"You mean the world," Jack insisted.

"Yes, of course. Force of habit. I mean the world, young man. And I'm going to personally hold a special medals ceremony for each of you and the entire CAST army as special guests. And we'll give a unique tribute to Gen. Childress. His sacrifice was pivotal."

"That'll be cool!" Jack said. "You wanna throw down some basketball in the White House after?"

"Jack!" Ryker chided. "Dude, you don't invite yourself to something like that."

"Ah, there's no harm," the president said. "You've earned it. Of course we'll play. Tell you what, when we rebuild The White House, I'll have a basketball court put in. I'll name it after you, Jack."

Jack smiled. "Whoa. Awesome!"

"We're here!" Ryker announced.

The helicopter began its descent into an opening between trees.

Ryker saw the ruins of their bed-and-breakfast, and the destructed appearance of his childhood home. However, he sensed it wouldn't be long before everything was repaired and back up and running.

He saw Grace throw open the front door of the house and rush down the porch steps. Jessie trailed her. He could tell his mom was wondering what was going on; he had purposely asked that no one prime her of their arrival. He wanted their return to be a surprise.

"Let me go first," Ryker said after they landed.

He slid open the helicopter door and made eye contact with his mom. He watched her sink instantly to her knees and put her head in her hands. She couldn't hold back the tears.

Ryker ignored all the trauma-induced pain in his body and ran to Grace and picked her up in a bear hug.

"Mom! Mom! We're okay. We're okay. We did it!"

Grace wrapped her arms around Ryker. She couldn't get a word out. She could only look to the sky and cry.

"And I brought something for you," Ryker said.

He grabbed Grace's shoulders and turned her body so she could see Jack emerging from the helicopter.

"Jack!" Grace screamed and fell to her knees again. She tried to stand. She got to her feet and stumbled forward.

Jack held his side as he jogged to his mom. "Mom! Mom! I wasn't sure I'd ever see you again."

They embraced and held onto each other like the world was ending. Yet they knew that life would soon renew.

"Jack, welcome home," Grace cried. She grabbed Jack's face and looked into his eyes. "Jack," she said then looked at Ryker, "Ryker, I love you two more than I can say."

"We love you, Mom," Ryker and Jack said together.

"Thank you," Grace said looking to the sky. She whispered, "Dear God, thank you for bringing my boys home." Grace went back to hugging Jack.

Ryker watched as the president, Brighton, and Dr. Sharp approached. The president thanked Grace for her willingness to let her family serve in the armed forces.

Dr. Sharp went on again about how good it was they didn't need to blow up the FORM ship because the survivors had surrendered. He couldn't wait for the host of research that would be done on the FORM ship, and the FORM themselves. The data would influence interstellar travel, medical advancements, technological innovations, and more. Grace seemed overwhelmed by it all but smiled politely.

Ryker chuckled. Dr. Sharp had been a good companion. Without his mad scientist quirks, none of them would be alive.

Ryker left the group and walked over to Jessie.

"If I didn't know any better," Jessie said, "I'd say you look like a FORM." She smiled teasingly. "I heard from some friends about what you did. Not too shabby, soldier." Jessie closed the gap between them and patted Ryker on his chest and looked into his eyes, then at his lips, then back into his eyes.

"Well, the good news is, I didn't turn into one," Ryker said as he pulled her into his arms. "And I may or may not have heard about what *you* did, putting your life on the line to save a fine group of people."

"All in a days' work, soldier."

They stared at each other longingly.

"So," Jessie probed, "what's next?"

"I *think* ... this is where we kiss," Ryker suggested bluntly.

"I think so, too," Jessie whispered.

Ryker squeezed Jessie tight and angled his head downward. She met him halfway and wrapped her arms around his neck. They kissed passionately, not caring who saw.

"Now *that's* what I'm talkin' about!" Jack hooted and hollered toward Ryker and Jessie, breaking up the other group's conversation.

Ryker continued the kiss a moment longer, then broke away with a smile and shook his head. "I'm going to kill that kid," he teased.

"But you just saved him."

"Ah, true. I guess I'll give him a day."

They kissed again and held each other close.

"You two are absolutely adorable," Grace beamed.

Ryker and Jessie looked at Grace and smiled.

"I imagine you're all famished," Grace said to everyone and motioned for the group to follow her into the house. "What do you say I whip something up for everyone to eat in our partially functioning kitchen?"

The group obliged without hesitation.

"Thanks, Mom," Ryker said as he and Jessie trailed the group. "But I tell you what, I need something first!"

"What's that?" Jessie asked as she slid her arm around Ryker's waist.

Ryker followed her lead, put his arm around her shoulder, and said, "A drink of *water!*"

THE END

About the Author

Dustin Williams, PhD, is a Professor of Orthopaedics at the University of Utah, formally educated as a Biomedical Engineer and Microbiologist. He was a member of the research team that developed osseointegrated implant technology for transfemoral amputees in the USA, the endeavor that inspired this project. He is a bona fide scientist by day and a novel writer, script developer, and occasional gamer by night. His passion lies in developing medical technologies to help heal those who suffer. Writing is a secondary passion as the outlets of story and imagination are morphine for the mind.

He has published over fifty scientific papers, one previous novel, holds thirteen patents, is the editor of one textbook, and enjoys mentoring graduate students, undergraduate students, lab technicians, project managers, and, most importantly, his five children. He fully admits that his wife is a far better mentor to their five kids than he is. They live their dream together in Utah.

For more information about osseointegration, to buy copies of *Return to Duty* or Dustin's other books, visit:

www.DustinWilliamsAuthor.com

Follow Dustin on X @DustinWAuthor, Instagram @DoubleODarkwing, and Facebook @Dustin Williams - Author

List of Characters

Ryker Vaughn (24): A captain in the U.S. Army. A grit-filled, well-built soldier who becomes a double amputee, losing both legs above the knees in an explosion. He is one of the first to receive Ozzies (osseointegrated implants). Ozzies give him a leg up in the fight against the FORM.

The FORM (age unknown): Fused Organic Machines. Interstellar water seekers and planet dominators.

Maazi (age unknown, thousands of Earth years old): FORM leader. A brilliant, yet maniacal engineer from deep space who discovered several keys to modifying biology for improved longevity. Using this tech, he refined his people's otherworldly bodies, fusing metals with biology to advance function and life. Though ancient, he hasn't learned to bridle his ego, which often overpowers his discernment.

Samuel Brighton, MS (50s): Colonel in the U.S. Army. Director of the Deployed Experimental Telemetry for Exploration, Combat, and Telecommunications (DETECT) initiative. A combat-seasoned leader whose military acumen shines throughout.

Steven Sharp, PhD (60s): MIT professor and inventor of the various DETECT initiative technologies including deep space and improvised explosive device (IED) recognition systems. A resolute character with an uncanny ability to understand software technologies. A quirky scientist with heart.

Van Childress (58): Former general in the U.S. Army. Current secretary of defense. A weathered man with grit and an experienced military strategist who can exhibit outbursts.

The President of the United States of America (50s):
Supportive leader who isn't afraid to be on the frontline. He sticks with Brighton and Gen. Childress through thick and thin.

Grace Vaughn (50s): Ryker and Jack's elegant, strong-willed, and proud mother. Her willingness to face fear head-on and serve her country while ostensibly living what may be considered a civilian life is a testament that everyone is anything but ordinary.

Jack Vaughn (15): Ryker's little brother, who always has needed protection and looks up to Ryker.

Jessie Bell (24): Rehabilitation specialist assigned to help Ryker through the early difficult days of recovery. Opportunity and intrigue of a different nature blossoms from the moment she gets to know him.

Acknowledgments

To Marianne, for the years of encouragement and support I needed to complete this worthwhile project. You are everything this world needs.

To my family, for your sacrifice, allowing me to carve time away from events, games, New Year's Eve celebrations, and ice-cream runs to focus on writing.

To my world-class mother, not only for being a model individual and matriarch, but for reviewing draft after draft of the manuscript, offering encouragement to complete the book, and providing expert insight.

To my father, who served in battle and was a real-life hero.

To my father-in-law, for your service in the Armed Forces and for taking time to read multiple drafts to provide welcome input on military matters and story intrigue.

To my mother-in-law, for supporting those who serve, raising some of the best people I know, and being a rockstar of motherhood.

To the osseointegrated implant research teams across the globe: Your experimental and clinical minds have improved the lives of many and will continue to enhance and inspire thousands more.

To osseointegrated implant patients, your courage and grit are commendable.

To my students, technicians, and lab experts, for putting up with my requests to review drafts, provide input, and tolerate my incessant mentions of how the book was coming.

To Kraig, for your essential coaching, story refinements, structure review, and creative eye. This book would not be what it is without you.

To Jake Clark, for capturing the imagination of my mind on the cover.

To Sage Taylor Kingsley, for your much-needed editorial eagle eye, keen questions, and catalyzing comments that drove me to take this project across the finish line.

To my friends, family, neighbors, and colleagues, for putting up with my at-times overexcitement as I worked on this book, shelved it, and repeated the process. Twelve years in the making: it finally happened!

To the reader. Thank you for joining my adventure.

To the men and women who serve. My gratitude for your service is deeper than words.